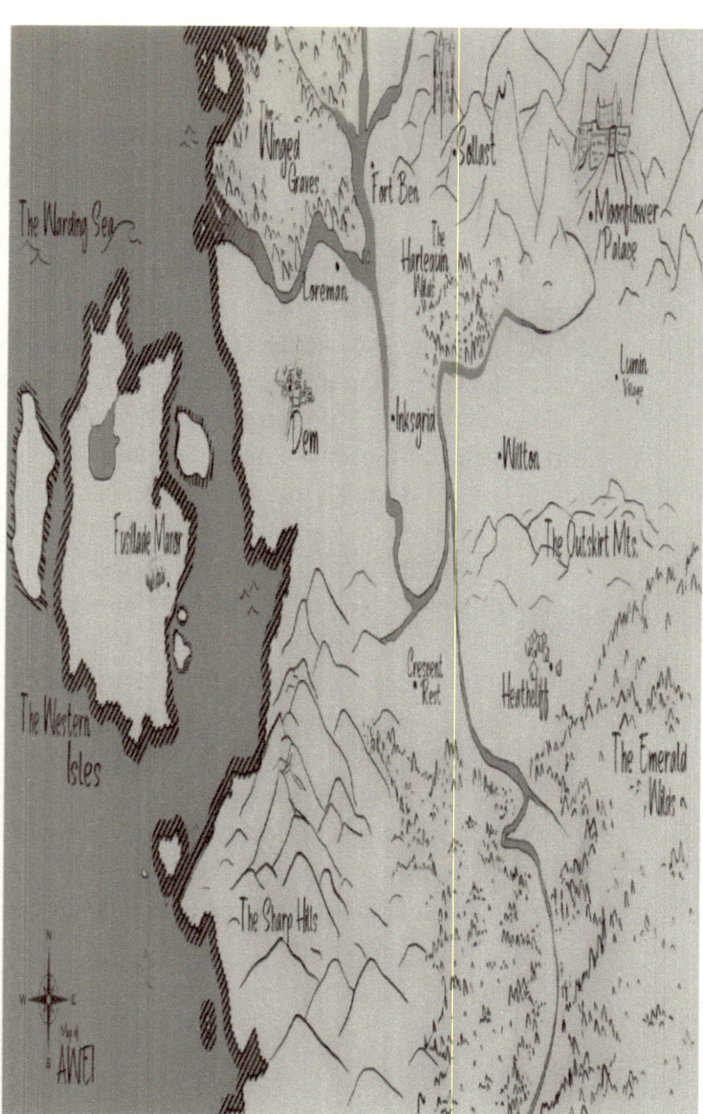

The Warding Sea
The Winged Graves
Fort Ben
Ballast
Moonflower Palace
The Harlequin Wilds
Loreman
Dem
Inksgrid
Lumin Village
Willton
Fustlade Manor
The Outskirt Mts.
Crescent Rest
Heathcliff
The Western Isles
The Emerald Wilds
The Sharp Hills
AWEI

Allison Stalberg

WANDER

Chapter 1
The Emerald Wilds

"A land of forgotten whispers, twisted with age, equal in both rot and splendor. That was the eastern forest. That was the Emerald Wilds," – Ivy's Compendium of Enchanted Lands

A naked girl opened her eyes to see pillars of trees in the sun. Emptiness stirred her stomach and her heart pounded in her ears. Ferns, sage, white clovers, and spotted flowers blanketed the forest floor around her. Juniper trees covered in patches of sheet moss twisted above her. Their branches hid treasures like violet orchids and chickadee nests. Their roots weaved around patches of blush mushrooms.

Looking up, she watched clouds pass over the snaking branches. She did not know what they were. She did not know what anything was, or even what she was. Her hands petted the grass under her, just beginning to understand touch: what form was hers versus the world's.

Eventually she stood up and wandered. Whispers tickled in her ears, but she could not understand their words. Her hands gripped honeysuckle vines, saplings, tree trunks, and thorny rose bushes, anything to help her stand as her legs trembled and begged her to fall. After a day of drifting, she began to feel heavier and sat in a grove. The air cooled and the world darkened. In a shivering ball, the girl tried to sleep through the night. She heard howls and crickets farther in the woods. Ants crawled over her feet, and spiders hid in her hair.

When the sun rose, so did she, and she roamed again. At night, she fell.

Three days passed of her wandering before she stopped. After trekking through what seemed like a never-ending forest, she collapsed at a tree base. She breathed through a dried mouth and hugged her aching body. Every movement began to hurt, and she felt heavier each day. The emerald world around her had dimmed, becoming as still as a painting.

She felt as though her body was caving in at the center. Her forehead heated up, and she experienced random waves from warm to freezing. Despite the sun being up, this time she remained curled under the tree. Maybe if she waited long enough, she'd disappear just the way she had appeared.

When night came, she felt like she was closer than ever to disappearing. Her body became numb, and she found it easier to fall away from the world. Rain fell from the dark sky and broke through the forest canopy, a tropical storm where no leaf could provide shelter. To the girl, it was like the entire sky fell. Despite her numb state, her body began to shiver violently. She curled up as tight as she could, hugging her knees to her chest and tucking her head inward.

The rain brought pain that pulled her away from disappearing. She tried to shut it out, constricting her grip on herself and closing her eyes. Every pelted drop splashed from her shoulders to her face. Her hair dulled and sank until it was pasted to her skin.

After rustles in the grass, the rain stopped hitting her. She could still hear it, though. She could hear the sounds of it falling all around her. Opening her eyes, she looked up at bright flame that blinded her. She blocked it with a hand to see a pair of red eyes looking at her beyond the lantern. A wing as black as the night sky stretched above her, sheltering her.

"Who are you?" the winged being asked.

Keeping his wing over her, he kneeled and put his warm hand on her wet forehead. She got a closer look at him. A head of dark shaggy hair, brown skin, and a heart shaped face. He wore sandals and ragged pants. His chest and arms were bare and toned with muscles and scars.

Shutting her eyes, she fell away.

The winged spirit's hands pulled a rope. A raccoon jumped at the sight of a bucket rising from the river and bounded back into the darkness of the forest. Filled with river water, the bucket rose up toward the cloudy sky, toward the branches the old oak tree the spirit lived in. Past the tree's leaves and through its shade, the bucket reached the window.

The spirit unwrapped the rope attached to the bucket before taking it inside. He pulled a fabric curtain shut to keep the cool night air outside. The bucket water sloshed back and forth, dribbling some drops onto the wood floor as he walked into another room. He heard a soft moan from the corner. Setting the bucket on a wooden stool, he turned to the shadows where the girl he found laid down.

"Are you awake?" Shadows danced around the room as he took a lit candle from a table. Folding his legs on the floor, he positioned himself next to a layered heap of furs. His wings folded at his back.

The girl lay with only her breath to move her. Her long golden hair had dried into a tangle. Her pale body was slim with various light brown moles on her body. The spirit put his ear to her bare chest, her rib cage pressed to his cheek. She had become warmer.

He put his hand on her shoulder. With a light shake, her eyelids fluttered and opened slightly. He inched himself forward and moved some of her tousled blonde hair out of the way of her sight. Her eyes were like bright green leaves in the sun. Based on her size and flat chest, the spirit guessed she might be between the ages of nine and twelve.

"Hello," he greeted. His own voice sounded odd to him, as he did not remember the last time he had spoken. "Right now, we are in my nest, where I live."

The nest was only two rooms big. The smaller room was used for cooking and the other for sleeping and storage. The doorway was unevenly carved out with just a tattered blanket as a makeshift door to block the wind. There were two windows with no glass, one with a view of the river and the other facing the inner part of the giant oak tree. There was no furniture. Not even a single chair. All the spirit had was what he had found with luck: blankets, pillows, bags, and tools. No one would bring furniture on a journey to the woods, only camping supplies. He could barely recall how he built his nest. He remembered using pieces of broken construction he found around the woods, from wagons and homes long abandoned. It was a pitiful place for a poor soul to wake up. The nest was little more than a shack.

Remembering his reason for waking her in the first place, he picked up the soup he set aside and brought the wood bowl close to her face.

She glanced at it before looking back at him.

"Do you want it?"

No answer.

"Can you talk at all?"

She just stared at him. Her unreadable gaze sent a chill down his spine.

"Can you nod or shake your head?"

She did not move. Maybe she went through something so traumatic that she was in shock? Her family or friends could have met a cruel fate by animals, venom, poison, or illusion.

A spell could have been cast on her to make her behave in this way. It was possible in this place. She could have eaten berries from vines or fruit from the trees and have a magical influence grow from inside her stomach.

The winged man scooped up a spoonful and brought it to the girl's mouth. Her jaw remained tightly shut. He thought of pushing the spoon against her lips, but that would just dribble into a mess. "Hey," he got a little harsher, "I don't know what your problem is, but if you don't eat you will die. Look." He ate the spoonful of soup himself since she seemed to be paying more attention to him than the food. When she saw that, she began to stare at the soup. With more hope, he attempted feeding her again. This time she opened her mouth and took the spoonful.

With that one slurp, she gained color. Her body shifted toward the spirit. Her bright eyes smiled at him. He kept feeding her till the soup was finished. As he guessed, she was starving. He retrieved a cloth from his kitchen and wiped her face. "Where are you from?"

Despite being fed, she did not speak. She laid her head back down on the mattress. Her arms closed into her chest, and her legs curled as she shut her eyes.

The girl could be a wind-born human. Wind-born humans, unlike the blood-borns, had no origin or family. It was as though the wind itself brought their bodies to this world. Sometimes they came as children, rarely babies, but many times they were adults, kids, or teenagers. No matter what body they had, their minds were clueless, speechless, almost like an infant's, yet they learned very fast. The first humans were wind-born, and spirits like him taught them how to live in this world. They began to have babies, making the blood-borns. The wind-borns never stopped coming, though.

But then how could he touch her? Nature made it so humans and spirits shocked each other if they tried to touch. He would have not been able to save her if that was the case. Despite that inconsistency, he became more and more certain she was wind-born. This girl may have just appeared here, far from other humans to take care of her. How rare were they? How many blood-borns and wind-borns made the human race? Wind-borns were likely to die if they could just appear in the middle of nowhere without someone to take care of them.

The spirit rubbed his forehead. He could not remember meeting a human before. He himself was alike to wind-borns, with no past to recall. Maybe this girl was a strange spirit. It was hard to tell. Many things were possible in this forest. His head ached at times when he thought too hard about possibilities.

Chopping through carrots and celery with a knife made of bone, the spirit prepared more soup. The cicadas and frogs sung through the night. With a new pot of soup, he returned to his bedroom and sat by the mattress. The girl slept on her side. His hand scooped her head up and tucked a pillow under. He unfolded a cotton blanket and tucked it around her.

The spirit raised the human, and the girl's ribcage faded under a well-fed body. No longer in danger, her personality began to show. She approached everything out of curiosity. She often stared out his window with the view of the river, yearning to go out. She would hold his baskets upside down, pouring all his collections and tools out, sit down, touch and examine everything they contained. She never spoke, but her body language told the spirit enough.

Her fascination with his wings was one of the few things that bothered him. She loved to grab at them, often pulling his dark feathers out, causing him the same amount of pain as would yanking out someone's hair. He disliked punishing her or yelling too loud, so he came up with an idea.

With one of his shed feathers, he made a bracelet. The bracelet itself was made out of deer leather. With a needle, he pricked a hole in the feather's shaft and looped the bracelet through. He tied the bracelet around her left wrist. "There, now you will always have a feather so you can stop plucking at mine."

The spirit was no small bird, so the feather was quite a large accessory. If she raised her hand, his feather nearly reached her elbow. But the girl seemed to get the idea and never plucked at his wings again.

With time, he found clothes for her. Most were baggy, dirt-stained shirts, pants too wide for the girl's hips, and clunky boots. It was quite the spectacle when she first put on clothes. The spirit had to help her, making her spread her legs and raise her arms. He crafted a rope from vine for a belt to tighten the pants to her bony hips. Once fully clothed, she looked down at her own body with wonder. She acted as though the spirit had cloaked her with a robe made of jewels. She spread her arms and skipped around the nest, her boots stomping up the dust from the wood. She looked like an ordinary peasant, but she danced with joy, believing she was beautiful and to the spirit, she was.

Like most things he had, her clothes came off the dead who had risked exploring the forest. The spirit often found their corpses, killed off in a variety of ways. The forest was a warped place. There were plants the size of men with teeth like daggers. At times, music could be heard resonating in the woods, or the voice of woman singing a lullaby, but the spirit knew never to follow the sound. When the moon was full, wolves the size of small homes would sweep through, eating all they could sniff out. There were monsters that oozed like tree sap and brush that would be rooted one day, gone the next. Serpents dropped from the high branches upon their victims, and there were frogs poisonous to the touch. For that, the spirit feared letting the girl wander outside the nest.

But there was also beauty, which was why so many came to explore the forest. Flowers with petals that shimmered like glass grew by the riverside. There were trees with deep-green moss and red orchids growing on their twisted trunks. Gentle creatures roamed like black deer, rainbow fish, hummingbirds, ferrets, butterflies, and rabbits. At night, the sky was speckled with planets and stars, enough to make the saddest or most angry person lose themselves in the sight. There were stones in the river which, if cracked, showed their insides filled with purple crystals. Ruins could be unburied, filled with strange treasures like faded scrolls, broken flutes, and ancient statues. These things made the spirit want to take the girl outside.

Eventually the he took her to the roof of the nest. On a day with no clouds, he decided it was time for her to join him outside. The spirit held her in his arms and flew her out to roam. When they took to the sky, her eyes expanded, and her mouth opened breathlessly. Since then, she would often hold him, hoping he would fly her somewhere. The destination did not matter, as long as she could fly with him.

Letting her wander outside turned out to be a challenge as she constantly got herself into some sort of danger. Her weakness was her lack of fear, poking and prodding everything she came across. She once stuck her hand into a hole at the base of an oak tree despite the spirit's shouts. The girl flinched and pulled her hand out with a snake chomping down below her thumb. The snake's broad head and tan color suggested a copperhead. The viper let go of her hand only for the human to try and grab it with her other free hand.

"HEY!" the spirit ran over and stopped her.

He sucked at her bite wound and spat a mixture of blood and venom onto the earth. The rest of the day he constantly checked her hand for swelling. She lived to see another day, but she vomited after a trout dinner in the nest.

Another time the girl thought the berries of a rosary pea looked appetizing. She walked out of some bushes with a handful of the red bead shaped berries to offer to the spirit. She must have been surprised when the spirit pinned her to the ground and shoved his fingers down her throat until she vomited out every berry. Too young to understand that he saved her life, she avoided him for the rest of the day.

There was also a time when she nearly drowned in the river by the oak tree. The spirit never understood how she managed such a feat in shallow water that only came up to one's knees. He had to pull her face out of the river, resuscitate her, and hope she learned a lesson.

Another evening he lost her and found her stuck in a tangle of thorn vines from which he had to cut her free. Then there was the time she found quicksand that the spirit did not even know existed. She had sunk down to her hips in the murky earth. The spirit was lucky he could fly and pull her out. He surrounded the quicksand with a fence of rocks as a warning for himself and the human. She even got caught in one of the spirit's own hunting traps a couple times. Luckily they were harmless, and he could cut her down.

There were times that saving her hurt him. Larger animals like wolves, bears, tigers, and certain snakes, like the girl, did not know of fear. Incidents happened where the girl wandered off and bothered dangerous creatures. The spirit usually could scare off the lesser animals, but the larger ones had to be escaped from or killed.

The girl's body became marked by the wild in the form of scars, more scars than normal for anyone. He had his scars, but for each one of his, she had three more. Most were on her legs and arms.

Eventually the spirit came to name the girl, "Wander." He became certain she was an abnormal human, since she bled red instead of black. Spirits like him bled black. They could touch that which regular spirits and humans could not. Wander could touch spirits, but bled and acted like a human.

The first time he heard Wander's voice was by the river while they were washing clothes. For his own amusement, he splashed her with water. She flinched, her blonde locks dripping, her green eyes wide. Her moment of surprise transformed as a smile flashed him.

She splashed back in the face. He flinched and his feathers fluffed up. Then . . . she laughed. At first her laughter scared him, hearing a voice other than his own. It was not some timid giggling; Wander's laughter came out in a booming, abrupt burst.

Not long after her laughter, Wander's speech began. She usually stated the obvious and could tell the spirit when she was hungry or tired. He began to help her with the names of things.

A day came when the spirit was given a name. "Masu," she called him. Unlike her name, his was meaningless. He was unsure at first. Spirits often named themselves words like Sunny or Willow, while humans named each other names with less or no meaning like Jonathan or Megan. Despite it not being a word, Masu came to accept his humanistic name.

Eventually, he could not imagine living without her.

With a stick in hand, Wander drew circles on the river's sandbanks. She picked daffodils from the near brush and set them in the circles' centers. Masu once asked her what all her drawings were supposed to be. She did not know. She just liked drawing circles and filling them with flowers, stones, seeds, or whatever she could find at the time.

Every morning the sand was wiped clean by the river's ebb and flow, and Wander would redesign the riverside all over again while Masu tended his garden. She was not allowed to go to his garden because that was near where she found the quicksand. Even when Masu made a rock fence, she would end up stepping in it and calling out for rescue. Masu eventually lost his patience and ordered her to remain at the riverbank until he was done.

Sitting on the sand, she tried to put the extra flowers in her hair but they all fell out. She stepped into the river and her pants flowed with the current.

Following the current, she clung to one of the humongous river rocks and hid. She waited until her legs numbed from the frigid water.

"Wander?" Masu walked out onto the bank with a basket of what he had harvested.

Wander let out a scream as she splashed out from behind the rock. She slipped and fell into the water.

"Wander!" Masu set his basket down and helped her out of the river. "You know you should not go into the river!"

They sat on the rock that looked over the sandbank as they ate strawberries, potatoes, and carrots. Masu prepared wood for a fire to cook the potatoes. Knowing strawberries were Wander's favorite, Masu let her have more.

"Masu," Wander said, "what is outside the forest?"

She had begun to ask a lot of questions like how far the sun was or how plants grow. Thinking of what was beyond the forest made Masu's head ache. "The forest is all I know," he answered as he snapped a stick. "So I don't know."

"Don't you want to know?"

"Not really." He snapped another stick.

"Why?"

"Everything I need is here. Why would I ever want to leave?" Masu took out his knife to prepare a fire starter with a dry piece of wood.

Wander ripped off the green part of a carrot and flopped it around. "Maybe there are more people or maybe different foods."

"I have no desire to ever leave the forest."

"Why?"

"Wander!" he put down his knife. "Enough with that question! I gave you my answer."

For a moment, he feared he was too harsh. Wander pouted, curling out her under lip. Whenever she did that, he knew she wasn't hurt. She was just teasing him now. "Don't give me that lip," he said.

She then stuck out her upper lip.

Masu smiled and shook his head as he continued working on the fire. "Or that one."

When the sun was highest in the sky, Masu went fishing. He had a long stick to hold while a rope of sinew with a hook made of rabbit bone sat in the water. He brought bits of meat or fruit to lure fish to the hook.

His fishing spot was a riverside rock under a pink silk tree. Wander loved the pink silk tree the best because of the fluffy pink flowers that it grew. Masu forbade her from climbing the tree since she usually fell and hit the earth below. He feared she could hit the fishing rock and crack her skull.

She shook the tree for the pink flowers to fall. The puffs of pink floated down like dandelion seeds. They landed among Masu's dark wings and hair, the stone, and river. Brushing the flowers off his head, Masu turned around with a smile. He was in a good mood, but she knew he would not be if she didn't remain quiet. He always yelled at her for scaring the fish.

"Masu?" Wander sat next to him and spoke softly. "What were you like before we met?"

"I was not so different," he answered. "I lived here. I hunted. I scavenged."

Wander frowned. "What about family or friends?"

"I was like you. I didn't have any."

"But you said that's normal for me because I'm born from the wind. You are a spirit, don't they have families?"

Masu's fingers clutched his fishing rod and his voice hardened, "I don't remember."

Wander laid on the rock warmed by the afternoon sun. She scooted to Masu's folded legs and set her head in his lap.

When it turned dark, Masu and Wander retired to the nest. After a dinner made from the hunts and harvests of the day, they'd lie down on a pile of furs, pillows, and blankets.

The nest had a window on the wall above their heads so they could see the moon and stars. Some came in purple, red, and blue. Others shot across the sky like a hummingbird.

Wander turned to Masu who lay with his red eyes open. He also watched the stars.

"Can we play the word game?" Wander asked.

"Sure, what letter?"

"S."

Masu and Wander developed a game to help her learn words. They picked a letter and said a word that began with that letter back and forth until one of them got stuck. Of course Wander always lost, but the point was for her to learn more with the goal of one day beating Masu.

"I'll start with the word *start*," Masu said.

"Stars," Wander said.

"Signs."

"What are those?"

Masu sighed. "Um, signs. They are . . . complicated. A sign is like . . . the rocks I set out to warn you about the quicksand. It's something that means something else."

"Stars."

"You already said stars."

"Um, sand."

"Sap."

"Sit."

"Sort."

"What's sort?"

The game was commonly interrupted by Wander's questions.

After Wander lost the game, they turned to fall asleep. Masu often faced away, and Wander pressed herself against his back between his folded wings. She liked to feel him breathe and feel his feathers against her cheeks.

"Masu?"

He did not answer. They both usually fell asleep quickly. Lately though, Wander had starred at the stars while Masu slept.

She turned and shook his shoulder. "Masu?"

He spoke in an exhausted mumble, "What?"

"What's your earliest memory?"

"I was under this tree, and I decided to build a nest."

"Why?"

"I needed a place to live."

"You didn't live anywhere before?"

"I don't know."

Wander rolled over to look at the ceiling. Masu did not know much about himself. What was odder to Wander was that he did not want to find out.

As Masu tended to his garden the next morning, Wander did not stay at the riverbank. She strode through the wilds to where she had never explored before. Past the juniper and oaks, the trees began to lessen in size. The land of lesser trees seemed to go on forever. It was the farthest she ever went without getting into a life threatening situation.

The forest was larger than Wander ever imagined. As she grew up with Masu, their lives seemed smaller and the world larger. What was beyond the forest? Was there only the forest?

She stopped to take in a bizarre sight. A large construct lay bare in the center of a grove. Light shined on what reminded Wander of her blankets, but they stood up and arched like walls. The blankets were built on top of a large wooden floor sitting on four wheels. A decomposing hand dangled down from a tear in the blanket. Little white maggots crawled over and around fingernails.

Wander circled around the discovery. It appeared to be some kind of shelter. She took the longest stick she could find and used it to open the curtain to the inside. No animals jumped out, so Wander peeked in only to turn her head and nearly retch. She could not see well, but the rank stench overpowered her senses. Beyond the construct, a body hung from rope on a tree branch. Flies crawled on the person's bald head. Wander approached and stared at the man's leather shoes.

It was not her first time seeing dead people in the forest. Dead people provided Masu with his most useful possessions. Perhaps Masu would be pleased if she brought him back something useful from these perished people.

She reached up toward the hanged man's shoes.

Flapping wings caused the branches of trees around her to sway.

Masu landed a distance away.

"Wander! What do you think you're doing? I've been looking everywhere for you."

"I wanted to see the edge of the forest, and I found this strange thing," she pointed at the wheeled construct. "There's at least one dead person in that wooden thing, and there is one hanging from a tree."

"That thing is a wagon . . . but that's not the point," he took a hesitant step forward and offered his hand. "Let's go back home. It's too dangerous here."

Wander remained rooted where she stood. "How do you know? Have you ever left?"

"Are dead people not enough evidence that it's dangerous? I haven't left because I don't need to."

"Don't you want to see more?"

He shook his head.

16

"If we go, maybe we can learn new things," Wander said. She spoke not only with her voice, but her hands moved, emphasizing every word. "Maybe there are spirits with wings like yours. There could be different foods and nests. I can meet other wind-born humans. I want to see a place with no trees or a place filled with people. I want to wear different clothes and hear different birds. I want more than this forest."

His knees bent a little. His red eyes looked larger than ever as he said, "I can't leave."

"Why?"

He attempted to step forward, only to stride back. "I just can't."

Wander knew Masu had never dreamed of meeting anyone else or ached to see a difference piece of land. Something in the way he looked at her said something more was going on. He suddenly looked small.

"Wander," he said. "I can't leave this forest."

"I don't understand."

"Neither do I. I just know I can't."

They walked back to the large oaks and juniper where the river ran.

As Masu put a knife to sticks to craft arrows, Wander sat by him and stared off into space.

"You don't want to go off and play?" Masu asked. "You look bored."

She shook her head and continued to watch the clouds go by.

After crafting arrows, Masu took an axe to chop wood for his fires. Wander watched his biceps tense with each swing down. Sweat rolled down the back of his neck. Rolling onto her stomach, she dipped her hand in the river current and sighed. She felt minnows nibble on her fingertips.

Masu sighed and threw the axe down on a stump where it stuck. "I'm going to go check traps and pick fruit now." Wander followed. Every time they stopped, she leaned against a tree. She followed like a shadow, and just as silent.

As dinner cooked that night, Wander stared out the nest window. A chipmunk crawled up the oak branches. Seeing Wander, it stopped and stared. The last time Wander tried to grab an animal on the tree branches, she almost fell out of the nest, and Masu had to pull her back in.

With a sigh, she turned around and planted herself face down in the bedding. She remained there until she heard the sound of wood bowls being set on the floor.

When she and Masu ate, there were only the sounds of crickets, frogs, and slurping vegetable and salmon soup.

Masu put down his bowl and looked at her, "You can leave whenever you want. You're intelligent and mature enough now that you don't need me. It would be wrong for me to make you stay."

She swallowed, "But you won't come with me?" "I can't," he said. "It's hard to explain but this forest . . . I think I'm bound to it. Maybe it's a spell, or I am its creature. I do not know."

Wander looked at the floor.

He continued. "I thought about it today, and the things you said were amazing. They were things I never thought of, maybe things I'm not even capable of thinking about. You should meet others like you and—"

She cut him off. "I'm not leaving you."

"You'd have to."

"Then I'm staying."

Masu's eyes widened.

"I don't want you to be alone, and it won't be fun to see anything without you," Wander said.

Masu looked at his lap, his hair hiding his face, but Wander could tell he was happy.

Many nights later, Wander watched the sunset. The forest turned shades of red before dark. Everything had become quiet except for the river and birds. They did not sing, but all flew out of the forest.

Masu lay on their bed, trying to sleep. Wander figured he was still awake as his breathing was not yet deep. She curled by his side and drifted to sleep with thoughts of why the sky could turn red.

"Wander."

"Hm?" Shaken from a peaceful, warm sleep, she did not open her eyes.

"I heard something strange."

She willed herself to listen. It was quiet, except for the soft whisper of branches in a cold breeze outside. Not even the crickets sang. "I don't hear anything."

"Stay here. I'm going to fly around."

She opened her eyes to see Masu's profile sit up and stand against the curtain that glowed with moonlight. It was not that first time he had heard something strange in the night and gone to see the cause of the sound. Sometimes it was a tree falling or a group of humans who walked under the nest or even screams of people or animals getting massacred by wolves. He never allowed Wander to come. "Never go out at night," he would say. "This forest has two faces, and the dark one is even dangerous for me." So Wander would wait fearfully for his return to the nest.

When he left the nest, she listened to the flapping of his wings till they faded. Despite her worry of what Masu could have possibly heard, she managed to drift back into a cozy sleep.

Wander awoke not to Masu's return, but an overpowering smell.

She never thought it was possible for a scent to physically sting her nose, but this one did. Her consciousness pooled back into her body, and she opened her eyes to find herself in a moving darkness. It was not like nighttime, but a dark cloud swirling around her. She clamped her fingers on burning nostrils.

"Masu—" she could only call his name once before her body erupted in coughs. Her prickling eyes squinted, looking through the darkness that moved around her like a snake in a tree. The cloud thickened like a river in the rain. Like the time she nearly drowned, she began to lose direction, sight, and breath. It was worse, though, as if bees had flown into her gullet, her throat throbbed. Her eyes squeezed shut, unable to stand the burning sensation the smoke gave.

She blindly rushed to find the window. Throwing her head and arms out, she let out a gasp in the night air. Opening her eyes, she saw burning colors sweep through the woods like dye on cloth. An all-consuming flame had taken over.

"Masu!" Wander called out.

A wind blew the smoke out the window, cutting into Wander's senses with nothing but stinging. The sound of cracking became louder, and the black cloud got larger. Attempting to take a deep breath, Wander belched out in a coughing fit. Her hands grabbed the window frame. Going by pure instinct, she swung her legs out to the open air, and let go of the nest. Her shirt billowed into her face as she fell into the river.

She landed with a splash atop the river stones of the shallow waterway. Her body trampled by the fall, she managed to get up with cuts, bruises, and a dizzy head. She called out Masu's name again and again, trudging through the river. She slipped a couple times, her hair dripping, body shivering as she emerged back into the cold air.

She could do nothing but watch the nest go up in flames, from the twisted roots, to the fat trunk, to where they lived, to the highest branches. It was not the only tree, nearly every single one had become a beacon of dancing light and heat.

She left the riverside to the heated woods, calling Masu's name. Flames licked at her knees. She could not tell the difference between the river drops and sweat on her body. Panic taking ahold of her, she started to run blindly through the streaks of smoke and flame.

Wander only got so far before she a strange sight made her stop, despite the chaos.

At first she wondered if the figure she saw standing in the flames was Masu, but it was not. There were no wings, only flames. A woman on fire stood between two trees. Her scarlet hair ended at her shoulders and had long glowing orange streaks that moved like wisps of flame in the wind. Her hand touched a tree and a burst of flame appeared where she touched, crawling up and around the bark.

Their gazes met, green and panicked against orange calm. The fire woman raised an eyebrow and began to approach in a fast walk, flames dancing around each step her pale legs made. She wore clothes that blended into the flames: a short dress of white and orange, dove feathers decorated her shoulders. Her pale arms and legs were guarded by long white boots and gloves, each adorned with long carrot hued ribbons. As she neared, the heat grew more intense.

Wander backed up from the woman and took off running.

Trees began to turn to ash, and branches fell onto the paths Wander ran. She had to twist and turn to avoid catching fire. Then flames began to chase her. She could not afford to stop or else they'd catch her by her heels and climb her like they did the trees.

Something cried, and it echoed through the woods. It howled over the crackling and Wander's heaving breaths. The sound clawed at Wander's chest. Her head began to throb. She followed the cries to a small den under a tree. The face of an unfamiliar creature peeked out. It was dark with splashes of orange and brown, pointed ears, and black eyes.

Wander scooped up the animal, its fur softer and deeper than a rabbit's pelt. To her surprise, it did not struggle. In fact, it embraced her touch, burrowing its head into her armpit.

In that moment of her stopping through, the fire that chased her finally caught up. It tore upward and all around her. Every nerve in her body cried in pain. All she could do was hug the animal, curl up over it, and fall.

Chapter 2
Heathcliff

"If it was a person, Heathcliff would be a poor and lost child. Someone who ran far away, hoping to forget the world only to find themselves just more alone and still trapped," – The Diary of Mr. Flinsler

Roslyn woke up in her room to voices downstairs. Slipping out from her pink quilted bed, she rubbed her eyes. The far wall of her room was a shade of red she had not seen before. As she awakened, more voices could be heard from outside the window.

The little girl turned to the window to see the enchanted forest, the Emerald Wilds, burn. It looked like a portal to Hell from a picture in one of her mother's books. Fires lit in their fireplace blanketed the house in warm golden hues. The fire Roslyn saw outside was different. It spread a gray fog and violent red had caged the trees.

She fully awakened at the sight of the villagers. They coughed, shouted, and ran around. Taking her brown teddy, Tiger, she waddled out of her bedroom and checked her brother and mother's empty beds. She stopped at the stairs to see her brother and mother speaking to neighbors by the front door.

"We don't know how it started," said Ms. Engles. "Some are saying it was a fire elemental. It was Aura's Arm on a hunt for a guardian."

"If that is even possible, we should get everyone out of here," said Roslyn's mother.

"I think the plan is to keep the flames to the forest and away from us," said Mr. Engles. "Scouting parties will go off tomorrow to find what they can."

"I'll go tomorrow," said Roslyn's brother, Ethan.

"No," said Mother.

"Mama," Roslyn interrupted to have the whole party looked up the stairs at her. "What's going on?"

Mother pulled up her nightgown as she came up the steps. "It's just a fire, sweetie. I'll wake you up if we need to move. We should be fine." She took Roslyn's hand. "Let's get you back to bed."

In the morning, Roslyn walked outside to the smell of smoke and a fogged-up village.

"Roslyn," mother called from the kitchen as she washed dishes, "get back inside."

"When's Ethan coming back?" Roslyn asked.

"If he does not come back by lunch, I'll go into that graveyard myself and drag him back here."

Roslyn looked out the back window where the Emerald Wilds used to be. All the trees that stood no longer had leaves. They had become dried up husks. Anything green had burned away, the trees left cracked, blackened, and gray.

From the window, Roslyn saw villagers go in and out of the burned down forest with wagons and bags. She perched by the window to watch.

Percy, a friend of Roslyn's brother, came back with a pendant. A silver rabbit, the one his Nancy wore. Nancy had disappeared in the Emerald Wilds a month ago. Roslyn never learned why the young woman went to the Emerald Wilds in the first place. Nancy was nothing like the others. She was just a simple gardener.

Fanning smoke away from his face, Percy handed the pendant to Nancy's father. The man held the silver rabbit to his chest, and Roslyn saw him cry. She never thought Mr. Rean could cry. He usually seemed mean-spirited with nothing to do since his leg broke in a horse-riding accident.

Nicholas and Mr. Hoc came back with a bag full of gold. Nicholas was another friend of Roslyn's brother. Mr. Hoc was a hunter. As Mr. Hoc began to spread the coins around the villagers, Nicholas pulled him aside. A fight broke out. Roslyn saw Mr. Hoc give Nicholas a black eye before Percy broke the fight up.

There was a sword that took three people to carry, a two-handed, unsheathed sword. Why it took three people to carry just one blade, Roslyn could not guess.

After witnessing several waves of greed and grief, Roslyn's curiosity was settled. She was prepared to go color in her room until she heard shouts. Looking up, she saw her brother run out of the forest. He had never run so fast before. His arms held someone whom he had draped Papa's old coat. Villagers crowded around him. He shouted for a doctor, and they scattered.

With the person still in his arms, Ethan charged toward the house and knocked on the back door. Mother and Roslyn opened the door. Ethan stomped in, and with him came the stench of smoke and rotting meat.

"Ethan, what's that?" mother asked.

It was a person. Fire had branded the entire body into volcanic-like skin. He or she was hairless, dry, and bleeding from every pore with patches of uneven colors of scrambled skin. The only places Roslyn could possibly see a human was in the hand that protruded from under Papa's old coat.

"This person is alive," Ethan said. "I found them deep in the woods."

Ethan put the body on the couch and pulled off the coat. Mother tried to push Roslyn back, but she saw the whole body. How could it be alive? The skin looked as crisp as tree bark. Fluid oozed from some of the charred flakes on the shoulders. Whatever clothes it once wore were now tatters of singed rags. It smelled awful, enough to make Roslyn pinch her nostrils.

"Doctor Reiner should be on his way," Ethan said.

When Wander opened her eyes, she wished for death.

Every inch of her body screamed in agony. Attempting to move felt worse than anything she had suffered before. She could not relate the pain to any other, not the stings of a thousand bees or even the crunch of a bear's maw against her skin and bones. The pain was so overwhelming; she could not feel what was around her. She could not feel the bed under her charred back or even her fingers touching each other.

Out of the corner of her vision she grasped the image of a warm glow. Her breath hissed inwards as she twisted her neck to view a white candle lit on a bed stand. Wax drops had dried at the bottom of the plate it sat upon. She watched the little wisp of orange and recalled the trees burning, the snaps of branches and roar of heat against her skin.

"Oh dear, she's awake."

An unrecognizable voice. Wander listened more to the voice than what it said, a strange, nasal voice. A man with hair growing out of his chin and neck suddenly hovered over Wander. His black eyebrows reminded her of poisonous, hairy caterpillars. He wore strange, see-through petals over his eyes. His breath smelled sweet like the ooze squeezed out of sugarcane.

"Miss. Miss, can you tell me your name?"

"Where am I?" She coughed and pain rippled through her body. Her throat felt like as though it were a mossy stone that bristled when she spoke. She held back the animal in her that wanted to wail. She wanted to scream and cry until the agony was gone.

"Heathcliff. We found you in the aftermath of a big fire in the Emerald Wilds. You . . . are not well."

"Who are you?" her voice ached. It felt as though the flames not only burned her outsides but insides from the roof of her mouth to the pit in her neck.

"Reiner. I've been treating your wounds for the past week. The Flinsler family has given you one of their rooms and has been looking after you when I could not."

"I . . . have a friend," Wander said. "Masu. He—"

Before she could finish, Reiner was already shaking his head. "I'm sorry. We have not found a single soul besides yourself."

Her heart retched like her lungs when they coughed from the smoke. She wanted to throw up. She tried to move, only to let out a feral howl from her raw, crispy skin rubbing under bandages that stiffened her arms and legs. She had not noticed until her attempt to move that she was wrapped all over in cloth. She could arch her neck and see that she wore no clothes, only white bandages, like a deformed cocoon. Many parts of her bandages were stained red and yellow.

"Don't move! Please! You are in a very poor state!" Reiner's fingers spread out, lightly pushing Wander back down.

"I have to find Masu."

"Was your friend in the forest?"

"He . . . might have left." She took hope in that. He left her in the nest and he could fly, so how could fire possibly catch him? If she survived, there was no way he had died. Every day she fumbled to survive, while he always knew what he was doing. He had to live if she did.

"Well, I can help you send him a letter if need be. Just please stay still."

Wander had no clue was a "letter" even was, but she accepted Reiner's plea. She needed to collect her thoughts anyway. This was too much to take in all at once, meeting a whole other person, being separated from Masu, and these wounds.

Even more people came in, four more. Wander could not believe so many people could be in the same place. She rested her eyes as she listened to their voices.

"She's awake?"

"Yes, but I think it's best to leave her alone for now. She's in shock."

"Did she say who she was? Where she is from?"

"No. I'm not going to bother her with questions for now."

"It's not important, Ethan. Why are you so suspicious?"

"You weren't there when we found her. The entire forest was decimated, and she was just . . . lying there."

"You say that like she came out spotless."

"Fire like that doesn't leave spots, mother! It melts people and animals. We found the river dried up. There were no trees, not a blade of grass left standing. The Emerald Wilds was an enchanted forest, not your simple backyard garden! That fire was not natural, so anything that can walk out of it alive can't be natural, either."

So these are humans? Wander breathed deeply, her throat itching for water. Reiner did not have wings; did that make him like her? She had imagined meeting humans like her before. She imagined they would have things in common that she and Masu did not, like her terrible cooking or love of drawing shapes in the sand.

She shut her eyes. Sleep had never been so easy. She wondered if was actually sleep. It felt less like a choice, like the whole world would suddenly fall away from her. Only then was the pain not so hard to bear. She wondered if her time in the world had come to an end. Maybe the world would one day fall away and not return.

The days Wander lay in the bed were uncountable as she slept randomly both day and night.

Each moment was marked with searing pain. Reiner changed her bandages often, trying to be as gentle as he could. He would unwrap them, starting with her legs and arms. When naked, she felt sticky and strangely cold. When she craned her neck, she could not recognize her own form. Her skin had become a leathery suit of dark, red, and white splotches.

She began to ask Reiner some questions. "When will I be able to move?" She wanted out of the room. Out to where she could find Masu or he could find her. He must be past the panic point with worry. This did not compare to the other times she had gone missing. Masu wouldn't be happy to see how hurt she got this time. Maybe he had better ways to fix it than the humans.

"I've give you at least three months if you want to move without much pain."

"What are months?"

Wander could tell when she asked a strange question of Reiner. The man would squint and wrinkle his nose. "Three months can be around ninety days."

"Nine?"

"No. Ninety."

The room became as familiar as Masu's nest, especially the ceiling, built like many red tree trunks that were turned sideways and pressed together. Besides the dreams she could escape to, there was not much to entertain her.

One of the humans often peaked in at Wander. She was small, maybe less than a third of Masu's height. She and Wander had staring contests though the doorframe. Like Ms. Flinsler, the girl had short dark hair that curled around large ears. Her copper eyes had a talent for not blinking.

They often had their staring contests at dusk and dawn after meals. The Flinslers ate elsewhere, and then Ms. Flinsler would come in and hand-feed Wander. She was gentle and called Wander kind things like "honey" and "sweetie." She also apologized a lot. The food was better than Masu's. Ms. Flinsler used things like salt, butter, and seasonings that Wander had never tasted before.

After Ms. Flinsler left, the little girl would peek through the doorframe. One day Wander caught the girl's gaze and she finally broke their silence. "Why are you so small?"

The little girl hesitated, looking away as though thinking of escape. Looking back at Wander she said, "I'm six years old."

"Years?"

The little girl stepped inside; gray socks concealed her feet. She wore a thin, white gown. "You don't know?"

"No."

"Do you know how old you are?"

"No."

The girl tiptoed closer with her hands curled up against her chest. She and Wander went into a silent staring contest again. The little one broke eye contact and examined Wander's encased body up from her exposed face and down to her wrapped feet. "I'm sorry."

Wander understood the sentiment, but not the reason. She shut her eyes, feeling like the world could fall away at any moment.

"It is true?" the little one began. "Doctor Reiner said that you told him you lived in the Emerald Wilds?"

Wander had told Reiner all she could about herself. She overheard him speaking to the Flinsler family. They thought something was wrong with her, a curse, spell, or sickness. "No one can survive on their own there," they said. Wander told Reiner that Masu took care of her. What they thought of that, she did not yet know.

"I did."

"It wasn't scary?"

"The fire was much scarier."

The little girl perched in the wooden chair that Reiner or Ms. Flinsler usually sat in. "I'm Roslyn."

"I'm Wander."

"That's a weird name."

"Masu gave it to me. He gave me the name because I kept wandering everywhere."

Roslyn smiled, showing a large gap in her teeth. Wander did not know people could lose those. "Is it true he had wings?"

So Reiner did tell the others. Wander guessed that they reacted the same way as they did to her living in the wilds: disbelief. Roslyn appeared to believe her, though; she could see it in the girl's interest.

"Yes, big black ones like a vulture's. If he stretched them out, he could easily fill this entire room."

Roslyn's grin widened, "Really? That big? And he was a spirit? How could you touch him?"

"I always could. Masu thinks I'm just a strange human since I bleed like one."

"I've never met a spirit before. I've never left Heathcliff. Mama won't let me."

"Masu was like that with me, too. He didn't want me to leave the forest."

"Was he like a papa to you?"

Wander did not know what a "papa" was. She said nothing, realizing she wanted to change the topic of discussion. For so long she wanted eager ears to hear about Masu, but now that she had them, she felt stuck, like words were not enough. She missed him more than the forest or even her ability to move. He knew her, he understood her even when she was silent. She wanted to hear his voice. He could say anything right now and it would be a comfort.

Once she was so sick, she couldn't get out of bed like in this moment. He spoke to her, even though she was too weak to speak back. His hand would sometimes rub her stomach in slow circles. Other times he just set his hand on her head, and his thumb would caress her scalp. When she got cold hands, he'd hold them to his mouth and breathe warm air to them. When she threw up, he held her hair and stroked her back. He hated to leave the nest with her sick or hurt, waiting for him.

"Are you thirsty?"

Wander snapped out of her trace. Roslyn seemed to have gotten the hint of silence and changed the subject.

"Roslyn!"

Ethan, Roslyn's brother, came to the door. Wander recognized his voice, as it was the loudest in the house. He often smelled of sweat. Wander could even see it on his arms, face, and neck like dew on leaves.

"Come here!" he hissed.

Roslyn's smile disappeared. Dragging her feet, she left the room, Ethan shutting the door behind her.

"I told you not to speak to her." Wander could hear Ethan beyond the walls, as usual.

"But she's nice!"

"She's not in her right mind. Anything that comes out of those wilds is not completely human."

"What's wrong with that?"

"Don't be stupid, Ros! She's dangerous."

"You're just being mean!"

"I'm keeping you safe. If I have to be mean, then fine. C'mon, go back to bed."

Wander listened to their steps fade off. She shut her eyes.

Wander's eyes opened to the log ceiling. As her eyes adjusted to the night, she made out the silhouettes of the room. For the first time since the fire, she lifted her arm and looked at her hand. The fire was merciful to her palm and fingers. She clenched them into a fist and then stretched them out.

Expecting to scream in agony, she sat up.

But there was no agony.

She managed to look out the window that teased her each day by hanging over her head where she could only see sunrays or moonlight bleed through. Strange ground-built nests were outside. Did this mean she has been on the ground this whole time? The thought felt dangerous. How did beasts not claim these people?

Standing up, Wander dizzily swayed in the moonlight. The bandages had stiffened her knees and elbows. She un-wrapped them and saw her bark-like torn-leather skin. If only there were some way she could heal properly. The humans worked like Masu, using tools and such, but Wander's body never got fixed.

Wander lightly stepped through the strange nest. Squares of images hung on the walls. Wander recognized some of the images to be the Flinsler family. There was a strange one with Ms. Flinsler holding a bundle of something that screamed. A human? There was no way they could get that small.

As much as Wander searched the nest, she could not find a curtain to the outside. She found a strange part of the nest that formed a path up, but going up could not be the exit. She followed the walls, touching around for some hidden exit. Finally she found part of the wall that looked different from the rest. Her hand found a knob that stuck out. Pulling did not work, but when she twisted, it pulled the un-matching wall open to the outside.

Stepping out, Wander looked around in wonder at all the nests that surrounded her. Did people live in all of them? The thought overwhelmed her. Maybe if enough people stuck together, they were safe. She wandered out of the land of nests and toward what was left of the wilds.

She knew it was the wilds, as it was as scarred and dry as her singed skin. She bent over. Her hand caressed the corpse of what seemed to once a blade of grass. It crinkled at Wander's touch, breaking into crumbs.

Masu used fire all the time, so Wander always thought it was a good thing. Maybe too much of a good thing makes it bad. Fire though . . . was usually created wasn't it? So what created enough fire to burn everything?

She wandered farther into the wounded land. What were once trees were now little more than thin, black shadows. They crunched at the touch of Wander's hands. The horizon was nothing but hills, raked of what once was a forest.

She sat down on a rock, its moss now blackened. She felt tightness in her throat. Placing her elbows on her knees, she planted her face in her hands. In the darkness of her palms, she tried to imagine home. The discomfort of her changed body tried to pull her back to the present, her teeth clenched with the thought of wanting to rip her skin off.

Masu could not be here. He flew away. Unless he looked for her, then he would have returned to see the nest aflame. He must have seen the fire and flew back to save Wander. He must have searched and searched. He must think she's dead. Where would he go if that were the case?

There was a crunching noise.

Releasing her face from her hands, Wander saw a familiar animal, black with splashes of orange, and brown with large eyes, pointed ears, and a fluffy tail.

"You . . ."

She recalled holding the animal in the flames, curling up; her body became a barrier between it and the fire. The fire ate at her flesh with the creature safe under her. It must have run when the fire died out.

It did not look well. The animal shivered though the air was not cold. Its pink tongue hung out, along with something else. It dropped a single, large, black feather at Wander's feet. Taking the feather, Wander realized it was attached to a leather strap. With her mouth and her right hand, she tied the bracelet to her right wrist.

It was the feather Masu had given her when he tired of her poking and prodding at his wings. She always wore it, but it must have come off. Or maybe the animal took the trinket from her as she protected it from the fire.

Her fingers caressed the vane, hollow shaft, and the softer, downy bits at the bottom. She stroked her face with the feather, remembering the nights she'd bury her face into his wings when he had his back to her. It even smelled like him.

Her breath shook, then her shoulders, then down to her chest. An inhuman sound choked out of her as she crumbled down from the rock, onto her knees. She hugged the feather against her like a precious living thing. The burned skin of her cheeks ached as her tears were entrapped in her wounds.

The animal jumped, its front paws on Wander's knees. It licked the tears off her cheeks. Wander enveloped the creature, wrapping her arms around the animal as it continued licking her face.

"Thank you," Wander whispered. She let go. The animal agreed that they were done, jumping down. "You can come with me. I'll keep you safe."

It seemed to understand, as it followed her all the way back to the place of human nests.

As the winter air grew more frigid, Ethan, Percy, and Nicholas collected wood for the coming winter. Leaves had begun to brown, crisp, and fall.

"I heard your family adopted Wander," said Percy as he took a break to smoke.

Ethan swung his axe at a vertically adjusted log, splitting it in half. He rubbed his arm against the sweat on his forehead. "You know my mom," he said. "She thinks she's everyone's mother."

Nicholas sat next to Percy with his carving knife with the beginning of what would be a wood duck. "So, Wander is just suddenly fine now? Dr. Reiner said he did not expect her to live."

Ethan wished he could change the subject, but these questions were bound to happen eventually. "Yes. The girl claims that she no longer feels much pain." His mother allowed Wander to keep the extra room that she had spent time in while bedridden. Out of pity, she even let Wander keep her pet around the house in the day. At night though, she had to leave it outside. Roslyn loved the animal, though it ran at the mere sight of her after many abuses of tight hugs.

"So what is that animal of hers anyway? Some kind of cat?" Percy asked.

Ethan chopped another log. "It's a damn wild fox."

"Strange colors for a fox."

"It's from the Emerald Wilds, so I'm not surprised," Ethan said. "Nothing there is normal."

"Does it have a name?"

"Hell if I know. Roslyn likes to call it Smokey. Wander never calls it anything."

"She really is a strange one."

After a long day of wood collecting, the boys dropped the logs over in their backyards before going out for drinks. With his mother babysitting for Ms. Engles and Roslyn in school, Ethan had the freedom to stay out late. As for Wander, she either played outside or in her room. The burned wind-born could entertain herself for hours with Roslyn's toys.

To call Heathcliff a modest village was generous. It was a place meant for people looking to get away from spirits and other humans. Their tavern was someone's house. Mr. Chang dedicated what could've been a decent room into a bar. His tavern had been redecorated since the Emerald Wilds burned down. He used what he found in the dead forest as a way to liven the place. Strange idols sat on shelves and weapons hung on the walls.

As Ethan and his friends walked in, Ethan stopped to stare at a sword on the wall. Circular and triangle-like shapes were engraved into the beginning half of the steel blade. The grip was wrapped in brown cloth. The spherical pommel reflected candlelight from the bar.

"Do you like the Emerald Blade?" Mr. Chang called out from behind the bar.

"Emerald Blade?"

Mr. Chang came over to Ethan's side. "That's what I named the sword since it came from the Emerald Wilds."

"Why don't you sell it?" asked Nicholas. "It could be worth a fortune."

"Ah. I have other swords I can sell that we found. This one is not for sale. It's enchanted, so only spirits can use it. And the fewer weapons spirits have, the better. I'd prefer it on my wall rather than in some spirit's hands."

"How do you know it's enchanted?"

"Because it took three people to carry it for me!"

They sat at a table instead of the bar and drank late into the night. It was one of those nights that the three boys did not want to go home. They just wanted to stay together at that table and talk about dreams, grudges, and love. Two hours in, Wander came back to their minds again.

"I've seen Wander around at the edge of the village," Nicholas said. "I sometimes see her crouched, digging a hole in the ground or burying some rocks. Another time she was drawing circles in the dirt with a stick. She sometimes whispers to her animal, too."

Ethan shook his head. "I really don't think we should keep her. I should have left her in that forest."

Percy leaned forward. "That's kind of harsh."

"He's right, though," Nicolas cut in. "That girl is a witch. If she could survive that fire and the enchanted forest, she can't be human."

"My mom thinks the wilds messed with the girl's head," Ethan said. "She thinks that Wander will become civilized if we are kind and patient."

"Screw that," Nicolas took the last swig of his rum. "Wind-borns never grow up normal."

"She's a terrible influence on Ros," Ethan said. "She sneaks into Wander's room, and they talk. She's started to collect snakeskins, bird skulls, and bugs and keep them in her room. When Wander isn't round, she's all Ros talks about."

Nicholas frowned, "She could be teaching your sister witchcraft. I've seen that raven feather on her wrist. It's an ill omen."

Nicholas believed in witches and omens, but Percy did not. Ethan sat somewhere in the middle. He liked to have proof; on the other hand, he was cynical and could easily believe in evil.

"Wander?"

Wander awoke to little Roslyn tiptoeing toward her. The girl wore just her nightgown and shivered from the cold. She held her stuffed bear in a hug. "I had a nightmare, and Ethan isn't home. Mama doesn't like it when I wake her up. Can I sleep with you?"

Wander scooted over, and Roslyn got under the quilt with her.

"What's a nightmare?" Wander asked.

"You know how you sometimes go places when you sleep but then forget most of it when you wake up?"

"Yes."

"Sometimes you go to really scary places. That's a nightmare."

Wander wished to press against Roslyn for body warmth but refrained. She knew her skin scared Roslyn.

"If that's what they are, then I've actually been having nightmares, too."

The two of them stared at the ceiling together, unable to sleep. Roslyn placed her bear between them. She tucked him under the blankets and placed his head on the pillow.

"Can you tell me a story?" Roslyn asked.

Wander had already told Roslyn many stories about her and Masu, but just because she told many did not mean she was close to running out of them.

"Once there was a time that I saw a black deer. It was beautiful so I chased it and when I finally lost it, I realized I ran too far and did not know where I was. I was still in the forest, but I could not find my way back home. I wandered around until it got dark, and I started to get really scared. I knew there were giant wolves and other dangerous animals that came out at night. So I decided to look for a place to hide for the night. I found a cave. I went inside and tripped because it was dark. When I hit the ground, I made a loud noise. Then I heard growling. I ran out of the dark cave into the forest. Then the biggest animal I ever saw came out of the cave.

"It was a bear, a giant brown bear with claws as longer than my fingers. When it was on its four paws, it was taller than me. But when it stood up on two legs, it was taller than trees. I ran, and it chased me. I tried to weave through the trees, but the bear kept getting closer. Every step of its paws felt like it could be the one that got me. Then I heard Masu's wings. He dove between the bear and me. He had his fishing spear with him, and he stabbed the bear's shoulder. I stopped running and watched as the bear's big paw slashed at Masu, and he screamed.

"Masu's next stab sent the bear running away. But then he collapsed. I ran to him and saw he was bleeding with an open slash to his chest. He told me he would be okay, but I'd have to help him. I helped him walk back home.

"Though Masu built a ladder for me to climb up and down from the nest, I was always scared to use it, so he usually flew me up and down. It hurt him too much to fly, so I climbed up alone. Even while he was bleeding, he had to encourage me to climb. I got the things he listed, a bottle full of alcohol and bandages. When I came back down, he did not seem well. He sat down and said he felt dizzy. He told me to pour the alcohol over his wound. When I did, he screamed and his wings got all fluffy, which only happened if he was scared.

"I started crying and thought I did something wrong. Even though he was red in the face and in pain, he still comforted me. He said, 'You can do it. I'm not mad. That was good.' So I bandaged him. After he rested, he managed to climb back into the nest with me. The next day I helped him change his bandages, and he said he was proud of me. I was still scared, though. I always thought he could not get really hurt. Since that day he got hurt, I wandered off much less."

"That's the end of the story?" Roslyn asked.

Wander nodded. "He eventually healed up, but it left a big scar. There were other times he got hurt and needed my help. I think those were the scariest times for me."

"I know what you mean. It's scary when Ethan and my mom are hurt."

Silence hung in the air for a while.

"Ethan and Mom don't think Masu exists," Roslyn said. "When I try to tell them your stories, they tell me that the forest messed with your head. That since you are wind-born, you were raised on illusions."

"They're wrong. I've fallen under illusions in the forest before. Masu wasn't an illusion. Illusions don't save you."

"Ethan told me Masu couldn't exist because winged beings were all killed a long time ago."

"I don't know what that means, but he's wrong about Masu."

"I know," Roslyn said. "I believe you."

"Thanks."

Roslyn hugged her stuffed bear. "I bet you were really pretty before you got burned, like a forest fairy from Mama's book."

"What's a fairy?"

Roslyn gasped. "I'll get the book and read it to you!" She hopped out of the bed and Wander heard her feet creak against the stairs.

Wander had a period where she would not leave the house. She'd spend her days with Roslyn or doodling in a blank book the family gave her. Once when Wander was not home, Ethan opened her book. He recognized a stick figure with dark circularly colored in wings and the violent color of red for eyes. One page contained a black figure with round orange eyes. Another was of a tree house, a brown square layered on top of leaves of green on a brown trunk. There was one disturbing image of a woman and trees on fire.

When she did not doodle, Wander looked out of the window at the village life while stroking her feather bracelet. Ethan's mother became convinced Wander had become depressed. "The poor thing has no friends other than Roslyn," she said. She eventually made Wander do the shopping to get out of the house at least once a day.

"You trust her with our money?" Ethan said. "She doesn't even know what that is or how any of this works!"

"It's not that hard to understand. I just told her to get certain things from the store and give the money to the man at the desk as trade. I counted it for her. Besides, I'm sure Mr. Bindle would help her out if she had trouble. She can never learn if we don't trust her."

With that, Wander would go out shopping once a day with little trouble. But once she'd return, she would still remain in the confines of the home. She'd color more pictures, sleep during the day, pet the fox.

"She knows the other people don't like her," Roslyn said. "But Mom and I are nice, so she stays home."

Ethan once sat with his friends outside, drinking ale and watching the village life. Children played hopscotch. His mother's past friends gossiped in the square. A stray cat mewled for food outside the food market. It was a non-working day with the weather pleasant enough to play a game of cards outside. "Hey Ethan, isn't that Wander over there?"

He already knew he would not like whatever he saw. He turned his head and saw Wander physically attacking Nicholas. Ethan bolted up from his seat. Upon closer inspection, she wasn't trying to hurt him but attempting to take his bag. Before Ethan could get to them, Nicholas pushed Wander down to the dirt.

Some of Nicholas's brothers gathered around to protect him. One turned to Wander. "What do you think you're doing?"

Wander pushed her arms against the ground. "That's my bag!"

Ethan didn't move; it appeared the situation was under some control now that Nicholas's brothers were there. Ethan did not want to deal with Wander if he could help it.

"Your bag? I got this from the wilds!" Nicholas said. His hands clutched the strap of a brown leather bag.

"It was mine!"

Ethan noticed Wander's fox was watching from a distance. The creepy creature stood half in an alleyway's shadow.

"What? Is all the gold we all got yours too then because you lived there? You don't own anything."

"The gold isn't anyone's, but Masu gave me that bag!"

"Get it through your head; your spirit-friend never existed! The forest played you like it played all humans."

Wander leapt up and rushed forward. One of the boys swung a punch to Wander's cheek. She staggered backward. The brothers began to surround her, throwing more punches and kicks until she was on the ground. Everyone just watched. Wander curled into the fetal position, her arms trying to protect her face, and her legs shielding her stomach.

"HEY!" Ethan threw his voice. "That's enough!"

The boys broke away from her; one spit on her as the final insult.

Another walked up to Ethan, his breath smelled of alcohol and smoke. "Your family needs to learn how to properly control her, or we'll force her out!"

Ethan nodded, and they left to their daily business. The villagers kept staring. Ethan scooped her wrist up in a death grip, pulling her to stand. To get away from all the eyes, he marched her back home. Mother was out, and Roslyn was at school.

He hurled Wander into her room. "You stupid girl!" The fox skittered into the room from under his feet, nearly tripping him, and jumping on the bed.

Wander looked up at him. Her green eyes were on fire, a look of fury Ethan never thought he'd see in her. She sat herself on her bed by the fox's side, her hands clenched into fists that rested on her knees. She was crying. They were pathetic weeps, like little hiccups. She was trying to hold it in. "Why is he taking so long?" she asked.

She often asked strange questions, and Ethan would ignore her. This time though, he was fascinated by her sudden display of emotion. "Who?"

"Masu. He always found me no matter what." She looked at Ethan, regaining some control. "Roslyn said you and everyone else don't believe me."

"That's right. He'll never find you because he doesn't exist. You said he had wings? Spirits with wings have all been killed a long time ago."

Wander's weeping went silent; she looked toward the window. The fox stretched, its fur standing up and his jaw opening, showing rows of sharp teeth as it yawned.

"I'm hideous."

That was possibly the most normal thing Wander had ever said to him. He realized she did not look through the window, but at her reflection within. She was right; her skin was splotchy, bumpy, and wrinkled. Wearing one of his mother's yellow dresses looked unnatural, like a decaying corpse in a pristine gown.

He bent a little, examining Wander more. She was like a corpse, but she had one feature that was still beautiful: her green eyes.

Seeing Ethan glare at her, Wander looked down. "Even Roslyn said it, so it must be true."

"I have an idea."

Ethan went his mother's room and opened her drawer of cloth. She loved to sew her own dresses, clothes for Roslyn's dolls, and gifts for people. Most of the colors were bright blues, oranges, purples, and pinks. All cut up enough that they could not be used. Then Ethan found untouched black cloth along with some red strips to make up for the rest. He stopped by his room and grabbed his black cloak he'd wear in the winter. He gathered more of his darker clothes.

He came back to Wander's room with the clothes, cloak, and scissors. He cut the length of his cloak so it was not too long for Wander. She was a tall girl, but not as tall as he. He blanketed the cloth around her head and neck. He wrapped her up until all he could see was her face. That was not enough, so he wrapped it more until her green eyes was all he could see.

He put the cloak on her and took her to a mirror.

"Masu won't recognize me if I am like this."

44

Ethan played along with the thought. "Would he recognize you anyway?"

The realization could be seen in Wander's eyes, widening for a moment, and then watering up.

She accepted Ethan's clothes, and wore the cloak and veil every day. The villagers tended to leave her alone more as well. She no longer looked like a girl. Others could only remember she was a girl when she spoke in her innocent voice. But on the outside, she resembled a dark and intimidating figure. Sometimes she looked into the mirror to try to imagine that blonde, smooth, and bright-eyed forest-dwelling girl that she used to be.

It's only skin, Wander would tell herself. *I'm still me.* Though there were too many times she just saw an ugly figure staring back with no connection to her soul.

"And here is one for you."

Wander bowed as Roslyn put a crown of dandelions on top of her veiled head. They sat in the backyard together. Roslyn plucked dandelions and tied their delicate stems into knots around each other. Every time Wander tried to tie one, she pulled too hard and the stem snapped. Eventually Roslyn gave up teaching and just made a crown for her.

Wander tried to think of what she could make Roslyn. Her fingers searched the grass around them. A cricket jumped out, and Roslyn scooted away from where it landed.

Ms. Flinsler voice called from the window. "Dinner!"

Roslyn ran ahead, her pigtails wagging. Wander stood up and glanced at the woods. The fox had run into the woods earlier in the day. It usually stayed for dinner for the chance of leftovers that Wander sneaked out for it to eat.

The creature felt different from others Wander had met. It rarely made a sound at all. Not a squeak, a yelp, or even a huff. Shrugging off the thought, Wander went into the house. By now, she had gotten out of the habit of calling them nests. With the time that passed, she began to wonder if she'd ever see Masu again. Unlike in the wilds, the passage of time caused severe change in the village. The air got colder, leaves died and fell, trees fell asleep. Such things never happened in the Emerald Wilds. Everything stayed green with warm days and chilly nights.

Wander, Roslyn, and Ethan sat at the dining table.

Ms. Flinsler set out plates of fish patties, mashed potatoes, and steamed beans. Before they ate, the family always bowed their heads to thank someone, though Wander never understood who. If she didn't do the same, Ethan always gave her a death glare.

"Aw, I love your flower crown," Ms. Flinsler said as they began to eat.

"I can make you one if you want, Mommy!" Roslyn said.

With so much time hearing Ethan and Roslyn call her "Mom," Wander once called Ms. Flinsler "Mom" by accident. When she did, she felt her cheeks heat up. The word ached in her throat, like it was meant to be said long ago. Ms. Flinsler didn't even flinch; she just looked at Wander and said, "Yes?"

Once dinner was finished, the family retired to their rooms. Wander could hear the ceiling creak and groan from Ethan, Ms. Flinsler, and Roslyn walking above. Ethan's room sat directly above hers, and she could hear him move from his desk, to his closet, and out to hall toward Roslyn's room. Wander sat down on her bedside, caressing Masu's feather on her wrist.

Was it all just an illusion? She began to wonder. Everyone could be right and the forest had her living an elaborate delusion. But what is it that made something real? If she saw it and felt it, how could it be fake?

Illusion or not, she had settled that he could not find her. Maybe he had even died. She might never know.

Pulling her veil tighter, Wander lay down to sleep. She had begun to sleep in her veil and cloak, as she felt unnatural without them. The cloth began to feel like her new skin, and to take it off made her feel more naked and ashamed than ever. She stared at the moonlight coming through her window until sleep took her.

Throwing her quilt aside, Wander sat up, shaking.

Another nightmare. She went to a place in her sleep that shook her core. With her hand on her chest, she felt her heart race. Roslyn said whenever Wander could not sleep due to nightmares, she could try to sleep with Roslyn in her bed. She rose from the bed and paused with a moment of dizziness.

Then she smelled a familiar and haunting stench of stinging heat. It took her back to that moment when the woods glowed in flame.

She flung herself through her room door. The gray ghost of smoke slithered through the hall, and she saw the fire beyond the window climb the house across the street. It consumed wood and flesh, as Wander saw a charred person stumble out of the door and fall to the dirt.

Then the chaos of screaming came. Humans all running around like panicked torches. No one was free of flame. It attacked them, chasing their ankles and spreading over their clothes, hair, and skin.

It had to be the same fire from the forest. It came back for her. It wanted to find her and eat her.

Wander turned back and ran to the dining room where there was a back door. Fire had not surrounded the place yet. She snuck out the back door and turned to peek around the corner. The flames had not discovered her; maybe they would not recognize her under her veil. They still licked at the carcasses of the dead, distracted.

A woman on fire walked into the town square.

Wander sucked in her breath. It was the same woman she had seen the night of the forest fire. She recognized the woman from her pumpkin and cloud hued dress, tall boots, and bright eyes. This time she was smiling; she marched over a human who stumbled backward and fell to the dirt. Wander recognized him, Percy.

The woman cast her hand out to him and flames burst forth out from her palms. He screamed as they attacked him, twisting and sizzling.

Wander could not waste any more safety for curiosity. She took off for the woods, running blindly. Leaping over logs, dodging bushes, and the fox joined her out of nowhere, running at her side. She ran until her breath grew heavy. Stopping, she bent over, her hands on her knees. Her mind raced with her heart. Was she being hunted? The fire was the exactly same as the one that had chased her and consumed her skin. It smelled and behaved the same. If it was the same, then did it know where Masu was? Did it . . . kill him?

She had to go back. Only the fire had the answer to what happened to Masu. Turning, she felt a sudden bite of pain as the fox nipped her heels. She ignored the protest and ran back to the village, her cloak flowing behind her.

Every tree began to look the same, all pine, all still shadows in the dark. All was silent except for the crunch of twigs and leaves under her rushing feet. Her run slowed into a fast walk. She felt the heat of her breath against her veil. The village couldn't have been this far.

Of course she got lost. How typical of her. It's been so long since she ran through the woods, and this place was not familiar to her. The fox had followed, leaping onto a nearby rock, looking into the darkness.

"You!"

A force hit Wander, pushing her into a tree trunk. A muscular arm crushed itself against her neck while a hand held one of her arms down. With her other arm, she tried to push her attacker off. It was no use, like pushing a wall. "Ethan," she hissed as she could make out his face. His nostrils were flaring, eyes wide, mouth quivering, and eyebrows low.

"What did you do?" He put both his hands on her neck, pulling her away from the tree, and slamming her back into it. Her head throbbed. "You killed them! You monster! I knew it! I knew you were a witch!"

The fox bit at his leg, and he swung his foot to its stomach. Even then, the creature did not peep.

"It . . . wasn't me," Wander's breath became like a jagged edge. It was similar to suffering smoke or water but with a crushing feeling. Ethan let her go. She inhaled for her breath to return. Ethan guarded her, fists ready in case she made a single wrong move. "I . . . can build a fire," Wander breathed. "But this fire is not built, it's alive."

"It was just like the fire in your forest! Are you saying this was a coincidence?"

"No. The fire followed me here."

"You really are insane," he said. "I wake up to my sister and mother screaming. I can't get into their rooms and get you for help and you're gone. You murdered them!"

"Roslyn and Ms. Flinsler . . . ?" By some sick twist, she had forgotten about them until now. Not a single thought was spared for her new family as she escaped alone. How could that be? They were her only friends, and they were directly above her as she snuck out.

Ethan looked away, trying to suck in a sob.

"No," Wander got up. "I did not start the fire, Ethan." She gently approached him. "You have to believe me! I would never ever kill them. I loved them."

"Then where were you?"

She teared up. "I don't know. It happened so fast. I got scared, and I ran. I tried to go back but I got lost."

"Coward!" his voice rose louder than Wander had ever heard. She wanted to cover her ears, but he screamed, "They loved you, they trusted you, and you killed them!" His voice cracked into sobs. He hid his face in his palms. He sat on the earth, consumed with agony.

Wander sank down the tree trunk to the ground. Her legs ached from her running. Leaving Ethan to his sorrow, she hugged her knees to her chest and hid her face in the darkness of her legs.

Her crying could not be heard over his, but her knees dampened with tears. Roslyn and Ms. Flinsler did not deserve death. It must have not been slow, the flames liked to hear people scream and fizzle. Not just that but the smoke, she could imagine poor Roslyn choking as she cried for her brother . . . like Wander had once cried for Masu. Or maybe Roslyn cried for her.

Her fingers clenched at her legs, nails digging into her flesh. How could she have left them? How?

Then she remembered the woman of fire.

"It was a spirit."

"What?"

Wander raised her head from her knees. "The fire was a spirit. She was the one who caused the fire in the forest, too. In the Emerald Wilds, I saw her touching trees and burning them. In the village, before I ran, I saw her killing people. Fire came from her hands and feet. Some of her hair moved like the fire. Her eyes were bright orange."

"Are you serious?" The question did not seem sincere, but mocking.

"I know you think I'm crazy, but if you want someone to blame, it was a spirit. She came back for some reason." Wander stood up and swayed with dizziness. "I'm going after her."

"What? Are you going to kill her?"

"No, I'm going to ask her where Masu is." She walked away while touching the back of her head where it throbbed.

"What? You're going back? To the village?"

"Yes."

He stood up, "I'm coming too."

The land was scarred like the Emerald Wilds, only this time there were shadows on the ground in the shape of people.

"Where did their bodies go?" Wander asked as she stood over the dark stretch of dust.

Ethan did not listen, preoccupied as he was with staring at where his home once stood. The home had become a skeleton. It appeared the roof had been weakened by the fire, causing it to collapse inward. Only the stone chimney remained standing above the rubble.

Wander jumped over the dead shadow and glanced around corners of buildings. She could still feel weak heat trapped within the walls of the homes. The fire was near the end of its long sigh, dying down into nothing.

"Where is your damn spirit?"

"Shush."

"What?"

"Shhh!" Wander hissed. She never shushed someone before, though Masu often did to her. She listened closely to the wall of a building.

"Please . . . help," a weak voice, coughing.

Wander made her way to the house door, opening it and stepping back as the roof crumbled dark debris the size of crumbs down at her feet. Cooked bodies lay spread on the floor. One's skin still bubbled and popped. What was once furniture were now dark piles of crispy wood and ash.

A man lay in the corner. She could not recognize him; the burns were too severe. The whites of his eyes and chattering teeth greatly contrasted with the darkness and red that his body had become. He lay curled in a ball, shaking uncontrollably.

"What are you doing?" Ethan walked in. He followed Wander's eyes to the trembling figure in the corner. He sucked in a gasp. "Oh my god, Nicholas."

"E-E-Ethan."

He sat in front of his friend while Wander stayed distant.

"My throat f-f-f-feels like it's on fire. Water . . . please."

Ethan gave Wander a pleading look. She looked down and walked away in search of water. Outside the nest, she noticed the fox pawing at the tavern. It was one of the only buildings left standing. The door had a window with a crack in the shape of a lightning bolt.

Wander never went into the tavern. She knew Ethan, Nicolas, and Percy liked to go there near the end of the day. The owner rarely was seen outside. "What is it?" Wander asked the fox. "Is someone in there?"

She opened the door and the fox rushed in. Wander followed, looking at the things on the wall. She examined a portrait with a woman on a horse, curly red hair, blue eyes, and a half-smile in a world of white grass and leaves. Above the chimney was a mantle with pottery glazed with dark and spotted hues, half melted candles, and a stuffed squirrel. Wander poked it; it looked real but felt stiff. She touched its eye, realizing it was made of glass like Roslyn's bear's eyes. The floor was soft, covered in a blanket-like material with intricate blue and red patterns.

The fox's silhouette looked at a certain object on the wall.

Wander approached for a closer look. She had no idea knives could get so long and large. The weapon was propped up with a stand that held it horizontal. She ran her finger down to the tip, taking her hand back to see red drops slither down her finger. The brown handle was long enough for a two-handed grip. Wander saw

52

the reflection of her veiled face in the weapon, her green eyes blinking back at her through etchings.

She placed a hand on the grip and lifted up the large knife. With its length and her reach, she almost stabbed the ceiling. Pleased with the find, she kept the weapon and walked out of the tavern.

"Wander," Ethan was looking for her in the village square. He saw her and ran over.

"Is Nic—"

"He died."

Wander looked down. She had been so fascinated with the weapon, she forgot about finding water.

Ethan squinted. "Why do you have that?" He pointed to the weapon.

Wander shrugged.

"Better yet, how the are you holding it? With one hand, too!"

"What do you mean?"

"It took three people to carry that sword from the Emerald Wilds to the tavern."

"It's light." Wander offered the sword to Ethan.

Once he gripped the sword, Wander let go. The sword fell to the ground and took Ethan with it, his knuckles hitting the earth.

Ethan tugged his hands out from under the sword grip.

Wander picked the blade back up.

"The thing is probably cursed, coming from the wilds," Ethan said. "You shouldn't take it."

"No," Wander said. "I want to keep it."

"For what?"

"Protection."

"From what?"

"The fire."

"You think you can fight fire with a sword?"

"Maybe."

Ethan sighed. He turned to glance back at the remains of his home. Wander began to walk toward another building to continue searching.

"Before Nicholas passed, he confirmed what you said, about a fire elemental coming and killing everyone."

"A what?"

"An elemental. It's a type of spirit. It would explain the amount of fire she created. They don't usually have anything to do with humans, though. It's possible she could be Chant, Aura's Fire. But why would she target our small little village?"

"What?" Wander had no clue what he was talking about.

Furrowing his brows, he crossed his arms. "It's nothing."

"Where could the fire spirit have gone?"

"I don't know. Elementals live across the sea, and deviants live on the other side of the continent." Ethan sighed, "It had to be Aura's Arm. There was no other reason an elemental would attack us."

"What are deviants and Aura?"

"It's not like you'll understand if I try to explain it to you."

"Try."

Ethan rolled his eyes and began. "I'll make it super simple so you'll understand. There are humans and spirits. There are different kinds of spirits. We got elementals, lullabies, faceless, and rainbows. Elementals are assholes who destroy everything. Lullabies drink blood. Faceless wear masks and rainbows live in the desert. Deviants are the worst of them. Right now they are trying to kill all the humans. Their queen, Aura, has mind-control powers and uses them to kill everyone. Deviants have killed entire races of spirits before such as horned beings, shadows, and winged beings. They are able to kill everyone because the queen has a lot of powers. She uses the powers to make her Arms, which are basically mindless slaves, to kill people for her. Chant, the fire elemental, is one of those people. Except apparently, she's not mind-controlled! She's just an asshole! And none of this explains why they'd attack us! Sure, they want to kill all the humans, but we are the furthest and smallest village out there! Our capital city is still standing. It doesn't make sense. You know what? The reason doesn't even matter! What matters is that Ros and Mom are DEAD!"

Wander opened her mouth.

"No!" Ethan hissed. "No more questions. Just leave me alone." Ethan stomped off toward the rubble that was once their home. He kicked some debris and sat down.

Leaving Ethan alone, Wander wandered through the village. Approaching a house, she glanced into a window to see nothing but rubble. Her sense of smell began to numb from the constant stench of burnt wood and flesh. She did not want to see anymore, so she sat on the earth.

Roslyn and Ms. Flinsler, were they really dead? She could not process what had happened. Most of all, she could not believe what she had done. Why did she leave without them? Hugging herself, she let herself cry again with the fox sitting at her side.

Eventually Wander returned to Ethan.

The boy had planted himself over the grave of his home. His eyes were stained red, and he just stared at the earth with tears still rolling down. As Wander approached, their eyes met. "What do we do now?" she asked.

"We are in the ass-end of nowhere. The next human settlement is mountains away, a two-week trip without horses or wagons."

Wander had no idea what settlements were. Ms. Flinsler had taught her what weeks were though. Seven days plus seven more could not be so bad. Then again, she had only known the Emerald Wilds and Heathcliff. What else lay beyond?

"Let's go then," Wander said. "Let's go to the human place." She had decided it was best to get Ethan somewhere safe. She owed him that much. Once he was safe, she could find the fire elemental on her own. "And cross the mountains? Do you know how dangerous that is? There are spirits, wolves, bears, little food, and cold nights."

"I've survived worse. We can make it. Let's take everything we can from this place, whatever food, bags, and clothes we can find. Then let's go."

To her surprise, Ethan nodded. He got up and began to loot.

Chapter 3
The Outskirt Mountains

"It's just mountains for miles. Utterly unsettled except for the occasional lonely farm. The mountains have no owner, neither spirit nor human. Some of Awei is just so, untaken and free." – Awei Unsettled

"**W**ake up!"

Wander woke to a bag being thrown on her lap. She set her hands on fallen pine needles. A blue jay sang somewhere above. Ethan stood over her along with the mountain pines. "Since when do you sleep so much?" He had always woken before her, anxious to continue moving.

Wander shivered. Their mornings were fogged up and heavy with dew. Every day Ethan dragged her through the mountains, her legs grew sore, and he criticized her every action and word. Roslyn had told Wander Ethan didn't like her, but she did not know the full extent of his dislike until now. Over their days of walking through the mountains, he had told her to walk faster, talk louder, stop talking, stop kicking pinecones, stop complaining, stop sleeping so much, stop breathing heavily, stop asking questions.

"I think he's scared of you," Roslyn once said. "Because the Emerald Wilds killed Daddy. He just left one day to search for rare medicine for someone . . . and he never came back."

Wander dipped her hand into her bag and felt around. She took out a smaller bag and picked out some dried grapes. The fox emerged from a nearby bush, its dark and orange pelt sparkling with dewdrops. Wander showed her hand of dried grapes, and the animal ate the whole handful.

Ethan charged at the creature, causing it to run back into the greenery. He turned to Wander, "You're feeding that thing?"

"It's hungry."

"It can get its own food. It is a wild animal. We, on the other hand, need this food to survive. How long have you been giving it our food?"

A silence hung between them.

"Oh my god," Ethan laughed. He did not laugh like Roslyn. Roslyn would laugh when she felt joy, but Ethan seemed to laugh out of frustration. "You idiot! You've been feeding a third of all our food to an animal!"

"Sorry," Wander pulled her bag over her head and shoulder and ran to catch up. On her back, the sword rattled. She had wrapped the blade in clothes and secured it with belts so it would not cut her. With a surplus of belts, she had also crafted a long fastening similar to a bag strap so that she could carry the sword on her back.

They had travelled for five days now. It began to get colder as they climbed the mountains. The pine trees possessed pinecones the size of human skulls. Birds sang; they seemed happy here, echoing each other's voices.

Ethan had the remains of a map found in Heathcliff, so they kept on a dirt trail. He said it was a trade route, so they might eventually meet other humans heading toward a town or village. What he feared was meeting lullabies, the spirits whose land bordered these mountains.

The mountains they traveled through were called the Outskirt Mountains. Ethan attempted to explain the map and its locations to Wander.

"Awei starts at the Western Isles and ends at the Collapsing Sea. The map we have just shows the western lands though since the rest was burned away. That's fine though since we are moving west."

"What's Awei?"

"The world or at least what we know of it. It's here. It's every place you'll ever be."

"What's the Collapsing Sea?"

"It's the east ocean," Ethan explained. "It's no different than the Warding Sea around the Western Isles, all water and monsters."

"What's the Western Isles?"

"Could you just shut up?" Ethan said. "It's not like you're even going to any of these places."

Frowning, Wander picked up a pinecone. She threw it up and caught it to keep herself entertained while following Ethan. "What will do you when you find other humans?" She decided that she was silent long enough.

"When we get to the next town, I'll trade work for staying at someone's place. While surviving that, I'll send letters to my relatives in Sollast."

"What-last?"

"Sollast. It's where Queen Naktol's castle is. She is the leader of the humans. Sollast is a city, a place with the most humans, the most buildings."

"Can I come?" She had nowhere else to go. After all, she had no idea where the fire spirit went. They checked the outer edges of Heathcliff but found no trail. There were no more survivors after Nicholas who could give any clues either.

Ethan turned his head, and she could see one of his brown eyes. They reminded her of the color of a tree after she tore off some of its flaking skin.
"Sure," he answered.

He could not see her smile behind her veil, but she was beaming. She threw another pinecone up as high as she could and scampered to walk at his side.

She did not realize how much she missed the outdoors until she walked the mountain path: the columns of brown under a blue ceiling, guests of feather, scales, and fur, the soft green of mossy beards, and the trickle of river water. She wanted to swing on a passing vine, splash ponds with pebbles, or dig a hole. But the days were nothing but walking, with the occasional break for water or food.

Wander's legs ached by the time they settled in for the night. She and Ethan sat over the fire in silence for a long time before Wander decided to speak, "You don't think the fire will find us here do you?"

"It's not just fire," Ethan explained. "It's an elemental."

"Right. Well, maybe if we see the elemental again, I can ask them about where Masu is."

"That would be insane."

"Insane?"

"Crazy."

"I'm not crazy."

"Elementals are possibly the worst of the spirits. They take pleasure in destroying everything. They don't listen to people, much less answer their questions."

Wander scooted closer to him. The fox curled up, its tail covering its dark snout. "Why do you hate spirits?"

"Well, we are at war with a group of spirits who plan to kill us all. I just got attacked by a spirit. Spirits enslaved humanity hundreds of years ago. They think we are animals. They are capable of magic and use it to scare us."

"Masu wasn't like that. He—"

Ethan interrupted, "Masu wasn't real. Winged spirits were all killed by the deviants hundreds of years ago, the same spirits who are trying to kill all the humans right now."

"Then not all of them were killed."

"Even if he was real, he could not have been your friend. Winged beings were the ones who kept humans as slaves. The only reason we got free was because they were all killed."

"What is a slave?"

Ethan let out an exasperated breath. "Wander. Let's just go to focus on eating now, okay?"

She backed into a pine tree and folded her arms. Ethan got a fire started and took out a pot. He poured in water to boil for oatmeal.

Wander dwelled on what Ethan said. Maybe deviants hunted down Masu, and the forest was a safe place to hide. But why wouldn't he tell her about that? The world was more complicated than she ever dreamed. Masu once told her too much of anything, even a good thing, would turn it bad. She did not believe him then, but now there was too much of everything, too much to know, to care about, and to question.

"A lot of people think it's the end of the human race." Ethan broke the silence when he handed Wander some oatmeal. "Deviants have wiped three other races off the face of the earth: the horned beings, the shadows, and the winged beings. And we might be the fourth. I always thought we'd be safe because Heathcliff was so far from everything but . . ." His voice began to tighten, and he went quiet. His eyes sparkled with sudden moisture. His jaw clenched, and Wander saw the bulge in his neck bob as he swallowed.
Wander finished her oatmeal. The fox stood up and moved toward their bags. Ethan shooed it with violent waves of his hand.

They next day on the trail felt the same as the last. When Ethan was busy charging ahead, Wander withdrew some crackers from her bag and gave them to the fox. Its warm pink tongue licked her hand for any grain offered. Ethan and Ms. Flinsler didn't know that she and Roslyn sometimes snuck food for the fox after breakfast, lunch, and dinner. It seemed to like everything: meat, vegetables, rice, bread, and fruit. Roslyn loved feeding the fox. She adored the furry animal. "It's cuter than a cat or a dog," she said. "Why don't we have pet foxes?" The answer became obvious to Wander as the fox disliked Roslyn's tight hugs and attempts to dress it up in bows to the point it eventually avoided her.

"How are you feeling?"

Wander looked up to see Ethan stopped and looking at her.

"Bored."

"No. I meant physically."

"I'm fine."

"Your burns don't bother you? At all?"

"Nope."

"The doctor thought you would be in a bed for the rest of your life," Ethan said. "There is something you're not telling me."

"I don't know," Wander shrugged. "I just got better."

Both she and Ethan stopped at a clearing with a view. Wander never captured so much land in her eyes before—a flat green blanket of trees as far as the eye could see until the earth and sky met.

"Wander —"

She noticed before Ethan could finish. Smoke. Lots of it. It billowed up a short distance from the bottom of the mountain. No campfire could make that much, which meant it had to be an elemental.

Wander split off from the trail in a run. Her legs mastered the steep mountainside, stumbling down in a sprint. She stepped on ferns to remain grounded and grabbed onto branches when she felt herself stagger.

"WANDER!" Ethan shouted from behind.

She did not look back. There was no mistake. This fire had to be from the same spirit from the

Emerald Wilds and Heathcliff. The elemental was the only clue Wander had to Masu. She had no idea how big the world was, so she did not want to miss another chance.

A branch she grabbed snapped, and she fell. She rolled in the dirt until she hit a tree. Her veil unwrapped from her face, and the air felt unnatural on her marked skin. Her shoulder weakly throbbed. Looking over, she saw that her bag had torn open, and all the food was scattered. The fox had been following her, watching from a rock. No sign of Ethan.

Wander rewrapped her veil around her face and continued to run. The anticipation made her sick to her stomach. Masu had to be alive; he had to be. She lost sight of the smoke now that she was surrounded by trees but ran in the direction she recalled from the view.

The familiar smell of smoke came. As the smell got stronger, Wander could see Masu's nest on fire, the crispy corpses lying around Heathcliff, and her own hideous reflection. Her scarred and deformed skin came alive with shivers.

The mountainside ended, and she stood on flat ground. She followed her nose. Then the dark cloud appeared visible again over the canopy of branches. She came to a clearing. Bodies lay scattered like the lifeless dolls on the floor of Roslyn's room. Each was in the process of getting eaten by flame. Wander examined one corpse closely to see it wore clothes made of shining stone and held a bow with a quiver of arrows at its back.

"Who are you?"

The elemental's voice rose above the crackling flames. She stood in the center, her orange hair flowing in ribbons. She was almost hypnotizing to look at, like a candle. She took a step forward and fire burst from her feet. The flames slithered to Wander, circling her from behind, creating a wall of flame.

"You aren't like the other soldiers." As the spirit moved forward, Wander could feel her skin begin to warm from the heat the elemental emitted. "You are what, a cloaked assassin?"

"Where's Masu?"

Wander did not expect the question to have the effect that it did. The woman's smile sunk, and her eyes went wide. "What?"

"You burned the Emerald Wilds where we both lived. I saw you. Please, my friend, he has large black wings like a crow. His eyes are red. Your fire, you didn't kill him did you? Do you know where he went?"

The spirit appeared thunderstruck. "You're Wander."

"Yes!"

The elemental's fire suddenly grew. Wander felt the firewall behind her get hotter, making her back burn just by being near. The bodies in the field melted like wax. The spirit's hair and ribbons rose up as her flaming body appeared to change. As she became hotter, the grass around her disintegrated into dark ash.

Though her heart raced and her body shook, Wander did not move. The elemental burst into flames that charged forward through the grass. Reaching Wander, the fire rose and turned back into the woman. A sudden arrow hit her in the side of the head, immediately decaying upon contact like a raindrop hitting stone.

Wander turned to see Ethan. He had taken an intact quiver and bow from one of the corpses.

The elemental sent a fire in Ethan's direction, the red racing through the grass.

"RUN!" the word escaped from Wander's mouth before she could think clearly.

Ethan sidestepped behind a tree. The fire hit the tree, climbed up, and spread through the branches.

"Clever," the elemental said as she turned back to Wander. Flame cast forward from her body, like a cat leaping from its master's arms.

Wander took a step back, but she was already too close to escape. Her head throbbed and her hands grabbed at the sword's handle over her shoulder. With a twist, she tore it out from its sheath of bunched up clothes. She swung down at the rush of heat. Upon contact with the sword, the fire split into two smaller flames. The two flames died down like an untended campfire.

Wander looked back at the elemental that seemed to be studying her closely. The spirit's knees were bent, her arms out, ready to attack or move at any moment. Her warm eyes were fixed on Wander's blade.

Wander decided to try again. "Where is Masu?" She saw Ethan off to the shadows of the wood. He was aiming another arrow toward the spirit. Wander slowly shook her head at him.

When the spirit gave no answer, she continued. "If you know my name, then you must have met him."

The elemental's gaze moved. Wander followed her eyes to the fox that stood behind her. She looked back to the spirit to see the woman's eyes had become locked on the fox.

The woman's hand moved behind her hip. The singing of metal against sheath sounded as she pulled out a short, curved blade. The elemental then shot forward not for Wander, but for the fox.

Wander put herself between them, her sword met with the elemental's. The woman slid her blade up, pulled back, and with a twirl sliced across Wander's upper arm as she danced around her.

The fox ran around Wander, keeping her in between it and the spirit.

Wander felt hot pain where the spirit cut but kept her sword up and ready. The two faced each other, ready to move at any second.

The elemental's eyes suddenly crossed to stare at her weapon. Red blood dripped from its tip into the remains of charred grass. She looked back at Wander and whispered with quivering lips, "What are you?"

The two glared at each other. Wander hoped that any minute the spirit would start talking. Perhaps the woman thought about it? Her eyes kept darting between the fox, Wander, and the sword over and over.

The woman sheathed her blade back behind her. She stood up straight and stared at Wander.

Wander held her breath for an explanation.

The elemental's body went dark, and Wander's skin went cold from the sudden lack of heat. Her flaming body turned to dark wisps of shadow. The darkness encompassed her, covering her face and veiling her entire body till she was nothing but a smoke cloud. The smoke took to the sky and moved to the west. Once distanced, it looked like it could be a swarm of insects.

Wander poked at the earth with a stick as Ethan wrapped her cut arm up in the last of their bandages. The two humans sat back on the edge of the mountain trial.

"With your recklessness, we're now out of both bandages and food."

"She knew and she didn't answer me," Wander said. She put pressure on the stick, pressing it to the ground until it snapped in half. "I saw it on her face. She knew my name. She knew where Masu was."

"Yes, I get it."

The fox approached her and licked her hip.

"You still don't believe me, do you?" Wander said. "About Masu."

"I don't know anymore." Ethan stood up.

The rest of the day was more silent than ever. Wander crushed pinecones under her feet and kicked stones down the mountain. She walked faster than before, forcing Ethan to keep a quicker pace to stay ahead. After so long on straight ground, they began to descend. Ethan decided to make camp by a riverside at sunset. The river had an old bridge with moss growing on its rails.

Unveiling herself, Wander washed her scarred face with a splash of the freezing mountain water.

"I think when we reach the nearest town, we should part ways."

Wander re-veiled herself and turned around to see Ethan standing behind her.

He massaged where his neck and shoulder met. "I don't know much, but I do know that staying with you will get me killed." He looked away. "I also know deep down that if you never stayed in Heathcliff, Roslyn and Mom would still be alive.

"You got close to that elemental without getting shocked. That sword cut down her flames, so it's not a normal sword, it's a sword made by spirits for spirits. You've survived flames that decimated everything else around you. The elemental knew your name. So I don't know what you are, but you sure are not human. I—"

"But I don't have anyone but you."

After the interruption, he said nothing.

Wander stood up and felt tears well up in her eyes. "I'll try to be better. I won't feed the fox anymore and I won't run off without you again."

"It's more than that," Ethan said. "Wander, I don't know what you are. You not knowing either is a bad sign."

Unable to control her tears, Wander looked away from Ethan and charged back toward the camp. After reaching their camp, she walked farther into the woods where she could be alone. Leaning back on one of the thicker pine trees, she let herself cry alone. The fox followed and sat by her feet.

What hurt more than Ethan's decision was that she did not know how to argue against him. He was right. She had no clues about herself or the situation she was in. The little comfort she had was in Masu's feather. She stroked it and held it up to her face, hoping that they could reunite.

Ethan started a fire beyond the dark columns of trees. Taking some deep breaths, Wander tried to calm herself before returning to camp. Her feet crunching on pines and seeds alerted Ethan of her coming. He looked up from the fire with a tired look.

"I'm sorry," he said. "I know I've been an ass to you." He paused, carefully choosing his words. He added in a gentler tone, "Ros and Mom loved you so I want to give you a chance. Once we get to the next settlement, we can rethink our plans."

Wander stared at the flames from just above her knees as hugged her legs. Ethan took some sticks off the ground and poked them into the fire, watching them burn. "I'm sure my dad would have liked you." Light swayed around his face. "He loved strange things. That's why he went to the Emerald Wilds, like some curious, idiotic kid who wanted an adventure. Ros took after him. That's why she liked you. Spirits say humans hate anything different from them. That's not true though. Some of them love difference, and they wake up every morning hoping for difference. That was my dad. That was Ros."

"I wish they were still alive," Wander said. When she saw a tear stream down his cheek, she regretted saying anything.

Ethan rubbed his face against his arm. "It should've been me," he whispered, "instead of them."

"They would be very sad if that happened," Wander said.

When they lay down for the night, Wander stared up at the stars. She counted each color of the stars. Three purple, thirteen white, four blue, and seven gold.

Wander woke with an aching neck.

Ethan managed to hunt down a pheasant for breakfast. The morning consisted of plucking, cutting, and cooking the bird. As Wander plucked a feather, she stopped and examined it next to Masu's feather dangling from her wrist. Masu's was huge in comparison, denser, lengthier, no speckles either, just dark.

The pheasant feathers felt the same as the wings she'd nestle her body into at night. Under the feathers, she sometimes felt Masu's goosebumps. For the longest time she thought wings were made of pure feathers and magic. It was only when she sank her fingers deep enough in his wings that she realized they were skin, flesh, and bone just like her.

She suddenly couldn't bear to eat a bird. "You can have my portion. I'm not hungry."

Ethan gave her a confused look but said nothing. He and the fox ate the legs, wings, and breasts until there were only bones. While they ate, Wander took the feathers and stuck them in the ground around her. They left the campsite with the remains of a campfire, piles of animal bones, and feathers pointing upward from the earth.

Three days and nights passed. In the day, Wander and Ethan walked side by side with the fox behind them. They collected whatever edible food they could gather. Most often, they would find a bush of berries. Ethan would ask Wander if they were safe, to which she would shrug. "You were raised in an enchanted forest, for God's sake!" Ethan would shout. It wasn't like before though, there was playfulness in his smile. "You should know these things!"

They would talk about many things. Wander liked to hear Ethan's stories, like when a sickness took over Heathcliff or a controversial criminal was charged to stay in the Emerald Wilds for a week. He sometimes avoided talking about Roslyn and his mother. Sometimes it was obvious he was about to mention them, but he stopped himself.

Wander did not feel comfortable talking too much about Masu around him. Just because he was willing to listen and be kind did not mean he believed a word she said. They discussed the meanings of words Wander did not know such as *etiquette* and *religion*. Those made for the longest conversations.

They left the mountains and reached the crossroads in the flatlands. The grass grew gold and tall. There were no more pine trees, or many other trees, just golden swaying ground. At the crossroads, five paths split. There were wooden signs with arrows pointing in various directions. Words were carved into every arrow, but Wander did not know how to read.

By the time they entered a forest, night had fallen. Ethan did not want to camp. He had no plans of stopping anymore.

"The closest town, Willton, is just through this forest."

Ethan moved ahead as Wander's pace slowed. The idea of a new town made her anxious. Ethan said this one was larger than Heathcliff, a place with more people and buildings. She could tell Ethan was excited. Though they had a better relationship than before, he must have tired of them being stuck with each other. She had as well, but it was better than being alone or with strangers. She just wanted Masu.

The forest of maple trees looked thin and young. The path was worn with no loose rocks like there were in the mountains.

Any forest at night, enchanted or not, made Wander's back feel intensely vulnerable. She walked in front of the fox, hoping the animal would warn her if something were following them.

Ethan and Wander stopped at the frightening sound of something running and panting in the dark. Heart racing, Wander prepared to grab her sword. Ethan put his hand on his sheathed knife.

A young woman tumbled out of the woods. The loose bun of her brown hair came undone, falling to her breasts as she looked at Ethan and Wander. She wore one boot, her right foot bare and caked in mud. Her chest heaved with heavy breaths. "Please! Help!"

Without hesitation, Ethan let go of his knife came to the woman's side. "What's the matter?"

"My son, spirits took my son! They're that way! Please." Her teeth chattered, her hands quaking.

Ethan looked up at the dark forest. He took off, disappearing into the trees and bushes. The young woman tailed after him, her brown skirt flowing behind.

Wander reached out. "Wait!" Yet they were gone and did not hear her. Her skin crawled. She looked at the fox that seemed to desire leaving. The animal kept on the trail ahead, sitting; it waited for Wander to follow.

"Ethan!" Wander shouted toward the woods. She paced back and forth, her hand stroking her feather bracelet. Her head began to throb, a headache due to nerves.

She raised her voice to its highest. Straight-backed with fists clenched, she hollered, "ETHAN!"

A breeze rubbing against the forest leaves answered back. She looked at the fox, then back to the woods. Her head began rattle when she ran into the forest. She came to a clearing to see Ethan and the woman standing face-to-face with two people. One looked delicate, a woman with thick black hair in one long braid that reached down her back and ended at her knees.

All she wore was gray, a long-layered skirt that reminded Wander of flower petals, long in the back but higher in the front to show her ghostly legs. Her feet were bare, and one of her ankles was adorned with a silver trinket. She appeared cold, holding a darker gray shawl around her torso. She looked at Wander with amazing, large purple eyes.

The other Wander knew. It was the elemental. She stood a little behind the woman in gray. She had her arms crossed, bright and watching.

No child in sight.

Wander looked at the victimized woman just in time to see her fall face forward. She landed with her arms outstretched in the dirt. She seemed peaceful, almost smiling, like the happiest dream had kidnaped her from reality.

"Don't worry about her," the woman in gray said. "She'll wake up in a couple hours. She was only a messenger."

Ethan backed up to Wander's side, giving her a panicked look.

"I am Aura," the woman introduced herself. She nodded over to the elemental. "You've already met Chant."

Ethan turned to Wander. "Run!" he hissed.

Right as they turned, Chant burst into flame. The flame ran like a wild mouse, lighting up a wall of fire in its path. She circled around Ethan, Wander, and Aura.

Wander and Ethan backed away from the fire. With little choice, they turned back to Aura, who walked closer to them. "Don't be afraid."

"How can you be Aura?" Ethan asked. "Don't be ridiculous. What would the queen of the deviants want with us?"

"The war has nothing to do with why I am here. I wanted to meet Wander because I've heard so much about her."

"If you know the elemental," Wander said. "Then you—"

"Yes. He is with me."

"Masu? He's alive?" Wander thought she could die right there due to sheer gladness. For a moment, nothing else mattered but the fact that he was still out there breathing.

"Yes. He is not far."

"Can I see him? Will you take me to him?"

"Wander!" Ethan hissed. "Don't trust her! She blocked us from escaping!"

The flame wall opened like a gate as the fox got chased in by Chant. Chant pursued the fox as she formed into a dog made of fire. The fox ran behind

Wander as Chant turned back to her human-like form. She was close enough that Wander felt her face burn and her eyes sting.

"You can see him," Aura said, "if you make me a deal."

"Anything!" Wander said.

"You see, I just need that fox," Aura raised her pale hand to point at the dark animal. "Give me that fox, and I'll take you to see him."

Wander's excitement died down. She looked down at the pitiful animal shivering at her feet. "Why?"

Aura adjusted her shawl tighter. "Tell me, Wander, what are you to Masu?"

"He raised me. We lived together in the Emerald Wilds before it burned down."

"And what are you to that fox?"

"I suppose we're friends."

"Hm," Aura paused. It was like when Chant fought Wander, the spirit's eyes scanned her from top to bottom, then the fox.

"What are you thinking?!" Ethan hissed.

"I want to see Masu but—"

"Then give her the damn fox."

"What?"

"Give it to her. I mean, it's just an animal."

For the past week Wander had gotten to know Ethan better. She remembered the relaxed look of love in his eyes when he fed the fox some rabbit. Now he stood possessed by fear.

"C'mon," he said, "if you don't you may never see Masu again. After all, they could just kill us anyway and take what they want. All this time you wanted to be reunited with Masu, how can you just walk away from this? Think about him!"

Wander's head ached more. It was like her mind turned to many stones that bounced around in her skull. "I can't," she whispered. Something mercilessly tore through her mind. Tears began to pool in her eyes. "I can't give—"

"Then I will."

Ethan bent down to Wander's feet where the fox hid. He grabbed onto the animal by the scruff of its neck. The creature let out a shriek, showing pointed teeth, saliva drooling, its legs racing in the air to get away.

"ETHAN, NO!" Wander screamed. Her hands flew to her sword handle. With all her strength, she twisted the blade and sliced its makeshift sheath open in a rain of tattered cloth and broken belts. She charged forward. She ran in front of Ethan, between him and Aura. "Put him down!" she said. Her hands holding the sword shook. Her head throbbed. Her knee bounced. She felt like she was going to vomit.

The fox still struggled in his grip like a worm on a hook, still crying out. Ethan looked at the tip of Wander's blade, then directly into her eyes. As his foot stepped forward, hers followed. She felt as though a power stronger than her own thoughts pushed her forward.

It felt as though they just walked toward each other—until her sword impaled him through the chest. He dropped the fox, and it ran back into the safety of Wander's feet and cloak.

A damp darkness expanded from where the sword had stabbed him. Ethan's hands shivered as they reached up and grabbed the blade tight enough that his flesh sunk into the edges. Blinking, he looked up at Wander. Heaviness claimed his eyes, darkened, glassy. His lips quivered as they uttered a single word.

"Why . . .?"

Wander could no longer control herself. Everything rushed on without her mind to catch up. She could feel the tears falling down her cheeks, her breath shaking, her heart breaking.

She never thought of hurting Ethan. This was not planned or desired. Yet it somehow happened by her hands.

She pulled the sword out of Ethan's chest. The steel was coated in red, enough to drip like a leaf dense from rainfall. Ethan's hands immediately clutched his wound, but the blood gushed between the fingers. His breath shivered. He fell to his knees and then to his side. His hands pressed against his broken chest tightly. Tears rolled from his eyes before his hands fell away, and he stopped breathing.

Wander couldn't form words.

She burst into the fastest run she could, stumbling through the fire, past the trees, and into the darkness of the forest.

Chapter 4
Willton

"Few human towns do as well as Willton. They fall to spirits, inner fighting, or just mysteriously disappear. Whatever the case may be, Willton is an example of how humans can live well in this world." – Humanity: After Enslavement

"Okay everyone, we're closing!" Alice spoke over the cacophony of voices. She moved around her bar, collecting glasses empty and half-finished. She spent her time rinsing and rubbing each glass dry while the tavern emptied itself. She shut the red curtains. She paused at one window and squinted at some new graffiti etched into the wood frame.

With a sigh, she pushed all the chairs into the tables, deciding she would not sweep tonight since she had a lost item to deliver. Returning to the bar, she ducked below the counter to grab her bag.

She looked up and shouted, "UNDER!"

"YES?" a man's voice yelled back from the ceiling.

"I'LL BE RIGHT BACK. I'M GIVING EMMA HER RING BACK!"

"ALRIGHT."

Alice turned the knob and stepped out to Willton's town square. The town had already gone dark.

The children had made chalk markings on the cobblestone, despite many people's complaints. Alice did not mind through, images of stick figures, rainbows, and suns were far better than the things people carved into the tables and walls of her tavern.

She stepped over the chalk markings of an apple tree on her way across the street. A stray black cat sat outside the Daisydrop Inn. Its bushy tail swished back and forth. When Alice reached the entrance, she bent down and offered her hand to the cat.

Upon a closer view, she began to wonder if the cat was actually a dog. It had a snout more similar to a dog's. "Hello, sweet thing," she said as it sniffed her hand. After the sniff, the animal ignored Alice, so she decided it was a cat.

Opening the inn caused a little bell to jingle.

Emma stood at the counter arguing with a customer. "For the last time: no money, no service!"

The customer was unlike anyone Alice had seen before. He or she wore a cloak of darkness, concealing everything but their eyes. To make things even sketchier, the character carried an unsheathed sword.

"What's going on?" Alice walked in.

Emma sighed with relief. "See? I'm busy now. Shoo. Off with you."

The cloaked visitor's gaze met with Alice's for a second. She expected to see eyes that would send shivers down her spine, but instead she met the gaze of someone about to cry. The customer strode out the door.

"Thank God! Good timing!" Emma leaned over her counter and whispered, "Alice, that was the creepiest person. First she came in with this strange cat, and I told her no animals. When the cat left, I told her no weapons. I mean, I was scared, she came in holding a sword, and I thought she was threatening my life when she asked if she could stay here. Then I found out she didn't even have any money! Then she acted all confused, like I was the villain! If she had the audacity to dress so darkly with a sword in hand, I hate to imagine what she is hiding under that hood and cloak."

"Well, I came to drop something off. I believe this belongs to you." Alice fished around in her bag. "I found it on one of my tables and figured whoever left it would return sometime so I saved it. Then I realized you weren't wearing your ring so . . ."

Emma beamed when Alice pulled out a single gold ring. She returned it to her finger, pushing it past her knuckle. "Ah! I thought I lost it forever! I always took it off and played with it so it could have been anywhere. I owe you one, sweetie."

"Don't mention it. People've got to look out for one another. I'll see you tomorrow, probably."

When Alice exited, she looked right toward the town center. No one was there but the statue of the town founder, a bearded man with a machete. The bell tower stood over everything, now just a tall silhouette in the night. She looked left down the road to see the cloaked wanderer leaving with her animal trailing behind. The sword was still out, almost getting dragged in the dirt.

"Wait!" Alice called.

The cloaked figure stopped and turned around.

Alice ran over. "What's your name?"

"Wander."

"Are you a spirit?"

"I don't think so."

Hearing Wander's voice changed everything. She sounded like a child. Her tone was quavering and untamed. Was there a tall child under that cloak? Alice would bend her knees if they weren't already eye level with each other.

"What brought you here?"

"I came from Heathcliff."

"Oh my. That's a tiny village."

"It burned down so . . . my friend . . . Ethan told me we should come here."

"Where is your friend?"

That's when the cloaked girl released a sob. Alice found it difficult to tell what the girl was truly feeling with most of her face concealed under a veil. The sounds of crying made everything clear. Maybe that was why Wander sounded like a child, because she was holding in tears.

"Would you like to stay at my tavern for a while?" Alice asked.

She looked away, "I-I don't know if I should."

"Why? Is there someplace you need to go?"

The cloaked girl's weeping got stronger. They appeared to do so with each question. Hesitant, Alice reached out and touched the girl's shoulder. Oddly enough, the girl was human.

"C'mon then. Let's go. I'll make you some hot tea. You can sleep in one of our rooms, and tomorrow we can get you some help."

Wander nodded, rubbing her eyes with her free arm.

The two of them walked back to the tavern together.

Wander never knew so many tables could be in one room. It was an odd nest, or house, whatever it was.

"You can sit and wait here. I just need to talk to my fiancé. I'll be back down in a moment!"

Alice had hair as blonde as Wander's used to be, but it was short. She wore brown pants and a white baggy shirt. Over her shirt was a tight brown vest with brown lace, like shoelaces tied up on her back.

Once alone, Wander set the sword in a corner against the wall. She sat in one of the many chairs. The fox sniffed around the floor until it found a piece of fallen food to eat. Like the Flinsler house, the building had a place for fire, except it was large enough for two people to crawl in and stand up inside. There was a large counter, and beyond it Wander saw more bottles than she could count, each filled with dark liquid.

Paintings framed in smooth redwood covered all the free space on the walls. A small one contained a duckling among lily pads. There were bodies caught in dance, a man caressing a woman's thigh, holding her back secure as she leaned back. There were more: wolves in a white world with the darkest fur howling, a house with a mossy roof and glistening sunlight pouring over the yard, identical little girls except one with red nails and the other with blue, a pink and rose sunset over mountains, a bowl of assorted fruits, and a lizard with wings hiding under a table.

Alice returned with a tall, lanky figure at her side. He wore a long, ebony jacket. His black hair fascinated Wander. It reminded her of Masu's night sky hair, but straighter and less fluffy. One side of his hair was longer than the other, covering his right eye. His skin was pale as paper, bringing out the darkness in his eyes.

"Wander, this is my fiancé, Under."

Under sat himself down across from Wander, "So, Wander, you like to wander around a lot?"

Alice walked over to the counter, "You shouldn't tease."

"Masu named me," Wander said.

"Who is that, your father?" he asked.

She shook her head, and she caught Alice giving Under a concerned look. Wander wondered whether to even bother telling people the truth anymore. To them, the truth was ridiculous. They'd only ask more questions until they decided Wander was something like a witch.

"Well, I know what it's like to have a name like Wander," Under said. "Trust me, everyone in this town wouldn't let me hear the end of it. They kept asking if I had a brother named 'Over.'" He laughed, but Wander didn't get what was funny.

Alice returned with a thick ceramic cup. She set it in front of Wander. Wander looked down to see a sunset liquid. A vapor rose from the drink like a weak smoke.

"Don't touch it for a while. It might burn your tongue," Alice said as she sat next to Under. Wander noticed behind the table that the two were holding hands.

"So," Under's eye looked toward the sword that Wander set in the corner, "that's a decent sword. You must be strong to be able to lug that thing around."

"I don't know if I want it anymore," Wander said.

"Why not?"

Wander looked away, but her eyes must have already given away her emotion. Alice elbowed Under.

"Sorry," Under blurted. "That's none of my business."

"It's alright. I know . . . I am a little odd," Wander said. "I'm . . . wind-born so I'm younger than I look. I . . ." emotion clutched her voice, "have been travelling alone for a couple days now. Everyone I know is either dead or missing. I don't know what to do anymore." Her breath shook. For the past few days she had done nothing but wander and cry. She had killed Ethan and got lost in the woods. She ran until her legs got too tired to move. At two large protruding roots under a large tree, she curled up into a ball. She never wanted to get up again. She wanted to abandon herself, if that were even possible. The fox licked the tears off her face. "I killed him," Wander whispered to the fox. "I killed him. I killed him. I killed him. I killed him." She threw her sword to the side, Ethan's blood still on the blade. She refused to move for days; the fox brought her any food it could find. Then it bit her until she sat up. The fox ran forward, then back to her, then forward again until she got up and followed. The fox led her back to the path she and Ethan were walking on. She followed until she got into town. She immediately knocked on someone's nest and asked for a place to stay, they pointed her to the Inn.

"You poor thing!" Alice got up and went to Wander's side. Wander flinched at the woman's touch to her shoulder. She noticed and let go. "So you're wind-born and have no one to take care of you?"

Wander shook her head and covered her tearing eyes with her veil.

"Alright, alright, no need to tell us everything all at once. We'll stay with you while you drink the cocoa. Do you want something to eat?"

Wander nodded.

"I'll get something for your animal friend, too."

Alice came back with mashed potatoes and sausages for Wander. She set a bowl down on the floor by the fox. "This is usually what I put out for the stray cats, the leftovers off my customer's plates. Better than throwing it out."

Wander gobbled up the food faster than she wanted. Her fork scraped every little piece off the porcelain plate. She drank the hot cocoa to find some sugar at the bottom. With her hands, she rubbed the sugar off and sucked on her fingers.

Under and Alice saw Wander's lower face as she ate, the burned up scars. Wander did not care enough to keep concealing herself in the face of food. Much to her surprise, Under and Alice said nothing about the markings on her face.

"I like your feather bracelet," Alice said.

"Thanks." She already started feeling better after the warm meal. She re-wrapped her veil around her face. "And thank you for the food."

"I can show you to a room upstairs. We aren't an inn, but we have extra beds."

Wander looked at the fox. Its face was still in the bowl of food. She then looked at Under, who showed her a kind grin.

Wander followed Alice upstairs to a hallway. "Under and I sleep in this room," she opened a door to show a room centered with a large bed. A patchy blue quilt lay wrinkled and twisted, exposing the white sheets. Potted yellow flowers sat on a dresser under a window. A large mirror hung across from the bed.

"And you can sleep in this room, right across from us." Alice opened a door to a small bed under a window with a view of the inn across the street. The bed was covered with a pink blanket with little white bird figures sewn on. At the bedside was a small table with a candle and book. A red silk bookmark dangled out from the middle pages. Stepping in, Wander looked over to see a dresser. On its surface was a parade of stuffed animals: a rabbit with ears far too long for its body, an old pink cat that had been loved too much, a mouse wearing a striped sweater, and a horse with black bows in its braided hair.

"I'll leave you here to rest," said Alice. "Come find me or Under in the morning when you wake up. One of us is always here. And don't be worried about getting one of us up if you need something. Remember, our room is right across from yours. Oh, and our outhouse is downstairs. It's in the back with the crescent moon carving." Alice bid Wander a good night and left.

Wander kneeled on the bed to look out the window. Almost every building had two floors, some even had three. Heathcliff really was small compared to this place. Laundry hung on rope in between alleyways. She noticed someone was in the room at the inn's second floor, a woman and small child. She lifted him up and placed him in the bed by the window. Her hand patted his head.

Wander shut the dark curtains. She went to Alice's dresser and scooped up all her stuffed animals. She placed them all on the bed. Untying lace, she pulled off her dirt caked boots and they fell to the floor with a loud thud. For the first time in a while, she took off her cloak and veil. She lay down under the pink blanket and adjusted the stuffed animals to surround her. Once she was comfortable, the fox jumped up and curled up by her legs.

Wander woke with a start from a nightmare. Shaking off her fear, she and the fox jumped out of bed. One by one, she took Alice's stuffed animals and rearranged them on the dresser. She grabbed her cloak and veil. Opening the curtains, she used her own reflection to make sure the veil securely hid all but her eyes.

Her legs trembled as she cautiously traveled downstairs. In the Flinsler house, she scarcely used their stairs because she'd always trip. Roslyn would often want Wander to come up to her room though, so she would hold her hand as they went up.

Wander found the first floor filled with people, all sitting at the round tables. The room was packed with speech, murmurs, and laughter. Many took a moment to stare at the cloaked girl who descended from the stairs. Wander could smell baked potatoes, sizzling meat, and chocolate.

Alice sat behind the empty bar on a tall stool. She wore an apron like Ms. Flinsler in the kitchen, except this one had far more pockets. With her back hunched over, Alice appeared to be drawing. With a pencil, she sketched the beginnings of a woman in a feathered hat.

When Wander stepped in, she looked at the many people. They looked away when they caught eyes. The children did not look away; they stared.

"Ah, Wander," Alice smiled. "Give me a moment, and I'll get Tom to cook you up some breakfast. Did you sleep well?"

Wander nodded.

"Go on, have a seat!" Alice's hand motioned to the row of tall stools at the other side of the bar.

Hesitant, Wander circled around the bar stared at the stool.

"Just lift your butt a little."

Wander did so, sitting down. Her arms clung to the side of the bar.

Alice left through a back door and came back with leftovers for the fox. She walked around the bar and set down a plate of meat bits. A man eventually came out of the back door with a plate of scrambled eggs and set it in front of Wander.

Wander unveiled her mouth and ate quickly, hoping no one else would see her marked skin. Once Wander finished eating, she wrapped her veil back over her mouth. "I need to go."

"You're leaving? You just got here!" Alice said. Her voice was raised enough that Wander grew worried that it would attract more attention. She could already imagine eyes burning through her back.

"You've been really nice to me. But that's all the more reason that I've got to go. If I stay . . ." She went silent. Why were the Emerald Wilds and Heathcliff burned? They had two things in common. They were close together . . . and they both had her. What if she was the reason the place burned, like Ethan said?

"What?"

Wander looked at the fox. Its face was planted into the bowl of leftovers. She just shook her head.

"Alright. Where would you go?"

"I have a friend to look for. I know he's alive."

"Any clue where he is?"

"Spirits might have him. I met some that knew where he was, but they wouldn't tell me."

"Okay. I want to help, though. I'll get you a map and food."

Under returned through the front door with other people carrying large sacks. Wander saw Alice pull him aside to talk.

Alice went to Wander. "Hey, Wander. Are you going to take your sword with you?"

She nodded.

"Good cause we . . . can't move it. It's super heavy. You said last night you may not want it anymore?"

"I think I need it."

"Well, we can find a sheath for it."

"A sheath?"

"Something to cover it. We'll get a map, a sheath . . . do you have a bag?"

Wander shook her head. She had torn her bag while running down the mountain after Chant. After that incident, Ethan had carried everything.

"Okay. We'll get a map, sheath, bag, and food. Maybe some clothes?"

Wander shrugged.

"Grab the sword and let's go."

When they left, Wander kept close to Alice. She never saw so many humans at once. The wide street filled with people going all directions. Among them were carts pulled by horses and deer. Dogs laid down, tied up at store fronts.

It was crowded enough that Wander did not even worry about being seen. Bodies blocked her from other bodies, and everyone seemed busy enough to not care how shady she looked.

At every store they visited, Wander would browse the wares while Alice did all the talking and buying. She had a way with people. They all seemed to know her, beaming, and asking questions about her life. Alice was the perfect barrier for attention, allowing Wander and the fox to wander the stores freely.

Wander's fingers caressed scarfs folded and laid out in a row. Little baggies that smelled of flowers were tied up with bows on another shelf. Steel traps, cages, and reins hung from the ceiling of one shop. Nails of different sizes were presented in an open jewelry box. The shop was emptier than the food and clothing stores. The owner's mouth could not be seen under his mustache and beard.

To get the sword sheath, the shop owner had to measure Wander's blade. He wanted to hold it, but Wander told him it was too heavy. Of course he didn't believe her and tried to grab it only to fall to floor with the hilt crushing his fingers. Alice managed to sweep away most of his embarrassment through idle conversation.

The sheath that he found in his merchandise to fit was nothing fancy: black with a strap to go around Wander's shoulder. The shopkeeper kept scratching at and tilting his head as he watched Wander wear the sword he could not hold. Before they left, he pulled Alice aside and whispered something in her ear. Whatever he said, her expression did not change.

When Alice bought a map she sat down with Wander on a free bench. Unfolding the map, she showed the right side had the ocean and the rest was shades of green. Wander could not read, so the map meant little to her. She did not tell Alice, though.

She pointed to a dot and some writing around the center. "We are here, Willton."

"Where are the deviants?"

"Deviants? Why them?"

"I think Masu is with them."

"Oh, sweetie. The deviants would be most dangerous. They—"

"I don't care."

"Well . . ." her finger moved far west to a dot with short writing. "Dem is here. That is their capital. But Wander, going there would be suicide. If your friend is there—"

"I know he's alive."

"Well, I can't stop you."

By the end of the shopping trip, Wander had a bag tucked under her cloak with some money, a change of clothes, and a map. The last thing Alice did was pack her some snacks. Wander stood by the doorway with Alice at her side.

"There, you look ready for anything!" Alice said with crossed arms.

Wander looked at the fox. She realized she did not want to leave. She could not determine why Alice was so kind, but maybe some people were just like that. Masu was. Maybe Masu could find her here?

"Are you sure you want to go?" Alice asked.

"I have to."

"Well, just stay safe. Under is busy, but I'll tell him goodbye for you."

Wander left Willton with a heavy heart. The fox danced around, skipping ahead. Some other humans passed, immediately moving as far to the other side of the path as they could from her. Some held hands at the sight of her. It appeared that these trails were far more used than the ones Wander and Ethan walked. They had met no humans, and now they were suddenly everywhere.

Wander strayed from the path for some privacy. Finding a log with minimal mushrooms, she sat down. Her butt cooled and moistened on the damp log as she opened her pack for some peanuts Alice had packed.

Sitting in front of her, the fox stared up at Wander with its large black eyes. In its eyes, Wander could see the reflection of her dark silhouette and the maple tree branches.

She picked five peanuts in her palm and showed them to the fox. The animal first licked the salt off their surface before its mouth gently took them and crunched. After it swallowed, the fox returned its face to Wander's hand to lick the salt off her palms.

With her sticky, saliva coated hands, Wander pulled out the map and looked at the line Alice had drawn between Willton and Dem. Though she could not understand it, Wander liked the look of the map. It was beige like the inner flesh of a tree. The trails and rivers were like veins or tree branches—all leading into each other in a complex network.

Standing back up, Wander retraced her steps to the road. She looked both ways to see if there was anyone there. Her moment of relief to see no faces was short. She looked back toward Willton and began to shake.

A billowing cloud of smoke spread through the sky like a drop of dye in water. It was like the smoke she had seen in the mountains that lead her to the elemental . . . except this cloud was far larger and closer.

She ran as fast as she could back toward the town. It did not take long for the scent of ash to fall upon her. As she got closer, there were people who dashed the opposite way. Some carried crying children to their chests. Many held hands, one slower than the other.

"NO! HENRY IS BACK THERE! LET ME GO!" a man wailed, struggling in the grip of a woman. Another man ran to the scene and they both lifted the screaming one up in their arms and bolted into the forest. More screams wailed all around. There were so many people.

The people Wander passed began to look more and more hurt. A child was wrapped in a blanket in the arms of a woman, an arm dangling out with streams of blood falling to the ground. Others passed, limping, with arrows in their legs. A woman holding a blood-soaked cloth to her head dizzily wandered into the woods. A shoeless child stood in the center of the path, crying out for his mother. A man raced past with a gray puppy wrapped in his arms.

Wander slowed as fear began to grip her. She could not stop trembling. Looking behind, she saw the fox had not followed.

Nearer the town, dead people speckled the path. Wander stepped over bodies that had died from blood loss before they could escape. Blood stained trails lead into the town. She followed the trails of blood back to Willton's gates. At the entrance, she could already feel the scalding heat. Her skin felt thicker and hotter than ever.

A piercing scream rose above all else. A figure on fire sprinted passed her, falling on the ground and writhing. His screams kept going, his limbs fast flailing like spider turned over. Wander gripped the strap of her bag tight. She froze in complete terror. The town was all flames. Figures lay scattered in the streets. Some were filled with arrows like pin cushions. Others burned and popped like wood in a campfire. Bloody figures added deeper red smears to the scene. Some limbs were torn apart, broken, and twisted.

The town had become a dining hall for the feasting flames.

"Please! Someone!" A person with long flowing hair stumbled out from an alleyway.

Just then a black bird the size of a large dog swooped down from the alleyway behind her. Its dark talons tore into her arms, pinning her to the ground. It pecked straight for her neck, and she stopped moving.

Wander could not move as she watched the bird look up directly at her. The flames reflected in its dark eyes. Its beak was soaked in red.

Spreading its wings, it took to the sky. It flew so high that Wander almost lost sight of it in the smoke before it dove back down like a bolt of lightning. The bird darkened into a void before transforming into a gargantuan gray boulder. The stone crashed into a house, crushing roof, windows, doors, and whatever was within. It kept rolling, hitting and destroying all the others in a straight path.

The earth felt like it shook when the stone hit the homes. Wander slapped her hands over her ears, and her eyes filled with tears. She knew without a doubt that the boulder had crushed Alice and Under's place. Their place was in that path.

The boulder shrank down, and a dark horse galloped out of the dust and rubble. It whinnied, bloody hooves leaping over the fallen.

When Wander uncovered her ears, she heard familiar flapping, the rhythm of large wings. It was unlike the transforming bird. When she heard the flapping, memories of the Emerald Wilds came to her. The sound of Masu leaving the nest while she was sick. The sound of his coming when she was in danger.

She turned to where a two-story building still stood. A figure with wings stood on the roof. Her heart shattered the moment she saw him. His black tussle of hair shivered in the breeze with ash. Red eyes gleamed. He had dark wings larger than he remembered. He held a bow with a quiver of arrows at his back. He took an arrow to his bow and pointed south.

A human ran for the southern gates. The arrow hit him right in the skull, and he fell without even a scream.

The winged figure slid down the roof shingles and with a flap of his wings, landed on the violent street. He turned to Wander.

"Masu . . ." she managed to whisper. His name did not rise over the sound of crackling flames.

He never looked at her like he did now. He stood straighter than ever before. He wore strange, heavy looking clothes. His focused eyes looked straight at her, completely devoid of his usual gentle demeanor.

Wander put her hands to her chest and let out a shout with her entire body, "MASU! MASU, IT'S ME!"

He did not even blink. His hand reached back for an arrow. Setting it to the bow, he pulled the string far back to his right ear. A force slammed into Wander from the side, arms tight around her. She crashed into to the cobblestone. When she turned, Under lay on the ground with her.

She looked back at Masu, who now took two arrows at the same time. "Masu, wait!" She stood up and bounded toward him.

Her legs came off the ground as Under lifted her from behind. He fled into the alleyway with her captured in his arms. She heard the swish of arrows.

"MASU! MASU!" She squirmed in his grip. Under's nails dug into her sides. "He was trying to kill you!"

"It's him," her voice cracked. "He just doesn't know it's me!"

Under's grip tightened. "He's killing everyone!"

In her struggle, her mouth became free of her veil. She chomped down on Under's upper arm. She put in all her force, like biting a carrot. Her tongue hung back while she felt the warm blood gush on her teeth and lips.

Under immediately dropped her, hissing in with agony as he grabbed where she had bitten. She landed on the dirt, scrambling back up to return to the main street. She looked around the corner to see Masu still there, waiting with an arrow pulled back. The moment their eyes met, he released the arrow. She jumped back behind the building, the arrow shot through the wood wall, the silver tip sticking out.

While he prepared his next arrow, Wander jumped out and raised her hands. "Masu, it's me." She walked forward. "Look at me."

Like before, he pulled the string back, the arrow pointing at Wander. His eyes went to her.

"I know I don't look the same anymore, but listen to my voice. Look at my eyes."

Her heart jumped when his eyes snapped unfocused for a second. They looked into her eyes.

"It's Wander," she breathed. "You know me."

He began to shiver and the hand gripping the bowstring loosened. For just a moment he looked like he was all there, like he would open his mouth and say her name.

The moment was lost when he swayed. He dropped the bow and arrow. His eyes shut, and he fell to the ground. His dark hair blocked out his eyes and his wings lay limp. "MASU!" Wander ran forward only to leap back when a wall of fire ran between them. The massive heat made her eyes tear up.

Chant emerged from a crumbling building. In her hand, a plush doll fell apart in her flaming grip. She strutted over to Wander, her lip curled in a half grin. "Well, well, we—"

Wander pulled her sword from its case and charged. She swung down with all her might through Chant's head and down her entire body. Her fingers clenched, but the body was not as dense as she expected. Did elementals even have bones? The sword cut through like loose soil with lumps of stone.

The elemental fell apart, chopped in near perfect halves. Both halves turned to flame and clumped together. The single flame rose taller than Wander, arms stretched from it, then the base separated into legs, and it blew out to show Chant unscathed.

"Wow. Look at you," Chant laughed with an unharmed body. "You really want him, don't you?"

Wander slashed for Chant's stomach, but the elemental danced out of the way. With a stomp of her foot, a small flame burst out and ran around Wander. It claimed her feet and rose up her cloak.

Just when she was about to tear off her clothes, a weight and cool sensation splashed over her. Her cloak hung heavy with water. The fire extinguished. She looked behind her to see Under stood behind her with a bucket. Despite the brave action, fear had an obvious hold on him. He breathed quickly. His lanky legs were bent, ready to run off at any moment.

"Oh, you got another fr—"

Under cut off Chant by splashing the rest of the water on her. The woman sizzled and let out a scream as the water that touched her rose into the air as a mist. She covered her face with her hands. Her body darkened and shivered. Her lively hair sank down and dripped. Her skin that glowed was now just pale. Furious orange eyes flared from under her soaked hair. Taking steps back she hissed, "I'll remember that."

Chant dimed further, her form becoming gaseous as she took to the air as smoke. Wander prepared for an attack, her sword held in front of her. But the smoke flew off over the ruined town and toward the maple forest.

Under let out a gasp of relief, "She's retreating."

With its controller gone, the flame wall shrunk away. Wander's legs moved before she even looked. She ran to empty earth. Masu was gone.

"I . . . I think the others fled, too," Under said.

Wander cupped her hands and put them to her mouth. "MASU!" She took off running.

"Hey wait!" Under called after her, but she kept going.

She ran all around what was left of Willton. She looked upon the few still standing roofs. She checked every alley. She turned every corner. Everywhere was littered with rubble and bodies. She saw limbs sticking out of broken down homes, dead pinned to buildings by arrows, and the ashes of those the flames claimed.

The fox came around. It moved with a low head and fast paws from around the corner of the building.

She kept calling his name, wandering into the broken down buildings. Then she found Under. He sat in front of a rubble pile, his back to her.

"Under?" she approached.

Then she saw he found Alice. Her lower body was crushed under pile of gray stone of what used to be the chimney. She lay there flat on her stomach. Under's pale hands held her trembling ones.

"You're going to be okay," Under whispered as he stroked some tears off her face. He looked behind him, his eyes glassy. "Wander, will you help me get these rocks off her?"

"No, Under," Alice voice splintered with emotion. Speaking appeared painful for her. "Baby, this is it for me."

He turned back to her. Some silence passed before a weak, "No," came from him. Crouching further, he held her hands to his face.

"You're going to be okay," Alice whispered.

He shook his head and choked on a sob. "I can't."

"Love, you can be whatever you want to be now."

His hands clenched against hers. "I want to stay like this."

Alice sniffled and let out a pathetic weep. There were no more words. Under stroked her cheek while she slowly faded away. Eventually the sound of her little pained cries stopped. Under broke down. He bent low to the earth his nose and lips resting in Alice's blonde hair.

Wander hugged herself. Despite all the flames and her thick, deformed skin, it suddenly got cold. She thought of leaving right then. Under probably wanted to be alone. She needed to go to Dem, but she could not bring herself to leave him there crying. She did not know what to do.

Under eventually stood up and turned to Wander. He rubbed his face with his coat sleeve. He looked like a ghost, eyes strained red and skin white.

"I'm sorry," Wander whimpered. "This is all my fault."

His pain and shock could not have been fresher. He could only shake his head his response. The two stood in silence.

Wander overheard the sounds of people. She emerged from the rubble to see the survivors, the ones that had fled had returned. They came in a slow march. Many covered their noses from the stench of smoke and burning flesh. Some ran to the dead, shrieking and weeping.

Under let out a shaky sigh and whispered, "I can't do this."

The fox began to leave. Wander gave a hesitant glance at Under before turning and following the fox.

Under grabbed her arm, "Where are you going?"

She stopped. "I need to find Masu again."

"He's a spirit, what's your deal with him? Also, how were you able to get so close to that flaming spirit?"

Wander jerked her arm away from Under. "I can touch spirits," she said. "And Masu raised me. He's family."

"How can you touch spirits?"

"I don't know."

"Are you really human? You're . . . sort of strange."

"Does it really matter?"

"I guess not." Under went to her side. "So where will you go to find Masu?"

"Dem."

"The deviant capital?"

Wander nodded and continued walking. She moved past the crying survivors, stepping over charred corpses. With each body she saw riddled with arrows, she realized it was probably Masu who had killed them. He wasn't in his right mind. The Masu she knew would never hurt so many people without reason. He, the changing bird, and Chant were all attacking Willton. Were they working together? Chant seemed to work for Aura, the deviant queen. Did the bird and Masu work for her, too? But why would Masu do that? Ethan told Wander that all the winged beings had been killed by deviants. It made no sense. Whatever the case, she had to stay away from any human settlements. Everywhere she went, fire seemed to follow.

The air cooled as she reached the gates, but heat stuck to her deformed body. She always felt a little hot. Her scrunched skin was always with her, like a thick coat she could not take off to release heat.

"Wander!" Under jogged over. Yesterday his dark coat had been clean, straight, and in one piece. It had become tattered, wrinkled, and smeared in blood and dirt. He put his hands on his knees, breathing hard. "Please, let me go with you."

"No."

"Why?"

"It's not safe."

He dusted himself. "Trust me, I can handle myself."

Wander shook her head. She turned and continued walking.

"Alice—" He choked on her name. Wander stopped and looked back. He took a moment to compose himself. "You must know what it's like to lose someone. She was all I had. Without her I . . ." He looked away toward the forest, and his hands clenched into fists. "Please," he whispered.

For a moment, Under looked like a well-drawn sketch. There was something about him that charmed Wander, like a prince in Roslyn's storybooks. His tall, pale figure and the crow colored hair that covered one eye all seemed crafted by a delicate hand. He was the prettiest human Wander had so far met.

He seemed as kind as Alice. They appeared to love each other, too. In a way, Alice was Under's Masu.

"Alright, you can come."

He let a sigh of relief. "Thank you."

"On one condition."

He looked into what little he could see of her.

"Never fight me. Don't even get near me while my sword is drawn. Don't get near the fox, either."

"Okay."

Chapter 5
The Daisy Trail

"Don't let the name fool you. It's not named after the flower, but an infamous bandit who preyed on travelers. Many now travel the trail, but the bandits never left. They are only more careful" – Awei Unsettled

During the first day of travel, Wander and the fox walked ahead while Under lagged behind. The entire day of travel consisted of flatland forest. White wildflowers grew in clumps at the trail's edges. At times they passed other travelers: people riding in carts of goods pulled by mules. Some were entire families hauling large backpacks. Occasionally Wander would hear the crunch of steps in the woods. She'd turn to see brown deer gazing back with ears raised. The trees were short and thin, providing little coverage.

By the time the sun ducked behind the trees, Wander motioned Under to leave the dirt trail. She found a spot of flattened grass; probably a place deer loved to sleep. Under sat down on a rock and stared into space while Wander collected materials for a fire. She peeled moss from stones and collected sticks of various widths and lengths. Setting the wood by Under, she then collected rocks.

For the entire trip they had been quiet. At times Wander thought of striking up a conversation, but then she remembered his wide eyes and pale face. He was not totally there.

She dropped the rocks next to the tinder. With her feet taking four close steps in front of Under, Wander measured how much of the land to clear. Putting her hands to the base of the grass, she tore out handfuls until there was a rounded dirt spot.

Taking the stones, Wander began to make a circle.

"You . . . do this a lot?"

She looked up to see Under was watching her.

Looking down, she continued to place the stones. "I lived in the woods for most of my life. Masu taught me how to do this."

"I thought you were from Heathcliff."

Wander frowned and swallowed against her dry throat.

"I lived there for a time. Before that, Masu and I lived in the Emerald Wilds. We lived in a ne—a treehouse."

She realized she hated to summarize what felt precious. Her words did no justice to the warm light against green leaves in the day or the comforts of the sounds of the river at night. Most of all, she could not accurately summarize her relationship with Masu. She hated to dull the reality of him with a swift explanation.

"Masu found me the forest. I don't remember it all that well, but being wind-born . . . I guess I was born around then and there. He took care of me, and we lived together." She set the last stone down. "Until Chant burned down the forest. Then a family in Heathcliff found me. Then Chant burned that down, and I went to Willton."

"Damn."

She placed the moss and minor stems in the circle. "Everything connects to the deviants, though. I met their queen, Aura, and found out she has Masu. She's at war with the humans, so maybe she's forcing Masu to work for her in some way. That doesn't make sense though because other humans have told me winged spirits no longer exist because the deviants had killed them all."

"You don't know about Aura's Arms, do you?"

"I know a little."

"The deviant rulers have always had them. They're servants. They are leftovers from battles the deviants won in the past. That boulder that attacked Willton was one, a shadow, a spirit who can transform into anything."

"Does that mean Chant and Masu are Arms, too?"

"Chant is a little different. She's an elemental princess. The elementals have formed a recent alliance with the deviants and Chant was offered as an Arm for Aura. Then Masu . . . well, I've heard Aura's 'Wings,' but it would not make sense for him to be the Masu you're talking about. He wouldn't just live in a forest and raise you unless it was an order. The Arms are controlled by Aura."

"Masu didn't remember anything before the Emerald Wilds."

"I've heard of the Emerald Wilds. It was a powerful enchanted forest far east from here."

She nodded. "It was a very dangerous place."

"I've heard stories before of people who have wandered into enchanted forests. They eat the berries and drink from a spring and forget who they are."

"Do you think that's what happened to him?"

Under shrugged. "A great number of things can occur in enchanted places."

She finished building the fire and sat by Under. She opened her bag to find a sandwich Alice had packed for her. She showed it to Under.

"I don't know if I can eat," he said. "You can have it."

Despite his talking, he still appeared troubled. Since the sandwich was something Alice made, just in case Wander put it back in her bag for Under to have later.

The campfire reflected in his eyes. Wander snacked on fruits and nuts from the bag. She dropped some on the ground for the fox to eat.

Maybe Masu did lose his memories from eating something bad in the forest. There were a lot of things he told her she wasn't supposed to eat. But then how did he know that if he would not remember eating it?

She lay down in the grass with her face to the sky. Mist floated in the night, but stars could still be seen beyond it.

"You just lie down and sleep like that?"

Wander turned to her head to Under. "I just stare at the sky and wait. I eventually sleep."

"Well, when you put it like that . . ." He lay down by her side and faced the sky with her.

The fox came over and curled up by Wander's side, using its own fluffy tail as a pillow. She felt its soft breath against her arm.

Ms. Flinsler called out from her kitchen window.

Roslyn looked up from the patches of clovers. Standing up to show grass-stained knees, she smiled down at Wander.

They sat in the lush backyard of the Flinsler house. This was where Roslyn would pick wild flowers. The blossoms were tiny specks of purple, yellow, and white. Roslyn loved the area because she said it never had bugs.

When Wander stood up, Roslyn grabbed her hand, leading her to the back door of the house. The back window's white curtain billowed to show Ms. Flinsler smiling and waving. After Wander entered the house, she blinked and everything changed. It became dark. Roslyn disappeared. The table lay bare. "Roslyn?"

Wander walked pasted the table to the window. She saw nothing but blackness outside. It was not even a nighttime sort of darkness, it was the darkest dark where nothing could exist.

A sudden scream tore through the uneasy silence. Wander could not determine where it came from; it was all around her. Fire grew outside the window, a familiar crackling sounded. The room glowed red. Scratching sounds came from behind. Wander turned to see the floor had been clawed at, four nicks marked the wood. It happened again, the same mark dragged on the kitchen wall; this time blood stuck to the splintered wood.

"WANDER! WANDER, HELP!" The screams came from upstairs.

She sprinted and tripped in the middle of the stairs. Getting back up, she saw Ms. Flinsler's door shaking just above. The doorknob rattled, sobs and coughing came from behind. Wander grabbed the knob, but it wouldn't turn. She flinched as Ms. Flinsler started banging rapidly on the door. She started to hit the door and scream. Looking down, Wander saw smoke pour from under the door.

Then she heard weeping down the hall. Rolsyn's room.

She ran to the door, its front decorated with a colored drawing of a cat, Roslyn's favorite animal. Taking the knob, she turned it and opened the door.

There was no fire, just Roslyn standing in the center of the room, her back to Wander. The room glowed red like the rest of the house. Her window did not show fire, just the backyard at night.

Suddenly there was nothing but scratching sounds. The walls, ceiling, and floors all were dragged through, splintered and bloody.

Approaching Roslyn, Wander noticed the little girl's fingertips were torn up, dripping with blood.

"Roslyn?"

The child turned around. Her eyelids were red and swollen, masking her eyes. Her cheeks peeled like tree bark.

Wander shook her head, tears welling up in her eyes. She turned around to run only to meet Ethan in the doorway. He stood with a bloody chest, his eyes so wide that they were mostly white.

Wander shot up under the sunlight filtered through trees. Her chest thumped so hard it felt like a pulsating wound. The campfire burned out into a pile of dark ash. She realized she was covered in a dark coat. She lifted it up to recognize it as Under's.

"Are you alright?"

Under walked over from behind her, bending down to her level. His face seemed even paler than before, and darkness circled around his eyes. Coatless, he wore a buttoned up white shirt tucked into his pants with sleeves rolled up to his elbows. He was thinner than Wander had remembered.

"I couldn't sleep, and I noticed you were shivering so I covered you up. Sorry, the fire died and I . . . don't really know how to remake a fire." He squinted at her, noticing how she shook.

"I went to a bad place."

"Nightmare? I can't blame you. With what we saw . . ." he sighed. "Geez, and you're just a kid, aren't you?"

She shrugged.

"Hey," he said, "show me your hand."

Wander raised her palm. It was unburned, but still had the scars from the many times she gripped thorny vines and mishandled Masu's tools. Under placed a white star-shaped wildflower in her hand. The stem was thinner than a vein.

"They smell a little sweet. I don't know about you, but I can still smell the fire. These flowers help a little."

Wander liked the gesture, but her veil blocked the smell. Not wishing to unveil herself, she pretended to sniff the little plant.

When Under stood back up, he put his face in his hand. "Sorry, I'm just a little dizzy."

"You should eat," Wander pulled out the sandwich from her bag.

He wiped his watering eyes with his arm. With a nod, he took the sandwich. Wander stared at Under as he sat down and examined the sandwich. He lifted the bread top off, revealing the tomato slices, meat, cucumbers, and lettuce. He plucked off the meat and set it aside. He ate with no meat.

The forest went on for weeks.

With each sign of a village or town, Wander was sure to walk around them with Under following hesitantly behind. The most she would see were the chimney tops. She had no desire to repeat Willton. Though once she waited while Under went to town to buy food. Not even wanting to be near the settlement's entrance, Wander and the fox hid in the woods.

Under was different from other humans Wander had known. The humans of Heathcliff had connections to the land; the children chased bugs and took mud baths while the adults chopped wood and watered gardens. Every time Under got a smudge of dirt on his blouse, he would lick his thumb and attempt to rub it clean. When a cricket landed his leg as they camped, he let out a yell and jumped up and down. He had no clue how to make fire or what plants in the forest were edible.

He would not eat meat. The fox would bring nightly gifts of rabbit, rat, and fish and he would never partake. "It makes me feel sick," he said. Wander imagined he must often be starving. She tried to keep an eye out for any fruits or vegetables. They once found berries, but they were so sour that Under's mouth puckered for a whole day.

The fox once brought them a crow. As usual, it laid the creature at Wander's feet, expecting her to pluck and cook it. Under noticed something was wrong when Wander just stared down at the rigid dark wings, unmoving. "What's wrong?" he asked.

"Birds. . . makes me sick."

In the day during their travels, Wander would tell Under about the plants and animals. She talked more than she thought she could. She told him stories of the wilds, about chasing animals to dangerous ruins, seeing dead people float past in the river, and about the endless moments when Masu saved her from danger. She shared how enormous the trees were and how the flowers were more beautiful than glass.

In the night by the glowing campfire, Under would tell Wander about the humans and spirits. He told her of sports games with intricate rules, staged acts that people watched, and about bar fights that he had to break up. He talked about parades where children were celebrated with flags, and town feasts at which everyone brought food.

"Under, do you think spirits are bad?"

"Not at all."

"A lot of humans at Heathcliff did. I didn't believe them, but then I once was attacked by one in the mountains. I was starting to think Masu was different from everyone, but then he killed all those people."

"Humans and spirits are not that different," Under said. "Spirits have just been around much longer. I bet if humans stay in this world long enough, they'll become like the spirits. It just takes a while."

"Why do you think deviants want to kill all of us?"

"The deviants don't want to kill all of us, just Aura does. As for the reason, I don't think there is ever a good reason to kill someone."

Wander frowned. She wondered if she should admit to Under that she had killed someone.

Sometimes at night Wander saw Under cry. She would open one eye and see him still awake. He'd stare into the fire and weep so silently that Wander would not have known if she hadn't looked. Though he managed to smile and eat in the day, she saw him melt late in the night. She never saw him sleep. His eyes were always open, outlined in tired wrinkles of skin.

They still passed other humans on the trail. Once there were many. They all wore the same shining silver clothes, and the way their feet walked were identical to each other's. Each man and woman was equipped with bow, arrows, and a sword at their side. When Wander asked Under who they were he answered, "Part of the human army. We'd best stay out of their way."

Under always walked behind. Wander occasionally glanced behind to her make sure he was still there. He usually had his hands jammed in his coat pockets. He sometimes had a toothpick in his mouth. He kept the thing in his pocket, sometimes taking it out and just moving it around between his teeth and lips.

This time he didn't have his toothpick or his hands in his pockets. He appeared cold, hugging himself as he walked. When he and Wander made eye contact, he smiled. His smiles were never large, always gentle like a caressing breeze. Looking ahead, Wander saw that the fox had suddenly stopped. It looked to the woods, its black nose twitching. Then it took off into the forest of evergreens.

A whistle sounded.

A grid of ropes thicker than fingers fell down upon her. The net blanketed her where she stood. People dressed in rags jumped out from behind the evergreen, and others rose from the bushes. All of them were armed with blades tucked in their belts. All around her they took the rope ends and tugged in the same direction. The rope tightened, and Wander lost her balance, hitting the earth.

They moved like ants upon an unearthed worm, all working together to tangle Wander. She began to flail, unable to reach her sword, her right hand stuck through a square of the net.

"HEY!" she could hear Under. She turned to see two men pounce on him. Each managed to twist one of his arms behind him and hold him still. A third immediately felt around Under's pockets. His hand dug into the coat. He took out the small leather pouch.

Delicately opening the pouch, he looked at everyone with a smile as he overturned the pouch and poured gold pieces out onto his palm.

Wander counted six people around her and three with Under. With a good view of their feet, they all wore brown heavy boots, all attached to hairy legs. The one who took Under's gold turned around. She saw his lower face was veiled like her. His hair was so short that the top of his head he looked like a fuzzy peach. A scar marked diagonally across his forehead and ended at his faded eyebrow.

"Okay, okay, you got what you want," Under said. "You can let us go."

The man pocketed the pouch of coins and approached Wander. Wander saw the man's cheeks rise; he was smiling under his red handkerchief. "Not so fast, pretty boy. I haven't gotten to know your friend yet."

The net shook as one of the men peeled the dark veil off her forehead. Another pulled her veil down to reveal her nose and mouth. Wander managed to turn her head down and chomp down on his finger. She could almost hear the crunch between her teeth. He tore his finger from her with a yowl of pain.

The red handkerchief man bent over to Wander. He stared down at her revealed face, his eyebrows furrowed. His companion cursed as he held his quivering wounded finger to his chest.

"Damn, I'm not selling her. See those scars and burns? Too ugly."

Some of the other men laughed in a chorus.

"Search her, and we're done. Take the sword."

Suddenly six pairs of hands came down upon Wander through the net. They tugged at her cloak. The man whom she bit landed a kick on her stomach, causing her to curl. "Damn, this sword is heavy," one said. They managed to unbuckle her cloak from her neck. They scratched at her clothes and dug into her pants.

She slammed her eyes shut. She wanted to cover her ears but couldn't move her arms.

Just then there were screams followed by a roar.

All the men stopped searching her. They turned upward, and Wander opened to see the last thing she expected. A bear.

An enormous brown bear towered over where Under once stood. It landed on its front paws; its maw opened and showed fangs as it let out another roar.

The three surrounding men ran to join the six by the net. Wander no longer struggled. She looked into the bear's dark brown eyes.

The beast moved forward in frenzy. Paws larger than Wander's head kicked the dust off the path. A man charged with blade drawn. The bear raised itself on two feet, towering over the men. Its body eclipsed Wander and them in shadow. With a swing of its claws, the animal knocked the sword out of the man's grip. With that, half the men fled into the woods.

The bear pinned the red handkerchief man to the earth. The thug could see inside the bear's mouth as it snarled over him. The paws that pressed against his shoulders were adorned with claws that could tear him apart. Then the bear let him go. It got off and watched as he started to crawl away desperately. He stumbled and followed his companions.

To intimidate them all the more, the bear charged until it got to the edge of the woods. It turned around, large eyes placed on Wander under her net. In a slow walk, the bear approached her. She could only stare at its long claws getting closer and closer. Darkness rose from the paws and throughout the bear's body. The entire form dropped to the ground, leaving just a shadow. The shadow rose up to reveal a familiar form.

Under fell to his knees at Wander's side. "It's me," he whispered through heavy breaths. He untangled her from the grid of ropes.

The moment she was free, Wander crawled backward.

He picked up her veil and looked at her charred-up face. "I meant to tell you before but—"

"It was you!" Wander shouted. She stood up and her hand began to reach for her sword. "You were that bird. You were . . . that boulder. You were the one who killed everyone!"

"What? NO!"

She pulled out the sword and pointed the blade at him. "You are one of Aura's Arms, aren't you? The one that can change its body!"

"That was not me. You know me."

She let out a mix between a sob and a scream, "I don't know anyone!" That's right, she didn't know anyone. Everyone was different from her, so how could she? If Under should change his body, he could be anyone anytime.

"You think I killed Alice? You think I killed all those people?"

Her fingers tightened on the sword. "What are you?"

He spoke softly. "I'm a shadow. A shapeshifting spirit."

"One of Aura's Arms is a shadow. You're not it? I saw it turn from a bird, to a boulder, to a horse. Then you came."

"If I turned into a boulder I wouldn't be able to change back into anything."

"Why?"

"Because I'd be a rock! I wouldn't have a brain to think or remember who I am!"

"Then how did Aura's Arm do it?"

"I don't know! She mind controls them, heals them, does all sorts of things to them to make them do impossible things."

"You're lying. You lied from the beginning. Why did you keep this from me?"

"I kept it from you for this very reason." He lowered his tone. "I saw a shadow attack the town. I was afraid you would think it was me."

"Well, you only made this worse on yourself," Wander glowered. "If one of Aura's Arms is a shadow, then does that mean she went to war with them in the past? Shouldn't all of them except for the Arm be dead?"

"Your answer is as good as mine. I mean, life finds a way, right? I don't remember a war or anything." He squinted. "For the longest time before I met Alice I just shapeshifted into whatever animals I wanted to in the woods."

"Alice, did she—"

"She knew."

"Tell me who you are. Right now."

"I'm nobody!"

"If you want to stay with me, you have to prove that you aren't Aura's Arm. To do that, I want details to make sure you're not lying."

The fox emerged from the evergreens and sat behind Wander.

"Okay, okay, calm down," Under said. "In my earliest memories, I lived in the forest as whatever animal I knew about. I didn't really have a sense of identity or anything. I just sort of changed into what I felt like. If I felt like flying, I'd turn into a bird. If I felt like swimming, I'd become a fish. If I wanted to fight or scare something I'd turn into a bear. I never got to examine a human closely because I lived far out in the wilderness. It wasn't enchanted though, just a normal forest.

"I lived underground in a hole just big enough for a raccoon, though I often slept in there as a squirrel, weasel, or mouse. Well, one day I peeked out of my hole and saw a dog for the first time. You wanted details, right? It was a black dog with pointed ears, brown eyes, fluffy tail, and a tongue with purple spots. It was sniffing around. Never before seeing a dog, I climbed a tree as a squirrel to get a closer look. After watching it move around enough from various angles, I turned into an exact copy of the dog. You see, I can't change into anything original. I have to have an image and watch it for a while. So I ran around enjoying being a dog. And that's when I met Alice.

"She was a child, maybe seven years old back then. She looked for her pet dog in the woods. Once she found him, she took him home. Only it wasn't him, it was me. I didn't really know what to do because I had never seen humans before. After talking to me some and petting me, she put me on a leash and dragged me home.

"She lived on a farm around the Outskirt Mountains. When she unleashed me I followed her to her room where she lay in bed reading to herself. When she began to play with me and talk to me some more, I changed into a bird and flew around her. That's when she found out what I was. I just wanted to play and did not know that my shapeshifting abilities were something to have any concern over.

"I was kept a secret. Her father hated spirits. Alice loved me though, and she had a very lonely life with no living mother, siblings, or neighbors. She quickly found out it was risky to keep me around so she took me back to the woods.

"But she would come back to the woods every day. She found my hole and would call for me. She called me 'Fairy' because she read too many fairytales. Anyway, eventually I popped out of the hole and shouted back. I managed to change into her. I was naked. though, didn't really understand how to make clothes with the form yet. That took a lot of practice. While we were kids, I played with her as her and wore her dresses that she brought me.

"She taught me about the world. Eventually we both thought of the name 'Under' for me since I lived underground. It was paradise between us for a while until her father found out about me. He began to lock her in the house. Of course I would try to see her. I would turn into a bird and peck at her window, change into the dog and trick him into letting me in, and sometimes even change into her to trick him into letting me in.

"Then everything changed when he caught me being her while playing with her. I suppose it was his worst nightmare. He couldn't tell which one was his monster and which one was his daughter. Once he found that out, he became extra paranoid. One day, he hit Alice and threatened to kill her . . . thinking it was me. That's when we ran away.

"I soon realized how reckless that really was. What mattered to me was for Alice to be safe. She was still so young, so I managed to get her to Willton's orphanage. I told her I had to leave her there, and she started crying. She told me to live as her twin sister. I didn't want that. I didn't want to be her after seeing how that made her father turn against her.

"I moved into the woods behind the orphanage. She grew into a young woman. I would watch over the town as a street cat, bird, dog, or whatever. Sometimes I gave into temptation and changed into a human, though that often caused nothing but confusion and trouble. As Alice grew up, she became an artist. She started drawing people. Eventually she visited me in the woods and said she was going to give me a gift: my own body.

"I laughed at the idea. I have to see something from so many angles, spend time with it, and figure out its size, weight, muscle mass—everything. It felt impossible. Despite me poking fun at the idea, she began to obsessively draw a single person from her imagination. She drew it non-stop for years. I felt awful. She would bring me drawings and paintings every week of the body at different angles, naked, clothed, fishing, cleaning, eating, sleeping…

"I realized then that she wanted me to join her in the human world, and that is why she tried so hard. She wanted me to have my own body so I didn't have to worry about other humans getting confused or mad. When I realized that, I found out that's what I wanted, too. I began staring at paintings and drawings for hours and hours.

"Five years passed of this, and it just eventually clicked. I opened my eyes in this body. I ran straight to Willton. It was the best day of my life. Alice was out in the streets. I snuck up on her and tapped her shoulder. When she turned around, I never saw someone more shocked and happy. Everyone stared at us when she hugged me, nearly knocking me down. She immediately began to introduce me to people, and that's when we began our life together."

He went silent.

Wander lowered her sword, "And?"

"And you know the rest."

"Are you making all this up?"

"What? Who could possibly make this up on the spot?"

Wander squinted. She knew one important thing about everyone else: They were smarter than she. This world was full of things she did not understand, allowing her to easily get tricked. There was no doubt in her mind that he could outwit her.

"It's a good story," Wander said. "Maybe it was from a book."

"That's just ridiculous. You know what? You're sketchier than I, and I've trusted you. You make far less sense. You carry around a sword no one else can carry and have this wild animal following you around."

"Why did you come with me?"

"Because I thought you'd be the most likely to understand if you found out. The others in Willton, I love them, but if they knew what I was they'd probably hunt me down and kill me. You could touch spirits. You were raised by one. Even though we just met, I thought if anyone was worth staying with, it would probably someone who would accept what I am."

Wander took in a big breath through her nose and let it through out through her mouth. Under held out his hand to show her veil limp in his palm. Lowering her sword, she took the veil. She was so preoccupied with her suspicions that she did not think about how he saw her ugly deformed face.

A bird swooped down from the sky and landed on the dirt path. One had never landed so close to Wander before. It was close and still enough to see the golden designs on its feathers.

Wander never had seen a bird like it before. Its long neck reminded her of a stork, but its bright talons were like an eagle's. Its head wore a crown of gold feathers. The entire bird was black with what appeared like gold inscriptions at the end of every feather.

She and Under, completely forgetting their conversation, stared wide-eyed at the unusual creature. Even the fox seemed unsettled.

"What is that?" Wander asked. She noticed a beige letter had been tied to the bird's right foot.

"A phoenix," Under said. "They are magical birds from the desert. They are creatures capable of green magic, reincarnation."

Wander did not understand a lot of the words Under had just said. "The note . . ."

"Oh," Under then noticed the beige square at the phoenix's feet. "Is that . . . a letter?"

They cautiously approached the bird. It did not seem concerned as Under bent down and untied the note. Once free of the letter, the bird spread its wings to show striped feathers of black and gold as it took off above the trees.

Under daintily opened the letter, making sure not to tear any place but the edge. He pulled out a folded paper. He opened it and began to read. Wander pressed against his side to see. She didn't know why she bothered, since she couldn't read. The tan paper shined with gold lines and rich black penmanship.

"What's it say?"

"It's for you," he said.

"The bird wrote that?"

"Oh my God, no! The phoenix belonged to someone. Only really amazing people can tame a phoenix. The fact that it found you is amazing. I wish the creature could have stayed longer, I'd love to examine—"

"What does the letter say?"

"Oh. It says, 'Wander, you don't know me, but I know you. I have heard a lot about you, enough so that I would like to meet with you. I know what you are after, and I can help you get him back. I know him in ways you do not, and I wish to share his story with you if you will share your pieces of him with me. We must meet with discretion, as meeting with you could cost me my life. I will be waiting under the waterfall by the crossroads of Inksgrid, the Daisy Trail, and Twilight Forest. Meet me there, and you can save him. Signed: An Ally.'" Under folded the paper neatly back into a square. "Can I see the map?"

Wander pulled the map from her leather bag. He opened it up and stared at the continent surrounded by blue. His finger began on a word and moved up a dark line. "That crossroad is far, but it's in the direction we're headed. " He handed her both the map and letter. "It's probably a trap. We should ignore it."

"I'm sorry about not believing you."

"Nah. Your suspicion was probably healthy. I can imagine that shadows are difficult people to trust."

They continued on their journey, passing fields of wheat and corn. Sometimes a rabbit bolted across the dirt trail or a dog barked in the distance.

"So you're a spirit?"

Wander's questions had become never-ending. Each day was a blur of her and Under talking. Under didn't seem to mind, in fact, he appeared to enjoy talking about himself. They walked through green pastures. At times Wander would see clouds of sheep in the distance. Sometimes horses with tails swishing, faces down in the grass to graze. Once some cows were close to the wood fence, and a baby calf stood among them. Wander ran over to the fence, her arm outstretched. The cattle ultimately ignored her.

"Humans think we are spirits. But the truth is that I don't have an original form, at least not one that I remember. I am whatever I choose to be."

"How did you make a painting human? It could've been a spirit."

"Alice and I wanted to be human together."

The air began to cool as the sun sank under a horizon. Hugging herself, Wander could see the dark silhouette of a home beyond the fields. Warm blond light glowed from its windows. She looked up. With no trees, only fields, the sky looked like it could swallow her whole. The moon became more than an orb beyond a window or canopy, now it was a looming planet of its own. The stars reminded her of when a drunkard smashed a bottle in Heathcliff—all the little glass pieces scattered and glittered with light.

With no wood for fire, Wander and Under lay on the hillside of the path, looking off hungrily toward the cozy home in the distance. Under picked a long piece of grass and stuck it into his mouth. The fox lay a little distance from them, keeping its body curled on the edge of the trail at the top of the hill.

"You know, it took a while for me to get used to being human," Under said. "Back when I changed into this body and Alice took me in to live with her, I did not actually realize what I was getting myself into. All I knew is that I liked her and wanted to be with her and make her happy. I had never stayed one thing for so long. It wasn't until I had this body for a while that I started to think and feel more. My feelings for her were way less simple. I began to get mad at her when she talked to other people. I got upset when she wasn't around. It drove me so nuts, that I once lashed out at her. I told her I didn't like being human anymore. I regretted it immediately after I said it. She cried, but then she kissed me."

"A kiss?"

Under took Wander's hand and pressed his lips to her knuckles. "Like that, except on the lips. I didn't know what it was either until she did it to me. After she kissed me, she said she was in love with me. That kiss never had me so shocked and excited. I was so confused. She took my hands and talked to me for hours about my feelings. I realized later that all my complex feelings that were torturing me was just that I was falling in love with her. I did not know something like that could make me angry, jealous, and lonely."

"Why are you human still?" Wander asked. "You can be anything you want. You could be a bird and fly anywhere. You could explore the ocean as a fish or become a powerful creature like that bear you turned into. You could be anything, so why do you stay the same?"

Under withdrew the grass from his lips. "As a bird or fish, I could end up as someone's dinner. As a bear, I could be someone's game. There are many cons to being an animal."

"But you can fly in the sky or swim in the water. You can smell and see far!"

"You take what you are for granted, Wander. There is no greater thing than to be human. When I lived as animals, I went day by day just living. I'd eat, sleep, and just move around. As a human though, I began to have dreams. Not like sleeping dreams, but waking ones, as though I could just think of possibilities forever. I tapped into strange feelings I never had before. I desired and thought of things I never understood as an animal. For nights I was overwhelmed by my own thoughts, unable to sleep. To think so much made me feel an insufferable loneliness at first but then that led me to understand why humans talk so much. Ah, talking. I love talking. Animals can communicate, but it doesn't compare to human language."

"I never thought of it that way."

"The grass is always greener on the other side for humans for the exact reason I love being one. Your minds have such imagination that you can always picture something greater than what you already have."

Wander shut her eyes. There was a comfort in the hillside against her spine, how it propped her up to look out to the horizon. Through her eyelashes, she could still see the shine of the stars. She peeked over at Under. His back had turned to her. Did he sleep? She still had yet to see if he slept for sure. Every day he had dark circles around his eyes.

She could not sleep herself this night. The air had turned frigid. She regretted not packing blankets. She lifted her veil over her eyes to keep them warm. She emitted soft, warm breaths against the cloth to keep her face heated. Looking out between the cracks of her dark cocoon, she noticed Under turn, his arms tightly wrapped around himself. He shivered.

Wander rolled to his side. "Under?"

"Yes?"

"Just seeing if you were awake."

"I am."

"Okay."

"Okay."

She pressed against him. He stiffened for a while and slowly relaxed. The sides of their bodies that touched warmed a little.

Under moved to lie on his stomach. He growled, "I'm changing." She felt his body sink away and rise back into a fluffy sheep. His white ears flicked, and he laid his head down. This was the first time he had transformed since the bandit incident. Wander stared at the mess of wool in front of her eyes. Her hand moved forward and lightly touched his back. It was real, like the stuffing of a pillow. There were no sheep in the Emerald Wilds, but she would see some in Heathcliff from time to time. She even ate some once.

The memory made her sick to her stomach as she remembered Under telling her he could become someone's dinner as an animal. She closed the remaining distance between them, her arms and face nestled in his wool.

As she shut her eyes, she silently hoped to not go to a bad place. She prayed for no fire, only the forest and Masu. She used to dream of the Emerald Wilds and Masu so often. She could splash in the river, dig holes, try to climb trees, collect sticks, throw stones, and chase animals. Masu would scold her, sleep at her side, and play word games with her. Most of the dreams were like reliving memories.

Now almost every night she drowned in stinging flame and twisted breathlessly in smoke, if not her own demise, she would see the dead of Heathcliff or Willton.

She had dreams of Alice still trapped under the collapsed chimney. Her nails scraped against the dirt to pull herself out. She called out for Under. Wander would dream that she and Under traveled down a forest path. Wander turned around to see Alice dragging herself after them with mangled legs, leaving a trail of blood behind her. "Under!" she'd cry. Then Wander would wake with the cries still echoing in her ears.

Of course the ones with Roslyn, Ms. Flinsler, and Ethan were common. Ms. Flinsler and Roslyn rattled, sizzled, clawed, coughed, and screamed in their rooms. Ethan frightened her the most. Unlike the rest of his family, he would appear silent and bloodstained. The whites of his eyes were wide, his nostrils flared, his back straight. He would just stare, never breaking eye contact. He scared her so much that she would jump up, hug herself, and take a while to recover in the waking world.

Wander woke up with a shiver. Her veil had fallen away from her face in her sleep. Her entire body felt as though it had been covered in dew. Sitting up she saw the sun just start to pull itself over the horizon. Light stretched the shadow of a lone tree on the field and the fences that separated her and Under from the farmland. A rooster cock-a-doodle-doo'd. Their calls always sounded forced to Wander, as though it hurt to make the sound. Despite that, they loved to holler in the mornings. One in Heathcliff did so every morning until someone chopped its head off. The mornings turned quiet after that.

Opening her mouth, she let out a burst of breath. Just then she saw an eruption of mist. She breathed again and saw her breath come out in a soft puff.

Her heart quickened. What was this? Her breath became like a campfire, emitting smoke every time she let go. She shook Under awake and he turned back to his human form. She kept breathing forcefully to watch the mist she created. She caught Under watching and his neutral gaze turned into a smile.

The two walked down the path. Under picked another piece of grass to keep in his mouth. "So . . . Wander . . ." Under began. He had become a lot more talkative lately. "Do you know any games?"

"What kind of game?"

"One we can do while walking, I guess. Alice and I would play the color game. We'd pick a color and take turns naming everything around us that was the color we chose."

"Masu and I played games like that. It's how he taught me a lot of words!"

"Let's play one then."

Wander looked forward to see the path slink into hills layered with trees. "Words that start with S."

"That's a lot of words, Wander."

"Snake," she began.

"Fine. Sleep."

"Sky."

"Silk."

"Sun."

"Sand."

"Soup."

"Sheep."

"Shirt."

"Slim," Under kept up a fast pace, each word thrown like a rock to the dirt. It wasn't like Masu who patiently waited for Wander's answer, no matter how long she took.

"Slip!"

"Slice."

"Stairs!"

"Stars."

"Smile!"

"Silver."

"Stick."

"Stone."

"Stretch."

"Strike."

"Stream."

"Shoot."

"Scream."

"Swarm."

"Socks!"

"Song."

"Stars."

Under took the piece of grass out of his mouth, "I already said stars. It's too bad you don't have money to make bets, or I'd get rich today."

They continued with other letters such as T, G, and H. Under won every single round. Each time he seemed pretty proud of himself. Wander had never won a round of the game in her life. Then Under wanted them to do Q. All Wander knew was "quick" and she was done. Next came Under's color game using the color green, then brown, then black.

Under suddenly halted and held his hand out, "It's snowing."

She stopped and turned to see Under's eye focused on a small flake of white. The pale petal drifted down to the earth where it melted into water.

"Weird."

"You know about snow right?"

She only frowned, not sure how stupid she would seem to admit her ignorance.

"It is cold water, so cold that it has become solid." He put out his palm to her, and they watched the flakes land and melt. "See?"

The fox seemed unfazed by the event. It stood in the path, waiting for the journey to continue. As they moved on, the white rain gained weight. The flakes fell more slowly. Wander saw the tree branches begin to bend. The snow no longer melted. Each flake stuck to each other and covered the ground.

"It's not melting. Are we going to be alright?"

"Don't worry about it. Just watch your step so you don't slip."

After a while, Wander could no longer recognize the world. Every color was muted in white. Her feet sank in snow with each step. The fox didn't even lift its feet out of the snow, leaving a dragging path behind. It was how Wander imagined walking on a cloud would be like.

She touched the ground, her finger pressing an indent in the white blanket. Under was right, the snow was frigid. She took a handful. It clumped together like dough. She held it up to her face. Pulling down her veil, the sniffed the mass. It smelled like water. She licked the white crystals. Under was right again, it was water. She proceeded to eat the cluster with caution, making sure not a single snowflake touched her teeth.

"What are you doing?" Under approached with his hands deep in his coat pockets.

"It is cold water."

"You shouldn't taste things you know little about."

"Now you're sounding like Masu."

"Eating it is nasty. However, there are a lot of fun things to do in snow. Like this," his tall, dark figure bent down and clumped the snow into an orb. With a swing of his lanky arm, he hurled the snowball into Wander's shoulder. "Now try to hit me."

She figured it out immediately when Under started running down the path. It was like a game of splashing in the river, except with snow.

Her hands scooped the cold and molded the white into a ball as she took chase. She never saw Under move with speed until now. His long legs could carry him far. She threw the snow, and it hit him in the back. He turned and threw one right back at her, but it flew over her shoulder and missed.

The world became a blur of white, frosted breathing, snow flinging, and frigid hands. They began to use trees to block each other's throws. Wander kept hitting Under, and Under mostly missed with every throw.

"You're bad at this!" Wander laughed as she hit him a second time in the chest.

"Try this then!"

Under dodged back behind the tree. A chestnut hued deer leapt out the other side. It bounded across the path and weaved around trees to Wander. Once in front, Under changed back into his human self, his hands already in the snow. He splashed snow up at Wander.

"That's cheating!" Wander scooped a ball.

Under shot back behind a tree and a squirrel crawled around and up the branches. Wander threw her snowball, hitting the tree trunk. A bird flew from the tree and turned back into a human on his knees. He chucked a snowball, hitting Wander's knee. She tossed one back, but Under turned into a rabbit and sped away.

The chase laced them in and out of the woods and path. Under turned into a hummingbird and buzzed past Wander's ear. Twirling around, she lobbed him with a snowball. The snow hit the hummingbird that cried out with a squeak.

Realizing the sphere was twice the size of a hummingbird, Wander ran to where Under landed. Her heart dropped when she saw the little bird limp in the snow. He looked like a jewel, green shining feathers, red belly, and a beak like a sewing needle. Her hands dipped under his body, lifting it up.

"Under?"

He opened his eyes and rolled out of her hands, forming himself human in the snow. Back as a man, he held his hand to his head and shivered.

For a moment she thought she killed him. The second she saw that limp bird she thought the whole world ended again. Her body ached to hug him, but she swayed backward. "Are you alright?"

"Y-yeah. Just grazed me a little. Sorry, I got carried away. I shouldn't change into something so small." His eyes met hers. He must have seen the fear in her because he said with a smile, "Don't worry. I'm fine. It won't happen again."

His eyes suddenly darted upward toward the sky. Wander looked behind her and up.

Smoke.

Chapter 6
Inksgrid

"The burning of Inksgrid made me realize that spirits and humans are not meant for the same world. Spirits are monsters, utter and complete monsters." – Records from the War of Arrows

The sight of smoke over trees was all too familiar by now. It flowed up like a river in the sky and pooled into an omniscient cloud.

"Do you think that's—"

"It could be Chant's . . ."

Under rubbed the snow off his shoulders. "We should go around then."

"But Masu might be there."

"What would you do if he was?"

"I'd talk to him."

Under winced as he rubbed the side of his head, "That didn't work so well last time."

"He knew it was me. I saw it. Just for a second he knew. Then he fainted. Chant fought me, and when I looked back, Masu was gone. That won't happen this time. I'll go through fire if I have to."

"Let's at least check out what's happening before rushing into it. Let's keep to the forest edge and watch and make sure Masu is there."

Wander and Under moved toward the smoky sky. As they neared, the sound of metal clangs beat like hearts over the familiar uproar of shouting and screaming. The stench of fire began to rise in Wander's nostrils. Under suddenly stopped walking. Wander turned to see the spirit's face had paled. He covered his mouth and nose, his eyes beginning to water. She looked down to see his other hand quivered. He had begun to shake.

"Are you alright?"

He closed his eyes and said into his hand, "It's going to be just like Willton. We should go. It's too dangerous."

"Then wait here. I'll be back." She moved herself in front of him to make sure he agreed. Under's visible eye opened, rimed in red. The smell of fire and sound of screams was causing him to relive Willton, even from this distance.

"If you don't come back soon, I'll be there."

They parted, and Wander noticed that the fox remained with Under as she left. When she neared the sounds of wood breaking apart, she ducked down to the brush. Deer were fleeing, their forms popping out in the snow.

She made it to edge of the wood, and she raised her head above the shrub to see a familiar scene. All the buildings glowed with flames climbing like ivy. Bodies littered the streets. A few differences stood out. She recognized the human army she and Under had passed before. She could only identify them because they all wore the same shining silver clothes. They collided with people in regular, mundane wear. Humans were fighting each other.

Wander never thought she'd see such a sight. In Heathcliff, there were little fights that broke out in the streets that ended quickly. This was an entire town erupted with individuals trying to kill each other. A woman in white ran at a silver-clad man from behind, planting a knife right into the back of his neck between his helmet and armor while he was in the midst of grappling another man for a sword. An army man cleaved through civilians with an axe. An army woman with her hair tied back into a bun kicked at one of the walls of the buildings. The wall broke, and she stepped back as the flames roared in anger from the interruption. She jumped into the burning building and came back out with an unconscious child, a boy, dangling in her arms. She laid the child down. Her fingers brushed down his face and to his mouth, which she opened. Her face lowered to his, her lips parted. Just then an arrow shot through her neck. She fell on top of the boy, gone.

The arrow came from the roof of a building. Masu stood there, preparing another shot.

Wander's heart jumped at the sight of him. She was about to leap out from the wood and call out to him but she froze when a chain roped around Masu's right leg. Below, someone in army wear stood with the other end of the chain in his hands. He ran backward and jerked the chain with all his might. Masu's leg flew forward as he got yanked off the roof. He landed on his side in the dirt. The soldier threw the chain down and stomped his boot down over it. He reached behind to unbuckle a redwood bow from his back. He drew an arrow and took half a second to aim and shoot. The arrow hit one of Masu's wings. Dark feathers fell, and black blood trickled down onto the snow.

Masu tried to get up, but the human took the chain back and tugged, causing him to fall again and drag through the snow. His wings flapped. A second arrow hit his wing, and he flopped about in the white. The scene reminded Wander of a robin trying to fly away from cat's paws. The cat would be only playing, but the bird became broken.

"LEAVE HIM ALONE!" Wander burst out of the bushes. Pulling out her sword, she placed herself between the soldier and Masu.

She met the human's eyes, dark brown and wide as full moons framed by a helmet. She could see the puffs of his breath. He reached back toward his quiver of arrows with red fletching.

Snow kicked up behind Wander as she charged toward him. He stumbled back, dropping his bow. His back neared flames as he pulled out his blade. For a moment, his eyes darted away from Wander, behind her.

She turned to see another soldier a distance behind her down the street, the fire's glow dancing on his or her armor. The soldier pulled back the string and sent an arrow straight for Wander.

Raising her sword in front of her face, Wander blocked the arrow. Hearing snow crunch on her other side, she twisted away from the slash of the other soldier. The swing left him open, and her elbow smashed into his stomach. An arrow missed them both, disappearing into the flames of a dying house.

Wander flipped back to the archer and stabbed her sword into the snow. The ground shook, and the snow leading up to the soldier bumped up a couple inches, like a snake slithered underneath. Once the path reached the human, the earth below them ruptured with vines. They coiled up and around the legs, squeezing until the armor cracked. She screamed as the vines twisted around her arms, curled around her neck, and reached toward her opened mouth. Wander grimaced as the plants dove down her mouth. Her shrieks turned to choking, and her struggles became violent thrashes.

Wander's gaze turned back to the dark eyed man. He was gone, his footprints leading to him charging toward Masu who still lay on the ground. She bolted forwarded, body-slamming herself into the soldier. Both tumbled through the snow. Hitting him hurt more than she planned. His silver armor was like stone.

Stabbing down his blade, he pulled himself up. His helmet had been knocked off to reveal a head of black curls and brown skin. Stubble grew around his lower face. The soldier's jaw clenched, his dark eyes big but blinded. A screaming man on fire tackled the soldier back into the snow.

She did not understand why the humans were attacking each other. Was everyone out for themselves—or were there two sides? While the soldier and on-fire man fought, Wander scrambled back to her sword, drawing it from the earth. She glanced to where the plants attacked the soldier to see the haunting scene of a limp body immersed in a tangle of thorns, vines, and branches.

Just then more humans appeared, both armored and unarmored. Each attacked with knives, arrows, scythes, torches, and sometimes just their fists. Half of them went for each other. Wander had to slash through those that came at her, blood spattering in the snow. She could see the dark-skinned soldier beyond the chaos getting overrun with more enemies.

Masu. I have to get to Masu.

She rushed through the pandemonium. There was no sign of Chant or the shadow. Who started these fires? Maybe they made this happen and left since people were killing each other already. But why was Masu still here?

A soldier finished off a young girl and jumped in front of Wander. Wander spun and hacked through the already cracked armor. As the soldier staggered, Wander thrust forward in a stab. As she drew out the blade, the man fell.

Since when did this become so natural? Until this very night she had only killed Ethan, who didn't even put up a fight. Now the slaughter of people felt the same as that of an animal. No, different. It was easier.

Where Masu once lay was now just a pit in the snow with some dark feathers and black spatter. The chain that held him was loose. There were footprints. They had never before been so obvious thanks to the snow. They were darker, melting. She could track him down.

"You!"

Wander turned to see the dark-skinned soldier pointing one of his blades at her. He had become injured. Streams of blood slid down his face from his forehead.

Just then a pain exploded from her back and pulsated through her body. Letting out a cry, she fell to her knees and saw the metal tip of an arrow sticking out of her breast. Though it made her entire body shake, she turned, and Masu stood at the corner of the building. He was so real that she could see the wisps of his breath.

She fell into the snow and did not want to get up. She stared at her own hand festooned in scars. The sounds of crackling began to fade. The snow dampened the side of her cloak. She blacked out.

Darkness opened to blurred columns. A silhouette sat with his back against a tree, his head against his knees.

"Masu?"

He lifted up his head. As her vision cleared, she saw it was not Masu. Under crawled over to her. His face closed in, dark locks shifted to reveal reddened eyes. "Wander? Can you hear me?"

She tried to move, and her whole body clenched. She spat out in agony, her hands reached up to find an arrow head sticking out of her bare chest. She had not stared at her own naked chest in a while. It used to be smooth with little specks of moles. Since she burned, her chest looked like a rotten fruit, wrinkly, discolored in splotches. Her cloak hung on a branch behind Under.

Under's hands grabbed at her bare arm. "Don't move! I think that would be bad!"

As her mind bloomed awake, she could recall the branches reaching into the woman's mouth, the furious dark eyes, fire, and screaming. She burst into tears. Not silent, hiccupping. Every sob shot anguish through her chest as the arrow moved with her heaving breaths.

"Hey, it's going to be—"

She interrupted Under with a feral scream. He got the message and sat silently as she let out all her distress. For just this moment she needed to be wild and the pain to soar free.

"I don't want this anymore!" she cried. Her hands took her veil, shutting the opening for her eyes. She whispered, "No more. Just no more. I want to go home."

She heard Under from beyond the darkness of her veil. "Look. I need you to tell me how to save you. This injury needs attention. I'm clueless as to what to do."

"I want Masu . . ."

"I know, but you won't get him back with an arrow through you."

"Cut it on the back. There is a knife in my bag."

She kept her eyes in darkness as Under worked on the arrow. She told him every step she could recall Masu had done when she had been shot before. It was less painful than the first time. Maybe her thoughts overshadowed the hurt, or her body had grown used to punishment.

As Under washed the wound with their bottled water, Wander shivered. Her crying had lessened, so she drew down her veil to expose her eyes.

"Why do you ignore my skin?"

"What?"

"My burns. You never said a thing about them. You're just pretending they aren't there."

He took out bandages and said, "Your body is none of my business."

They stayed quiet as he wrapped her chest in white cloth. It reminded her of the Heathcliff doctor's visits. For so many days he would shed her bandages and rewrap her. Her skin sometimes stuck to the bandages, and she would weep as they were peeled off. The bandages would come off in colors of yellow and red. For the first week she thought it would be like any other wound, leaving just a couple of scars. Then she looked in the mirror for the first time and no longer recognized herself.

"There. Done." Under sat back to examine his bandaging work.

Wander looked down. Her naked and injured body shivered in the snow. She felt like a candle that burned brightly and furiously before completely going out. Her outcry left her empty.

"Hey. It's going to be okay." Something about those words hurt despite their kindness. She shook her head, holding back the tears his words summoned.

"I know. Let's play words that begin with O."

She shook her head.

"Object," he said. When she didn't answer, he said, "Oblivion." Still nothing. He continued with long pauses between every word, "Open. On. Out. Or. Odd. Own. Obscene. Obtuse. Omen. Obese. Orange. Off."

Wander finally picked up her head. "Open."

Under smiled. "Orchestra."

"That's not a word."

"Yes it is."

"You make words up. I've never heard of obscene, obtuse, omen, or oblivin. I can tell because I do it, too."

"It's oblivion, and did you not hear my whole deal about how I love language? No one can beat me at a word game. I have read Willton's entire library of books."

"I don't know how to read."

"I'll teach you sometime."

She noticed Under shaking. Nighttime had come, and they sat in the snow with no fire. Under probably had no clue how to make one despite watching her many times. Wander cloaked herself and instructed Under how to build a campfire. She helped him start the flame since her first try at making fire took an entire day. Once the fire was done, Under sat close to her side and she leaned against him.

For a moment Wander wanted to ask, "How are you okay?" But she quickly answered her own question. He wasn't okay. She had only seen him sleep once, he barely ate, and he would not go to the burning town with her. Regardless of those things, he managed to be fun. She would not know how to deal with someone like herself in his place.

"You cover yourself up to hide your burns, don't you?"

"Yes."

"I didn't talk about it because I imagine it's a touchy subject for humans. I mean, I'm a shape shifter. I don't have a permanent body. I can't imagine being stuck in the same one all the time and getting it permanently damaged."

She stared into the flames. "You're right. It's horrible, and I wish I could change."

"When I shape shifted in Willton, everyone would treat me differently. If I was a cat, people petted me. If I was a bee, they ran. As a child I would skip and dance in the street and people would smile. As an adult, though, everyone thought I was nuts. But my favorite people were the ones who always treated me somewhat the same. Dog, cat, or goat, they'd still pet and feed me. As a man or woman, they'd still be respectful. That's one reason I loved Alice so much. It didn't matter if I was an animal or human, she'd still sit down and talk to me. Good people don't judge on appearances." He smiled. "And the best are the ones who talk kindly to animals even though they can't talk back."

Wander shut her eyes and leaned her head against Under's arm.

"Masu shot me."

"I figured he did."

"I wish he would recognize me."

"I didn't want to mention it, but we can follow the letter. I mean, whoever wrote it said they knew all about Masu and could help you get him back."

"You thought it was a trap."

"I know. I'm right all the time aren't I? No, I could be wrong. We're near the meeting spot." He leaned against her, "Don't worry, Wander. If you don't find Masu, I'll stay with you."

The words wrapped around her like a blanket. A long rain had ended from a roof appearing over her head again. She opened her mouth to say something but couldn't think of how to respond. Closing her eyes, she leaned against Under's arm. His coat smelled of smoke, not like a campfire, or smoke emitting from the dead, but like the smoke from the tubes people breathed in Heathcliff. She saw Ethan breathe in through one of the pipes once. He then puffed it out like visible breath in the cold.

Chapter 7
Twilight Forest

"The orange leaves are like gold, but still no one lives in the Twilight Forest. It's protected by the deviants, who despise building in a location they already deem to be perfect." – Where the Stag Runs: A Guide to Deviant Customs

Under grew more concerned about Wander. The poor girl was just a kid. Despite her jaded eyes he heard innocence in her voice and laugh.

He had heard of wind-borns before. Some lived in the orphanage Alice grew up in. They never turned out quite normal. One became a fortune teller on the streets, and the other was arrested for murder. They were also a huge part of the human slave trade. What better way to get loyal, useful slaves than to capture those who come into this world able-bodied but unable to think for themselves?

It would be better if she just gave up on Masu, but he didn't have the heart to tell her. It was as though some force pushed her into the chaos, forcing a little girl to endure fire, bandits, loneliness, fighting, injury, and cold nights.

The next morning they set off to the crossroads. Under couldn't conceal his astonishment when Wander stood up and walked without even a wince. He thought she had died in his care before she regained consciousness. Shock numbed him as he sat there, unsure of what to do next. He almost got to crying, feeling aches in his throat and heat below the eyes. He was sure the arrow hit her heart, and he knew human anatomy well.

Nature versus nurture: Under knew both concepts well. Nature was destiny, what most people cannot control, like what they are born as. Unlike humans and other spirits, shadows like him could manipulate their nature. Nurture was complicated. People sometimes can change their fate: like a good-natured boy born with evil parents would become evil. Under tried to place whether Wander's peculiarity was due to her being raised in a bewitched forest or because she simply wasn't all human.

By the time they arrived at the crossroads, the snow had shrunk away into the earth. They stood in front of a wood sign with two arrows pointing in opposite directions to Inksgrid and Twilight Forest. The single path forked into two roads, one indented with footprints and wagon trails, the other shadowed thickly under orange canopies of leaves.

The fox began to walk toward the Twilight Forest path. Something about that animal gave Under the creeps. He could discern a lot about something just from watching its form at different angles. After his time spent with Wander, he could shape shift into her if he wished, but he could not figure out the fox. It was as though the creature consisted of many broken pieces that didn't form a single entity, like an undone puzzle. It also thought it was the leader of the party apparently, always charging on ahead.

"I hear the waterfall," Wander said.

Under heard the roar of water from behind the sign. "Stay behind me."

They pressed through the brush in between the roads. Beyond the bushes, the grass came close to Under's knees. Orange leafed trees met with pine above. They came to a river, perhaps a foot high, flowing fast.

Frogs leapt in with little plops. A breeze carried the cool spray of water. The water fell from a cliff side in a white rush. Ferns and pine gated the top. As the waterfall hit the earth, a foggy mist rose. The entire area felt damp.

As the letter said, they found the dark cave behind the falls. Peeking in, Under saw only the dark. "I don't like this." His voice echoed.

"I went into a place like this once."

"How was it?"

"Really big, fluffy bugs attacked me."

Under squinted. "I can transform and go ahead. I can see in the dark as a cat. You wait here."

Her felt her hands grab at his sleeve. "No. We stick together."

They shuffled into the darkness. Under kept his hand on a wall to follow, Wander's hands held onto his other arm by the coat sleeve. He could not hear the fox's steps. Did it stay outside? Maybe the creature knew this was a really bad idea.

Under kicked what felt like a stone but could not hear it due to the waterfall roaring behind them. The whoosh of falling water covered every other sound.

"Wander," Under spoke over the rushing falls, "I forgot to say, whatever happens, don't mention that I'm a shadow. We're supposed to all be dead. I don't need that attention. As far as you know, I'm a human named Greg."

"How about Samson?"

"Fine. Whatever."

"Who's there?" A third voice, a woman's, spoke in the darkness. Under pushed Wander behind his back, facing in the direction opposite of the voice.

A glow emerged, showing a corner of the cave. It expanded until a woman stepped out with a torch. A deviant. Under could tell immediately. She possessed dark hair in a tight bun. Fire reflected in her purple eye. A leather eyepatch covered the other eye with a briar patch design etched in. She dressed in typical peasant's clothes: brown pants, loose white shirt, and sandals. She was rather flat-chested and pale.

Despite her young face, she moved forward like an aching elder, a cane leading her as a third leg. Under sensed something horrid in her body, like a disease or sickness but worse. Being her would be painful.

"Who in blood's name are you?" she asked.

"I could ask you the same," Under said.

Her eyes traveled to his back and locked on Wander.

"Wander?"

"Yes?" she asked.

"You got my letter?"

"Yes."

"Quit hiding behind that man then. I'm not going to hurt you."

Wander stepped out, and the deviant hobbled in for a closer look. She examined Wander from her head down. She looked back at Under, obviously suspicious at the uninvited guest.

"I will only speak to Wander," she said. "No one else."

This had to be a trap. That woman was a deviant. He was certain of one thing: He could not leave them alone together.

"I want him to stay, please," Wander said.

The woman scowled. "I am already risking myself too much here. You have to understand."

Under had enough. "Let's leave, Wander."

"What? Why?"

"This woman's a deviant. She is an enemy, and this is obviously a trap."

The woman managed to intimidate him with a wildness in her eye as she looked up at him. She set her cane aside and reached out to touch him. She had beautiful nails for a peasant: glossy and smooth. Her hand flinched as it got shocked. She must have suspected he wasn't human and tested the theory. Luckily for Under, being a shadow meant he could be whatever he wanted. He was human through and through right now. He even bled red.

"I demand honesty," she said. "But I suppose you are right to be suspicious. Come, let's sit and discuss the matter at hand. There is a lot to say."

She limped back where she came from with Wander following. Under looked around to see he had been correct; the fox had not joined them. He skulked behind, keeping an eye on the deviant. She seemed frail, but a deviant's body could take much more pain than a human. She could put up a fight.

They reached a dead end with a fire glowing in the center. Groaning in agony, the woman lowered herself down to the stone ground. Wander sat across from her, and Under planted himself at Wander's side.

"I will tell you who I am only if you both promise secrecy. What you said is correct. I am a deviant. That means I could be executed as a traitor for meeting with you and telling you what I know. My information is to be spread among anyone you wish, but not my identity. Understand?"

"We promise," they said.

Wander gave Under a strange look, like she wanted to say something. He sensed the truth about him on her lips and shook his head.

The deviant looked into the fire. "My name is Myth. I am Aura, the queen of the deviants' twin sister. I have fought many battles until my body was broken in the war with the winged ones. I knew Aura's Wings since we killed his entire kingdom and took him to become an Arm. He is 'Masu' to you?"

"Yes!"

"Aura, Chant, and I knew you were connected because he mentioned you when he woke up. We found him after Chant set the Emerald Wilds aflame. She caught him flying around until he choked on her smoke and fainted. Chant brought his unconscious, half burned body back to the palace. When he woke, the first thing he said was, 'I have to find Wander.'"

Under looked at Wander. From where he sat, he could not see her eyes, only the dark cloak.

"Despite a broken wing from his fall, his burns, and weakened state, he struggled to get out of the bed. He kept saying he had to find you. My sister, Aura, gave him drugged tea to put him to sleep. While he slept, she used her powers to return him to as he was before."

"What he was before?" Under repeated.

"Before getting into Masu, let me tell you about my people. We deviants do not fight in wars. We win them with our ruler and their Arms. We have killed many with little sacrifice. We have eliminated three entire races. We are how we are because once deviants were enslaved by horned spirits. We were the same as the horned spirits but were born without horns. Thus, they called us deviants and made us slaves. My people had their blood spilt as though it were water to wash the streets. They were powerless until a woman by the name of Rumor found power. Rumor belonged to a noble horned spirit and was forced to help him on a hunt for a guardian, a ruler of an enchanted forest. The horned spirits killed these guardians to achieve status. Rumor found the guardian before her master. It was a large, dark-furred stag. The creature took pity on Rumor's bruised and sickly body so it offered her its blood. She drank and gained the same power my sister has.

"Rumor sparked a revolution that freed the deviants. She did so with the powers granted to her from the guardian's blood. With their freedom, the deviants built their own kingdom with Rumor as their hero queen. The horned spirits grew bitter over the deviant's victory. They believed they were divine people who were meant to rule others. In that bitterness, they slew a third of the deviant people in hopes of conquering them. Rumor had enough. She had seen many friends and family die. In her love for her people, she began to hate all else that disturbed them. The queen decided to kill every single horned spirit. She did so with her powers alone. She visited every settlement and every army to make them tear themselves apart.

"She killed all horned spirits but one. The princess of the horned people was taken as a trophy and jailed in a prison cell. Her name was Red for her crimson hair. Every night Rumor would visit Red and practice her mind-control powers on the princess' mind. Eventually the princess broke and became Rumor's pet. Her mind was so tortured that her hair became ghostly white. She became an Arm, a bodyguard and reminder of what happens if you mess with the deviants. Red had a lover who returned to save her from Rumor's control. He came to save her only to be killed by the one he sought to save. His story was immortalized to set an example to all other outsiders who believed they could free their minds from the queen.

"Before Rumor passed away, she wrote a creed. The ruler of the deviants had to drink the blood of guardians for power to protect the people. The power can never be used against a fellow deviant unless to heal. Due to mind-control's power to corrupt, a ruler must never fight. She or he cannot kill another. Their hands must stay clean. But when a nation strikes us, we strike back with vengeance that shakes and breaks every soul they have.

"Later the deviants clashed with another race: the shadows. They were shape shifters, able to turn into anything they desired. Our people nearly died out. They faced wolves, bears, elephants, dragons, sharks, and all sorts of beasts that possessed the minds of spirits. They turned into our own and spied on us, making us doubt each other. How does one defeat such an enemy? The king of our people during that time did something very simple. With the power of the guardian, he controlled the minds of the shadows and made them kill each other. He could control their minds to the point that they'd transform into inanimate objects, unable to change back. To copy Rumor's deed, he kept a single shadow alive, a prince whose name was Arrow. He became the second Arm."

Wander looked at Under. He wished she hadn't. She obviously wondered how Under could be alive if what Myth said was true. He had no idea himself.

"The next war was during Aura's and my time. I know all that I have told you paints a bloody picture, but our society is peaceful. Our people did not know pain. They lived without fear, with my sister healing them of any disease or hurt. Then the winged beings attacked. Our father, mother, and baby brother were murdered during a visit to the winged beings' castle. They were traveling to the northern snow mountains for a ceremonial guardian hunt and decided to tour the winged beings' lands on the way there. They were killed at the castle, their blood used for a dark ritual for power.

"Aura and I decided to fight back. Aura had already drunk guardian blood while our parents were still alive. She was crowned queen. I trained as a warrior, becoming the only deviant to learn combat in hundreds, possibly thousands of years.

"I wanted to kill the rulers the winged kingdom myself. The rulers were two women, Sky and Morning. They were like day and night. Sky was small, had blonde hair with light blue eyes and wings like a dove. Morning was like a crow: dark skin, dark hair, wings, and blood red eyes. She was a sorcerer, as some winged beings were. She mastered dark magic, a magic whose purpose is to poison lungs, summon the dead, and break bodies. Morning made her magic even more powerful by fueling it from the lifeblood of slaves . . . and my family. I fought her, and she cursed my body to always feel pain and struggle with movement. While we fought, Sky flew off.

"I killed Morning, but I lost my eye in the process. I chased Sky to the ocean. The woman dove into the sea. I realized she was trying to kill herself. One was lucky to dive into the sea and drown before one's body is claimed by a serpent or megalodon. I didn't want to swim after her, but then I realized her real goal.

"In her arms as she crashed into the waves was a child. Dark haired and raven winged like his mother Morning. They must have known that we deviants kept the youngest royalty as mind controlled trophies. Sky sought to kill her own baby rather than let us have him. After risking my life to swim after him, I took the child and pulled him to shore. Exhausted from my fight and cursed body, I still managed to climb the sand dune hills to safety. I breathed into the child until he coughed up sea water. He survived."

"He was Masu?"

Myth nodded. "He was a little boy then, the size that could sit on your knee. I brought him to Aura, knowing she would want to keep him. He was so young that he did not completely understand what was going on. For days my sister was too busy to attend to him. He stayed with me and talked endlessly. He asked me what happened to his moms. I told him they were dead. Then I convinced him that his mothers never loved him by mentioning that his mother tried to kill him.

"What little will he had to begin with probably died the moment I persuaded him that his mothers never loved him. Aura took his mind easily. She told me it was almost as if he enjoyed it. She said she could numb his emotional pain, and it was because of that he gave in so fast. Once the mind was taken, the Arm didn't display any emotion. They also did not talk, ever. Talking comes from a willful, emotional state that my sister numbs.

"With my broken body, I could barely do anything without feeling my muscles implode, bones shake, and discomforts that ranged from aching teeth, cramping legs, sickness, and pounding headaches. I became my sister's adviser. In the process I found a part of our palace that we never used. It was a collection of artifacts, books, and art from those we had eliminated. It was a labyrinth of items now forgotten. Our parents never allowed us in, but we opened it to store whatever was left of the winged beings.

"I then used my time to learn all I could about those we slaughtered: the horned beings, shadows, and winged beings. All my life I was taught that these were evil people, but as I flipped pages of their books, I began to doubt all I had been told. They were like us. They knew fear, love, and worry. It was like I looked into a mirror. What made us similar made me doubt, and what made us different only made me nostalgic for what we destroyed. I learned of all sorts of ideas that were destroyed with the people we slaughtered. The horned beings mastered sea travel. The shadows had the cures to so many diseases. The winged beings had blueprints to build a capital city in the sky. All these things were demolished with the people. That was when I doubted our creed even more.

"My sister has never faltered. After defeating the winged beings, she feared another war. She became certain someone else would attack us while we were weakened. With that in mind, she created the alliance with the elementals and received Chant as the first Arm with a will. Then she sent all Arms, Red, Arrow, Masu, and Chant to enchanted forests to hunt down guardians. She wanted more power, and that came from the blood of guardians.

"There were some successes and failures. By then Masu had grown up into a young man. He was sent to the Emerald Wilds but never returned. We sent the other Arms to find him or the guardian, but they all failed. Eventually we could only think him dead. After a couple years, my sister had the typical vengeful attitude that our history promoted. She decided it was best just to burn the Emerald Wilds to the ground since it had killed her personal Arm.

"When Masu was returned, he kept half-waking and mumbling about needing to find you. He explained some about you to us. That you were a wind-born human he raised in the wilds, one who could touch spirits. We concluded that the forest must have taken his mind. Aura told him that you were probably nothing but an illusion. He said he didn't believe it, but I saw in his eyes that she broke something in him.

"One day he woke up more quiet than usual. I asked him, 'Do you still want to find Wander?' and he said back, 'Who's Wander?'

"That's when I knew my sister won. That is until you came along. You turned out to not be an illusion of the Emerald Wilds. You are real. You can touch spirits. And you are the greatest threat to my sister. You see, she cannot control your mind. When she met you, controlling your mind was her plan. But she was terrified to realize she did not affect you at all. You are an enigma. That's why I am here to help you, because you are the greatest threat."

Myth's eyes were half shut, as though speaking made her sleepy. "Well?" she waited for Wander to speak.

Wander's silhouette shivered. Under's hand touched her cloaked shoulder. She turned to him with watering eyes. Looking back to Myth she said, "I'm sorry. I don't know why I'm crying."

Myth's face went slack. She must have not expected Wander to react in such a way. "No, I know it's a lot to take in. You . . . must really care about him."

Wander nodded, rubbing her eyes. "We lived in a tree house in the wilds together. I don't know how long, maybe years. He raised me. I was so troublesome, but he still took care of me. He had no memory of anything before the forest. He also would not leave. He had no name so I named him Masu. I had no name, either, and he named me Wander because I wandered around and kept getting in danger. Then the fire came, and I couldn't find him. I searched for him and saw him attacking a town. When I called out to him, he fell unconscious, and I couldn't get to him before Chant came."

"He fell unconscious because you probably managed to get to him. My sister uses sleep as a failsafe in case her mind-control is broken from an Arm. It might be as difficult to kill him as it would be to free him. People travel all around the world for my sister's healing. After every battle, she heals all Arms of any wounds, no matter how severe. The only thing she can't heal is what Morning did to me."

"I don't know why I can touch spirits. I don't know why Aura isn't able to control my mind."

"That's fine. You don't need to," Myth said.

"How do I save Masu?"

"There is only one way: Kill Aura. It won't be easy. She will throw everything between you and her unless it's against her creed. The humans—"

"Wait wait wait," Under interrupted. "You want your sister dead? No, I know exactly what you're up to. Wander, we can't trust her."

"Why not? I think she's telling the truth."

"Even if she is, she has a blatant ulterior motive. She wants her sister dead, so she can have the throne for herself. She is using you."

Myth's skinny lips curled into a smile. "So what if I am? In the end we'll both get what we want. I can rule the deviants, and you and Masu can leave."

Under shook his head. "And who is to say you decide to drink guardian blood and keep Masu for yourself?"

"You think I want my sister dead so I can keep things the same? No. If I were queen, things would change. No more Arms. No more guardian blood rituals. It's time deviants fight with their own power like the rest. If another nation commits a crime against us, I will not exterminate their entire existence. That is not justice. I will find those specifically responsible and punish them myself."

"So Masu would be free," Under said. "What about the other Arms?"

"Chant will be relieved from her role in the alliance with the elements. As for Arrow and Red, I will execute them. Their minds are gone, and we have only kept them alive so long with the magic of the guardian blood. "

This time Wander spoke. "Why don't you kill your sister yourself?"

"Succeeding would be difficult. If I did manage to kill her then I would not get the throne. I'm sure my people would find out it was me. I would be executed. Aura is well loved."

"And you think by killing Aura, Masu would return to how he was before?" Under asked.

He noticed that Myth did not even look at him. Instead she gazed at Wander. Myth's goal was not to convince him. She was trying to read what Wander felt.

"I know Masu loves you. As much as Aura tried to change him back, he is different from before. You can save him. I know you can."

She did not answer Under's question. She had one goal in mind: convince Wander to kill Aura.

"Here," Myth leaned around the flames, offering a rolled up paper. "These are instructions. You must go to the Harlequin Wilds. Aura seeks the blood of the guardian that lives there. The more blood she drinks, the more magic she gains. With enough blood, she could end up immortal. She has sent an Arm, Red, to the wilds to fetch the creature.

"It is not far from here, and that is why I picked this place to meet. At the edge of the enchanted forest you will find a camp of humans, part of Naktol's army. You and they will have a common goal: to find the guardian before Red. Join forces with them, and I'm sure you'll succeed. The Harlequin Wilds are enchanted, as the Emeralds were. You will probably be the best asset the humans could ask for as someone who grew up in an enchanted forest. You will recognize a fraction of the dangers. With their numbers and your knowledge, I'm sure you'll find the guardian before Red."

"What's a guardian like?" Wander asked.

"Guardians are animal like humans, but they are magical like spirits. A forest becomes enchanted, and a guardian is born around the same time. Once a generation of some animal reaches somewhere around the ten thousands, a guardian is born. They can be anything: a squirrel, beetle, or even a fish. Guardians possess magic like Aura's: healing, mind control, among other things. They are dangerous and unpredictable. The guardian of the Harlequin Wilds is not known. Look out for an animal of strange hue, or behavior, or movement."

"I don't think the army will accept me. I have fought against them."

"Why?"

"They tried to kill Masu."

"I see. Well, they don't have to trust you at first. What matters most is that Aura doesn't get the guardian. Once you complete that task, look at the scroll for more methods to weaken my sister's power. You must eventually get yourself on good terms with the humans. You are only one person, and the humans will have the resources and connections you'll need to defeat my sister."

As Myth led them out of the cave in the glow of her torch, Wander's heart raced.

She kept envisioning little Masu. Was he like Roslyn? Small and big-eyed with feet that did not touch the floor when he sat in a chair? Did he practice flying while holding his mother's hands? She could picture the winged kingdom; it would have been many tree houses. Maybe they had gardens of orchids and moss in the branches outside their windows. Maybe somewhere deep down Masu could remember that when he built his nest in the Emerald Wilds.

And now he belonged to Aura. Wander could imagine the violet-eyed woman snaking into his mind as he slept, her fingers on his cheek, plucking out every memory that made him himself.

Aura must have taken control of Ethan. There was little doubt. One moment he said not to trust Aura and the next he began to obey her. Did that mean Aura could just make anyone attack each other? She could make someone like Under kill Alice? Make Ethan burn his own house down? Could she make Wander kill Masu herself if she had the chance?

The waterfall's roaring amplified as they reached the cave opening. Wander strained to see at the light of day. Myth's finger's caressed Wander's back. "I want to speak with you alone, just for a moment."

"No," Under said.

"It's alright, just for a moment," Wander assured him.

With a groan, he moved outside. His silhouette blurred across the rush of water, arms crossed.

Myth brought herself closer to Wander, her hand against the cave wall for support. Her body twisted, hunched. Wander had to bend her knees to allow their faces proximity. Myth's breath smelled of honey.

"My sister will use everyone against you," she whispered to Wander's veiled ear. "You cannot trust him. You ultimately cannot trust anyone but me and yourself. Aura is adamant about her creed, so she does not control the minds of the deviants, and you are abnormal. Everyone else will be possible victims to her power. You must be prepared to kill anyone you meet if they turn against you."

Wander recalled the sight of blood on her blade after slicing Ethan, his eyes wide in her nightmares. She looked at Under's dark shadow beyond the falls.

Chapter 8
Sollast

"A walled off city cornered against a mountain. It's a city of lost souls. Or maybe the last city of souls. That's what the name tells me, and I believe in it. I believe it."
– Travels of Manger

Vincent's body felt lighter than ever. For days he had been weighed down by imperial armor.

News of humans losing their minds to Aura's mind control and setting their own homes on fire spread quickly in Sollast despite the orders that no one in the army was to tell civilians that information. It was no surprise; something like that could not be kept secret for long. It did make matters worse. People had started to lock themselves in their homes. There had been endless reports of mind-controlled spies in the city. Far more than the army could handle. Most would say the city had changed, but Sollast was always ugly to Vincent.

He approached the castle gates where two guards saluted. Sollast Castle was built on the side of a mountain, so the stairs would seem endless for a newcomer. Everyone born and raised in the walls became strong by default. The air was thinner, making their lungs tougher as well. As Vincent passed fellow soldiers, they looked as though they wanted to say something, but when their eyes met, they looked away. They already knew what happened at Inksgrid. Vincent was the sole surviving soldier. He, his captain, and comrades were on their way to where they predicted the deviants would strike next. Inksgrid was nothing but a stop along the way.

He reached one of the roofless castle halls outside. The halls were not straight but curved and modestly blanketed with greenery. Violet flowers shaped like bells hung down, still too high for anyone to reach without a ladder. It was half garden, half castle, with the ground still consisting of grass and dirt.

Past the stairway up was a small alcove with a round iron table on a four-curved center leg. Two chairs: one taken, one empty. Two cups of tea were out. Queen Naktol sat in one of the chairs. She was as the rumors said. The right half of her head was shaved, the other half possessing long silver hair to the base of her breast. She possessed a heart-shaped face and had large gray eyes like storm clouds. Despite the safety of her castle, she carried a mace. Unlike her three daughters who were all said to be flowers of femininity, Naktol never wore dresses or delicate shoes. She dressed in pants and stomped through her castle in boots. She always wore clothes that were the colors of storms: gray, black, and silver.

"Vincent is it?" Naktol's hand waved to the chair. Her thick lips curled with a polite smirk.

He sat down straight backed. He hated this intimidated feeling. Of all people, he never wanted this but once news of his being the sole survivor reached Naktol's ears, she wanted him to report to her personally.

"I've read all reports and files with your name. The more I learned about you, the more excited I was to meet you. It's truly an honor that you fight in my army."

"Thank you."

"I wish we met on brighter terms, of course. Please, speak. Tell me what happened." She took the teacup and slurped.

"After having some time to think, I realized the people of Inksgrid were a little odd when we arrived. I noticed people were too quiet. When I spoke to someone, it took a couple tries to get their attention. Their bodies also swayed a little.

"But everything went to madness when someone screamed in the street. My squad and I were together and ran out of a local shop to see a woman had sliced her own neck with a knife in public. Then a man took a torch and began lighting buildings on fire. Our commander chased him down, but he wasn't the only one: many more civilians started doing it. More began to kill themselves. Children included.

"The rest of the civilians were either burning to death or began to fight against us. We weren't sure what to do. Putting them down was easy at first. Then Aura's Wings appeared and began to pick us off one by one while we were busy either fighting civilians off or trying to pull them out of the flames. I managed to drag him down and injure him. Before I could get to him though, a stranger ran out of the woods. I thought she was a spirit. Everything about her was covered in a cloak or dark cloth except for her eyes and hands. She protected Aura's Wings and said 'Leave him alone.'

"When we began to fight, I realized she wasn't a spirit. She was a child. I could hear it in her voice. Despite this, she had a large, two-handed sword meant for close combat. When we fought, we did not shock each other. My commander tried to shoot the stranger from behind but missed. Then the stranger—this may sound insane—stabbed her sword into the ground and plants rose up and killed the commander."

"How?"

"The ground shook and vines, wood, plant stuff grew quickly from the ground. They strangled her and grew down into her mouth. If her neck didn't break, she suffocated."

"You think the sword did this?"

"I am unsure. I lost the stranger in the midst of more civilian attacks. I think her main goal was to keep me away from Aura's Wings. Then something stranger happened: the Wings shot her. He shot her from behind with an arrow to the chest. He then flew away. I tried to get to the girl but then . . . well . . . this is probably the strangest part."

Naktol leaned forward.

"A bear tumbled out of the woods and would not let me get near the girl. The creature stood over her and roared at me, slashing its paws anytime I stepped near. It would not attack. It simply guarded her. I had no choice but to leave her if I wanted to live. I then ran through the town to find everyone dead. I was the only one left. I checked back on the girl and bear to find them gone. That's all. That's what happened."

Naktol leaned back. "It may surprise you, but I've heard some of these insane reports before. Aura is making our people kill each other. However, the cloaked figure and bear are new."

Vincent bowed his head. "I wouldn't believe this story if I was in your place. It is what I saw, though, and I'm still trying to process it."

"I'll tell my spymaster about this strange girl, and see if we can get any reports on her."

"She's probably dead."

"We thought the same of Aura's Wings for a while, yet he returned."

Vincent clenched his hands into fists.

Naktol set her elbows on the table and rested her chin on her hands. "From now on, I'd like you to take orders directly from me."

"What?"

"I want people to fight even if they are the last ones standing in the end. That's what this war will take to win: survivors like you. I will send you on special missions from now on."

Vincent got out of his chair and bent down on one knee. He arched his back into a bow. "As long as those who slaughtered us are destroyed, Naktol, I will follow you."

"Then you will go to an enchanted forest with more of my most trusted. You will seek a guardian. Aura drinks their blood in order to gain mysterious power. Rumor has it that she has sent her Horns to hunt the guardian of the Harlequin Wilds."

"I will go.

Chapter 9
The Harlequin Wilds

"We forget too soon how nature sees us. To it, we are nothing. It rules over us and we cannot separate from it. The Harlequin Wilds reminded me of this in the most terrifying of ways." – Ivy's Compendium of Enchanted Lands

The Harlequin Wilds reminded Vincent of a surreal dream. Not the sort of dream where one's deepest wishes came true, and not a nightmare in which every fear became reality. It was more like the bizarre dream that you'd try to make sense of for the rest of the day. The moss, leaves, and brush were dark green like the end of a broccoli flower. The amount of moss that carpeted the trees seemed unnatural. Vincent wondered if trees could even be alive with that amount of green. Every tree seemed to have its own forest growing on its trunk and branches.

Earlier that day he heard a report from one of the scouts. Nobody seemed calm when they returned from a walk in the woods. They constantly scratched at their own skin, kept peeking under their clothes as though looking for something. Their own bodies seemed to disturb them. One claimed that he ripped some moss from a tree trunk, and it revealed not bark, but pulsating flesh. "They're not trees," he said. "It's meat."

Vincent's fingers touched a moss-infested tree. With a deep breath, he peeled off the layer of green.

Bark. Gray bark. No skin or veins.

He sighed with relief and returned to camp. The people Naktol assigned him to were based at the eastern edge of the wilds. None were dressed for combat like Vincent had grown used to. Their bodies were light with leather, like typical adventurers. The tents also lacked Naktol's patriotic silver shades. These were brown and green, probably for camouflage.

Walking past the shelters Vincent could hear the shaking voices of those who returned from the woods. These were only a fraction of the people that made it back. When asked what happened to the rest of their team, they'd cry and clamp up.

This mission was going to end in failure. Vincent knew it. Not only had they not seen the guardian, they had not seen a single animal. The forest seemed devoid of movement. The stillness gave Vincent chills. He could only pray they'd give up the mission before it was his turn to lose his mind.

"Vincent!"

A still sane scout jogged over. "Some bizarre people have come offering aid! We think they're spirits! Commander Neil is speaking with them."

"Spirits? We can't trust spirits." Vincent continued walking toward his tent.

The scout kept to his side. "One claims to know enchanted forests. I think she's faceless. She's completely covered up in a dark cloak."

"Wait. She wore all black?"

"Yes! The other was a dark fellow as well, tall, pale, sort of sketchy looking. Oh, and they have a strange pet."

Vincent did not know what to make of the pet and the tall one, but could the girl possibly be the one who attacked him in Inksgrid? Or were there more like her?

He followed the scout to the edge of camp. It seemed everyone still able-minded had clustered to see the strange visitors as well, as Vincent stopped in front of a crowd with their backs to him.

Vincent, not being the tallest fellow, had to stand on the tips of his toes to see over the shoulders of soldiers and scouts. Commander Neil sat on a stump conversing with, as the scout described, two dark figures. One sat on their legs with hands folded in their lap, a bastard sword sheathed at their back. Of course, the most noticeable attributes the person had was their cloak and veil. Only the hands could be seen. Even the faceless spirits didn't normally cover themselves to such an extent. Upon a longer glance, Vincent noticed the hands began to mess with something. Was that a black feather?

Behind the cloaked one was a lanky man. He remained standing behind her, leaning his left shoulder against a tree. His skin appeared as pale as paper, his dark eyes sunken. He chewed on the end of a dandelion stem.

One by one, Vincent tapped shoulders to get the soldiers and scouts to let him pass by until he got to the front of the crowd.

"I am not a spirit, see?"

The cloaked figure reached forward. As the hand extended away from the cloak, the arm was revealed. The skin of the arm looked like overcooked bacon. The commander removed one of his leather gloves and took the hand. Whispers erupted among the scouts and soldiers who watched.

"She's not a spirit?"

"I think she's burned..."

"That's a woman?"

The lanky man came next, bending over to offer his hand. Neil was able to touch him as well. More mumbles surged among the crowd.

Vincent noticed a creature sitting by the cloaked one's legs, a black fox. Foxes reminded him of the marketplace from his youth. There was a salesman who kept various odd animals in cages to be sold: bobcats, peacocks, otters, snakes, and foxes. Vincent would watch their shaking bodies through the two rows of bars that separated them from the crowds.

The cloaked one turned to glance at the crowd. Vincent saw the same eyes he met in Inksgrid: bright green like the sun shining through two pairs of leaves. Seeing them left him with no further doubts.

"Commander!"

Neil and the strangers looked at Vincent. He marched forward, his hands clenched and his heart racing. "I know this woman, sir. I met her in Inksgrid. She attacked me and was responsible for a fraction of soldier deaths."

"You did what?" To Vincent's surprise, it was the lanky man who reacted first.

The cloaked girl stood up, "They were attacking me! They were attacking Masu!"

"And they were defending themselves from him!" the man said.

"What was I supposed to do?"

"I can't believe this."

The cloaked girl turned to Vincent. "Masu. You know him as Aura's Wings. He's my friend. Aura is controlling his mind. That's why I attacked. I was trying to protect him."

Vincent folded his arms. "That monster has a death count of humans high enough to fill a city. That's your friend?" As the girl struggled to answer, Vincent turned to Neil. "I say we turn them away, kill them, or torture the girl for information. A friend of any Arm is an enemy to humanity."

The tall man threw away the dandelion. He pushed the girl behind him. "No one is killing or torturing anybody. Look, we'll just leave."

Commander Neil leaned back. "Yes. That would be best, I think."

The cloaked girl stepped forward but the man clutched her shoulder and whispered, "Don't."

Her wild eyes met Vincent's once more. The man took her hand, and they walked away. The fox followed behind the flow of her cloak.

Vincent waited until their figures were completely swallowed by the forest. Once gone he said, "We should've killed or captured them, sir. I have no doubt they will cause trouble."

"I would say the same thing in your position. But you didn't notice, did you? The woman, her body is covered with burns. I saw them all over. Her legs as she sat down, her arms as she reached to me, her face as she moved her head around. When a human or spirit suffers that much injury and still possesses enough determination to stare an army down you don't want to make enemies out of them. I may have been able to touch her, but some pains can take the humanity out of people."

Once they had gone far enough that the humans couldn't hear them, Under dropped Wander's hand. "I can't believe you killed people who were trying to protect themselves."

"I couldn't tell the difference between good and bad in that town. Everyone was trying to kill each other. Masu was caught up in it. He was the only one I knew I wanted to save."

"Well, we tried your plan. Now I say we give up on Myth's plan and go our own way."

"You should do that. I'm going into the wilds alone."

"What? No!"

"You and I want different things. I want to save Masu and you . . . Well, Myth also said you'd be in danger of Aura's mind control. I don't want you involved in that."

"Without me you'd be dead."

"I've survived before without you."

Under squinted and looked over her body.

"You should want to kill Aura," Wander said. "Aura killed Alice. She killed your friends. If she did that to Masu—"

"I don't like fighting and killing people. It's not right. If I kill Aura, wouldn't that make me more like her? Revenge is a cycle. If I killed Aura, someone close to her would seek to kill me, and then someone close to me would seek revenge. Violence just doesn't work."

"It could work if no one cares, or maybe if they fail or are too scared."

"You don't think critically, Wander! Your mind is still maturing. You'll understand in maybe ten years. Killing Aura won't bring Alice back. Nothing will."

"I'm sorry," Wander said. "I have to do this. I'm going to get to the guardian before Red does. At least that way, Aura will be less powerful. If she is less powerful, fewer people may die."

"Fine. I'm going with you."

"You shouldn't."

"I want you to be safe, so I'm coming."

"I—" Wander tightened her veil around her face. He was too good, like Roslyn and Masu. Like them, Under managed to crawl into a warm space in Wander's thoughts. But what if he ended up like Roslyn? Like Masu? No. Under was different. He wasn't a child. He was a shadow. He was smart. He saved her life more than once. Aura wouldn't be in the forest to take his mind, either. For the moment, he could stay.

"Alright. Let's go. We'll enter the wilds at a different side from the humans."

Wander could tell when the Harlequin Wilds started. There was a feeling in the air that reminded her of home. It felt like wonder. It made the mind feel dreamy, like more could make sense. At the moment the sensation felt nearly imperceptible, but it thickened toward the west.

Under did not seem to notice the feeling. He tilted his head as he tried to figure out where they were on the map. "How do you know where we're going?"

The fox trotted ahead of them, sniffing at the moss covered soil.

"I can feel it. The enchanted woods feel the same as home."

"So we are in them?"

"Not so much yet."

They stopped together at an edge. The soil ended with vines blanketing the forest as far as they could see. Every rock, tree, bush, and patch of ground was covered in both vines and moss. Some branches were broken under the weight of the greenery, dangling in midair, still captive by the vines.

When she stepped forward, Wander's foot sank half a foot under the vines. Raising her foot back up almost caused her to trip as the creepers tucked themselves over her foot and wouldn't let go. In her next steps, Wander made her feet stomp on top of the vines instead of dipping through them.

"I've never seen plants like these," Under wandered over to examine a tree. His eye fixed in on a pale flower that sprouted from the moss.

"This isn't like the Emerald Wilds," Wander hugged herself. The fox had to leap through the earth draped in green tangles, like Ms. Flinsler's needle weaving up and down from two pieces of cloth.

"What're we looking for again?" Under asked.

"The guardian. Myth said to look for an unusual animal. Aura sent Red to capture it, and we need to save it, because if Aura drinks the guardian blood then she'll get more powerful. Then saving Masu would be harder."

Wander's next step had extra crunch. She picked up her foot and peered down at the darkness between the vines. Something was down there under the green. She looked up at the fox whose face ducked under the vines, sniffing. Hesitating, Wander dove her hand under the brush. Her hands met with many fragments of something. The soil under the fragments felt lukewarm, like the outer edge of a bowl of hot soup. She scooped the fragments and lifted her hand from the vines. The back of her neck prickled. When her hands felt under the vines, she felt as through something living breathed against her fingers. Opening up her hand, she saw white pieces of tooth and bone. The teeth were easily recognizable, their roots cracked and filled with dirt. The bone shards were familiar. She'd find bones often in the Emerald Wilds. She must have shattered a skull or something with her foot.

She turned around. "Under, we should stick close together."

Her heart fell away from her chest to see he was no longer there. There were no sounds or movement. She scared herself by taking a step forward, as though she attracted all attention to herself. But whose attention? Even her own breath frightened her. She wanted to be silent and still.

But Under.

"UNDER!" she screamed.

Nothing. No, no, no, no, no, no. Her head roared with panic. Moving with sudden recklessness, she tripped on a vine. Her body hit the earth. Her stomach and chest felt the vines and below, a crawling sensation, like millions of tiny insects crawling into her cloak. Vaulting back onto her feet, her hands swept through her clothes. Nothing.

She moved toward were she last saw Under. No use. The entire forest looked the same. Glancing at a tree, she noticed a jade beetle. The bug immediately crawled beneath the canopy of vine leaves.

"HELP!"

Another voice erupted from the wild's silence. Wander turned a full circle, trying to determine the direction the shout came from. The voice did not belong to Under.

The shout turned into a scream of desperation. "IS SOMEONE THERE?"

The fox moved to Wander's feet. She lifted the creature into her arms. Holding the fox to her chest, she felt more secure. "HELLO?" she called.

A man tumbled out into view, his arms outstretched for balance. He looked around with a reddened face. His clothes matched those the humans wore in their encampment. He had a head of curly red hair, freckled skin, and green eyes. He stood about the same height as Wander.

Wander stomped over to him.

"Oh God! Don't tell me you're a spirit!" He stepped back, his eyes moving from hers to the fox in her arms. "I-I'm seeing things again aren't I?" He rubbed his face. Wander noticed small sprouts grew out of his hands.

"I'm real. And I'm not a spirit."

"If that's true, then you have to help me. My friends are all asleep, and I can't wake them up! Also, these plants, they're growing on us!" He showed Wander his hands. The skin bumped up as the weeds burst forth from the flesh. They were bright baby green, curling, almost delicious looking.

"Why don't you just pull it off?" Wander asked as her hand neared his. In panic, the man took back his hands.

"DON'T PULL IT! Whatever you do, don't pull them. Varnel did that and he . . . The roots pulled his muscles, bone, and skin up with it!" The man's teeth chattered. "B-But if you don't pull them out then you will fall asleep, and they'll keep growing! This forest is a deathtrap. We're probably walking on corpses right now! That's what all these plants are. They grew off of flesh. That's why there are no animals. There is no life here besides these plants."

"Have you seen a friend of mine?" Wander asked. "He's very tall, has dark hair, and a long torn up coat?"

"No. I've seen others, but they weren't real. The wilds show you visions. They aren't real. Please! Help my friends! They're not far."

Wander followed the man through the wilds. She ignored the occasional snaps and crunches under her feet. She lifted each foot high above the vines with each step she took. Looking at the man's back, she noticed a little yellow flower grew from the back of his neck.

"D-Do you hear those whispers?" he asked.

"No."

He mumbled something that she could not hear. As they walked, his fingernails dug into his ears. Sometimes Wander did that, too, to get out earwax, but he tunneled to an extent that it frightened her. She began to see blood on his finger. He either did not notice or did not care.

"There. There they are!" His strides became longer and faster as he went to two bodies in the distance. They leaned against what could be a fallen tree; it was difficult to discern what it could be under all the vine and moss.

The man bent over; his fingers checked the pulse on their necks. He let out a groan of relief. "They're still alive."

Wander crouched in front of them. One looked peaceful. She even seemed to smile in her sleep. The woman had a clover bloom from her chin, some little white flowers from her neck, and moss on her forehead. "Her legs are hogtied by the vines. The plants curled around them like a goddamn snake," the man said.

The woman's eyes moved under her eyelids. Was she dreaming? Her lips parted a little as though she were about to say something, but there was nothing. Even how she lay down seemed serene, utterly relaxed with head dangling to the side and arms out with palms facing up.

The second one was a man. His condition seemed far more disturbing due to moss growing on top of his eyelids. A spider the size of a coin crawled through his head of brown hair. Out of his arms grew various weeds.

"We should take them back to camp," said the man. "I can't carry both of them, though, and I'm lost. The fog makes it impossible to tell where the sun is."

"Fog?" Wander looked up and squinted at the sunrays. Even the sun could not erase how dismal the forest was, but it was there.

"The deeper we went, the foggier it got."

"You're near the edge of the forest."

"What?"

Wander reached into her bag and took out her knife. The man crawled back in panic. She started with the woman, pinching the clover on her chin between her thumb and knife. She cut through the tiny stem toward her thumb. The clover fell to the ground, leaving a small green stub.

"Oh. You're t-trimming them. That's a good idea!" The man laughed nervously.

She remembered how delicately Masu tended to the berry bushes in the Emerald Wilds. He cut toward his thumb but never managed to cut himself. He never trusted her enough to give her a knife. "When you're older," he said as he'd wipe the blade on his pants and sheath it back in its case.

After cutting off all the plants from the man's arms, her hands trembled when she reached his moss coated eyes. The man noticed her uncertainty. "Best leave that as it is. Too risky."

Wander turned to him and put her hand out. He looked at her hand and back to her face in confusion. Revelation finally came over him, and he placed his hand in hers. She examined the sprout and placed it between her thumb and the knife. The man regained some composure, his eyes less mad. "I'm Felix, by the way. Felix Kroswin." Wander got him to turn around to get to the flower at the back of his neck. He had many freckles, like a bird's egg.

"I'm Wander."

"Just Wander?" He gave an anxious laugh. "I really am going mad."

He thought she wasn't real. At least he gave her a chance despite that.

"You carry one. I'll carry the other. I'll lead you to camp. I know where it is. It's not far from here."

He whispered something to himself that she couldn't catch. He lifted the woman into his arms. Wander pulled the moss-eyed man over her shoulder.

"Watch your step," Wander said as she raised her feet high with each advance.

As they paced toward the encampment, she kept her eyes wide and moving for Under. How fast could someone get plant infested? She was wrong to let him come. Only minutes into the thick of the wilds, and he was gone. After she saved these people, finding him would be her first priority.

Her steps grew more labored. She never imagined another human being could be so heavy. Masu made carrying her seem easy. As she carried the man, she noticed little white insects tangled in his arm hair.

Halfway to the camp, Wander heard a crash behind her. She turned to see Felix face down in the moss and vines. At first, she thought he tripped. She stood there, thinking he'd pick himself up. When he didn't, she set down the man she carried. She flipped Felix over to find he had fallen asleep. Some new fern-like plants had sprouted from his cheeks.

She shook him. "Felix! Felix! Wake up!" His head rocked. For a moment his face tightened, but returned to its slackened state. Wander stood up and looked at the three bodies around her. There was no way she could carry two. She was struggling enough with one.

She'd have to leave two of them. There was no doubt the plants would swallow their bodies while she was gone. She drew out her sword and stabbed it into the ground as a marker.

Felix's body seemed the lightest. She took him into her arms and moved in long strides toward the camp. She lost her balance a couple times, plummeting forward and crushing Felix and the plants. He did not wake despite the abuse. The fox kept a fast pace ahead of her. It knew where they were going. Wander could feel the sensation of the forest become dimmer. The forest thinned out, and the amount of growth lessoned. The outer edges were only moss.

By then she could smell the campfires, the food, even hear the people. She tumbled out of the woods. "HELP!" she shouted the moment she saw a tent. Whatever they were doing before she came ended. The humans all reacted. They emerged from tents, stood up from sitting, some rushing to her, others running off to get someone else.

"Felix!" A man tore himself from the crowd.

Wander did her best to gently pass Felix onto the concerned man, bending her knees, and making sure Felix's head was supported by the man's upper arm. At the sight of his friend's plant-infested condition, the man fell to his knees.

"What happened to him?" someone shouted from the forming pack of people.

Wander caught the eyes of the man with curly dark hair and dark skin. He joined the inner circle of Wander, Felix, and the concerned man. She had yet to know his name despite this being their third meeting. His hands reached for a sprout emerging from Felix's cheek.

She slapped his hand away. "He told me not to pull, that the roots will break through the skin and rip away your pieces. There . . ." She had to take a deep breath. Carrying Felix and tumbling through the forest had exhausted her body. "There are two more in the forest. They won't wake up. I can take you to them. We have to hurry."

The dark man stood up over her, "And what's to say this is not your doing?"

"My doing?"

"You killed part of my team with plant-based magic!" His eyes darted to her empty sheath. "You used your sword for that magic. Where is it? In fact, where is your friend?"

"I used it to mark the spot your friends are. Under went missing in the forest! Please, you have to trust me. The plants could be getting worse as we speak. They put people to sleep and kill them."

The concerned man looked up at the dark one. "Why would she bring Felix if she did this to him?"

"A trap."

Wander jumped up, causing the dark man to step back as though expecting a fight. "Forget it! I'll bring them to you one by one!"

"I'm going! Someone take care of Felix!" The concerned man stood up.

The dark one groaned. "Fine. I'll go, too."

"Whatever you do, keep following me. Stay close."

Already the fox dove back into the forest. Wander followed, the two men's feet beating against the ground behind her. As the forest thickened, Wander would often glance behind her to make sure they were still following. Any minute they could end up like Under.

They traveled fast and concentrated enough that they reached the area in no time. She almost laughed with relief at the sight of her sword still sticking out of the ground like a beacon. "There it is!"

She came to where she left them. Tearing her knife from her sheath, she tore at the vines that began to claim the sleeping bodies.

"Oh God have mercy on us." The concerned man took the moss-eyed one into his arms.

Wander lifted the woman's torso and turned to the dark man. "Take her. Take them back to your camp. I have to go find Under and the guardian."

He hesitantly took the woman in his arms. He looked for something to be wrong, a reason for his suspicions to be right.

"Let it go, Vincent! Ines and Patrick need our help!"

Vincent scowled and gave Wander a final flaming gaze before they turned back to camp, the bodies of their friends held close. Eventually a fog enveloped their bodies.

Wander raised up her hand from her cloak to feel the air. Despite a thick fog coming suddenly upon the woods, there was no dampness in the air. She tore her sword from the earth. The tip of its blade looked bloodied; she stabbed into the earth again to see a crimson pool in the slit. Her breath quickened as she looked back to her sword to see soil instead of blood.

The fox nipped at her feet. "Yes," she said as she sheathed the blade, "I'll follow you." As she trailed behind the fox, Wander's fingers searched against her charred skin under her clothes for plant life. Nothing so far; perhaps her body was too damaged to be claimed. Despite finding nothing she swore she felt crawling sensations similar to ants. She could imagine their little legs trailing on her back, inner thighs, and neck.

A figure off to her left leaned against a tree. Another human? No.

"Under!" He did not answer. Was he hurt? Sleeping? She had to check. The fox charged back to her and chomped at her ankles. Ignoring the beast, Wander ran over to her friend. His eyes were shut, his face lax, long legs outstretched.

Wander's hands ran around his face, the back of his neck, down his shirt in search of plant life. His smooth skin gave no evidence of roots, stems, or buds. His flesh felt heated, but not sweaty. She pinched his cheek. "Under! Wake up!" He did not respond. Unlike the humans before, his eyes did not move under his eyelids. He was stone still.

A centipede emerged from under the vines of the tree and crawled across his neck. Wander clutched the insect, which curled and thrashed upon her touch, and threw it behind her. She grabbed Under's upper arms and shook him. "Wake up, wake up, wake up." His body flopped in her arms. She kept shaking and repeating. "Wake up, wake up, wake up, wake up."

"WANDER!" Under screamed in her ear.

Her body tensed. Hands from behind clutched her shoulders and shook her. She saw that her hands didn't clutch Under, but a boulder. What was once his warm flesh before her eyes was now cold gray stone. The fog disappeared.

"Under?" she looked behind her to see he was the one shaking her.

"Oh, thank goodness. You were scaring me. I found you, but you wouldn't respond. You were just touching that boulder while repeating 'wake up' over and over."

"I thought you were—" Wander stopped herself, realizing she had fallen for an illusion. She stood up and felt down and around her body.
Under watched with his arms folded. "Are you alright?"

"Where did you go?"

"I . . ." Under looked away, "got distracted. Sorry."

"We can't get separated again. I met some humans who were not well. Plants grew out of their skin, the roots curling around their insides. If not removed, they are put to sleep, and the vines move over them."

"That's horrifying."

"It was. I helped carry them back to the human camp."

"You did?"
Wander nodded.

Under smiled, "That was really nice of you. Good job."

Wander looked off in the distance. The forest seemed to get thicker. "We need to keep going. The guardian will probably be around the center."

She took Under's hand. Their thumbs curled around each other as they began walking.

"How do you know where we're going?"

"I have a gut feeling."

As they trekked deeper into the wilds, the vines both thickened and darkened. Wander and Under's legs sank further into the vines than before, greenery reaching their shins. Wander had to carry the fox in her other arm so as to not lose it. The swelling of green forced them to travel slower. They often almost tripped, but the other would keep them stable. Many times one would see or hear something and try to wander off. The moment Wander or Under felt the other's hand loosen, they would tighten their grip and jerk them out of the trance.

Under didn't seem to notice, but more insects were appearing. Wander could see their bodies move with the faintest tilt of a leaf. It became more likely that the guardian was a bug of some sort. If that were so, then this mission seemed impossible. She looked to her left, her hand tightening around Under's as she felt him sway a bit. She saw what she thought to be a small bare tree—until it moved.

The silhouette looked as though it had branches that reached upward toward the sky. Wander than recognized those as horns atop a head. The horns were like that of the black deer from the Emerald Wilds. The tips looked sharper, like daggers. Wander counted ten points to both the horns combined, far more than she had ever counted before. This was no deer.

She propelled herself and Under behind a tree.

Under stumbled, nearly falling down into the sea of vines. Wander put her back to the trunk, holding the fox closer to her chest. Under copied her, but looked around, obviously confused. "What are we—"

"Shhh!" she hissed.

They stood in silence. Her heart pounded as she heard the crunch of footsteps in the distance. Under appeared to hear it as well and put his free hand over his mouth. The grinding of vines seemed to get closer and closer. Wander felt a tickle against her neck. An insect probably just crawled onto her. It made its way down her chest. Whatever it was, it moved fast. Despite the scuttling against her skin, she had to keep still.

The horned spirit walked out from Under's side. Without her horns, she stood shorter than both Wander and Under. She was perhaps around five feet tall with the horns giving her an extra foot. Her snow-white hair reminded Wander of the rush of a waterfall. Hitting the rocks, the water would bounce and wave just like her wild locks. Upon closer examination, her horns were decorated with rings of colorful paint: sky blue, black, gold, and rose red. She wore light clothing with many pockets, similar to the humans' clothing in the encampment on the wild's edge. The humans mostly wore brown; this spirit dressed in dark green to match the wilds. She wore no blade, only a wood shield at her side carved with the image of a stag.

She walked right past them, keeping her face forward. Wander and Under squeezed hands as they watched her moved away. Once she was far enough to no longer be seen, Wander reached under her cloak to grab whatever insect crawled on her. Its legs flicked and squirmed in her grip, wings fluttering against her palm. She pulled out a cockroach and threw it to the vines.

Under spoke. "That was Red wasn't it? The first Arm? The horned being."

The fox struggled to get out of Wander's arm. It leapt from her grip and dove beneath the vines. Under kept speaking. "Should we follow her? She probably has a better idea of what she's doing than any of us. I mean, she's being controlled by Aura, and Aura probably knows what she's doing."

"This way." Wander tugged at his hand. She saw movement in the vines; the fox trailed a different direction from Red.

The fox managed to move quickly under the tangles of plants. Wander and Under made clumsy movements in their attempts to keep with the rustling movement.

The movement went still at the base of a tree. Wander and Under stopped. She looked down to see the fox's black eyes gleaming in the darkness of the brambles. She looked up at the tree heavy with moss and vines. It wasn't the largest or the smallest tree in the woods. Under reached for the trunk, but she took his hand away.

"She's here," Wander whispered.

"She?"

Wander felt the presence and name on the tip of her tongue. It felt fuzzy in her mind, as though the knowledge came from a dream. Letting go of Under's hand, she motioned for him to step back. She got down on her knees, the vines up to her stomach.

"Wander!" Under hissed. She ignored him. Her hand reached, palm facing up, and sank her hand through the moss and ferns. Then she waited. Her head ducked downward, and her arm began to feel heavier with time. Then she felt it: something prickly that dug into her skin. It moved up her arm with many legs. Each leg felt like one of those seeds that clung to her skin. She pulled her hand from the tree to see a spider unlike any she had been before: white like a cloud, large as her hand, and hairy with eight red eyes. Wander had the feeling that if she made one wrong move, she'd die. Her heart quickened at the sight of its sharp fangs, hooked like fishing tools.

She looked at Under who stepped farther back with a fist over his mouth.

"It's okay."

"That's the guardian?"

She nodded, careful not to make any sudden movement.

"Of all things, why does it have to be a spider?"

"You don't like spiders?" With her other hand, Wander lifted the cloak on her arm as an invitation for the guardian to be a guest on her body.

"Is it not pure human instinct to find them unsettling and unpredictable?"

Wander watched the spider slowly make her way under the cloak. Once under, she let the cloak down and felt the spider move up toward her shoulder. Even Under could probably still see it moving under the darkness of her cloak.

"So now what? Take it to the humans?"

"No!"

"What?"

"They'll kill her!"

Under took a moment to process what she said. He did it with a judgmental look. She wondered what he was thinking. "You don't know that."

Soft aches rocked in Wander's skull. "I do know."

"One of your gut feelings again?"

"We take her to an un-enchanted wood. Aura will never look there."

"What makes a forest enchanted anyway? Can a guardian live without one?"

"Myth said the age of the place led up to enchantment. Maybe how many lives and deaths happen in one place. Maybe . . ." her breath shook "it is ghosts." She looked down and blinked a lot. Her gut churned. The spider had reached the center of her stomach and rested there.

Under crouched to look at her face closer. "Are you okay? You're getting pale."

"My head hurts."

Under almost touched her shoulder but then jerked his hand away. His eyes scanned her body, trying to determine where the spider lay. "We need to get you out of this forest, c'mon."

He hurried ahead with Wander languidly following. She feared moving fast as she felt the tips of the fangs nearly touch her abdomen with each step. The fox kept near her side, appearing to stop and wait every time it got even a little bit ahead of her.

Under delayed for her to catch up to him. "You look faint." He went to her and took her hand for support. "Can I carry anything?" He gestured to the handle of the sword.

"I'm going to need my sword. Take my pack." She unlatched the strap and passed the case of food, water, and Myth's scroll to Under.

"YOU!"

Both Wander and Under flinched when the quiet atmosphere shattered. To the south appeared to be a group of humans. She counted five, recognized two. Vincent and the leader, Neil, stood straight with little fear unlike their company who scratched at their necks and rubbed their legs together. It was Neil's voice that boomed through the wood.

"HANDS UP!"

Under whispered, "Do as he says."

Her head rocked, and the forest became blurred, like when she'd close her eyes just enough to look through her lashes. Taking in deep breaths, she raised her quivering hands. The guardian crept around her body to her lower back.

The humans approached. The three scouts followed Vincent and Neil but looked in various directions. "Found your friend, huh?" Neil gave a nod to Under. "What about the guardian?"

Wander opened her mouth, but Under spoke, "It's impossible. There is no life but the plants and insects. If the guardian is an insect, it could be anywhere beneath the vines or even burrowed in the wood of a tree."

Neil placed his fists in his pockets. "Perhaps it would be simpler if we just burned this entire place to ash."

"We're leaving," Wander said. "The quest is impossible on all sides. No one will find the guardian, not you, not me, not Aura." Her eyes focused on a small tree behind the humans. Familiar branches reached up toward the sky. That's not a tree. Before Wander could warn them, Red's arm threw itself out. Something escaped her hand, too small to see.

One of the scouts let out a hissing slip of breath, his hand shaking as he reached for the back of his neck. A needle stuck into the man's skin. Just a needle, like Ms. Flinsler used to sew Roslyn's bright dresses. Wander had pricked herself with one a few times; it never hurt. Yet the needle seemed to cause this man torment. He dropped to his knees, skin faded pale to the point that his blue veins seemed bright. Red threw another, hitting a scout in the cheek.

Wander's body shook under her cloak. The guardian sensed her pain, its eight hairy legs, skittering around her body as though seeking an escape, its fangs dragging lightly against her skin.

Vincent and Neil already began shooting toward Red. Their bowstrings tightened, each arrow decorated with a silver feather. Red moved like a leaf loose in wind, dodging and ducking. When she could not avoid an arrow, she pulled out her shield and the arrow stuck in the wood.

A plant grew out of Red's cheek, a light purple orchid. The flower flopped on her face as she ran behind a tree for cover. The orchid was far larger than the plants that grew on Felix and his friends. Red would not fall asleep, not when the mind controlling her body was elsewhere safe and sound. Maybe the flower grew so large out of a desperate attempt to conquer the body.

Wander turned to Under. He watched with a racing mind. She tugged on his sleeve to get his attention. "Take her," she whispered.

"What?" It took a second for him to realize what Wander meant. His eyes widened. "No."

Wander's hand extended out of her cloak to him. The guardian seemed to understand the plan, already moving to her arm. "I have to fight. I can beat her."

"I can't!"

Red got closer, rushing from tree to tree for cover. Her needles must be poison-dipped, but also limited. If Red was skilled enough to hit a target with a needle just by throwing it, then what could she do up close?

"I'm running out of arrows!" Neil's hand groped behind at the three last nocks in his quiver. The two hit with the needles had sunk into the vines. Wander could see the plants already begin to snake around their arms and legs. The sight of their weakness and the plants' unrelenting clasp made her want to tear someone to shreds. The vines wove between their fingers with their bodies too busy fighting the poison to struggle. Wander wanted to rip it all apart. Something in the sight of them getting conquered set her on fire.

She looked at Under, prepared to scream at him if she had to. But she didn't have to. He took her hand. Perhaps he realized the gravity of the situation, or maybe it was the madness in her eyes. She squeezed his hand and looked into his eyes, hoping something in her stare could calm him. The guardian ran across her arm to his. His body went frigid the moment the spider's legs reached his knuckles and slinked under his coat sleeve.

Right as they let go, Wander wasted little time. She turned, pulled out her sword, and charged.

"What are you doing?" Vincent shouted as her body sped past him and Neil.

Red's hands plunged into her pockets, drawing out two shining needles. Wander held her blade in front of her eyes. One needle pinched into her right shoulder, the other jabbed in the center of her chest. Upon impact, her entire body turned cold. The cold felt like the first seconds of plunging into a river on a cloudy day.

Despite the sensation, she kept running. Her feet stopped in front of Red, and Wander raised the sword high. She braced to feel the skull crack under the blade, but Red clapped the steel between her hands before it could reach her head. Clenching her teeth, Wander's arm muscles stiffened as she tried to force the sword past Red's grip. The sword's edge sliced into the woman's palms, black blood drooling past her wrists and down her arms. No matter how forcefully Wander pressed the blade against her flesh, Red did not let go. She did not even seem to feel pain. Her apple-red eyes just stared up, focused on what she was doing.

Red threw the sword to the right and twirled. Her white locks flowed liked a whirlpool in front of Wander's eyes. Her leg rose up and spun, smashing the side of Wander's knee. As Wander faltered, Red smashed the side of her shield against Wander's face. Half of Wander's head pounded with crushing pain. The metallic taste of blood surged from biting her cheek. By some miracle, she was conscious and still standing. She thrust her blade forward. Red moved aside, but Wander could feel the tension of flesh against her weapon.

The horned woman's hand brushed her upper hip to feel the stick of her own blood gushing. Wander could not begin to know how Aura's mind control worked, but it looked like Red had come to a revelation. Her red eyes moved from the blood on her fingertips to Wander. Her eyes darted to Under, Vincent, and Neil. Vincent prepared his last arrow, waiting for the right moment. Neil attended to the fallen scouts. Under stood there watching from behind, his body stiff.

Wander did not give the spirit time to look anymore. She swung her sword at Red. During mid-swing, Red's bloody hand clenched into a fist and sent a punch at the blade's flat side. Losing her momentum, Wander wavered for a moment, just enough to let Red kick her in the stomach. Next the shield buffeted the side of her head. Everything went black.

When the world returned, her front was pressed against the tangle of vines. Her hand slipped underneath her veil and caressed her scarred scalp. She pulled it out to see blood. Rising, she saw Red had moved on toward Under, Vincent, and Neil, the spirit's shield outstretched and ready for Vincent's final arrow to fly.

Wander felt as though she could fall at any moment as blood slunk down her face and neck. Her body heated up, unable to sweat for a release. Just below, her sword lay in the vines. Taking in a deep breath, she used both hands to grab the blade's handle.

She rushed at Red from behind. Her hands lifted the sword up and swung sideways. Red noticed too late to dodge the hit. She lifted her shield, and the wooden plate broke along with her arm, the elbow snapping like a twig. In the same moment came the whistle of Vincent's arrow. Red's fingers snatched it by the shaft.

Wander swung the sword up and left toward Red's neck. She ducked and crouched far down enough so even her horns were not caught in the steel wave. She looked downward, horns pointed forward, and then she lunged. Her rack of decorated horns impaled Wander. With Wander speared, Red continually charged forward. Wander dropped her sword, and the world went dark with agony for a few moments until her head whiplashed against a tree trunk. Moths fluttered out from the vines her head had crushed.

She was pinned. Red kept on the pressure, her horns digging deeper into Wander's chest and shoulders. Red began to maul Wander, her horns twisting and goring into her. Wander never expected mere antlers to hurt more than a vicious bite, but they were far worse. The pain was so great that she couldn't even scream. She could only softly cry as her hands grabbed the horns and attempt to push them back.

It was no use. One of her hands moved off the horns and reached toward Red's face. Her fingers caressed a soft, familiar touch of petal. As her fingers curled around the flower, Wander already prepared a breath of relief.

With all her might, she jerked the orchid from Red's face. She watched as the flower pulled up the flesh. The roots followed, pulsing upward in the skin like sudden thick veins. The flower popped out, along with half of Red's face.

Black blood splashed onto Wander's hand and down on jungle-green leaves. Red's eyeball dangled among the roots that rapidly ate into her exposed meat and muscle. Red pulled out of Wander, ripping her clothes in the process. Red's face looked like something out of Wander's nightmares: an empty socket, torn lip and nose, and her whole cheek looked like a monster had taken a single chomp at her.

Wander dizzily slid down the tree, half of her body consumed by the forest's growth. She saw the horned woman regain composure as she pointed her face down, her horns facing forward. Wander shut her eyes, ready for the deadly impact.

She heard the rush of someone else. Opening her eyes, she saw Under throw himself between her and Red. Red smashed into a shock of blue that pushed her back. Shaking off the force that pressed her away, she put her hand in her pocket.

An arrow hit her square in the hip. She moved like a tree hit by a sudden gust of wind. Vincent stood defiant with his bow, standing over the fallen scouts. He took their arrows and prepared another.

Red staggered away and broke into a run. She fled toward the north. "Oh no, you don't!" Vincent took chase. Neil called after him.

Under lifted Wander off from the tree, using himself to support her weight. His dark eyes scanned her. Wander attempted to say something only to erupt in wheezing coughs.

Under's eyes began to redden. She closed her eyes, and he lightly shook her in response. "Stay with me."

"Is . . . she . . . okay?" Wander whispered.

"Who?"

"The guardian."

Under checked around him to see that the humans were busy. He nodded.

"Take it somewhere safe."

"That's your job."

The fox had come to her side, its face peeking out from the vines. Its front paws jumped onto her leg, and it licked her wounded chest. Her breath shook with a soft cry. Under brushed away a tear that escaped her eye. "You're going to be fine. Just hang on. We'll get help." He wrapped his coat tightly around her chest and lifted her up in his arms. Her head rocked between his arm and chest, legs dangling out. It was like how Masu would hold her when he flew. She could almost imagine the stroke of wind on her face.

Chapter 10
Sollast

"Sollast Castle is humanity's grandest structure. It showed the spirits that they were now equals. They too, can rule. They too, can fight."- Humanity: After Enslavement

Wander's eyes fluttered open to a high ceiling. Her hands moved to her chest to feel the familiar woven strips of bandages. They were wrapped tightly enough to feel like someone was hugging her.

"Under?" she turned her neck right to meet a wall. She spun left where sunlight filtered through tall arched windows. Each window framed in long white curtains, the draperies billowing with one window left open. Two doors stood on different walls, and a stand held folded sheets.

Her face was bare. All but her lower half was exposed. She shivered from the open air touching her charred skin. A soft weight hit her feet. Craning her neck, Wander smiled to see the fox lay its body over her ankles. At her slight movement, the fox stretched and let out a yawn.

She lifted herself from the bed. Her teeth clenched as her chest ached. When she stood straight, her vision blurred. Her hand grabbed the nearest drape, and she looked down until her sight cleared.

Outside the window, the entire horizon of hills was blanketed with buildings. Every space her eyes moved had a roof, chimney, and street. The people were as small as earwigs, traveling on the roads as small as clover stems. Wander's fingers grabbed the window to pull it up further. She stuck her head out to taste a whole new air. Directly below and around was the colossal gray construction she stood within. The place seemed to be made entirely of stone and glass. She could catch glimpses of other windows with rooms filled in furniture and people. She twisted her neck to look up. A flag billowed in the wind, blue with silver twists and waves. A silver wolf sat center, howling upward.

"You're up!"

Wander pulled herself back inside. A woman in a brown dress and white apron stood at an open door.

"Where am I?"

The woman backed up, preparing herself to flee. "You are at Sollast Castle. Queen Naktol's scouts brought you back here. You should really be in bed!"

"And Under? Is he here?"

"Under? Oh, your friend. He is being interrogated presently."

"Interro-what?"

"Oh dear," the woman looked around the area behind her. "You stay here! I'll get someone else to help you!"

"Where is my stuff?"

The woman ignored the question and shut the door. Wander heard a bizarre crank and the knob shook. She tried the door to find it would not open for her despite the woman having just used it.

Wander hissed and found blood starting to speckle her bandages. The woman was probably afraid of her skin, just like the people in Heathcliff. That would explain why she had left in such a hurry.

Wander moved back to the window. At the castle's edges she saw green. It was nothing like the wilds. The wilds were like windswept curling hair with tangles, and what she saw was more like Roslyn's braids. *Tamed*: that was a good word for it. The flowers were grouped together by color and a path of stone wound through the shaved grass. Someone tended to the flowers with a pair of scissors. A black bird landed next to him. The person waved their arms at the bird until it flew away. Its dark wings carried it high up enough to level with Wander's window. The creature soared away to the city.

Lifting her wrist to her eyes, Wander checked on Masu's feather. She could remember plucking them from his wings in her early weeks of life. They were always fascinating. She wanted black wings to match his. She could fly over this city, over roads, over enchanted forests, over to him right now.
With both hands, she pressed the feather to her blood-soaked chest.

Two men opened the door. Wander recognized neither. Both were dressed in all white with black boots, their long hair in buns. One held folded cloth of black and salmon-pink and the other held a dark case that resembled a purse.

"Who are you?"

"Dave and Sal. We are Queen Naktol's personal doctors. She assigned us to take care of you upon your arrival."

They entered, one placing the folded cloth atop the towel set and the other setting his bag on the bed. "Please hold still while I check your vitals," said Sal, or Dave, Wander was unsure who was who. He pulled tools from his black bag, some familiar from Doctor Reiner's examinations and others not so much. The other doctor began to cut through her bandages with scissors. "The queen is very excited to meet you."

"Where is Under?"

The doctors moved quickly. After poking and prodding her body, one took a notebook and pen to scribble notes down. "She has already spoken to him. He is settling into his room."

"His room?" Her chin touched her charred chest to see six puncture marks. The higher up her chest, the larger the holes got. The two highest lesions oozed with blood.

From the black bag came new bandages. One doctor picked her arms up while the other wrapped the white cloth on her wounds. The familiar cocoon tightened around and around.

"Here." Once finished, Dave or Sal handed her the folded cloth. "Get dressed. Someone will lead you to the queen soon."

"Bu—" Before Wander could get in another word the doctors took their leave.

Taking the cloth by the corners, Wander saw the fabric fall into a black dress-coat. Pink roses layered on ferns were embroidered on the sleeves and long skirt. The salmon-pink dress that came with it felt like silk. A pair of black slippers fell out from the dress. As she set the clothes on the bed, she noticed a black veil decorated with various shades of green beads.

"These aren't my clothes," Wander said aloud. They were too fancy to be hers or anybody else's she knew for that matter. Given no other choice, she pulled the clothes over and around her. Her feet slipped into the shoes. They felt the same as being barefoot. She was used to clunky boots.

When she looked at her translucent reflection in the window, she marveled at herself. The beads knitted into the veil matched the embroidered ferns and her eyes. She recalled Ethan telling that her eyes were her best feature. It was not much of a compliment as Wander had never seen an ugly pair of eyes. She adjusted the veil to cover any sign of her burned skin.

She opened the door, the fox at her heels.

Vincent stood out in the long hallway. He looked different with a baggy shirt, brown pants, and buckled worn boots. She recognized the curly dark hair that bounced against his shoulders.

Without a word, Vincent pushed her back in the room.

"What?" Wander staggered back and away from him.

"You put on your dress backward."

"It's more like a coat, but it's as long as a dress."

"Whatever. Switch it around."

Frowning, Wander took out her arms and turned it around. When she looked in the window, she thought the outfit looked less beautiful this way.

"Follow me."

Wander smiled when they stepped into the castle halls. Sun shone through windows that looked out to the sky like the room she woke up in. She stopped at the window. Looking out she saw a giant stone bowl in the center of a grassy tower porch. The bowl had a pool of water that danced, spurting up, out, and down like a flower.

"C'mon!" Vincent hissed.

"What's that?" Wander pointed to the bowl.

"A fountain."

"The windows over there are rainbow!"

"That's stained glass. Let's move!" he grumbled.

"I'm wind-born," Wander said. "So I don't know a lot of things."

Vincent stopped walking.

"No one is telling me what happened," she continued. "The last thing I remember is Under picking me up."

Vincent said nothing. She came to his side and leaned forward to see his face. His mind was in another place. "Vincent?"

He managed to snap out of the trance and continued moving. "Long story short: Aura's Horns fled back to Dem. We deemed our mission victorious despite not finding the guardian. Aura probably won't send another Arm to the Harlequin Wilds after she sees the state you put her Arm into. We put you and Under on one of our wagons and brought you back here to Sollast. Commander Neil believed you proved yourself a worthy ally."

Vincent couldn't see the grin that stretched on her face. She did it, she gained their trust. Now she had a better chance of freeing Masu.

"Don't get smug though," Vincent muttered. "Queen Naktol may fall for mysterious allure like all the others, but I won't. Other soldiers and I know you are not on our side."

Under must have succeeded in taking the guardian to a non-enchanted place. She'd have to thank him later. Even she didn't like those spider legs on her skin.

She admired the paintings they passed. Some were so large, she felt like she could step into the tinted world. One depicted a little girl carrying a raincloud, her eyes a bizarre fade of crimson over cracking dry lips. A smaller one had a woman sitting on a bench with a dead wolf draped on her back, its paws over her shoulders and head resting on her curly brown hair. A colossal painting showed a mountain-sized monster with glowing blue markings. A man the size of the monster's toe faced it with nothing but a blade.

At the far end of the hall, a door opened, and Felix stepped out. Wander recognized his freckled face and disheveled red hair. He lazily ran toward them. He had white bandages taped to his cheeks. "Wander! I was told you were awake and—"

Vincent interrupted. "We're busy. The queen wants to see her."

Wander beamed under her veil. "I'm glad you're okay!"

His cheeks went rosy and a smirk stretched one side of his face. "All thanks to you. Neil told me what happened. You saved all three of us, and you took down

Aura's Horns! After you meet with Naktol, drinks are on me! Come by the barracks later, alright?"

Wander nodded and continued to follow Vincent. When they came outside, stairs reaching down curled against the stone wall like a cat's tail. Wander squinted at the sunlight and a breeze welcomed her, billowing against the redbud trees and her dress. Going down the stairs, Vincent sped ahead of her as she cautiously placed her every step. The steps were far shorter than the ones in the Flinsler home.

"Hurry up!" Vincent barked. She trotted to his side once the stairs ended to a path of stone framed by sky dyed hydrangea. Every plant they passed possessed some form of order or shape. The redbud trees had no low branches. Wooly thyme blanketed earth fenced with smooth stones. The placement of the verbena flowers seemed organized. The blades of grass all came to the same height, short like a carpet.

"Are the plants real?"

"Yes."

"Everything here is like a bracelet, or necklace, or tablecloth. It's all designed and pretty."
They passed other people. Some carried umbrellas even though just the sun beat down upon them. Some wore feathers in their hair, and their shoes clicked with their steps. Upon passing them, Wander found that they smelled more like flowers than the actual flowers did. Roslyn would have liked some of the dresses; she liked ones that turned people into hourglass shapes. There were also soldiers. Wander could recognize the armor. They had a very different way of walking, using more of their heels than the balls of their feet. They seemed more distant as well, moving along the walls rather than on the paths. Both the soldiers and fancy people stared at her. Some would stop talking to each other and glance.
"Why does that creature follow you everywhere?"
Vincent gestured at the fox.

Wander glanced at her companion that kept close to her heels. "I don't know."
Vincent looked like he wanted to say something more, but he let the topic go. Wander never thought the fox to be strange. What an odd question to ask.

They came under a green archway that led through a corridor made of blue clematis flowers. Wander stopped to examine how the humans managed to make the plants act like a doorway. They made an arched wooden fence for the plants to climb as if they were trees. It was like the wilds and human society collided in this one structure.

At the end of the passageway was a woman sitting at a table. She had the largest gray eyes Wander had ever seen. Her hair color reminded Wander of metal like a spoon, blade, or a cooking pot. Perhaps her oddest feature was that half of her hair was long and wavy like a river, but when she turned her head she revealed the other half of her head was shaved down the length of a bumblebee's hair. She dressed like a soldier but with more elegance. Her chainmail shone more than the rest. The woman's long fingers held a dainty teacup with petal-like edges. A rigid man a distance away from her offered food from a silver-lidded pot.

Seeing Wander and Vincent come, a smile stretched the woman's thick lips. "Ah! Finally awake. Please, have a seat."

Wander sat down on the metal chair. It looked like lace with many swirling designs and tiny holes, like something not meant to be a chair. The man to the side came over and poured a steaming liquid the color of chocolate into a teacup.

"Where to begin?" the woman said as she leaned forward.

Wander looked over at Vincent who was already leaving.

"Introductions are in order. Given your character, you may not even know who I am. I am Naktol. This is my city. I rule over the humans."

"I've heard about you."

"How fortunate."

An awkward silence fell. Naktol seemed to be waiting for Wander to say something. At this point though, she only looked down at her teacup. Wander was unsure of how to proceed. If this woman was queen of the humans, then she was Aura's greatest enemy. Wander and Naktol had to be allies if she wanted to save Masu.

Naktol's fingers caressed her cup. "Before we talk, I have an important question." She refused to break eye contact. "Are you human?"

"Yes." Wander made sure to look into the queen's eyes when speaking. She could not allow any doubt.

Naktol sighed and quit leaning forward. "I'm in doubt though. My commander reported that you told him that you were human and proved it through physical contact. He still turned you away because you just gave off an otherworldly feeling to him, and I have always trusted his intuition. And he found that his intuition was right. Despite your claim to be human, you were able to touch a spirit, Aura's Horns, during a battle. Vincent, Neil, and your friend Under were witnesses to the close combat. Getting that near a spirit would be impossible for any human without getting a shock."

Naktol took something from her lap and set it on the table, a white cloth with smears of crimson. "You have been full of surprises, though. You bleed red, the same as my people, and Aura's poison that killed my men within moments failed to even sicken you. That poison is no joke. The spirits named it 'Hydra's Tears' because it's said to make even the most ferocious of monsters weak. The Hydra Tears were layered on the needles Aura's Horns used. One is enough to kill any human no matter how willful or strong they are. You were hit with more than one, yet Vincent, Neil, and your friend claimed you continued fighting. Even after being bashed in the head with a shield twice you managed to stay conscious."

"I—"

Naktol raised her hand. "My people brought you back here for medical treatment. After all, you saved them. For that I thank you, no matter what you are. Despite that act of heroism, we experimented while you were being treated. I had my doctors inject various poisons and venoms into your bloodstream. You were not in any danger, as we had all the antidotes. But the antidotes were unneeded as you were unaffected by everything we injected.

"Then there was your sword. Once Vincent told me of its magical abilities, I sent soldiers back to the wilds to retrieve the weapon. Three of my people had to carry it, yet all witnesses said you could carry it on your own. I found that interesting. Don't worry. The sword is currently under my care. I know what it's like to desire a weapon at your side at all times, but I decided our meeting without weapons was necessary.

"Your burns fascinated my doctors as well. They believe that your ability to move around, let alone fight, without being in intense agony to be against all logic. I interrogated your friend, Under, about your identity. He told me you are a wind-born human under unfortunate circumstances. Raised in an enchanted forest that was burned by Chant. I am no stranger to wind-borns and their unusual circumstances, but never before have I met someone like you, spirit or human. So tell me honestly, why are you sure that you are human?" "I—

" Wander lost herself. Why was she so sure she was human? Masu sort of decided it for her. What made him certain? Just because she bled red? Just because she was wind-born? Are there wind-born spirits? If so, what spirit was she? If she claimed to be anything but human though, what chances were there of working with Queen Naktol? Why did the truth have to matter? Why couldn't she just decide?

"I-I'm . . . special," Wander managed to spit out. "A special human. M-Masu always told me I was human, so I believe him. I'm just special is all."

Naktol rested her head on her hand. "What does that mean exactly?"

Wander looked away. Her mind could not stop racing. She searched for a word, any word to show her humanity. If only she knew Naktol better, she would then know the right thing to say. In Naktol's eyes, what did it mean to be special? Bad? Good?

If only Under were here, he'd know what to say. What would he say? Maybe his mind would race like hers. His shape shifting abilities made it so he would not be in these situations. Despite being the one who was actually a spirit, Naktol seemed to lack any suspicion of him. What would Ethan say? That's when the strangest thing came out of Wander's mouth.

"A witch," she whispered.

"A what?"

Wander's wandering gaze shot back to Naktol's. The queen saw only Wander's eyes, so Wander made sure they were wide as she said, "I am a witch. I am a human witch. That is why I can touch spirits. Being born in an enchanted forest made me a witch."

She clammed up. What was she thinking? The people of Heathcliff called her a witch as an insult! They were afraid of her. The witches in Roslyn's storybooks were all evil. The word was terrible.

"So you know magic?"

"No. It's not like that."

The queen raised one of her thin, dark eyebrows.

"It's more like . . . magic knows me."

"Tell me more."

Wander feared making no sense as she said, "It's like something is with me. I wasn't born with it, but it came to me."

"Witch or not, if you are human then you are one of my people, so I'd like to hear all you have to tell."

Wander told the queen everything she could, from her life in the wilds, to Heathcliff, to travelling with Under. She surprised herself with the amount of information she withheld, though. She did not tell Naktol about ever meeting Aura and killing Ethan; in fact, she told the queen that Ethan died in the fire with the rest of his family. She avoided telling her that Under was a spirit. She kept quiet about her alliance or any mention of Myth. She also did not dare admit that she actually found the guardian of the Harlequin Wilds.

"So you're telling me that Masu and Aura's Wings are one and the same?" the queen asked.

"Yes, but she's mind-controlling him now. The Masu I knew would never kill anyone without a good reason. He was kind-hearted, loving, and responsible."

"Trust me. I know the extent of Aura's mind-control. I'm getting reports of more and more of my people slaughtering each other every day. The deviant just folds her enemies against themselves.

"You haven't had any coffee. You should try some. I promise, I'm done testing poisons." When Wander hesitated, Naktol added, "I've already seen the degree of your burns, so there is no need to be shy."

Wander pulled down the silk pink veil to reveal her nose, cheeks, lips, and chin. Her eyes wandered to the man holding the silver-lidded pot. He quickly looked away. When she took a sip, she tried her best to swallow without her face crinkling from the bitter taste.

Naktol laughed. "Ah, you truly are young. Younger than my daughters."

"How old are they?"

"Sophia is the youngest, eighteen years old. Mae is nineteen. My oldest, Gwen, is twenty-three."

"Uh-um." Wander struggled with words. Would it be strange to ask for an alliance with Naktol to save Masu?

"Yes?"

"I-I would be happy to help you in the fight against Aura."

"Good. I'll talk to my generals for a coming plan. Battlegrounds are hard to pinpoint. I'll tell you when I have a plan."

"Thank you!"

Naktol stood up tall and offered her hand, "I'm happy we've met."

Wander bounced up. "Yes!" She took the queen's pale hand in her scarred fingers and they shook. Wander had never before shaken hands with someone. When their hands touched, she wanted to pull away. She realized she was not so used to physical contact anymore.

"Under?" Wander knocked on an arched wooden door.

One of Naktol's servants lead Wander to Under's room upon request. Apparently the castle had an entire section dedicated to visitors. The hallways were centered with a purple rug and a scenic painting hung between every two doors.

The door cracked open to show a single tired eye looking down upon her. "Wander?" Under threw the door wide open. "Oh, thank goodness! You're up!" His arms wrapped around her in a hug. Wander tensed up. Under lifted her feet off the ground in the tightest embrace she could recall. She let out a gasp of pain, feeling her injured chest crushed against his. When he heard the wheeze, he quickly set her back down. "Sorry."

He invited her into the guest room, immediately jumping up at the foot of his bed with legs tucked in. "I've been sleeping like a rock since we arrived a couple days ago. I just couldn't sleep on the road. I'll never take beds for granted again." The bed looked large enough to fit three people. There was a mahogany dresser and vanity in the room.

Wander looked out the window to see another side of Sollast. All the buildings sloped upward like an anthill. The city appeared to be built on a mountainside.

She leaned her back against the stone wall and took a breath of relief. In this room with Under, no one stared at or questioned her. For the moment, she could just be herself with little consequence.

Seeing Under, she realized how strange he looked compared to other humans. It was funny that his race was called a shadow, because he looked like a shadow, extended and thinned from the sunlight. His hair began to remind Wander of a dark and wilted flower. He sometimes looked . . . vague for some reason. Maybe it was the black colors he wore, or it could be because his entire body was born from Alice's imagination. It seemed no one else thought Under to be strange. Under truly was a shadow to others. Wander took in all the attention instead of him. Maybe it was the same for Alice. He was Alice's shadow and now he was Wander's.

"Nice outfit."

Under broke the peaceful silence, hanging his head back to look at Wander.

"Naktol gave it to me."

"She kept asking whether you were human or spirit. I kept telling her you were a wind-born human, but that wasn't enough for her. I began to wonder if it was a mistake to bring you here. I mean, I sort of panicked after that fight with Red. I never saw anyone fight like you did before, and the moment she impaled you I thought you were gone."

"You ran in between us."

He turned his whole body on the bed. "Well, she was a spirit, and I was human. I realized she couldn't touch me if she tried. And if she gored you a second time, I think we wouldn't be having this conversation."

"It was brave."

Under looked away toward the red rug. His voice took a lower tone. "I should have been braver."

"How so?" Wander plopped on the bed next to him and the mattress sank a little. She stared at the back of his head.

His fingers clenched the white sheets of the bed. "Alice," he managed to choke out.

Wander's heart sank, and she regretted asking.

"They say endings don't matter, but how can I just get that out of my head? I just don't want to see anything like that again."

"I'm sorry." Wander wanted to say more, but what? Why did Under even want to talk about it? She understood agony but did not want to summon words to give it more shape.

Under looked back at her, and she was glad to see he did not weep. Despite his lack of tears, all his features were sunken. "I saw Alice. That is why we got separated in the Harlequin Wilds. I saw an illusion of her and followed her. She sounded just the same, even walked like the real Alice, and made me forget for a short time." He began to speak faster, his breath shaking. "The only reason I was able to snap out of it was because I could not be happy. I remembered her blood under the rocks and—"

"Under, you're making yourself sad."

Venom colored his tone. "And what *should* I be doing? What if Masu died, what would you do?"

His question caught her off guard. She could not conjure an answer. The fox jumped up to her side and tried digging into the mattress with no luck.

Under sighed. "Damn. I'm sorry. That crossed a line." They sat in silence before Under spoke more, "I may return to Willton one day. As much as I've complained to you, I do actually have friends there. I just sort of panicked, not wanting to find out who else died. They are good, hardworking people, and I'm sure they are currently rebuilding . . . thinking that I died with Alice."

"You could even go now if you wished."

Under shook his head. "No. I want to go home when things are peaceful again. Aura won't stop until she's killed every human she can find. I'm not about to let that happen. I'm better off with you. Besides, you are the only person in this world who knows what I am. That's what made me so close with Alice and distant from everyone else. I'd like to see you safe when this is all over."

"I'm glad." By now, Under was the one she trusted the most. "I just spoke with Naktol about helping her fight Aura. She also asked me about whether I was human or not. Honestly, when she told me all of her suspicions, I got confused as well. I don't know what I am anymore."

"If you're not human, then what would you be?"

"I don't know, but I knew Naktol wouldn't trust me unless I had a good answer. So I made something up. I told her that I'm a witch."

"A witch?"

"When someone doesn't fit into a category, why not just sort of make one for yourself? That's what you do isn't it? You chose to be human." She played with her thumbs, one circling the other. "A lot of people in Heathcliff called me a witch, so it just came into my head."

"Calling yourself a witch will probably get you more attention than you'd want. I'm sure Naktol liked it. It seems she enjoys the abnormal."

"Is the guardian safe?"

"Yes. I put it on a random tree outside the Harlequin Wilds. It immediately crawled up."

"Good."

Under laid his back down on the bed, his hands tucked under his head. "I'd tell you I'm not doing that again, but I have a feeling hard times will be ahead of us. If you secured an alliance with Naktol, then this is the calm before the storm."

"Would you like to get drinks with me?"

Under already knew where the barracks were after strolling through the castle. He led her through the maze of stairs and halls. Occasionally Wander stopped to examine a piece of art or view from a window. He would join her, both staring thoughtfully at a statue, painting, or upon Sollast through stained glass.

One life-size sculpture depicted a woman with wings. She wore a dress carved as though it flew in the wind with a sash. Her hair was braided around her head like a crown. One of her hands reached out downward while the other held a book. Like most of the art, there was a plaque on the wall by her.

"Winged beings were the ones who educated the first humans," Under said as he looked at the plaque. His hands dipped into his pockets. "It's says that a lot of human history got lost because of fires during the Horizon War. That's when the deviants led by Queen Aura destroyed winged beings and their forest-based cities."

"I didn't know that." Wander felt the fox lean against her ankles. The animal did not wander as far off in this place.

"We need to get you in school once this is all over. History is important, especially in times like these."

"Only if you go too!"

Under laughed, "Sure. I'll turn into a kid for you. We can go together, and I'll be the smartest in everything."

Half the corridor fell away to sunlight and the outdoors, the stone floors coming out into a colossal balcony with a view of the castle gardens. Without a doubt, it was the barracks. Soldiers crowded the area. Some sat at long wood tables with food, maps, and weapons. Two rows of silver and blue tents, larger than the ones used in the Harlequin Wilds, lay sectioned off to the left side.

The center of activity was in the archery. Men and women lined up to hit various targets. Some of the targets were strung up into the sky while others were propped up on the ground. They reminded Wander of scarecrows. Red paint smears colored the placement of the head, neck, and heart. Blue paint covered the knees, hands, feet, and elbows. Wander couldn't help but notice the figure that hung in the sky had large wooden boards attached to its back, barely resembling wings. Was that figure meant to stand for Masu? Upon the sight of an arrow hitting the figure right in the neck, she turned her attention elsewhere.

She found Vincent. He held a long chain and faced another solider with a large group watching him. He took the chain and swung it over his head, a small metal ball linked to its end. The other soldier looked prepared to run at any moment. His legs bolted but Vincent immediately threw the chain. It looked like it could barely reach for a moment, but the solider fell. The chain had curled around his ankle like a snake, jerking him down. Those watching clapped.

"Are you . . . Wander?"

Someone tapped her shoulder. Wander turned to see the woman who slept under the spell of the Harlequin Wilds. She recognized the coarse, straight dark hair and almond shaped eyes. Now that she stood, she seemed much shorter. A bandage lay across her chin.

When she met Wander's eyes, she quickly looked away and scratched the back of her head. "You may not remember me, but you saved me in the wilds. I just wanted to thank you."

"I remember you. I'm glad you're alive."

Her small mouth burst into a smile, "I'm Ines, by the way! Let me know if I can help with anything."

"How did you get the plants off you?"

"We waited until we came here where the medical care is best. The castle doctors put some vinegar on the plants to kill them and get them loosened before operation."

"What about the guy who was with you?"

"Oh, Patrick? His eyes couldn't be saved so he went home. It's alright, though. He was happy just to get out of there alive. He has a family that will take care of him."

Ines looked up at Under and blushed. She began pulling her fingers through a piece of her hair. He introduced himself, and they began their own separate conversation.

Wander looked back out toward the soldiers. She met at least twelve other pairs of eyes. Whispers began to go through them like a passing breeze. "Is that her?" "Her clothes are different." "I thought she died." "She can touch spirits.'

A voice broke the whispers. A hand waved out from the masses. "Wander!" Felix darted past the soldiers to her. "Are you ready to go out for drinks? It's out in the city, so it'll be a bit of a walk."

A whole new aura overtook the barracks. New mumbles hissed around them. "Is that Felix?" "I could go for a drink." "Is he really?" "She's actually kinda cute."

Just then another man approached, his features blue eyed and gold-skinned. "Are you Wander? The one who cut down Aura's Horns?"

She nodded.

A group of four more people approached to join the conversation. "How'd you do it?"

"There was a flower in her face like the plants that grew on Felix, Ines, and Patrick. I pulled it, and half of her face came off with it."

Gasps erupted among them. Even more humans joined in to see what the fuss was about. Wander grew anxious that the fox might get stepped on. She picked the creature up in her arms. Felix got pushed aside by one larger man. "You can touch spirits?"

Wander decided to stick to what she told Naktol. Her body puffed up as she said, "I'm a witch. I can touch both humans and spirits." More inhalations of surprises vented from the crowd. Wander noticed some looked concerned and backed away, but most the humans remained.

"What a cute animal!" A woman tried to touch the fox. The creature's lips curled as it snapped its jaws at her. Others laughed. "It only likes Wander!"

A voice rose up. "Can you teach others how to touch spirits?" She shook her head. Too many people began to speak at once. Their skin smelled of sweat, their breath like damp meat. The fox tried to bury its face in her armpit. She lost sight of Under.

Felix pried himself out from the crowd. "Let's go!"

"Where are you guys going?" a woman asked.

"To get drinks."

"Can I come?" several voices asked.

"Yes."

The voices picked up a higher tone, like bird songs in the morning. Realizing she was leaving, a large part of the crowd dissipated, leaving five individuals, Ines, and Under.

"Whew," Felix let out a long breath, "you're as popular as the princesses."

The group traveled through the castle, Felix leading the way. First were corridors, then stairs, then gardens. The fox stayed closer than ever, wary of the humans around them. Wander did her best to not get distracted and keep up. In her attempts, she nearly tripped down the stairs. Stairs were already difficult for her, but the fox keeping to her feet did not help. Under managed to grab her hand to prevent her from toppling over. He held it to keep her steady as they walked down.

"Are you both . . . courting?" s woman in the group asked. Wander had no idea what that meant. "Oh heavens no," Under laughed. "We're just friends. We met in Willton, just a day before Aura's Arms attacked."

"I heard about that. It was a devastating attack."

"Yeah . . ." Under trailed off. Wander saw that he was already going to a bad place in his head like earlier that day.

"That damn deviant likes to scare of crap out of people," said one of the men.

In the gardens, Wander no longer listened to their voices. She gazed upon the flowering rhododendron, where swallowtail butterflies danced and played like fairies. A cage hung down from a pink-berried rowan filled with seeds. Robins and cardinals clung to the metal bars outside and feasted. A couple of humans sat upon a fountain's edge, one dipping her dark hand in the pool of water.

Despite its more natural aspects, the fox still did not seem to like this place. It still kept near Wander's skirt. The wilds were no garden. Perhaps the fox missed the tadpole eggs or the howls of the wolves rather than the flower petals and bird songs. With Wander's time spent around humans, she realized there was a certain catch to what they loved in nature. The castle garden was a collection of all they loved like sweet smells and clear water without the bad things like flies or mud.

There were constructions that added to the outdoor wonders: stone creatures whose mouths flowed out with water into a pool, octagonal wooden shelters with no walls, more corridors of flowers and vines.

"So," Felix walked to her side, "how has the castle been for you so far?"

Wander's mouth hung open, trying to pick an answer from many that buzzed in her head. "It's very different from what I'm used to."

"What are you used to?"

"The wilds."

"Come again? Sorry, this ear got severely damaged. It can be hard to hear."

Wander recalled how Felix's nails dug into that ear until they came out with blood. She raised up her soft voice. "The wilds!"

"Like the Harlequin Wilds?" This time he heard her, his tone thick with shock.

"No. I lived in the Emerald Wilds. It was different. I wasn't alone, and there was nothing to be sad about."

"You sound homesick."

"Homesick?" Wander never knew those words could be combined.

"It's alright," Felix said. "I'm sure it'll all grow back one day. If I know anything about nature it's that it's stubborn."

Wander could tell that Felix was trying to be kind. She would not mention it, but she knew the woods would not grow back. Death happened in an instant while life occurred so slowly it was nearly invisible to the eye. Wander felt as though she had been alive for so long, yet she did not recognize growth in herself. She wondered how long it took for the juniper and oak trees to get as large as they were, surely over a span of time she did not have on this earth.

That was alright though because Masu was her home. He had not burned down like the flowers, bushes, and trees. Once he was free from Aura's influence, she'd be home again.

The castle exit was an arched bridge, the biggest Wander ever crossed. Unlike the wooden planks on trails, the bridge had blue railing on the sides. She looked off the sides to see still water with speckled fish. Lily pads lay upon the water's surface. In the distance on another bridge, a human and her child threw breadcrumbs into the water. The fish splashed around the spot the crumbs fell, their mouths gaping. The child grabbed the whole loaf from his mother and threw it below. She grabbed his wrist and proceeded to yell at him.

Wander ducked to Under's side once they crossed the bridge. There were far too many buildings and people for her to process. She picked up the fox and buried the animal in her dress coat, nearly feeling the creature's anxiety from its quivering body. People in the streets were as crowded as ants on spilled sugar. Horses rose above people's heads, carrying men and women in uniforms. Wagons pulled boxes filled with food, clothes, and household goods. The buildings bordered every street, some with chimneys that emitted smoke and others with porches. Signs hung on entrances, wagons, and even some people, but Wander could not read a single one. She sensed eyes on her but could not identify them in the moving masses of people.

Wander's eyes fell to the road. Not a single bit of green grew. On the roads she walked, the edges were bordered in plants. Here the roads were enclosed by buildings. No rocks or pebbles even; the earth was like hardened garden soil without seed. Nothing could grow with this many feet passing by.

Her mind went numb as she tried to process everything they passed. Children laughed and clumsily pushed their way through the masses of people. An old woman with a missing leg sat in the dirt with a bowl out front and a blonde pup in her lap. A man walked past with a bird screaming in a cage, its claws locked against the bars with its head darting various directions. Wander caught the smell of meat so strong she could almost hear it sizzling. A young boy juggled balls, throwing them through his legs and catching them with ease as a crowd watched. Everyone was talking. "You need to think about what you're doing." "She said what?" "Where's Conrad?" "The elemental attacked near Tillstrast." "Mama!" "Ew, it's sticking!" "We'll talk about it later." "I hate that blouse." "It tastes good!" "You mean the bookstore down the road?"

Felix's familiar voice blew the others out like a candle. "Here it is: The Wolf and Banner."

Wander looked at a wood building with a bunch of jolly people sitting in chairs, leaning on rails, and standing around the porch. She could not read the sign above the entrance, but it had a painting of a grey wolf holding a blue flag in its jaws.

"And animals are allowed!" Felix smiled as he brushed the fox's coat in Wander's arms. The animal was too traumatized to care, its head buried in the darkness of her coat. Its fur began to shed on her dress.

Entering the tavern, Wander found it disturbingly similar to where Under and Alice lived. Stools lined up against a tall counter. Heavy wooden tables scattered the building. Under and Alice's tables had chairs, while this place held benches. Instead of paintings, there were corpses mounted on the walls. Elk heads with eyes that didn't move and bear pelts. It was a wonder why the place didn't smell of death with flies and maggots.

The group sat themselves at a table under a stag head. Wander nestled herself across from Felix and between Under and the wall. She looked at the deer piece fastened above. Red's horns had more points and looked like daggers. The deer horns looked almost fuzzy like moss in comparison.

The fox slipped under the table by her feet. It remembered the routine of Wander's table manners, and probably expected food to drop down at any moment.

"Under, did your place have a name?" Wander asked.

"Name?"

"Like The Wolf and Flag. Your place was like this."

"Oh. It wasn't mine as much as Alice's. She called it The Queen's Boot."

Felix inclined forward across the table. "Like I said before. Drinks are on me. Under, I can buy for you, too."

Under shook his head. "I really don't think I should drink."

One of the soldiers who placed herself on Under's other side gave him a nudge with her arm. "No need to be shy! Let's get you some Sollastian ale."

"I suppose as long as I don't get drunk . . ."

"Drunk?" Wander questioned.

Under looked up as he thought. "Fuzzy minded? I guess?"

"No one is getting drunk. We're busy people who can't afford hangovers. Besides, we need to stay sharp minded in public. As soldiers we are part of Naktol's reputation," Felix said.

"Reputation?" Wander was more lost than ever. She began to wonder if she even knew what they were doing here.

Under looked up again, summoning a way to explain the word to her. Instead of his answer though, Felix spoke. "You probably don't know. Naktol hasn't ruled for very long. Her brother, Lethran, died three years ago from illness. He was our king, but had a very weak body. Having no children or brothers, his older sister Naktol took his place. She has had a very difficult reign, as no queen's rulership has ended well in the past. Not just that, but rumor has it that she killed Lethran, that she was power hungry. Lies of course. People are also spreading lies that she wants to start alliances with spirits. Of course the rumors are ending now that we are at war with the deviants."

"How was the king's body weak?" Under asked.

"I think he had a disease."

"It was inbreeding," Ines said. "People aren't meant to make babies with their siblings, so their children turn out sickly. It's what they get for being greedy and trying to keep all the wealth in their family."

"That's not true!" one soldier laughed.

"It is!" Ines's eyes narrowed. "I heard the doctors talk about it. That's why Naktol's daughters all have different fathers. She's being smart."

"That's right. Everyone was calling her a whore for that."

"They're idiots. Naktol is changing everything for the better. Besides, I think one of the daughters is adopted. In fact, there is a rumor that they all are. They do all look very different."

As Ines spoke with her companions, Under tugged at Wander's dress. "Order something small. A lullaby's wink."

One soldier laughed. "What kind of sissy lady's drink is that? Does it come with a cherry?"

Wander tugged on Under's sleeve. "I can't drink something small. I'm thirsty. I didn't drink anything today since I knew we would drink later."

"Oh my god, it's not thirst-quenching!"

That's when she concluded she really didn't know what they were doing. She felt relieved when Under laughed.

Drinks came in open glass jars. Wander did as Under suggested and ordered a lullaby's wink. As he said, it was in a smaller jar than the rest with two cherries. The cherries still had their stems, the split of the stem straddling the edge of the glass. She sniffed the green content. "It smells like stuff for wounds."

"This is your first drink?" a soldier said.

"She's wind-born isn't she?" Ines mentioned. "Is she even old enough to like it?"

"How old are you?" Felix asked.

"Three years?" she guessed. She had no reason to think so. A year was four seasons, but the wilds did not have seasons. There was no way to tell how long she lived there with Masu.

Felix's brown eyes got wider. "Wow, I've never met someone wind-born before."

"You probably have," Ines said, "and you just didn't know it. Being wind-born isn't exactly something someone would announce, especially in Sollast."

"Yeah," another soldier spoke. "Human trafficking wind-borns is a big business here."

"Really?" Under said. "That's awful."

"What better people to be slaves? Adults born without the brains to think for themselves. It's easy to train them to do anything. They learn and imprint on masters fast."

Wander took a sip of her drink and immediately spit it back into the cup. It tasted of poison. How could it not be poison? She regretted making herself thirsty. Maybe the other drinks were better? Under's was the color of tree sap with foam caking the top.

She asked to try his, but it tasted even worse. The group giggled, finding her predicament amusing. "Yeah. That's expected with someone's first try." Felix fetched some water, and she drank the whole glass. She ate the two cherries, spitting their pits into her hand and setting them on the table. Under took her lullaby's wink and drank the entire glass. With both her drink and his own, his usually pale cheeks began to look as though they were blushing.

A soldier across from Under took out a pipe and tobacco to smoke. Wander would watch people smoke in Heathcliff, loving the sight of the vapor they breathed out.

The soldier noticed Under and Wander staring. "Want a puff?"

"Yes!" Under's voice rose in volume.

Watching Under smoke interested Wander. His lips went to the tip of the pipe and he pulled smoke inward. When he exhaled his entire body seemed to melt a little. The vapors from his mouth smelled foul though, and gave Wander echoes of Chant's smell. Once she smelled the stench, she immediately knew she did not wish to try.

The fox jumped into Wander's lap, giving up on the possibility of food. She petted the creature to calm herself. The room was all chatter with little she could understand fully. Some people at other tables were loud, and she wondered if they were angry. Her comforts were Under, the fox, and Felix's random questions.

"So what is that animal?"

"It's from the Emerald Wilds, like me. I saved it from the fire."

"That's why you're all burned up?"

Wander nodded. She remembered how she curled around the animal, which made her back and legs get the worst burns and her stomach and chest the lesser. Under turned, listening to their conversation.

Felix's joyful face turned somber. "That must have hurt so much. Why go so far for an animal?"

Wander's fingers caressed from the fox's nose to up between its eyes, to the forehead. Her fingers spread behind its ears. It never had ticks, its colorful fur perfect as a plush toy. Her mind scattered for an answer that she did not have.

"I don't know. I wasn't really thinking."

Something creaked in the dark.

Under half-opened his eyes, his arm outstretched over the bed, fingers just at the edge. He had drunk just enough to sleep soundly. His mind was numbed past its sharp nightly torments. He dreamed of something warm and wanted to go back. Nearly drifting back, he heard a small gasp behind him.

He wasn't alone.

In moments of fear, he wanted to change into the largest thing he could think of: a bear, a cougar, a wolf—an animal with teeth and claws and a loud roar. Even in his numbed state, he managed to stop himself from transforming. That's why he didn't usually drink, too easy to lose himself and change shape.

He flipped his body over to see Wander standing in the moonlight. She looked like a ghost, wearing a white nightgown. The scarred burns on the right side of her cheek were most visible. She sobbed and trembled as though she were in physical pain. She stammered his name. He noticed a wet spot near her crotch. Did she wet her bed?

Under tried to shake away any sleep or numbness. "Wander? What happened?"

She tried to speak but the words came out as gasps. She hyperventilated, her body seemed to quake more as she attempted to speak.

"Another nightmare?" Though he was troubled with little sleep, Wander was cursed with nightmares. It was like a sickness; she'd cry in the night and wake up with a scream. That's what happened when a young mind got caught up in a brutal war.

Under scooted his body to the edge of the bed and opened the blankets for her to join. She crawled into the bed and pressed her face against his chest. Once with him, her sobs increased but muffled against his body. Her touch surprised him at first. Wander wasn't much of a touching sort of person. Anytime someone touched her, she would tense up. Maybe it was her burns, did they hurt?

Cautiously he put his arm around her. "It's okay," he whispered. "Shhhh. I'm here."

Rather than tense up, this time she melted into him, placing her arms between their bodies. Her fingers clutched to his shirt, and her body hiccupped with weeps. Alice's cries were similar when she was a child. He could usually cheer her up by transforming into something: a dog that would lick the tears from her face until she laughed, or a bird to fly and steal something pretty for her, or just a soft rabbit for her to hug. He had a feeling his shape shifting abilities would not calm Wander at this point. She seemed barely intelligible.

"Today was fun, right? Those people really like you."

Her head shifted, rising up to show her face. She never looked more like a child with a face of snot and tears in the dim silver light.

"You're not alone anymore. Think of that."

A soft, "Okay" left her lips. Her face betrayed her word though, as her eyes went wide and teeth chattered. What could she be thinking of?

Entering the war room, Vincent shook raindrops from his dark hair. Outside the nobles scattered but the soldiers kept the same pace as rain soaked into their hair and slipped down their cheeks. The war room always felt hot. It needed to be larger, as bodies fresh from training and sweating would emit heat as they discussed battle plans shoulder to shoulder.

Whenever the queen was there to plan, only five of her best generals were invited. So why invite him? Surely it could not be just out of fascination. He was no leader and no ambassador to the human race. Naktol had to have something specific for him in mind.

The room lent little light with the storm clouds. There were bookcases lined up like a library, each one piled with rolled up maps. A table cut from what must have been an enormous redwood tree spotlighted the chamber. Stubby candles were lit, so melted that they seemed attached to the table.

Naktol stood tallest and center. She was the tallest woman Vincent had ever met, at least six feet. That may explain why she rides the most frighteningly large horse in the stables, Wolf. Rumors said that it was not a horse, that it never slept, never neighed, and only let Naktol ride it.

By her side was one of her trusted generals, Sara. Sara was famous enough for rumors as well. It was probably only due to her rough appearance, but many whispered that Sara used to be a torturer. She grew up in a fishing town by the sea. Anywhere near the sea was one of the most dangerous places in the world, so people from there were never humble. Rather they were known as the bravest warriors. People from there have endured sea monsters that could swallow whole cities. Those things could never be killed, only survived. The sea constantly clawed at the shores with waves as high as the castle towers. Only fools and madmen built homes and towns by the sea, though Vincent heard from fellow soldiers that they had a fascinating culture.

Sara's background showed. Her black hair was probably only an inch long. She had four rings sticking out from her eyebrow and a scar that began next to her nose and sliced diagonally across her lips and ended at her chin. Her skin obviously had been long exposed to sun, speckled with dark spots and freckles.

On Naktol's other side was Devon, another female general but far different from Sara. Devon was noble-born and a life-long friend of Naktol's. She kept her night-sky hair long, layered, and curly. She put on makeup with her armor with red-wine lips and rouged cheeks. Her silver and black coat of armor resembled a dress from the back.

Someone else was there: a dark figure by Devon's other side. Vincent clutched his teeth when he recognized the cloaked girl. Wander. She dressed as fancily as yesterday, a sky-blue dress with gold lace and a matching headscarf. If he didn't know what was under the cloth, she could have passed for a princess. Naktol was treating her like a doll. What was she doing here?

"Ah," Naktol noticed his entrance, "Devon, Sara, this is the man I told you about. Wander, I believe you've already met Vincent."

Vincent leaned forward into a bow before approaching the table. They had laid out a map that read LOREMAN VILLAGE. A place he did not recognize. "What is this?"

"A deviant village. We have decided to try offense as a defense. Both Sara and Devon will take separate troops to attack the settlement from both sides. The goal will be to eliminate as many civilians as possible, save some for interrogation. What this will do is force Aura's Arms to defend her people rather than attack ours. This way we will have the advantage."

"Why this village?" Sara said. "It's deep in spirit territory. There are better options. We should cut in from a border where retreat is easier." Upon a closer look at her mouth, Vincent noticed one of Sara's teeth was blue like lapis lazuli.

"I got a tip that Loreman is home to a family friend of Aura. His name is Pitch, and he lives in a manor. I want him alive. If anyone has information on deviant weaknesses, it would be him. Other prisoners would be meant for experimentation of deviant physical weaknesses."

"What about children?" Devon asked.

"I won't use them for experiments, but I can't afford to step back after what Aura has done to us. If you find children, kill them swiftly."

"And what is she doing here?" Vincent asked as he looked from Naktol to Wander.

"She is able to touch spirits and use magic, so she is our wild card if close combat or magic is needed."

Vincent crossed his arms and glared at Wander. It was impossible to discern what the girl felt with all but her eyes covered. All he could see were lines of exhaustion.

"If Masu comes to protect the deviants, I will use myself as a distraction." Wander pointed to the edge of woodlands drawn on the map. "I will make him chase me into that forest and keep running south, away from the village. That way, no one will need to fight him."

Vincent shook his head. "Tell me, if your plan were to fail and Aura's Wings ignored you, would you then become our enemy as we fought against him? Your goals do not align with ours."

"Please, Vincent," the queen cut in. "I already had a chat with her about that. She knows betrayal will be punishable by death. That's where you come in. I want you to make sure her plan succeeds. She needs to know how to ride a horse before the battle, as I'm certain that Aura's Wings would catch up to her in a matter of seconds if she tried to run ahead by foot. Troops have notified me that you are a good teacher, and she will learn the fastest under your watch. She needs to learn quickly as I want the troops set for the road in three days."

Vincent sighed. "That's pretty soon."

"The trees in the forest will greatly slow his flight due to his large wingspan," Devon said. "She may not need a horse."

"I won't chance failure. If she wants Aura's Wings to live, she'll have to learn. Riding a horse is as easy as a walk up some stairs. Have her ride Barney. That horse is fast, tame, and has run in forests, so he is fit for the plan. Teach her and aid her in distracting the Wings."

He wanted to refuse. But he bowed. "As you wish." Naktol would just find another teacher if he rejected her request. This way he had some control over Wander. If she committed wrongdoing, then he could finish her off.

"You and Wander are dismissed. Best start lessons right away. Do not tell a soul of what was said in here, as it all is confidential. You hear me?"

"Yes," his and Wander's voices joined.

They left the room together and went out into the rain. With a lighter setting, Vincent saw the dark fox was behind her. That animal was her shadow.

Wander followed him in the rainfall. She walked like the soldiers, not seeming to care if she got her new clothes wet.

"Well," he sighed, "let's get started."

On the most western part of the castle grounds, anyone could smell the horses' sweat, even in this rain. Wander and Vincent went through a veil of trickling water to get under the arched roof. The fox shook the raindrops from its body, making its dark pelt fluff up.

Each horse had a nametag at their door, named by soldiers: SNIPS, CASPER, FROST, MARLEY, SOOT, CHASE, HUNTER, and the list went on. Wander attempted to touch Frost, the horse's snow-white mane braided. The horse sneezed, and Wander jumped back. "They're bigger up close," she said.

Her voice was always so soft that Vincent had a hard time hearing her. He marched down the stables until he found Barney, a brown horse with a black mane; it looked utterly average save for the scar across its cheek.

The horses paced in their stalls and many whinnied. It must've been about Wander's presence. There was no way she was human. Even the animals could sense that. All the more reason for him to keep a close eye on her. Wander seemed to catch on that the horses disliked her. She approached the stall in labored steps. Her hand reached out to the horse's nose. "Hello, Barn." The horse turned away from her and whinnied.

"It's Barney. Wait here while I put the saddle and reins on." Once Barney was dressed for riding, Vincent turned to Wander. He nodded toward her blue dress. "Are you wearing anything under that?"

"Just pants."

"Dresses aren't meant for horse riding. Take it off. You can use my shirt." He pulled off his shirt and handed it to Wander. He expected her to at least turn around to change, but she immediately started stripping before his eyes. He turned around and rubbed his face. Just as she pulled up her dress, he caught a glimpse of her burns. They were all over her.

When he looked back at her, she was dressed almost like a normal person—almost. She still wore her ridiculous headscarf, its elegant blue color and gold lace clashing with his simple brown shirt and her peasant pants.

He pointed to the veil. "That can blind your vision. Take that off, too."

She tightened the cloth with a tug. "No. I am better like this."

She would not show her face. What fool would trust someone who would not even show their face?

"What are you hiding?"

"My face."

"What about your face? Are you a wanted criminal or something?"

She shook her head, "It's just . . . burned."

"Same with your arms, and you have no problem showing those."

She pulled on her sleeves to try and cover her arms. "Not my face."

Vincent saw this would get nowhere. To force the issue would make him seem like the villain. "Fine, keep it, get on the horse. You step here and swing your foot around." He pointed to the stirrup.

Holding her hands to her chest, she stepped toward Barney. Vincent clutched the reins so that the horse's movement was limited. Barney jerked against the reins and nickered. His feet stepped around, seeking escape. Wander stopped moving, perhaps hoping for the creature to calm down.

Taking a deep breath, she picked up her foot. Barney screamed, fighting Vincent's grip, hooves pounding against the dirt. Placing her left foot on the stirrup, Wander threw her arms around the animal's neck in an attempt to get balance. Right when she picked up her second leg the horse managed to shake her off. Her body fell to the dirt, immediately rolling away as to not get trampled.

It had stopped raining. Vincent lost count of how many times Wander fell off the horse. She eventually stopped his strategy and tried to grapple the horse in her own way, from flinging her entire body over its back to distracting it with apples while trying to get on. Nothing worked. Wander had exhausted herself, her clothes layered in the dirt she fell on over and over. Her shoulders heaved and her breaths grew heavy. Wearing the headscarf in such a state must've been hot.

"Let's try a different horse," Wander said.

"No. Naktol said this one would be best. To outrun the Wings, you need this horse."

"I can manage with a different one. Please."

"You can ask the queen, but I'm sure she'll say the same thing. Don't waste your time, you have only three days."

Unlike the rain yesterday, the sun beat down hot with no clouds. The horse Wander tried to climb began to feel more slippery with each attempt to get on its back.

She used a haystack to climb up to Barney's level and leap onto his back. The horse let out a scream and she clutched the saddle, her nails pressed into the leather. Barney raised his front hooves, and Vincent backed up, letting go of the reins. Without Vincent to hold him, the horse broke into a gallop that threw Wander off the saddle and rolling on the stable floor. Sitting up, she saw the horse corner itself at the far reaches of the stable, its face to the wall.

"Enough." Vincent marched over with his hands balled into fists. "That's enough for today. The horse's behavior toward you won't change. I don't know what you are. I don't buy that witch bullcrap, but the horse doesn't like it."

"Maybe if I climb from behind then I—"

"No. His back legs will kick you. A horse's kick can injure you."

"There has to be some way......"

"The plan would have gone poorly anyway. You worry about Aura's Wings getting killed, but he is known as immortal. Aura's Wings is a monster. He has killed entire towns on his own. Controlled or not, nothing can redeem that."

"It's not him. Masu doesn't know what he's doing."

"That doesn't even matter."

Leaving her with those words, Vincent took Barney back to his stable. Wander's throat clenched.

She marched in a fast pace back to the castle. Her surroundings felt invisible in the light of her bursting mind. She should feed the horse, brush it, and braid its hair, anything to get it to like her. If only it could bond with her as easily as the fox.

Her fist knocked on Under's door.

"Come in," Under's voice spoke beyond the door.

He was just as she left him, sitting up in his bed with his back against the wall. A stack of books lay next to him on the bedside table. The books he read had thick worn covers. Roslyn's books had images to at least give Wander a clue about what she read. What Under read had nothing but writing. The fox lay by his side; it had probably tired of Wander's castle adventures.

Under wrinkled his nose. "You smell like manure."

"Poop?"

"Yes. That's what manure means."

"The horse threw me in it. I think I'll go see it tonight with apples to get it to like me."

"I thought the armies were leaving early tomorrow morning. If the horse doesn't warm up to you by then, then you'll have no chance."

"What else can I do?" Wander asked. She shed her filthy cloak and veil, exposing her burned body. Under went quiet. With a sigh, she sat on the edge of the bed with him. "Since coming here, I have lost certainty of my humanity. Now I'm surrounded by humans and whether people treat me with kindness or cruelty, I feel like I don't belong."

"Of course you don't. No normal human would." Under folded a corner of a page and put down his book. "Wander, we are surrounded by soldiers and nobles!" he laughed. "We are in a castle! Of course you don't feel like you fit in. Most humans don't live like this."

"Oh."

"As for your horse problem . . ." he trailed off. "Nah, it's a dumb idea. No way."

She scooted closer to him, "Wait, you have an idea? One to get the horse to like me?"

"No."

"C'mon, you can't just not tell me!"

He looked away.

"Please, Under? I'm sure it's not dumb. Any idea would be good. If I'm not there for the battle, Masu could show up and kill more people. He could get killed."

Under's dark eyes trailed back to her. "Take me to the horse."

The sun set over the castle walls, making the horizon glow. The stables were dim with no one in sight but horses. Some nickered and stomped their hooves at the sight of the fox sniffing by their doors. Wander wore a freshly washed pale blue nightgown with a white veil; her bare feet evaded any horse poop. She reached the door she recalled from earlier today and saw the familiar brown horse. It recognized her as well and moved to the furthest wall. "This is him," Wander pointed.

Under opened the door and Wander took four steps back. The horse did not seem to mind Under. His fingers reached out and caressed the animal's cheek. He looked down at the hooves and then bent his knees to look under its stomach. Under circled around the horse, his eyes as focused as when they read the pages in his books. His hands brush the horse's sides. His fingers explored the insides of its ears. He pulled on its lips to see its crooked teeth.

"What are you doing?"

"He looks simple enough to turn into."

"Turn into?" Wander took a moment to understand. Once what he meant hit her, she let out a gasp. "Wait a moment. You can turn into this horse? That's the idea?"

"It's not like one look and I can turn into something. I need to see it at different angles, shades, positions. I need to see him move." Under folded his arms and looked at Wander. "I need more light. We should get a lantern."

"Leave it to me!"

Wander searched the castle grounds until she found a servant and asked for a lantern. She returned to see Under had moved the horse outside its stall. He fed it some hay from his hand. As it ate, he bent down to watch. He looked as though he were in a trance, completely unconcerned with anything else around him.

When the light of her lantern reached him, he snapped out of his focused state. "Good. I'm figuring out this form pretty quick since it's similar to others I know."

"You can really turn into anything if you look at it enough?"

"I have to understand a lot about the body as well, but I already know a lot of it by instinct. It helps to touch the form as well. Once you learn one form, it opens doors to other possibilities. For example, this form would be difficult if I didn't already know how to change into a different breed of horse."

"Can you turn into me?"

"Easily."

"Into Masu?"

Something about the question broke Under's concentration. He looked at Wander from over the other side of the horses back. "No." He started to brush the horse. "And even if I learned, I would never do that to you."

She and Under watched the horse graze just outside the stable. They sat with their backs to the wall and the lanterns glow between them. They discussed the battle plan together.

"So I just have to run into the forest?" Under asked.

"I'll talk you through it. You'll still understand me, right?"

"Of course. Changing forms messes with my mind a little, but I can definitely still understand you. Horses aren't stupid enough to make me forget who I am and what we're doing. In fact, you can ask me questions. I'll stomp my foot once for yes, twice for no, and three times for maybe."

Wander looked off to Barney. "So I'll meet you here tomorrow morning. You'll be a horse, and I'll ride you. But what will happen to the original Barney?"

"I'll just put him in an empty stall under a different name. Hopefully no one will notice."

Wander began to go back to her room. She stopped for a moment and turned her head over her shoulder, "You don't have to do this you know."

He lifted his head, "I know. Don't worry, this is my choice."

The barracks had a different energy from the last time she was there. No one sat down or trained. They were packing their possessions and weapons and sharpening arrows.

"Vincent!" Wander spotted him from behind and caught up to him. He was in the middle of some conversation with another soldier, half dressed in chainmail. He looked none too pleased with her sudden appearance. "The horse," she smiled. "I can ride it now."

She led him to the stables. The whole walk there she feared that Under could have somehow failed. She wouldn't know if the horse was actually him until she tried to get on its back. What if Under changed his mind? What if she was too heavy for him to carry? What if someone saw him transform? Each question made her walk faster, speeding ahead of Vincent.

The stables seemed nearly empty. Maybe most of the soldiers had taken horses from there already. Wander sighed with relief at the sight of Barney's stable possessing a horse. She could barely contain her mix of excitement and anxiety as she approached the stall door. The horse stood at the opposite end of the stall. Their eyes met.

"Under?" she breathed out his name. She reached her hand out. Vincent walked over behind her to watch.

The horse walked over to her and sniffed her hand. She beamed and proceeded to pet him. Under pressed himself against her strokes.

"So he likes you. That doesn't mean you know how to ride him. Wait here while I get the saddle."

As Vincent left for the storeroom, Wander opened the stall door for Under to walk out. He was the mirror image of Barney. Backing up, Wander took him his whole appearance. "This is amazing," she whispered. He even nailed it down the horse's scar.

Vincent came back and put the saddle and reins on Under. Wander watched as Vincent tightened leather straps around Under's face and around his mouth.

"Do those hurt the horse?" she asked.

"No. They're used to it."

Under wasn't. She looked over at him, but he gave her no clues as to what he was feeling. No wonder he loved being human, he could express himself far easier.

"Now prove it. Ride him." Vincent clutched the reins in preparation.

Wander hooked her foot on the stirrup and lifted herself. Her hands clutched the saddle horn for balance as she threw her leg over Under's back. She felt herself begin to lose balance the moment she threw up her leg. Under bent down and swayed toward her to help her on. Once she was secured, he rose back up.

The look on Vincent's face was worth the trouble alone. He looked like he needed to be pinched just to snap out of his shocked stare.

"Now what? Where should I ride him?" Wander asked.

"Do you even know how to control a horse and tell it where to go?"

"Yes."

Vincent's tone went flat. "Really?"

Wander took the reins from him. "I do it in my own way. Just tell me what I should do, and I'll prove it."

"Fine." Vincent looked around. His eyes locked on the outside. He pointed to a tree. "Get him to walk over to that tree and stop on the right side."

Wander straightened her back, hoping Under understood. "Fine." She hooked her other leg in the stirrup and petted Under's neck. He walked out of the stables. Riding him was far bumpier than Wander imagined. She'd have to hang on super tight when he galloped. He stopped over at the right side of the tree.

Vincent did not stop his test there. Next he told her to circle around the tree four times. He made them jump over a bench, which Under seemed hesitant about. The final test was to make Under gallop from one end of the courtyard to the other. Wander gripped the horn and reins firmly as her body rocked in the saddle seat.

When they made it back to the stable, Wander jumped off the horse with a gawky stumble. Brushing herself off, she said, "See? I can do it. I can come."

"You didn't do anything," Vincent hissed. "The horse did all the work. You didn't even lightly kick its side to go or tug the reins to make him stop." He lowered his tone. "What did you do to the horse?"

"I just fed him some apples last night."

He grabbed her upper arm, his fingers burrowing into her skin. "Do you think I'm that stupid?"

"You said I could figure out something because I'm a witch," Wander looked calmly into his dark eyes. "And I did."

"Then you better succeed," Vincent said. "Because if I see that winged beast on the battlefield, I'm going to kill him like he did to so many."

"If anyone wants to kill Masu, they'll have to kill me first."

Under whinnied and stomped his hoof twice. The hostile exchange probably disturbed him.

Vincent let her go. "Then I'm looking at a dead woman. Everyone wants to kill Aura's Wings. Those soldiers you went out with? Aura's Wings have personally killed some of their friends and family. You can't be our ally but fight for him."

Wander went silent and only glared. Her hand covered where he clawed into her arm.

"I'll see you on the battlefield," Vincent said as he marched off.

Chapter 11
Loreman

"Deviant citizens know nothing of battle. Aura and the rulers before her made sure of that. It was out of love and kindness, but I always found it cruel." – Myth's Journal

Wander's sword was never returned to her. When pressed, Naktol said, "Until I understand the weapon and your connection to it, I'm afraid I will not allow you to handle it. It's okay. I'll give you a fine blade. Maybe if you return victorious, I'll return your magical sword as a reward."

Instead of having the weapon strung on her back, it was sheathed to the side of her hip on a belt. The placement made her feel off balance, like she swayed to one side of the horse more than the other.

On the journey toward Loreman, Wander found no familiar faces among the soldiers except for Sara, Devon, and Vincent. Sara and Devon were never alone, always surrounded by people and busy. Whenever Wander saw Vincent, they made eye contact; he watched her all the time. There was no Felix, Ines, or any of the soldiers she had shared a drink with. These ones felt different, heavier like a storm cloud. They were always sharpening arrows, layering arrowheads in poisons, or staring off with a frown.

Dogs walked among the soldiers. They weren't like the small and thin hounds of Heathcliff. These ones were built like wolves. On the second day, one dog, Sister, seemed most aggressive. She attacked another dog and killed him. Sara leashed that hound later and took her out in the woods. She returned without the dog and a bloody knife.

They did not walk on paths and made scarce use of fire. There were no wagons, only backpacks. The nights were cold with little flame. Much in contrast to the castle, the meals were lukewarm if you were lucky. Wander fed most of her meals to the fox. The animal seemed to prefer this life to the castle.

As a horse, Under seemed desperate for expression and conversation. He constantly stomped his feet, rubbed against Wander, and even so as far as to pick up a plum tree blossom in his mouth and drop it, covered with saliva, on her hand. Realizing how lonely he must feel, Wander tried to stick with him as much as possible, trying to ride him, feed him, groom him, and even sleep in the woods with him when no one watched.

Camps were made outside of Loreman in a forest of juniper trees and bamboo. Wander loved the thick clumps of bamboo where she could just dive in and be submerged in green with only her thoughts.

Wander was called to meet with Devon and Sara who met behind a fifty-foot juniper. Devon's armor shined in the sun while Sara wore leather. Both women had bows and quivers fat with arrows. Sara wore a belt of bottles, many soldiers did. Wander figured that they would dip the arrow tips in these bottles of poison before shooting.

"Wander, as our close combatant, you will come into Loreman on the east with me and my people," said Devon. "Unless you see Aura's Wings, your primary job will be to eliminate all deviants in the village. You will be stationed outside. We have groups that will kick down doors. You will kill anyone who manages to escape outside. Anyone who escapes from you will meet a third party of soldiers circled in the woods. If you see Aura's Wings, you will do what you must to get his attention. Run south back toward camp. Our soldiers will make an opening for you."

"I understand."

"The deviant Pitch is not to be killed, but captured. It is unlikely you will see him. But just in case, he is white-skinned, looks to be in his mid-thirties, will probably wear fancy clothes, has red eyes and black hair with a long rat tail."

"A tail?"

Sara laughed. "No you doof. It's . . . How to explain? It's his hair! It looks sort of like a tail though because it's long and thin!"

Wander bit her lip, hoping she would not meet him. She did not know she would be ordered to kill deviants. The thought of coming into a village and killing everyone didn't feel right. Under wouldn't be able to stand it, and he had good sense.

She walked away from Devon and Sara with a tightening throat. How could she explain killing a village to Under? She could barely explain it to herself. Under's reins were tied to a bamboo shoot. He must've been bored out of his mind with nothing to do but stare into the dark wilderness.

"Under." Wander greeted him.

He turned his large head and snorted. Wander stood in front of him, trying to collect words. "I don't feel good." She looked at her dark reflection in Under's eyeball. She had to lower her voice, as people could be listening from camp. "They want me to kill a lot of people. Not soldiers, but people in their homes. They want me to wait outside and kill anyone who tries to run away. I don't like this!"

Under stomped once.

"You, too? Then what do we do? Myth said I can't fight Aura alone. I can't mess this up!"

Under began to jerk fiercely against the reins that held him. Wander untied and took the reins from the branch. Under lightly tugged for her to follow. Wander circled a glance around them to make sure no one was watching. With no one in sight, she followed Under deeper into the woods.

He circled behind a large juniper. The reins fell through her hand as though it were mist. The horse's face darkened and shrank away as through it shriveled. The body became a shadow that fell to the ground and rose back up into Under's human form.

He blew some of his dark hair out of his eyes. "I have an idea."

She expected him to tell her that they should go. She thought his face would look scared, tired, or concerned. Instead he seemed confident. "You won't kill anyone," Under said. "But they won't be able to blame you, because you'll still try. Just act like you are trying. I'll help you and misbehave as your horse. How's that?"

"I think they'll get mad at me."

"Who would be staring at you in the middle of a battle? They'll have other things to worry about. I noticed that Vincent guy has been watching us, but even he'll be busy. You shouldn't worry about him. If someone does see it, you can tell them it's because they didn't give you your magical sword back! That makes sense, right? You're used to being dependent on magic."

"I suppose that makes sense."

Under put his hand on top of her head. "What would you do without me?"

Wander smiled under her veil. With Under, the world was not such a cruel place. He was like shelter in a storm.

His hand left her. "Now I'll change back. Don't worry, we can do this, I'm with you."

When they returned to the camp, Wander laid down by Under's side. No fire, only a blanket. She covered her face from the light of day. She had to sleep under the sun, because the battle was at nightfall. She and the other humans would leap upon the village in the dark.

Sitting on Under's back, her heart pounded as she was surrounded by other humans on horses. The sun had begun to set. The nightly raid reminded Wander of Aura's attacks. Did she wait to strike from the shadows like this? Did Chant lurk in the Emerald Wilds or circle around Heathcliff before setting it all aflame? Did Masu and Aura's Shadow do so before the attack on Willton?

The fox stayed behind at camp. Wander did not worry, the creature always found its way back to her.

Devon sat in front of Wander. Her white horse had a dark mane and gray spots on its rear-end. Wander stared at the silver colored bow Devon held, it was carved to look like an art piece rather than a weapon. The engravings reminded Wander of rings worn on people's fingers, like little vines. Devon's white arrows contrasted to her dark quiver, their fletching decorated with dove feathers. Upon closer examination, Wander saw that every soldier's arrow was different at the end. Different feather, differently cut, variously sized, and some dyed or painted. Did they do this so they could determine who killed whom or what?

The dogs were released and stood alongside the soldiers. It was as if they were people, patient, silent, and waiting for orders. Devon turned her horse, her long dark hair pulled back into low ponytail. "There are no words to warm you for this night. This night we are not soldiers, we are killers."

A sobering silence blanketed the humans.

"Tonight, your resolve must be stronger than ever," she said, "because our enemy seeks to end every single human life for the benefit of her people, and tonight we show her that we will take her people with us." With a pure white flaming arrow, Devon shot upward as a signal to attack. The arrow shot across the night sky like a shooting star. The charge began.

Under galloped with the others. Surely the village would hear them coming. They sounded like rumbling thunder. Soldiers lit arrows on fire and aimed at the first sight of buildings. The constructs differed from human ones. All human buildings were squares and rectangles. These were circular with roofs of moss. The round walls were built of stone with diamond shaped windows. The green rooftops were the first to catch aflame.

The small army spread out, soldiers meant to break into the homes moved on foot. They opened the doors and charged in with the dogs. Screams followed. If the entryways were locked, the humans broke windows, kicked the door, anything to scare the deviants into coming out.

In human towns, trees were organized. It wasn't so in this village. Large trees grew in the middle of the streets. The humans shot fire arrows at these as well, lighting the night in golden waves of heat.

Wander saw her first deviant make it out of her home, a tall woman with hair like moonlight. Her red nightgown billowed like a flag in the breeze. The steel hissed as Wander drew out her sword. Under galloped toward the woman. Wander prepared her sword to look as though she meant to attack. For a moment Wander thought she would be successful at lopping the deviant's head from her neck, but Under performed as he said. He let out a whinny and twisted his body around, jerking Wander's blade away from the woman. The deviant ran a couple feet away before getting shot through the eye with an arrow. Her body fell upon tree roots. Wander met Vincent's dark eyes. His arrows all had red feathers, perhaps cardinal. The next one he prepared he dipped in poison.

An entire wave of deviants managed to pour out from one of the larger homes. They were of every age: elderly, babies, young adults, children, and middle aged.

At their backs were human soldiers armed with crossbows and bloodthirsty dogs.

She had to keep appearances. Wander nearly shut her eyes as she swung her sword down upon them. Under reared up, and she almost fell off the saddle. She threw her body forward and her hands clutched at his reins, nearly dropping her sword.

Smoke swelled up in the sky. Wander kept up swinging her sword. At times she felt flesh, but only left injury. No one fell from her sword. Most of the ones she did not get were killed off by others, by those on horses with bows or on the ground with crossbows.

There was a calm moment when no deviants ran the streets. Bodies lay about with bolts and arrows sticking out of them as though they were pincushions. Wander trembled on Under's back. The smell of smoke, sight of death, and the chaos of Under's movement shook her heartbeat and breath.

A horse approached her from behind. "Hey, are you alright?" A soldier noticed either Wander's shocked state of mind or her horse's strange behavior. Before Wander could answer, an axe spun into the back of the soldier's skull. The man fell off his horse to show the weapon had split his head open from behind.

Wander looked over to see a familiar face. Aura's Horns, Red, she stood in the street. Her face looked as though Wander never ripped it open, not even a scar. She held up an oddly thick gray bow, its center like a plank of wood. Three arrows hit her bow as she twisted the bow to align with her arm and used it like a shield. Wander realized with was a multi-purpose bow and shied, crafted with a wooden disk outside of the arrow's rest.

After defending herself, Red moved like a flash of lightning. Drawing an arrow from behind, she shot at a ground soldier who just stepped outside. The arrow danced and spun. Its design was not like the humans'. Some white material twisted around the shaft like a vine that caused it to twirl. When the arrow hit the soldier's chest, it drilled through him, blood spattering on the doorframe. Glass shattered as she fired a second arrow through a window, hitting a human square in the ear. Next she shot a dog outside, which let out a piercing cry.

Under sprinted away, and Wander clutched the horn of the saddle. "The Arms are here!" the fleeing deviants shouted with hope.

One human ran to another on a horse. "Impossible! How did they get here so quickly? Did they know we were coming?"

Upon hearing that, Wander shouted, "Are the Wings here?"

One answered back. "Other side of the village! He planted himself in front of Pitch's mansion!"

They passed Vincent as he galloped the opposite direction. Wander said nothing, but he obviously noticed her. Deviants still scrambled. One jumped out of a second story window, falling to the ground, not getting up. A woman held her children's hands and sneaked as they sought the cover of an alleyway. One tried to plea for mercy as she came out of her home with her hands up. None of these people seemed to know how to fight back.

They came to an opening where no trees grew. It seemed like a marketplace. Most of the buildings were equipped with signs. The grass seemed beaten down by constant walking around of citizens. A small pond sat in the center. Human, dog, and deviants' bodies had strewn the place. At the far end of the market was a home taller than the rest, perhaps five stories high. The stones that built the walls were more like boulders. Ferns grew on the roofs that divided each floor. A dark silhouette watched from a diamond shaped window on the third floor.

Masu stood in front of the building spattered in red. He held a bow-shield similar to Aura's Horns. From over his shoulder Wander could see he had similar drill arrows. Not yet seeing Wander, he pulled on his bowstring.

Wander froze up. Despite the torched buildings, the sight off Masu made her feel cold. As she saw him now, he almost seemed like a stranger. His dark fluffy hair had grown, almost hiding his eyes. His dark wings were spread out when they were usually folded.

A human screamed as Masu sent an arrow through his stomach. She doubled over, hands where the arrow hit. He appeared to have killed her horse as well. The creature lay by the woman's side with three arrows in its flesh.

Masu prepared another arrow to fire. Under whinnied as if to say, "Do something!" He ran between the injured soldier and Masu. Masu's bowstring loosened as he processed his new targets. She got to see his eyes. They had changed, looking like the glass eyes of the stag head in the Wolf and Banner. He had gotten worse, more distant. Could his mind get further and further away with each day?

"Masu," her voice came out softer than she planned. What could possibly get him to follow her? Could a single word even reach him? She did not want to use her sword. Something harmless to throw?

Her mind twirled to the large house. Masu was protecting the place. The person by the window caught Wander's gaze. She saw a pair of red eyes beyond the glass. Pale, dark hair, he was Pitch. The one person ordered to not be killed. Was Masu protecting him?

Drawing in a sharp breath, Wander jumped off Under's back and onto the bloody earth. Under screamed, tormented from the sudden change of plan as Wander jolted for the mansion. Masu burst into action, shooting an arrow. Wander twisted out of the way and tripped over a dog's corpse. The arrow shafts that stuck out of the dog's body broke against her as she landed.

She knew Masu could fire more shots at any second. Her hands clutched at the dog's collar and pulled. Three consecutive arrows hit the dog's corpse.

Using it as a shield, Wander jogged to the mansion, unable to sprint with the dog's weight.

"WAIT HERE FOR ME, UNDER! I'LL BE BACK!" Wander shouted across the bloodbath to him.

Under whinnied in response.

Wander pressed against the mansion entrance. It would not open no matter how hard she banged her body into the door.

Masu gave up arrows and began to charge at Wander with an intimidating flap of his colossal wings. Under galloped and hit Masu with a head-butt. Masu was hit on the right side and fell on the trampled grass.

Under circled around to Wander. She got out of the way of the door as Under turned around and kicked with all of the might of his back legs. With four powerful kicks, the door broke along with the bureau and chairs that blockaded it from behind.

Wander ducked out of the way of another arrow. Masu crouched on the ground, readying another.

She dove into the mess of broken door and furniture. Wood splinters cut through her arms and legs as she shoveled through the mess into the home. Inside the house was dark. Nothing but diamond shaped filters of firelight came from the windows. Behind a bookcase, stairs curled up the round room.

Wander slowed as she walked up to the third floor where she saw Pitch. He was gone. Of course he'd be gone. He would see her entering and hear her feet upon the stairs. Anxiety clenched at Wander's inaction as she tried to think of what to do next. He must have gone—

Wander staggered forward as a blunt force pounded into the back of her head. Dizzily turning around, she saw hands clenching the marble bust of a woman's face. Beyond the hands were two frightened red eyes framed in pale skin. He wore a white long coat, and his dark hair was tied into a thin tail at the back. He stood the same height as Wander. Despite the fear in his eyes, he smiled.

Drawing her sword, Wander pointed it at the deviant. "Come with me."

Dropping the marble bust, Pitch attempted to get away downstairs. Wander tackled him, causing them both to tumble down the stairs. As they landed at the bottom, he tried to crawl away.

Grabbing her sword, Wander turned it around and hit the back of his head with her steel pommel. He stopped moving. She immediately turned him around and checked his heartbeat. It still thumped. She dragged him through the broken furniture and door to the outside where Under waited.

Under kneeled to help her throw Pitch across his back. Behind Under, Wander saw a group of humans were keeping Masu busy.

She climbed on Under's back.

"Masu!" she called.

She held her hand up to get the soldiers to cease firing. Masu looked back at her, his eyes locking onto Pitch laying between her and Under's neck.

His wings flapped as he charged forward toward Wander, and he took to the air as Under shot into a fast gallop toward the woods.
She felt the air move from the power of Masu's wings. An arrow hit the ground by their side. Masu attempted to aim from the air. Under began to run in zigzags.

Leaping over bodies and roots, they left the village and moved into the woods. Masu did not slow down. He managed to dodge branches at a fast rate, sometimes flying vertically and horizontally. He seemed to have given up on shooting them. Now he only followed.

She looked out to the side of the forest. As if in slow motion, she saw a face above the bushes.

"NOW!" Sara's voice hammered down. As Under leapt over a log, Wander turned around to see Masu fly lower to dodge branches. As he swooped down, an enormous net followed by a dozen arrows came upon him.

Under stopped and turned. Sara and twelve other humans emerged from the brush. The soldiers held down the net while Masu struggled like a bird, his wings trying to flap with no room. One human tried to touch Masu only to get shocked and stumble back. Sara held a crossbow and watched.

"What are you doing?" Wander inelegantly let herself down from Under's back.

Sara smiled, her blue tooth looking like a gap in the dark. "You did great! You even have Pitch." She approached the unconscious deviant and felt the pulse of his neck. "And still alive.

"As for what's next, we're taking Aura's Wings with us. Naktol said everyone gets killed, unless we take them alive as hostages. And this Arm is way more important than Pitch. He is sure to know more about Aura. He must know everything there is about her."

"Masu is mind-controlled! He can't say anything!"

"Now that he's ours, we can find a way to break that."

"You can free him from being controlled?"

"Of course. Enough pain should snap him right out of it."

Wander stood there, trying to process what was happening. Sara watched Masu under the net. She approached, her feet a half-foot away from his face. "Those wings are really something."

Wander tore forward. "Don't hurt him!"

Three soldiers came upon her. One grabbed her left arm, the other her right. The third grappled her from behind, his arms locking her into place.

Sara approached. "Just as I thought, you're on the deviants' side." She pointed her crossbow to Wander's knee and released the bolt. With a scream, Wander's body twisted in the soldier's arms. It felt as though her leg had exploded.

"So many people had hope in you, too. It's okay though, I'm sure you can still be useful." She turned to her soldiers, "Keep holding her. She'll sleep soon."

Sara was wrong. Wander glared, fully conscious. Besides the agonizing pain in her knee, a cold wave flowed through her body. She tried to kick the soldier behind her with her good leg. No use, even as she hit him, he seemed unaffected.

Sara kneeled by Masu's face. She stared at him as he thrashed in the web of rope. Cautiously, she attempted to touch his face only to get a blue blast of shock to her hand.

"Why would you hurt him?" Wander asked. "If he's mind controlled, then he's innocent!"
The warrior stood up and her neck twisted to face Wander. "We have gone beyond caring about innocence! We just killed more than a hundred innocent people today."

"Masu can't say anything!"

"Even if you're right, Aura cares about him. With both the Wings and Pitch, we can have power over her."

"And what? Do you think Aura is controlling me, too? I'm not on her side! I want her dead just like the rest of you. I just want to save my friend!"

"Where is your friend, Under? We received a letter from Naktol's hawk that he has been missing since we left the castle. Did you really think we would not notice? Is he with Aura now?"

"Under, he's—" Wander stopped herself. "He has nothing to do with this."

Sara looked at Masu. He kept trying to flap his wings and the soldiers struggled to hold onto the shaking net. "The sedatives don't work on the Wings." She looked at Wander. "And they don't work on you. Is that really a coincidence?"

Chapter 12
Fort Ben

"Once a manor, Fort Ben came to life at the beginning of the War of Arrows. Ben donated it after his family was killed by Aura's Arms. Thanks to him, dozens of souls were tortured in the basement." – Records from the War of Arrows

The army separated, most to return to Naktol, and the other to a place that resembled a castle. There were only soldiers. Many who came in were injured, carried in on stretchers or with a friend's shoulder to lean on. The blue human flag billowed upon the fort walls. There was the smell of cooked meat and steel.

They brought Wander in chains. The metal hung heavy on her wrists. She hobbled with each step due to her injured knee. A soldier had cleaned, applied ointment, and bandaged the wound, but it felt like the leg was no longer a part of her. Rather it felt as though it should fall apart from her, and then she'd be better off.

There was no sign of familiar faces. No Vincent, Under, Masu, Sara, or Devon. Wander was relieved to not run into Vincent. In the end, he was completely right. She was in denial the whole time. She should have recognized the moment Naktol said she tested poisons on her body that she could not trust them.

All the signs were there, such as not giving her sword back and making Vincent watch her.

The soldiers and Naktol only liked her out of some bizarre fascination. Humans sometimes liked difference, as Ethan said, but why did she automatically think that was a good thing? They didn't care about her as a fellow human. She was like an animal to them. Maybe they felt superior to her, and that's what they liked. Maybe Naktol enjoyed dressing her up as a way to empower herself. *Look what I can do,* she must've thought, *I can make this savage witch beautiful.* And the moment Wander tried to have a say in something, to have her goal met, it was over.

The soldiers led her through a wooden door. All that was in front were stairs into the underground. The two soldiers were kind and patient enough to aid Wander with each hobble down to make sure she did not fall.

At the end of the stairway was a corridor lit by torches. A woman sat in a chair with a wolf-like dog sitting at her side. She provided one of the soldiers with a key ring. "Check for rats before leaving her there," she said. "That Pitch bastard screamed bloody murder when he saw a rat, and I had to take care of it to get some peace."

The soldiers ushered Wander down the hall. The sides of the walls had small arched barred doors with little rooms. The rooms looked impossible to stand or stretch in; one would always have to sit or lie down with knees bent. Some people were cramped in the rooms. Deviants. Wander could tell from the inhuman colors of violet, lemon-yellow, and red in their eyes. Chains constricted their ankles and wrists. One even had a cloth jammed into his mouth.

"Here we are," one soldier said. He sat down to open the barred door with a silver key. When it opened, he peeked inside. "No rats. Maybe a cockroach or two."

They stuffed her into the cell. She curled up into a fetal position, her face close to the cold metal bars. "What's going to happen to me?" she asked.

"Captain Sara is leading the fort for now. She'll decide."

"I'm so hungry. Can I have something to eat?"

"We'll let Deb know on our way out." The soldiers left her in the dim and cramped hole. She turned her body to face the wall.

Under had been taken. The last time she saw him, a soldier had taken his reins and led him away. Wander had faith that he'd transform and look for her. The real question was whether he could find her. She never thought she could be this deep under the earth.

It was cold. Wander ducked her hands under her cloak and up through her veil to her mouth to breathe warm breath on them. Hissing from her hurt knee, she curled tighter until her heels touched her butt. "Hello?" she called.

There was no answer. As she thought, they had put her farther away from the other prisoners.

Food never came. She had not eaten since before the battle. It had gone beyond aches in her stomach. Now all she felt was weakness. The smell of meat on the way to the prison made her feel even worse as her mouth watered.

Masu. He was probably getting hurt as she lay here.

She stuck her hands out of the cell. She let her sorrow out. With a shaking gasp, she blinked and tears streamed down. She was so happy and hopeful that the humans trusted her; she never questioned whether she could trust them. She did not know what she was but human or not, she decided she did not want anything to do with humans anymore. The people she could love or trust in the world were spirits, like Under and Masu.

Wander heard a scream. It sounded distant, as though it were on the other side of a wall. She could not tell if the sound belonged to a man, woman, or even an animal. As she lay there, the screaming repeated. Sometimes there would be about five minutes of silence, but then it returned. The screams were sometimes in short bursts, but most of them were long and wailing. With those sounds, she could not sleep or have any peaceful thoughts. She wished her hands weren't chained so she could cover her ears.

Wander attempted to extend her injured leg, but there was not enough room to unbend the knee. In a sudden fit of rage, she smashed her back into the wall to create enough room for her legs to stretch. Even then she could not unbend. Never before did she so badly want to straighten out her body. She tried to stick her feet through the bars with no success. Her kneecap shot pain through her body, as though to groan at her unfruitful attempts.

"Wander?"

An unfamiliar voice broke her thoughts.

She turned too quickly, hitting her injured knee on the low ceiling. Her mouth opened in a soundless cry, pulling her leg inward to her chest as she rocked in pain.

"Are you hurt?" The voice spoke as if he knew her, as if he cared.

"My knee."

"Oh, right."

She looked out to see a soldier on his knees by her cage. He wore a helmet with a metal piece bridging his nose. He had a brown beard and mustache long enough to hide his lips.

"Who are you?"

The soldier looked both directions down the corridor. He brought his face closer. "It's me. You know who I am."

Her heart skipped with hope for a moment. No. It could still be a trap. She couldn't repeatedly trust just anyone. "Prove it," Wander pleaded. "Something only you and I know."

The soldier's seemed taken aback by her mistrust. He brought his face even closer to the bars and breathed. "I'm a shadow."

She let out a gasp of relief. Her hand reached outside the bars to him. "I knew you'd look for me, but I didn't know if you would find me."

Under took her hand in his. It was so warm. "Let's get you out of there."

In his other hand he held a ring of keys. Not knowing which key was correct, he tried them one by one.

"Did they hurt you while you were here?" he asked as he tried the fourth key.

"No. I feel sick, though. I haven't eaten since before Loreman. Also it's very small in here. I want to stretch my legs."

"I'm so sorry. I just stood there and watched you get captured."

"It's okay."

"It's not okay. I should've been braver. I could've helped you. I'm a shadow! I'm not powerless." He tried the seventh key. "In the moment I was just scared. All I could think of was that if I changed form, then everyone would know what I am. They'd think I was a monster, like they do with most spirits."

"I want nothing to do with humans."

Under tried the twelfth key. "Don't say that."

"No. It's always been like this for me, ever since I left home. If you changed into me for a single day, you'd understand. You'd understand that people are scared of you, distrust you, think they can fix you, or only like you because they know they are better than you."

"You won't find any better behavior with spirits, trust me. People of all backgrounds are capable of being jerks."

The lock clicked as he turned the right key. The barred door silently swung open. Wander crawled out, and Under helped her stand. Picking up her hurt leg, she leaned against him.

Under took up her hands bound in cold metal. His thumb caressed the lock. "Damn, I don't know if I have a key to unlock your chains." He looked down at her bloody pants. The blood had dried brown around her knee. "You need a doctor."

Wander looked down the hall to see the fox had followed Under. It ran over to her and licked her leg.

"What now?" she asked.

"I don't have any medical supplies or food. We could get out of here and get you attended to but . . ." Under trailed off. He looked off to the left side of the hall. He sighed, "I heard they're keeping Masu here."

"We have to find him."

"I was afraid you'd say that. This place is a maze. Also with each door I'll have to try all the keys because I don't know which key is for which door."

"Sara is going to make him talk by hurting him. If what Myth said about Aura's mind-control is right, then Masu can't speak. If Masu doesn't talk, I think Sara is just going to hurt him more. We have to save him."

"You're in no condition to—"

"I'm not leaving him."

Under kept on hand on her arm to support her as she limped down the hall. As usual, the fox trailed behind. It sniffed the ground and sometimes chased a rat or roach that moved from one prison cell to the other. Nearly all of the prison cells were empty.

"What's even the point of trapping people like this?" Wander asked.

Under never responded to her question. Maybe he didn't have an answer or he was deep in thought.

Wander stopped for a moment to breathe warm air on her hands. It would be tricky to get the chains off with no key. They did not bother her as much as her thirst, hunger, and leg.

Suddenly something clutched onto her injured leg. Looking down, Wander saw a single hand extend from between the bars below. The fingers curled around her ankle. Before she could react, the hand jerked at her leg. Pain burned through her body as the knee got tugged. She let out a howl of agony that echoed through the halls. She nearly fell to the prisoner's level.

Under held Wander up as she tripped away from the hand. "Let's stay away from the walls." He pulled her back to the center of the hall. The way in which he held her up felt familiar. His hands on her upper arms, gentle but strong whenever she swayed. In her earliest memory, Masu had done the same thing. She remembered that her legs trembled, and the smallest dip in the floorboards would cause her to stumble.

Eventually the cells ended and were replaced by regular-sized wooden doors. Each door had a barred window. With her hurt leg, Wander could not stand straight enough for a decent view of the rooms. All she could see was a wooden table at the far end, nothing more.

"These are larger cells," Under told her. "I see chains dangling on the wall. Empty though."

"Masu has to be here. With his wings, they can't fit him in a place like I was in."

"Yeah. Let's check each one."

They went door to door with Under looking in. They'd start from the left door, then the one across, then up, then right, then up, and then left in an almost zigzag pattern. With each one they checked, Under would just look at Wander and shake his head. That was until he looked into a room and someone spoke on the other side. "I see you."

Under immediately ducked his head down.

"Too late," said the voice. "I know you're watching me."

"Who is that?" Wander whispered.

Under lifted his head back for another look. "That Pitch guy. He's pinned up. Let's move on."

As they walked away the voice called, "Leaving so soon?"

Wander looked at Under, wondering if they should speak with the deviant. Maybe he knew where Masu was taken? As if he read her mind, Under said, "Let's ignore the crazy man."

Pitch seemed to be the only person in the large prison cells. They checked around ten more doors, reaching a dead-end. If Masu wasn't here, then where could he be? Maybe on the way back they could ask Pitch. It was better than nothing.

As Wander approached the second-to-last door, Under's hands suddenly abandoned her. Looking back at him, she realized he had begun to shiver. "Under?" His soldier body was difficult for her to read, but it had become obvious that something was wrong.

"He's back there," Under pointed a couple doors down.

"What? Masu is? But you looked in and shook your head."

"I'm sorry. I panicked. He's not alright. I didn't want you to see. He's—"

Wander hobbled to the wall and used it as support. As fast as she could, she limped to the doors Masu pointed at. "Right or left?"

"Left, but wait!"

Wander stretched up to peek in. There was just a table but upon a closer look she saw feathers around the floor. Putting her injured leg down, she tried standing up straight. Breathing through the pain, she looked in and saw a black wing. Immediately something was wrong. The wing wasn't supposed to bend like that.

Wander hands attacked the doorknob. She shook the locked door. Already she had lost her breath to a flow of panic. "Under, the door!"

With shaking hands, Under took out the key ring. The first key didn't work; the second key didn't, either.

"What did they do to him? Can you see?"

"He doesn't look good. His wings are on . . ." Under shook his head. "I think they tortured him."

"What's that?"

Under hesitated to answer. His mouth hung open for a moment, his face twisted as though it pained him to even think of a reply. "They hurt him a lot."

Her bound hands pressed against the door, wishing she could just phase through. When she heard the lock tick, Wander pushed the door open.

Masu was on the far left side of the room. He sat on his legs with knees bent. His hands were up above his head, one layered over the other with a spear through both of the palms, pinning them to a wooden board. The flesh on his arms, chest, and face were coated in lacerations. Black blood still freshly oozed from the wounds. Two more spears were through his elbows. His wings were spread out and speared to two giant wheels similar to the ones on a wagon. At the very end of each wing they were speared to another set of smaller wheels. The wings were shaped like Ws, the bones broken in at least four places. Perhaps the most visually disturbing was the flesh of his wings. His feathers were plucked to the point that Wander could see the bumpy and bloody skin. His wings looked like the meat sold in markets, like the dead geese, chickens, and turkeys.

An inhuman sound left Wander's mouth. Under's hand touched her shoulder, but she pulled away, stumbling toward Masu. The smell of blood was so strong that she could taste the metallic tang. She let herself fall in front of him, letting out a cry of agony as her suffering knee hit the stone. She sat on loose feathers and blood spatter. Was he dead? She gasped. His eyes were closed. Her thumb barely touched his cheek when Masu opened his eyes and flinched. His entire body began to tense up and tremble. Wander's eyesight blurred from tears.

"It's okay. It's Wander," she whispered. "You know me. I'm not going to hurt you." That's when he looked at her, but seemed to see nothing. There was no expression. No relief. She wanted to wrap her arms around him, but her chains did not allow her hands to part. She looked at the ground and cried. Under sat by her side. His hand reached out to console her, but Wander twisted away.

"Bandages." The word was hiccupped through Wander's sobs. "We need bandages."

"We don't have any."

"Then let's just get him down!"

"Wander, even in this state, he's still mind-controlled. He would possibly try to attack you. Even if he didn't do that, he could bleed to death from the wounds and—"

"No!" Wander cried "No, no no!" She hit her face against her chained hands. Her cries became hysterical. The entire world collapsed into this room. Her scorched throat ached in her screams. She would set herself on fire all over again just for this room to not exist.

"WANDER!" Under grabbed her chains and jerked her hands away from her face. "Calm down!"

Her screaming only worsened. She tried to writhe out of Under's grip. "LET HIM DOWN!"

Under forcefully embraced her, locking her body in his arms. She struggled until she gave in, bawling into his shoulder. Each time she tried to form a word it got lost among her cries. Under's body did not feel familiar and his armor felt cold. "Pulling those spears out could kill him," Under whispered.

"This is all my fault. I got him here." She calmed enough for Under to let her go. "I'm not leaving him."

"Then wait here," Under said as he stood up. "I'll explore and see if there is anything we can use to help him."

When Under left the room, he let his back fall against the wall. Tucking his face in his hand, he needed to think. He had to let the horrors of what he just witnessed sink in and settle.

Wander was just a wind-born kid. There was no doubt she wouldn't be the same after all this. No one could be. If that were Alice—he choked up at the thought. That must be what it's like for Wander.

He had to think. He could turn into anything. Sara? She had the run of the place. He could go out as her and get Masu medical care. Too risky, it would be a disaster if the real Sara saw him or if they were seen at the same time. Even with medical supplies, he wouldn't know what to do. It might not even help. Under traced his steps back down the hall. If he took too long, Wander was in a mental state to do something chancy.

Just then he heard a voice further down the hall.

"You're right. You're far chattier. But at the same time you say nothing."

"That's because humans only hear what they want to hear."

The voices came from the door Under passed earlier with the deviant. He stood up to the barred window to see Sara. She sat on a stool. Bent over, she held a clamp that gripped a metal claw. She stuck the claw in an alcove in the wall full of hot coals. The metal began to glow orange. A soldier stood by a table full of sharp implements and bottles.

They weren't too far from Masu's room. It was a miracle they did not hear Wander's cries.

"Hey!" Under jumped when Sara looked right at him through the window. "This isn't some theater show, soldier. Either state your business or get out of here."

"Um," Under opened the door. He saw that the deviant, Pitch, was in a position similar to Masu's, his hands speared up on a wood board. So far he was spotless. They had only just begun. "Queen Naktol sent a messenger. He said it's urgent. He's outside the gates."

Sara looked to the soldier at the table. "This could take a while. You are relieved of duty. I will seek you out when I'm done."

The soldier bowed, and they both walked out.

Sara turned around, her brown eyes on Under. "You."

"Yes?"

"From today forward I have created a buddy policy for security measures. No soldier comes into the prisons without a partner. I will look over your being here since this rule is recent. Next time you come here, you'll need a partner to get entrance."

"Yes, ma'm! I'm just here to pass the message to you and to . . . find some missing equipment."

"We have equipment missing?"

"Well," Under thought his chest would explode. He wondered if his face was red. He was used to lying but not with so much pressure. "I'll be honest. I lost my wedding ring." He fumbled with his hands to show empty fingers. "I checked everywhere but here."

"Check the storage room. It may have been placed with prisoner belongings."

"Thanks, Captain!" Under made an awkward and delayed salute. Sara must be used to soldiers being either scared or awkward around her, because she just ignored him and walked on. He pretended to walk the opposite direction. Once Sara and the soldier turned out of the hallway though, he stepped in a light run back to the room they were in. He went straight for the tools on the table. Holding the bottles to his eye, he read the label, "Boil sap." No idea what that entailed. The tools lay on top of a cloth. He could use that to bandage at least one of Masu's stab wounds. It didn't look clean though, quite the contrary, it had blood smears.

"You're up to no good."

Under looked at the deviant, Pitch. He would be seen as handsome to girls like Alice: tall, pale, with dark lavish hair. He smiled like a trickster and his rat-tail reminded Under of the seedy drunks at the Queen's Boot. No good could come out of listening to him. Under slide the tools off the cloth and placed it in his pocket.

"Are you with that Wander girl?"

When Under looked at Pitch, the deviant's smile broadened, knowing he'd hit on something. "The moment I heard the humans imprisoned one of their own, I knew things would get interesting! That's what makes you guys so miserable, no trust, no loyalty. If it wasn't for us deviants, I'm sure you'd be fighting each other."

He had to get back to Wander. She could not be doing well alone with Masu. But just as Under began to walk out . . .

"I can help, you know. A temporary alliance if, you will. Get me out of here, and I can do you a favor. As a friend of the royal deviant family, I am a man of many talents."

"You don't even know what's happening."

"I can piece things together. I've heard a little from Myth about Wander. She's after the Wings isn't she? Except I don't think she'll be happy when she finds him. I heard the cries from his torture hours ago."

"She already found him..."

Wander felt a smidgen of relief when Under left. She did not want his pity or his touch. He could only help by helping Masu. The fox sat in the corner of the room as if knowing her desire for space.

Masu must've been freezing. She was cold and covered in her cloak and veil while he was shirtless. Her bound hands shakily reached up for his cheek. She cleared a trickle of blood that oozed down from his forehead. He recoiled at her touch, like a worm twisting in the sun.

She could no longer see through her eyes, like looking through a wave of water. "I—" she choked and looked down. Not looking at him helped. "I'm sorry this is happening to you." She crumpled up into a ball, her forehead on his knees. "I'm sorry I ever wanted to leave. I never wanted this. I want to be with you. I want to go home."

Masu did not respond. She did not want to look at his expressionless face. If she saw those blank eyes while she poured her heart out, she would probably lose all hope.

Under came back, but he wasn't alone. A shorter man stood behind, straight-backed with bloody hands balled up at his sides.

"Did anything happen?" Under asked.

She shook her head.

"Pitch said he would help us if I released him."

Wander looked over the deviant. He stared at Masu, not appearing all that shocked from the winged being's wounds. "Whoever did this torture committed a terrible job. They wanted to keep him alive, but Aura's Wings can die from injuries like these."

"Can we really trust you?" Wander asked.

Pitch examined his bloody palms. It looked as if he squeezed a bunch of blackberries in his hands until they burst. "Look, I'm not one hundred percent certain of trusting you, either. You're the reason I've gotten into this mess in the first place. We're both taking risks here."

"What's your connection to Aura?"

"We were childhood friends. My family has connections to the palace and royal family because of our trade business with the elementals. I must say I'm closer to Myth than her sister. The Queen is somewhat of a recluse."

"How can we help Masu?" Wander asked. "I'll help you get out of here if you can help Masu."

Pitch held out his hands to show Wander his wounds, as if she failed to notice already. "We only have one set of hands out of the three of us, and that one set can't touch spirits like me. Let's remedy that. I'll get those cuffs off you, then you bandage me, then we'll take care of Aura's Wings. Deal?"

"We don't have a key to unlock me."

"I still have a pin that the humans didn't find. You," Pitch pointed at Under, "get the human torture tools from the room I was in. I'll teach you how to pick a lock."

When Under returned, he laid out a cloth full of tools.

Pitch almost grabbed one only to pull back. "I can't use my hands, so you do it. Take this pin and use the needle for the bottom part of the keyhole. Then use the flat end of that clamp and jam it there. Not too hard."

Wander placed her bound hands on Under's lap. He fit both objects in the lock and began tweaking around. Whatever picking a lock took, it wasn't easy. Wander grew anxious as Under worked on her chains. She could tell he was getting stressed out as well. "We got to work fast," he began to twist around the lock with more aggression. "Sara will come back once she discovered I lied. We may need to have getting out of here be our first priority."

"Wonderful," Pitch sighed. "I'm a terrible runner by the way."

Just when Wander was about to suggest forgetting about her hands, there was a click as the lock opened. With her hands free, she immediately tore pieces from the ends of her cloak. She scooted over to Pitch, holding in a cry from her knee scraping the stone. Taking his left hand, she began bandaging. She pulled the dark cloth tight between his thumb and index finger. Pitch tried to look into her eyes, but she avoided his gaze, rushing to attend to his hand. They were soft, the fingers turning pale to contrast with a tan wrist. The nails were spotless and even. Wander never clipped her nails. Ms. Flinsler tried to trim her nails once, and

Wander screamed. She did what Masu did in the wilds: bite them whenever they grew too long.

"Yikes, not so tight!" he complained as she pulled at the cloth. She tied a knot below his knuckles.

"Now we take care of Masu," Wander said.

"Yes, I see where your priorities are." Pitch got up and examined Masu's condition. His face closed into the wings and where the spears hit. "Damn, he's really harpooned. How long has he been bleeding out?"

Wander noticed that Masu had shut his eyes.

"He's fainted. That's okay. It'll make this easier." Pitch's hands both grasped one of the many spears that lanced through Masu's wing. Placing one foot against the wooden wall, he pulled and twisted the spear out of the wing. Dark feathers floated down and blood trickled.

"What are you doing?" Under tried to grab Pitch's wrist. A blue shock briefly lit up the space between them. "We can't have him bleed more!"

"You said Sara could be back any moment. We need him free if we got to run. If you want him to stop bleeding, go heat up that clamp you have in the room I was in. Sara's coals may still be hot. Heat it and take it out just before it starts glowing. If it's red, it's too hot."

"What? How will that help us?"

"We're going to cauterize."

Wander had no idea what that word meant. Under left in a hurry.

"Pull that spear out of his hands, but hold him up. His wings could break a second time if we're not careful." Pitch nearly fell backward when getting out his second spear. "Hopefully the he will stay unconscious for the procedure."

She started with Masu's hands. They looked like meat rather than a part of his body. Like two patties held together by a silver toothpick. Then she realized her hands were shaking. Her entire body quivered, and it wasn't from the cold. *Get a hold of yourself.* She took the spear's wood handle and pulled with all her might. The moment it released, she set it to the ground.

"Hold him!"

Masu had fallen forward. With his wings not fully release from the wheels, they tugged with his falling body. More blood pooled and trickled out from beneath his feathers.

Wander wrapped her arms around him and held him back up to ease the tension on the wings. His blood stuck like sap against her cloak and hands. Closing her eyes, she sniffled. She held his completely limp body, as if he were dead. She could not feel or hear his breaths over her shaking body and hyperventilation. Pitch finished freeing the wings as she kept up the position. Masu felt heavier the longer she held him. She moved all her weight to one leg, the injured one unable to stand two beings' mass.

"Now let him down easy," Pitch said.

She sank her knees down and placed Masu against the wall. When she backed up, it looked like a scene from her nightmares. Black blood and feathers were all around, like the jaws of a monster just took him and shook and shook and shook.

Under returned with a hot clamp, like what Ms. Flinsler used to serve salad, except this one was metal. It reminded her of a crawfish claw, the little creatures that would pinch her on the riverside.

"The pain might wake him up," said Pitch. "I need something wooden for him to bite on. Both of you will hold him down while I burn the wounds shut."

"Wait, we're burning him?" Wander positioned herself between Pitch, Under, and Masu. "There is no way we're hurting him more."

"Trust me," Pitch said. "This is a last resort for survival. He will die if we don't do this."

Wander looked at Under, someone she trusted. He did not seem sure. He held out the hot clamp far from himself.

Pitch picked up a spear. "It might be too thick for him to bite down on, but it's our best bet."

"Bite?"

"If he wakes up we don't want him chomp or swallow his tongue while screaming. If we jam this spear in his mouth, he'll bite that instead, and it'll lessen the screaming."

"Under!" Wander looked back at him, desperate for him to say something.

Under took a gaze at Masu, "I don't think we have any other way."

With that conclusion, Wander helped Pitch spread Masu out on the cold stone floor. Pitch positioned everyone. Wander sat on Masu's legs. Her right hand held down his right wrist and her left hand held down his left. Pitch sat below the left wing, armed with the hot clamp. Under was placed by Masu's head and held the spear.

Before the procedure even began, Masu's eyes fluttered open. He did not seem completely there. His consciousness was probably like a leaf floating on the water, sometimes rising and other times sinking. Did he see them? Did he have any clue as to what was happening? Under began to push the spear's midsection into Masu's mouth, his arms far apart on each end as to not touch him and get shocked. He tried to be gentle, gradually easing the spear between Masu's jaws. Wander looked away and toward Masu's thighs.

"I'm going to begin now with what's bleeding the worst," Pitch said.

Wander slammed her eyes shut and tensed. It was like bracing for impact, like she would feel the pain as well. She had no idea what hot metal could feel like against the skin, but she could remember the sense of drowning in flame, to feel the skin bubble and pop.

The sound that came from Masu sounded like an animal. His wrists warped madly in her grip. His knees tried to bend, but Wander pressed her weight firmly against them. She briefly opened her eyes to see the clamp pressed down on a chest cut. Under pressed the spear down on Masu for him to scream against.

Pitch picked up the clamp and moved it farther down the gash, leaving behind a hideous and ragged burn. He moved on to the next wound on Masu's shoulder.

Masu's wrist twisted out of Wander's clutch. She managed to grab his hand, making him let out another gurgling, muffled scream as she squeezed where the spear impaled. She repositioned her hand, slipping around in his blood. Letting go, she grabbed his wrist again. She closed her eyes, focusing on her own breathing over the struggle, over the shouts of agony. If he died in this much pain, she would never recover. She wanted to wrap him in a blanket, let him sleep, and feed him soup like he would when she hurt.

Soon Masu's struggles ended. He wilted, knees unbuckled, arms limp.

"He should have fainted for good now," Pitch said. "Makes this much easier." He held the clamp over to Under. "Should be fine to let go of him now. Please reheat this."
Under obeyed, took the clamp, and left in a hurry.

Pitch rubbed his forehead with his arm. "Can't say I want to do this ever again. You guys better be good on your word."

"If Masu lives, I'll make sure you get out," Wander promised. She let go of Masu's wrists and looked at the black, warm ooze on her hands.

Under returned, and Wander could feel the heat emit from the clamp on her eyes as he passed her. Pitch finished off Masu's stomach and torso injuries. Masu did not struggle, but Wander held his bloody hand just in case he could feel anything. Pitch offered to cauterize the hands, and Wander agreed. With Masu unconscious, Under no longer had to hold the spear. Instead he sat back, and the fox moved to his lap. It seemed to begin warming up to him.

"What about his wings?"

"I don't know how to even begin fixing that. They're broken in around four different places. He won't fly again unless you take him to Aura."

"There is no way we are doing that."

"You might not have a choice," Pitch said. "Cauterizing isn't a permanent solution to his condition. I'm sure that human captain did more than just cut him up and break his bones. He might have internal damage, head trauma—all sorts of other issues that can kill him. It would be just cruel to not heal his wings."

When Pitch finished cauterizing, he set the clamp down on the stone. "Now let's get out of here. We need alcohol for me to drink and to pour on this bird spirit. We don't want his wounds to get infected." Pitch stood up and looked over Masu, his fist against his chin. "He won't be easy carrying. Those wings are a piece of work."

The fox jumped out of Under's lap as he got up. "I'll do it."

Pitch gave an amused snort. "You look strong, but you're human. You can't even touch him."

"I'm not human."

"Under—"

"It's alright, Wander. I'm fine. I have to do it if we want to get out of here."

Pitch's eyes widened and his hand fell away from his face. "What do you mean?" He seemed like a man not ordinarily caught by surprise, but Under got him.

"I'm a spirit. I just decided to be human for a time. If I turn into a spirit, I can carry Masu's body on my back, and you both can take a wing so they don't drag."

"Go ahead then," Pitch said. The deviant's face was like Roslyn's whenever she heard a story of Masu: utterly astonished.

From the tip of his head to the bottom of his steel heels, Under's body faded to black and fell away like ash onto the ground. The ash turned to a murky and round smear and it billowed like smoke. Pitch took three steps backward. From the dark hole a silhouette of a body built up from the bare feet to the upper legs where the beginnings of fingertips began at the sides. At the back, long hair flowed out and reached up to the skull. The darkness lifted to show the form of a woman.

Wander never saw someone who looked quite like what Under turned into. She reminded her of certain birds she'd see in the Emerald Wilds, the ones that had every feather a different color. Or maybe of butterflies with flowers of many different shades all at once. Under turned into a rainbow woman. Her hair was the most colorful thing about her, splashed with moss green on the front, yellow speckles all around, then sky blue down the toward the shoulders. The underside of her hair was red, and a longer layer of gold strayed down to her lower back. One of Under's eyes was orange and the other was dark blue. To contrast with the bodily iridescence, he wore a tan long shirt and pants.

"I can't believe it!" Pitch laughed. "A shadow, of all things! Of course!"

"What do you mean 'of course'?" Under asked. His voice was female, as though an entirely different person spoke.

"Well, we knew not all of the shadows could be dead. After all, they just appear, they don't breed or anything."

"What?"

"You mean you don't know? I suppose you wouldn't without a family to tell you what's what. Shadows never have families."

"What else do you know about shadows?" As rushed and panicked as Wander was, she could not blame Under for asking. If what Pitch said was true, then she and Under had more in common than she thought.

"Other than your people lived in tents and loved to have transforming parties, play tricks, and had barely any system of government, nothing."

"Where do shadows come from?" Under asked.

"You know, I'd love to chat about you but we're kind of in a hurry?"

Wander stepped around the amazing looking woman Under became. "Under, what body is that?"

"A rainbow. A type of spirit from the south. I have only met one, and trust me; they are very hard to get down."

He ducked down. The rainbow flow of hair against the ground layered into a puddle. "Lift him onto my back."

Wander's knee began to feel better. She put more weight on the foot and little pain shot up. Maybe seeing Masu's condition sobered her own. Still, holding Masu's wing while moving would be a challenge.

Under's arms locked around Masu's legs, and he leaned far forward so Masu would not fall back. Wander lifted Masu's left wing over her head. Some feathers floated down to the floor and blood slid from his wing to the tips of her fingers, down her wrists and arms. Back in the wilds, his wings were like shelter, always between her and the cold or danger. Now it seemed like a broken home.

"However we are getting out of here, we'd best be quick," Pitch said. "If anyone even sees us in the dark, we are undeniably suspicious."

"I saw something while walking around," Under said. "A grate, probably to some sewers. It won't be fun, but it's the safest way."

"Then you lead, shadow."

Just getting through the doorway tested them. With Masu's wings broken and spread, they had to move him through left wing first, then body, then right wing. Under instructed where to go. Masu's huge wingspan made everything trying, forcing them to walk like crabs down the hall. He certainly was never meant to be underground.

"There. Under the torch there."

"We need to put him down."

The three of them set Masu aside, his back to the wall. His head dangled down like a rag doll's. Wander sat by him while the two spirits examined the grate.

"You're kidding, right? To fit the wings through here we'll need to mince them!"

The grate was rectangular, about the width of a wagon wheel and the height of a stool. Small size aside, it was barred more than the prison cells, with both horizontal and vertical iron slabs to prevent even a rat's entry.

Pitch bent down, his fingers ran across the four corners. "I don't even know how to begin opening this thing."

"I could turn into a snake, explore the other side. See if there is another way."

Pitch's body tensed. "Wait," he whispered. "Do you hear that?"

Wander stopped breathing for a moment. Footsteps, a couple sets of feet echoed through the halls. Voices too, but she could not make out what they were saying.

"We have to hide!" Pitch hissed.

"They're probably here for you or Masu. You both are the only prisoners in this area," Under whispered. "Maybe I can turn into something and distract them while you guys figure out a way in."

"What about you?" Wander asked.

"I'll catch up."

"No!" Wander spoke a little too loudly, causing both spirits to flinch.

On her hands and knees, she crawled over to the grate. Her fingers curled around the small squares of open space. She jerked back without the grid budging, her fingers cutting against some ragged steel. Looking up at Under, Wander said, "I'll kill them if they find us. I'll kill them." Under's lips parted, but no words came out. The face she made must have frightened him, though all he could see was her eyes. They must've been huge and stained red from the torment of this place.

Her fingers clenched around the grate. A little white flower grew in the cracks that separated the grate and the wall. A root creeped through by the flower's side, then more plants grew, each thickening and emerging from the cracks. With the plant's presence, the grate's attachment to the wall weakened.

With all her strength, Wander tore the grate from the wall. The spirits were left astonished.

"I guess you aren't human, either," Pitch said. "But I've never seen someone do that."

"Wander, what did you just do?" Under asked.

She looked at her own hands. "I thought only my sword could . . ." What did she know? Nothing since the wilds had been expected. Whatever she was, whatever was happening to her, she had no idea. Perhaps calling herself a witch to the humans was close to the truth.

The voices that came from the other halls were clear and close. Sara's familiar voice spoke, "The wings were more fragile than I expected. I'm going to need a doctor down here."

Wander turned around to see Masu still unconscious with a dark abyss of a hall beyond him. The torches further down looked like fireflies.

Under ducked his rainbow head into the open grate. "It's like a slide down. I don't know where it goes."

"I don't care," Pitch hissed. "The humans are coming. We have to go. Let's get the wings in first."

Wander looked at Masu's wingspan and back at the hole. "There is no way he'll fit."

"We'll make him fit," Pitch got up and grabbed one of Masu's wings, near where bone stuck out. "We'll break his wings a little more. They are already messed up anyway."

Wander was about to object when a voice boomed down the hall.

"WHO'S THERE?"

Three silhouettes blocked some of the distant torchlight.

Without any more time for hesitation, Wander and Under grabbed Masu's wings. Pitch pushed the right wing against Masu's body. The white and bloody bone fragments twisted away from each other. When Wander pushed on the left wing, she could feel a snap. Masu was so gone that he did not wake as they broke him more.

"THEY HAVE THE WINGS!" Sara shout echoed through the hall. "Shoot them!"

Arrows shot toward them. Under clutched the grate cover and held it up like a shield. The arrows caught in the metal grid.

Feet first, Wander and Pitch stuffed Masu into the hole. They crushed the wings into him, folding them over like flesh and feather blankets. Breath barely flowed from his lips. Then he fell away through the grate, gravity doing the rest of the work.

Realizing their arrows wouldn't work, the humans ran down the hall. Their silhouettes grew larger and larger, the footsteps beating.

Pitch leapt in next. Unlike Masu, he slid down easily as though he were buttered. Wander took the fox in her arms, sat on her butt, stuck her legs in the grate, and held her breath as she scooted down until she slid down a slippery slope.

Her body submerged into a thick, swampy pool. It felt disgustingly warm, gooey, and the smell made her retch. Luckily her head did not sink under. She had fallen into a tunnel with no light except for grids from other grates.

The fox struggled out of her grip and swam through the muck toward Pitch. His figure stood holding Masu's upper half out of the bitter muck. He shakily breathed, coughing from the vile stench and taste of the place.

A chickadee flew in and transformed into Under's rainbow form at Wander's side.

Above them, they could hear the humans.

"I'm going down!"

"Wait," Sara said, "we don't know who we're dealing with. They're all below, and we'd have to get down one by one. We'd be at a disadvantage. Find another entrance."

Pitch let out a frustrated sigh. "This is the worst day of my life."

Wander shifted through the piss and dung tainted water toward Pitch and Masu. Her hand moved over his mouth. His breath quivered. When she touched his cheek, his dark skin lacked warmth.

"He's near death," Pitch said. "There's no denying it. Aura will be your best hope if you want him to live. People from all over the world make journeys to seek her healing. You have me. I can take you to her. I am going to her, with or without any of you."

Wander's nostrils flared. Pitch could not see her raging eyes on the dark. She had no words to give him a clue. She feared that if she opened her mouth, all that she would conjure would be a scream or sob.

"Let's worry about getting out of these sewers first," Under said. "We're being chased now. Pitch, Wander, can you carry Masu on your own? I think I'll scout ahead as a bird and try to find an exit. You guys follow the right wall, and I'll follow the borders back to find you."

Wander ducked herself under Masu's left arm and held him up. It was easier to lift him in the putrid waters. Under wasted no time turning to a chickadee and flying off into the dark maze. Pitch put his free hand on the wall, and they followed the structure's lining. Masu's broken wings dragged behind them.

"At this rate, all of his wounds will get infected," Pitch said. "If you don't want to give him to Aura, we should just drop him here and not burden ourselves with dead weight."

Wander ignored him. The silence only lasted shortly though. He kept speaking. "If we escape this place, anyone will be able to smell us from a mile away."

When she burned and Masu disappeared, Wander thought she could not despair more. Now she would give so much for anything simple. Just a bed would be nice, it didn't have to be warm or have blankets. Naïve friends like Roslyn to smile for her. Any food, anything to get rid of her dizzying weakness. Masu to be safe, maybe gone, maybe even mind-controlled, but safe.

Chapter 13
The Emory Road

"The road to Dem is typically bustling, but not during wartime. During wartime, the gates close and do not open until they win." - Where the Stag Runs: A Guide to Deviant Customs

Warmth and the smell of salt rose into Wander's nose. Something heated pressed against her lips. Parting them, the taste of tomato soup made her insides melt.

"Are you okay?" Under's voice whispered. It was his voice, his actual voice from his body. She did not want him to change ever again. The relief from his voice was enough to pull her out of darkness. Opening her eyes, she saw Under's pale face, shaggy dark hair, and vague demeanor. He offered her another spoonful with a wood spoon.

As the comforting contents eased down her aching body, she remembered the vivid image of goosebumps on winged skin. "Masu—" She broke into a cough, some soup going down the wrong way.

Under put his hand on Wander's shoulder. "You fainted before I returned to the sewer. We made it out okay. We are a ways away from Fort Ben now. We are on Emory Road in deviant territory, toward Dem. You and Masu have high fevers from infection. Pitch just returned from a deviant village not too far from here.

He brought back supplies. I disinfected and bandaged up your knee the best I could. As for Masu, he is barely alive."

Wander shook her head, her mouth opened but she kept listening. "Pitch was right. Masu suffered hits to the head that a normal person can't see. His body is bleeding in places on the inside. We are taking care of what we can. Pitch stopped in a town and brought more medical supplies."

Wander leaned further against the tree behind her, as if to distance herself from the information. Her body was damp with chills. The fox slept curled at her side. Beyond Under, she could see Pitch's back and Masu's wing. "How do you know?" she asked. "How do you know his insides are bleeding?"

"I'm a shadow. I see a body, and I can tell. I see a lot in order to turn into someone, including their insides if I look long enough. Masu is not well. His head looks as though it's drowning."

Placing her palms down in dry grass, Wander attempted to get up. Under gently pushed her back. "You're not doing so well, either. Finish that food. There's a cup of water right there."

Wander took a heavy gulp. She felt as though her head were cooking, yet she shivered. Her throat welcomed the rush of water. She tilted her head back and raised the cup as she chugged down the all the water.

Placing the cup down, she rewrapped the undone veil around her chin and mouth. "Has Masu woken up at all?"

"No. He is barely functioning. I don't think he can hear us."

Pitch felt Masu's forehead. He took a wet cloth and dabbed it around Masu's body. Masu's wings hung from his back like broken branches on a tree. His skin had been graphed with diagonal and horizontal lines and spots of burn scars. Pitch paused from his care to swig a sip from a bottle. Under stuck a piece of grass

266

in-between his teeth and gnashed it lightly while watching with Wander.

Without breaking her stare at Masu, Wander said, "We're taking him to Aura, aren't we?"

"No. That's your call. I've only moved us in this direction because the humans would have more trouble getting to us."

Her eyes moved to Under. "Will he die otherwise?"

Under faced downward, his hair moving over his eyes, "To be honest, he could die before we even make it to Aura."

Wander squinted and leaned her head back against the tree trunk. In a fit of dizziness, she thought she might fall away from her own body. It took effort for her to summon the words. "Take him to her."

"Are you sure?"

A tear ran down her cheek, and she nodded. Without a life, there were no more chances. She could save him from Aura later. For now, she had to save him from what the humans had done.

Under looked over his shoulder. He withdrew the blade of grass from his mouth. "What would Masu want?"

"Who doesn't want to live?"

Under seemed so tired with the dark lines under his eyes. Maybe even he was sick. His back curled like an elder, his elbows on his knees. "There are things worse than death, you know. If I was mind-controlled like him, I know I'd want to die. I mean, what's the point of living when you can't control yourself? When you can't be you?"

"He can live and be himself. I am going to save him."

"Even if I was saved, I still might have wished I had died."

Wander forced herself to stand. She swayed, and Under twitched to help her, but her hand swished him away. "How could you say that? No, I'm doing whatever it takes to save him. If that means taking him to Aura, then fine!"

Under got up, towering over her. "Has it ever crossed your mind that you could be acting selfish? You are only caring about how you'll feel if he dies. If I was in his place, I would want you to kill me!"

"Since when have you decided this? When did you care? Where is this coming from?"

"From seeing him like this! Look at him! You would make him endure more pain and war so you can have him longer?"

Pitch stood up and approached them both. "What happened to this being her call? She's right, Aura should have him back. Aura is a healer above all things. She'll set him right. Besides, maybe she'll parlay with those who return him."

Under let out a sigh, his shoulders easing down. "Even so, I don't think we'd make it in time. Masu is near death. He'll die today if not within the hour. We can't move fast carrying him."

Pitch shook his head. "The wings will last. I had him drink a sylvina potion. It's an elixir that should hold back death, but only for a short time. Luckily a shaman lived in the village I visited. He recognized me, and I convinced him to give me elixir along with the medical supplies. I think he'll last long enough for me to run ahead and get help. If I can find someone with a bird, Aura can know her Wing's situation in a matter of moments. She'd meet you here. I'll give her your location. She'll come fast to save him, I'm sure of it, probably with the help of magic or an Arm for transportation. She has her ways."

Under shook his head. "You mean you're just going to run on ahead, and we'll just stay here? We'll just sit here and hope you don't just leave? Just play with our thumbs while you possibly set up a trap? Hope the brain-washing Queen comes to help us in time?"

Pitch folded his arms, unfazed. "Well, I know you'd rather not just let him die. If it helps to trust me, I am doing this for the Queen and my people more than I am doing it for you two. I'd rather not let the Wings, a part of my people's attack and defense, die."

"I believe you," Wander said. She rubbed her fingers against her forehead. "Go. Be quick."

"It was very fascinating to meet you both." He turned and took off running. Her eyes stayed on him, making sure he did not slow when he thought he was out of sight. He didn't, he kept on running until the young forest swallowed him up.

Already feeling a sense of relief, Wander turned to Under. "You should go. Aura can't control my mind, but she can yours."

"What if that changes? What if she does somehow control you? Myth could have lied to you."

"I'm not leaving Masu alone. I want to talk with Aura. I want to see if I can get her to set him free."

"Even if she couldn't control your mind, she can kill you."

"Myth said Aura is traditional. She follows a code and doesn't kill people."

"She can get someone else to kill you!"

"You're right. She could get you to kill me if you don't go!"

Under let out a frustrated breath. "I'm staying. I want to make sure you are safe."

"Why don't you trust me?"

"You're wind-born. You're just a kid! You trust too easily."

She realized she could not stop him. There was no way to make him go. "Just promise, whatever you do, don't betray me."

"I won't, Wander. You know I won't."

The surreal wait for Aura left them silent.

Wander sat next to Masu under the shade of the tree. She found peace only in the slivers of light across his dark skin that shined down from between the branches. The touch of his hand felt like a splash of river water, cold. His breath became softer than a whisper.

Once in a while his breath shook, and his teeth chattered, pain wrinkling his face. Wander took his chilled hand in hers. If he were to die in this moment, she could at least be with him. Pushing herself against his side, she placed her face against his shoulder to warm him.

The fox's snout pushed her arm up and crawled into her lap. Maybe it envied how she treated Masu. Remembering the day it licked her tears in the ashes of the Emerald Wilds, Wander petted the fox. Through it all, the animal understood her pain and stayed. Now, as Masu may be taking his last breaths, she needed the comfort of the fox's breaths against her folded legs.

Under sat a couple feet away, his knee bouncing. He stared at the earth, avoiding the scene of Wander and Masu.

"What have you done?"

Wander and Under's heads yanked up. A woman tumbled from the bushes. Her thin gray dress reminded Wander of spider and butterfly nests. Her dark hair nearly hit the blond grass. Large panicked purple eyes, quivering rouge lips. "Get away from him!" she said.

Its fur standing on its end, the fox jumped out of her lap and fled behind Under. Wander had no such privilege to say a goodbye or sorry. Caught in the urgency, she crawled away from Masu.

Aura's sandaled feet rushed to Masu's side. She reached to touch him, but flinched at a distance from his wing. Shaking her head, she sat on her knees across from him. Her smooth hand caressed his cheek and moved hair out from his eyes. For the first time all day, Masu's eyes opened a little, showing slits of their red color. The deviant queen enclosed him, her lips pressing on his forehead. He shut his eyes, the rise and fall of his chest deepened.

Turning around, Aura faced Wander with eyes filled with profound emotion. Tears smeared down, and she shook with wrath. "How could you?" she asked. "You're supposed to be on his side!"

Wander backed up until she bumped into Under. His hands gently held her shoulders. "It wasn't her fault," he said. "The humans tricked us. They imprisoned her and tortured him. There was nothing she could do."

Aura rubbed the tears out of her eyes, and she stood up.

"Are you going to help him?" Wander asked.

"It will take time, but he will be fine. Better than fine. I won't let him out of my sight again. But before that, I have to deal with you. I know what you're doing, and we're ending this now."

"I just want Masu free."

"Your actions last time we met prove otherwise. I offered you a deal, that fox for Masu. You didn't just reject the deal, you killed your friend who tried to help you."

"What is she talking about?" Under asked.

Aura crossed her arms, her smooth nails glossing against her skin. "Of course she wouldn't tell you. This isn't the first time we met. Last time she had a human friend with her. Ethan right? I told her to give me the fox, and I'd give her Masu. She wouldn't take the deal. When Ethan took the fox and tried to give it to me, she stabbed him right through the heart and ran away."

Under let go of Wander. "Is that true?"

She had never wanted him to know. She never wanted to even hear it, think about it, or speak of it ever. That night should not have happened. It should not have existed. She spoke quickly. "I wasn't thinking! Ethan acted strange, and he was scaring me!"

Aura shook her head. "Masu obviously isn't so important to you. You won't even give me a simple animal for his return."

Her head pounded. "He's more than an animal! I need him."

"And why is that? Do you not hear yourself? Do you know what's happening?"

Wander bent down, her head aching like a heavy stone rolled around her skull.

"Wander!" Under touch her shoulder and checked on her.

"Even now you are struggling," Aura said. "You are fighting for the freedom of my Wings, but who is going to save you?"

"What are you doing to her?" Under hissed.

"I can't do anything to her, never could. Do you want to know why? It's because she is already a puppet for someone else!"

Aura let her words sink in. Wander hugged herself and backed away from Under. She could not look at him or anyone.

"After our first meeting, Wander, I stayed awake in the night wondering why I could not get into your head. I searched all our records to try and find how a human could somehow touch spirits. I had weapon specialists try to determine how a human could wield a spirit blade. I asked the elementals for all their knowledge on wind-born humans, or spirits that bled red. Then it came upon me that the answer was obvious. I should have known from the beginning of how you have such abilities. It was that you are the opposite of me."

Aura pointed at the fox that now stood between Wander and Under. "It is no secret that I drink the blood of guardians for my power. Guardians have the power to heal, haunt, and control the hearts and minds of humans and spirits. I get a fraction of that power, which is why I drink from multiple bodies. My Wing's mission was to find me a guardian in the first place. That is why I sent him to the Emerald Wilds six years ago. He never returned, I lost control of him, and he forgot who he was. That fox, the guardian of the Emerald Wilds, did that to him. I misjudged how powerful the guardian was. It saw that he came to take its life for me to drink, so it took control over him. It made him forget and made him a prisoner of the forest.

"After so much searching, I decided to just burn the whole forest down. The guardian lost everything, save for one small thing . . . you. I've dominated countless guardians for my magic, but you, you have been dominated by a guardian for yours. That creature is using you as a tool for revenge. It wants you to kill me. It doesn't care about your goals; it's just using them to disguise its true intentions. Guardians care for nothing but themselves. That's why you killed Ethan, isn't it? The fox made you do it. That's probably why you've done a lot of things, even probably why you think certain things.

"At least I'm ethical with my powers. Guardians however, they're wild. I make my Arms stop feeling emotions, speaking, and possessing memories as a mercy to them. The fox doesn't lend you that, so you wander around like a tormented ghost. After finding out the truth, I really pity you. Maybe you don't even care about the Wings, and it's all just the fox's trick to push you toward me."

"You're lying!"

"I know for a fact that the fox is too weak to do much. The Emerald Wilds were the base of its power. You are the corner to which I pushed."

"Under, I—"

Aura spoke over her, "What do you call my Wings? Masu? The man you thought was Masu never existed. It was just a persona the fox gave him to keep him in the forest. Any decision he made, what he said, any love you think he had for you, you best forget it. He was hypnotized to be that way. It was not him. You call me the enemy, but you're just wishing he were in a different prison. You fight for freedom, not realizing how imprisoned you were in the first place."

Wander lurched forward, her hands tightened into fists. Under clasped her from behind and she squirmed, her legs kicking at Under's. Her throat ached with each word she screamed. "YOU'RE LYING! IT WAS REAL!!"

"I know the real man. If I set him free, the Wings would not know you or himself. He would be like his mothers and fated to possess an evil soul. In my controlling him, I set him free of that awful fate."

Wander's face felt as though it were red from the heat and tears. She shook her head. If Under would let her go, she'd run. She would run and not look back. She could not fight or reason this away. Run, she had to run. It did not matter where.

"Let's give her the fox."

The hauntingly familiar words reached Wander's ears, but a hissing rolled in her head. Her entire body tensed up. Under promised he wouldn't betray her. This was a repeat of Ethan. That's what happened. Aura must have mind-controlled Ethan. Now she was doing the same to Under.

"No," she whispered. "Under, you promised not to do this."

"You're mind-controlled!"

"She's lying!"

"It explains everything that you've been asking yourself!"

"She's controlling your mind so that it makes sense. Trust me!" Wander wrenched herself from his arms and stumbled forward. The fox immediately set itself behind her feet. Instinctively, she reached behind her back to the empty air. No sword.

"It all makes sense, Wander!" Under said. "Remember when you explained how you got your burns? You saved the fox from the fire! You said you weren't thinking, but to go through all that agony and remain there . . . you had to be controlled! And you killed a friend? It made you kill, didn't it? That's also why you fight so well."

Wander shook her head. "Let's leave, Under. We can talk about this later, after we get away from Aura." She dipped down, scooping the fox into her arms. She sprinted for the woods. A weight knocked her forward. Her arms threw the fox. As her chin hit the ground, her teeth clenched against her tongue in a gush of blood. The fluffy black tail vanished into a bush.

Twisting her head on the ground, Wander saw a paw larger than her fists against her upper arms. Fading to black and shrinking, the paw turned to a hand scrunching her skin.

Aura walked over. Her hand moved up for a robin to land on. Bringing the bird to her lips she said, "Hunt the guardian." The bird fell away to a shadow on the ground and rose up to a large bodied cat. Wander never saw a cat so thin and tall. The blonde fur's speckles seemed unusual, as the small cats in the streets never had spots so small and specific. The great cat took off in a run, each step like a leap across a river.

Under got off Wander's back. Sitting up, she saw a look of horror plastered on him. Aura's Horns, Red, emerged from the bushes and grabbed Wander's wrists. She forced her to stand.

It was a trap. The Arms, the Shadow, and Horns had been in the forest this whole time.

"Under!" Wander shouted. He had to see now that this was wrong. Aura was wrong. This was a setup. But Under did not budge. He remained frozen, eyes wide like he saw something the rest of them didn't.

"Let's go to the palace," Aura said to Wander. "If you struggle, I won't be able to heal my Wings so soon."

Wander tried to coil her wrists away from the Horn's grip. Aura's Horns smashed her skull into Wander's. Dazed in a blur of dizziness, Wander found herself getting led away. Her stability regained enough to turn around, she saw Aura and Under left with each other.

Chapter 14
Dem

"Dem's Palace is known for its murals. History, culture, and battles scatter every wall with no frame to limit it. It's beautiful and daunting all at once." - Travels of Manger

Wander's mouth flooded with a metallic taste, and her tongue swelled, feeling more like a lump of meat rather than a part of her. Hands upon her shoulders forced her down. Her butt hit what felt like a wooden platform, her tailbone grinding against the flat surface. Her wrists unbuckled from their chains. Sharp nails dug into her skin as her hands were pulled backward. With the click of a lock, her wrists could no longer separate, hugging around a plank at her back. Fingers attended to her ankles, tightening them with rope to chair legs. Footsteps smacked against ceramic tiles and disappeared.

Blindfolded, Wander could not determine anything about the room. It smelled of paint and dust. She did not dare speak. Aura was skilled with words and would only drown out Wander in doubt.

A clicking of steps came forward from the right. A thumb tucked under the blindfold and pulled it up. Wander squinted at the sudden light. Under a glass ceiling, the light shined and danced as though she sat at the bottom of a pool of water. A large glass table lay out in front of her; she could see the white tiles underneath.

The walls were painted in shades of green and violet, like rolling hills with a purple sky. A woman with horns like a ram lay by a tree. In her arms, a hornless babe. A horned man sat feet away, his face with blue smudges turned downward.

The human castle kept their art in frames but the deviants had none. The amount of wall was the only limit. There was more, and Wander's eyes followed the path of painted narratives.

Her eyes met with Chant's. The elemental stood cross armed in the corner of the room, one of her feet up against the mural. Her flowing bright hair moved like a candle, but it also reminded Wander of how hair flowed when underwater. She wore an orange dress that ended at her knees with layers like flower petals. Gold bangles glittered around her ankles.

Aura walked around the table. She had changed clothes to wear a thin shawl over a gray gown. Wander saw the beginning of her breasts, like two eggs peaking from a nest. Her gown dragged across the tiles like tail feathers. Her hair framed her face elegantly, like a mask complimented by silk layers and waves.

"Well, Wander, even as prepared as I was, you managed to surprise me," Aura said. "A shadow in your company was certainly something I did not expect. The moment I touched his mind, I saw into his history."

The corners of the chair began to cut into Wander's wrists. She attempted to adjust herself, twisting her arms. "You made him turn against me just like you did with Ethan."

"He made the choice to believe the truth all on his own. I just gave him a little push so you wouldn't escape."

"Where is he?"

"He will have a private execution tomorrow morning. Do not worry though. He will not suffer. With my power, I can make sure someone is as at ease without a care in the world. He was a little hesitant at first, but he gave in once he started to feel comfortable and relaxed."

Wander wanted to twist like a worm in the sun. "You're horrid."

"I'm only horrid to my enemies."

"Under has never hurt anyone!"

"You know nothing. Shape shifters once thought they could rule the world. It's the responsibility of the deviant royalty to keep them down. No matter how pure of heart one is, they can change, and I cannot let them exist for that chance. Think of it like killing a snake before it grows into a man-eater."

Aura leaned forward, a long dark lock falling from her shoulder. "But don't worry. I'm not going to kill you. I wish to make you an offer. Wind-borns like you are not so different from us deviants before we won our freedom from the horned beings. Wind-borns are usually taken, raised, and sold as slaves to blood-borns or spirits. You are exactly the same as other humans save for how you came into this world. We deviants have a similar story. We were the same to the horned beings but we were treated differently all because we were born without horns. Hence the name they called us: deviants. We had no rights and were sold into slavery. We were treated so differently that everyone became convinced we were of another race.

"I want to give you a chance, the chance to be a part of the future of humanity. Once I kill the fox, your mind will be free. You could work with me. You could gather the wind-borns and rid yourselves of human identity. Then I'll kill the blood-borns and you could be an ambassador for your people. They can live in peace."

"With the fox dead, you'd just control me."

"I don't control Chant. The elementals became an ally of their own free will. We had a fair bargain of resources."

Wander looked away to the left wall: a mural of rain and shadows. "I can't feel myself being controlled by the fox. So how does Chant know if she is controlled or not?" Her eyes shifted to the elemental princess. "

Aura did not waver. "I would die before I broke my word to the elementals."

"If I may cut in, Aura." Chant set her leg down and walked toward Wander. "We have solved nearly every mystery but one. It's the reason I'm here. I want to see what's under the mask. It's very rude for your guest to hide her face from you."

Aura's purple eyes scanned Wander and ended in a focus on her cloaked face. "You're right, Chant."

Chant's hand hooked into Wander's veil. Her nails, sharp like claws, raked against Wander's scalp as she jerked the veil down. At the first sight of Wander's branded skin, Chant drew in a fast breath. Suddenly gentle, she unwrapped the rest of the veil like a delicate package.

The dark cloth fell to Wander's neck and slipped down to the floor. Aura and Chant stared at her with owl-like eyes. Whatever they expected, it was not the burns. She wished she didn't see it, but her face was reflected in the glass table. She had a corpse face, cheeks like crumbled paper, lips like chewed and spat out meat.

"Ancestors . . ." Aura looked away.

Wander turned away as well. She squeezed her eyes shut, wanting to forget what she just saw. She wanted the face that reflected in the Emerald Wilds' river long ago, smooth, smiling, and bright.

"This is from that day," Chant said. "When I set the Emerald Wilds aflame, I saw a girl run away. I didn't know it was you."

Wander kept silent.

"I could heal you," Aura said. "If you take my earlier offer, you could have healthy skin, a home, leadership, and save all the wind-borns."

"No."

"Forget it, Aura," Chant said. "All this girl cares about is the Wings. She doesn't think about things like right and wrong."

"Chant, could you give us some privacy?"

The question seemed to have caught Chant off guard. "Uh . . . yes." When she opened the door to go out, Wander saw that outside it was dark.

Aura placed her palms on the glass table. Her usually sweet-toned voice became deeper. "I told you before. The man you want to save does not exist. The Masu you knew in the enchanted land was just a persona the fox gave him to keep him imprisoned. If you freed him from me, he would not know you. You don't know anything about the real man like I do. He would not be the man you wanted.

"His mothers, Morning and Sky, were monsters. They planned to take everything from the deviants. We were an innocent nation. We had peace since the War of Shadows. My mother, father, and little brother all were murdered just to be used in those bird spirits' dark ritual! I was just a teenager when I had to call a war on them. Morning was the worst one. She had the dark magic and cursed my sister into an unending pain! She used the blood of my people to raise the dead for an army to take the world! Your precious Masu was going to be that dark nation's king!"

"Winged beings couldn't be all so bad."

"The first humans were enslaved, brainwashed to worship winged beings as gods. Nearly every winged being home had human slaves that were mistreated. They saw you as animals."

"You weren't there when Masu raised me. He was nothing like—"

"He was hypnotized! You weren't there when he was a child. I raised him! After his parents died and we won the war, he was taken to me to become an Arm. He inherited the same dark magic as Morning. He was fated to become just as evil as she. Dark magic does that to the user. It corrupts the soul. Luckily it hadn't fully developed, so I numbed it away with my power." Aura stopped talking. Her face had become a light shade of red from raising her voice. Wander swore she could see the deviant's heartbeat in her chest. Small shadows passed through the room as a flock of birds flew over the glass ceiling.

Regaining some calm, Aura tucked a dark lock of hair behind her ear. Her eyes drifted. "I love him, you know. But when I first saw him, a little boy with downy, feathered wings, I was scared. He had the same evil red eyes, dark hair, and wings as his black mage mother. I had to control his mind and make him my Arm, but I was scared. I tried to control his mind with so much fear in my heart. I expected him to attack me, kill himself, or scream and thrash around. He didn't. He gave in immediately. There was not a single struggle.

"All my life I had minds push against my will. It was like being put into a room with a bunch of wild, violent, and untrusting dogs and being asked to tame them. During the war, winged beings would try to kill themselves or me before falling under my influence. I was only a young girl, and I got so scared. I felt like a villain, and I was told that was just part of being a queen.

"My Wings changed me. I could make him feel anything I want, do anything and I would not feel guilty, because I knew deep down he liked it. With his parents dead, his people gone, he had nothing left. I offered his heart healing, and he took it without hesitation. I love him because he accepted what I've done to him."

Wander looked down at her lap.

"Well, we can continue our discussion after your mind is free. For now, I'll have you locked up in the Painted Prison."

With perfect timing, Aura's Horns entered the room.

She released Wander's legs from the chair. Her wrists were untied around the chair back and retied to her back.

Every word said within the past day pulsated in her mind. She paired everything Aura said with evidence. Under was right, it all did make sense.

The fox was a guardian. She was currently controlled by the guardian. She burned her entire body to protect it and killed Ethan to save it from Aura. If she had a sword, would she have killed Under? How much of her was actually her? Was it her choice to keep the fox, or was it the fox making her? The concept overwhelmed her.

The guardian was using her to kill Aura? She was not so sure. She set on a quest to kill Aura because Myth said that was the best way to free Masu. The fox seemed to just be in the background since then. Maybe Aura was just paranoid.

Masu was controlled by the guardian. The idea fit with why he had no memories from before, also why he would not leave. The fox controlling him would also explain his bizarre amount of knowledge of the forest. Did that mean the fox did not control her until the fire when it lost Masu? She had no knowledge of the forest. The forest tried to kill her innumerable times.

She realized that during her time in the forest, it was Masu who could touch her, not the other way around. The fox's magic let him touch humans. During the fire, when the fox took over her mind, it must have given her the magic to touch spirits.

With the evidence aligned, Wander could possibly accept everything Aura said as true, save for one thing: that what she and Masu had wasn't real. That couldn't be true. That life they lived together could not just be irrelevant. Aura had to be wrong.

The prison cell of Aura's felt preferable to the one the humans had stuffed her in. The cell presented itself more like a bedroom with marble floors, a mattress, sheet, and flattened pillow. Wander was grateful for just being able to stand up and pace around.

Aura's Horns even untied her before throwing her inside the room. After the door shut, Wander tried the doorknob to find it was, of course, locked.

The room lacked any window or crack. Wander imagined herself in the tightest weaved basket with only candles standing around with no pattern, like a scatter of stars. How long had they burned?

Caresses, splatters, and notes of paint caked the four walls. Buckets of gray, red, and black were provided, giving the room an aura of death and danger. Had past prisoners decorated these walls? Why were they invited the opportunity?

Wander so wished she could read what prisoners of the past had scribbled on the walls. The room provided limited entertainment. Wander could make out a black sun, a red fish, and possibly a dog, cat, or donkey painted around the bed.

Under could not save her this time. With each moment, the fox's control over her could end, and she'd be at the mercy of Aura's mind-control.

Moving to the back corner of the room, Wander charged at the door. Her body slammed shoulder first. Her right side beat itself into the wood. She did not even feel the door rock with her force. She tried to run faster her second time, crashing even harder. That time she let out a cry as her body bruised from the impact. Clutching the silver knob with both her hands, she tried to use all her strength to turn it left and right. The attempt resulted in sore, red palms. She pulled next, throwing all her weight backward.

Putting her face to the cold floor, Wander tried to see beyond the door from the small space under. The space was no bigger than an ant, and she saw only darkness.

She thought of calling for help, but the sound of her own voice in this room would haunt her. The silence would become stronger with each sound she made with no one to answer.

I have to stay me. Wander could not leave, so she decided to endure. Having used all her remaining energy on the door, she crawled onto the mattress. The pillow had been flattened. Her hand clutched at Masu's feather attached to her wrist. Placing both hands on her chest, she curled into a ball. She would not allow herself to sleep for fear she could wake up different.

Masu changed, even when he wanted to find Wander. Aura had taken control.

Eventually Wander could not stop touching her own face. Her fingers dragged their nails across her wretched skin, wishing she could tear it off with ease like skin peeling after sunburn. She wondered how she lived shameless with such a face before she covered herself up. She clawed at her face until her nails were lined with blood. Her lips bled, then the creases of her nose, and lastly her chin.

Stopping herself, Wander dipped her hand in a bucket of red paint, and it felt thicker than she imagined. She had never touched wet color before. She thought color would feel warmer than water, but instead her hand felt as though it sunk in mud.

Pulling her hand out, she smeared the paint at the bedside. As her hand slid down, she sighed.

Just then the doorknob rattled.

Wander sat up, her back pressed into the corner.

First the door cracked and an eye peeked in. "Wander?"

Her head raced. The visitor spoke, so she couldn't be an Arm. Maybe Wander could overwhelm her and push past to freedom. The thought seemed ideal, and she stumbled up, prepared to charge.

A shadow stretched on the walls as the short figure stepped in. Her hair was bunched up into a low but tight bun. Brown slippers scooted on the floor with a deep green dress flowing after. The identity was obvious when Wander saw her eyes: a single purple eye on the right and a black diamond-shaped eye patch on the left.

"Myth?"

Myth's teeth clenched as though stepping inside caused her pain. "Are you alright?"

Her face warmed and she shook her head.

Myth grabbed her wrist and tugged her forward. "I'm getting you out of here. You have to save the guardian before my sister catches it. It's your only hope of saving Masu."

Wander pulled away and stepped back.

Myth scowled, "What's wrong?"

She could do what Myth said and save the fox. Then it would continue to control her. She'd kill Aura, free Masu. Then what? Aura proved to Wander that they were never free. What would freedom do to them? Would Masu be evil? What would she be?

"I don't know what I'm doing anymore." Myth stepped forward, and Wander backed up.

"I don't know who I am! I don't know what's real anymore!" she cried. Her teeth gnashed together with the words. "The guardian has been controlling my mind all this time. Same with Masu. We're both the same. I'm the same. These aren't my thoughts, my feelings, or my goals! I never even knew Masu, did I?" Her breath shifted in and out so fast she thought she could explode. All the memories she held dear twisted. "It's all been a lie. There is—"

Myth's hand slapped her across the right cheek. The force reminded Wander of tripping and her face smacking against the earth. Falling silent, she touched her cheek and gave Myth her unbroken attention.

"You just want to sit here and wait until my sister takes your mind?" Myth said. "Even if everything is a lie, so what? You think that's a reason to stop everything?" Her last words were feral, her lips curled like a dog. "If I were you, I would die to fight. After what you've been through, I would want to tear the entire fucking world apart!"

Though she could not shake off the misery, Wander slowly nodded.

"Good. Then let's get you out of this place. I have keys to an underground passageway. No guards. It's a straight route to the outer edges of the city. My sister mentioned the hunt taking place in the Sax Woodlands."

Myth opened the door wider. The arched hallway possessed a brighter dark, the sort of night that turned blue from moonlight. Wander followed the border of the right wall, her hand trailing against a mural of fields and dancing figures.

There were other doors, each with a symbol painted in black.

"What is this place?"

"The Painted Prison," Myth stepped on the balls of her feet as she walked down the hall. "It is where we locked up those whose minds are to be broken. We give them a place to sleep and paint in order to make mind-control easier. Minds weaken in sleep. It's the same when they concentrate on something other than themselves. My sister also tests how much control she has over them by making them paint different things."

The opposite end of the hall opened out to a glass-roofed courtyard with a view of a nearly full moon. A stream trickled through and past a tree heavy with wisteria. The sweet smell of the light purple petals could take Wander home if she just closed her eyes. The marble ended on a dirt path.

Myth flinched and rubbed her side. Trying to ignore some sort of physical pain, she moved forward. "Let's hurry. I chose this time to help you escape because the guards are switching up their posts."

"Wait," Wander stopped where the dirt path met the marble. "What about Under?"

"Forget him. I warned you about keeping him along."

"I'm not leaving him!"

"Finding him will mean going to the other side of the palace. There will be many guards, and I don't have the authority to waltz around the halls with prisoners. Even if we made it to him, he will be in my sister's control and will not come with us."

"I am not leaving without him."

Myth walked back to Wander. "I get it. He's your friend. But is a friend really worth the possibility of failing? Is he worth losing your mind? Dooming Masu? All of humankind getting killed?"

"I'm not sure about many things now," Wander said. Her hands clenched. "But Under is someone I am sure about."

The shadows around Myth's eye thickened and her mouth hung open. She must have thought Wander to have already lost her mind. "I see." She regained some composure. "If you are willing to lose so much over one spirit, then fine." Her hand dove into her cleavage, and she pulled out a rusted key. "Forgive me if I do not wish to do the same. Here," she dangled the key in front of Wander, "this key unlocks a closet in the storage room to the southeast. Use it if you become wiser and decide to leave. I am having no part in helping you find the shadow. He is in a guarded guest room, I'm sure. Probably locked as well, and I have no such key. Maybe only Aura herself has it.

"I'll admit that though his mind is controlled, he may not be lost. Some people can easily snap out of my sister's magic if they've only just been introduced to it."

Wander took the key, the rust scraped against her nails.

"Good luck," Myth said as she turned and strode away in the moonlight.

Staring at the key, Wander realized her hand was shaking. Her fingers curled shut and tucked it in her pants pocket. Crossing the garden, she entered another hallway that seemed the same as the last, except the murals became birds in the sky. Passing large doors as tall as trees with diamond-shaped locks, Wander could not imagine what lay beyond them. The maze-like palace dizzied her with courtyards of water, flowers, halls of paint, and locked doors. She began to think she walked in circles, having taken both rights and lefts.

"HEY!"

Wander flinched, and her feet stopped on the marble floors of one of the halls. To her left was a mural of flames and the right, waves of water. The forceful voice echoed from behind. Balling her hands into fists, she burst into a run. Whatever the guard shouted, it sounded more like the roar coming for her in her panic. Her feet reached the soil of another garden room. She swung left into another hall. Every door could be locked, so she didn't dare try them. She wanted to scream, as though anyone would hear and help her.

She reached a crossroads, and another guard appeared on her left. The sound of steel rung as he drew a sword. Wander twisted to the right and sprinted. She tightly shut her eyes and reopened them to the abysmal marble path. The murals became screaming blurs. More feet began to gather behind her. They gathered like a pack of wolves in the wilds. She could hear them shout to each other. Passing through a gold gate, she tore into a garden with a sky unblocked by glass. Violet, blue, pink, and many white stars shined like holes on a curtain. Vines glazed over the murals.

More trees had been placed within than in the earlier gardens. It almost seemed like a forest. Every tree's trunk had a snowy hue and orange leaves. She twisted around one of the trees and put her back to the trunk. She could still hear jingling of the guards in their armor. She sunk down into a crouch and crawled deeper into the forest-garden.

"She's definitely in here. Check everywhere."

Wander touched the white bark of one of the trees. It felt warm, as though it breathed and pulsed inside with blood. Nearly bonking herself into a low branch, she stared at a cluster of human-shaped leaves. What *was* this place?

She tensed as a boot stepped out from behind a tree, nearly crushing her hand. She scooted away, picked a stick off the ground, and threw it across the garden. All the guards began to move toward the sound. Taking the chance, Wander carried herself away with light steps. As she moved, she grabbed another stick from the ground.

She went straight as far as she could until seeing the back of one of the guards. Before he could turn around, she backtracked and took a right. Her vision blurred, and her body swayed. There was only so much running she could manage. She could picture herself in a bed, safe, a blanket covering up to her shoulders.

Unable to run anymore, Wander walked with heavy breath. Eventually, after innumerable hallways, chases, and close calls, Wander finally got somewhere promising. She peeked around a corner to see two guardswomen, complete with stag crested shields and spears crossed in front of the door they secured. The walls were painted with deep green vines, red roses, and dragonflies. Myth had said where Under was kept would be watched over. Under could be beyond those tall doors. Wander gritted her teeth. Leaning against the wall, she rubbed her face. Her body shook with anxiety.

Sucking in all her fear, she walked out into the hall. The guards clearly saw her, their heads turned, then their bodies. Wander's knees bent as she set off into a sprint toward the armed lookouts, both her hands gripping tightly to the stick she picked up.

One guardswoman ran up to meet Wander, and her spear thrust forward. The weapon advanced farther than Wander imagined. Attempting to back away, she slipped on the marble floor. A second spear came down from the other guard, piercing her leg.

Wander sat up, grabbing the spear impaling her with one hand. In her other hand she drove the stick up into the guard's left eyeball. Blood poured down her cheek as she screamed and staggered back. With both hands, Wander pulled the spear from her thigh. While the skewered guard twisted and called out in agony, the other watched in a moment of shock. Wander scooted backward, blood trailing from her injured leg.

Using the spear for balance, Wander got herself up in time for the intact guardswoman's attack. The guard plunged her spear forward. Wander did the same, immediately falling off balance. By her falling, the guard's spear missed her. Wander's spear lurched through the woman's lower abdomen.

Landing on her face and hands, Wander lifted her head to see the guard collapse. She dropped her spear and her hands shakily worked their way to the one impaling her. Taking the dropped spear, Wander sat up. She thrust down at the woman's neck and ended her life.

Wander hobbled to the half-blind woman. The stick still stuck out of her eye. She cried from the pain. Perhaps the stick went even past her eye. Stepping to the guard's blindside, Wander lightly set her injured leg on the floor. She pointed the spear tip toward the guardswoman's neck and pushed forward. The guard fell and more blood pooled and ran through the cracks of the marble floor.

Wander fell to her knees. She spat on the floor, feeling like she could vomit. Her breathing began to squeak through her mouth. Tears, drool, blood—she could taste, feel, and smell it all.

Crawling on all fours, she got to the door and turned the knob to a disheartening stop. It was locked. The keyhole was eye level with her.

She skulked to the bodies. Her quivering hands checked their pockets. One had a locket, the other had a filled water skin, but neither had a key. "No . . ." Wander's hands moved to their belts. She pulled a knife from a sheath and looked at the door. A dizzy spell fuzzed her vision. Dangling her head down, she waited for the unsteadiness to pass. Making it to the door on her hands and knees, Wander slipped the knife between the door and frame. She wiggled the weapon up until she hit what she guessed was the lock. She had no idea how such devices worked, but perhaps they could be cut.

Pulling the knife out, she placed it back in above the lock. She heaved down with all her might, but what was in the way did not cut. Maybe it was like thick rope and the cut would slowly work through. With this in mind, Wander jiggled the knife back and forth while dragging down.

She heard a click and the knife slipped through. Without a moment's waste, she turned the gold knob and threw the door open. "Under?"

She scuttled into the dark room with no windows. Closing the door behind her, she leaned back. Her free hand covered the stab wound in her thigh. Blood gushed onto her palm. Staring into the dark she called out, "Under?" Her leg throbbed as she crawled forward. As her eyes adapted to the dark, she saw furniture. She made out a single bed in the far left corner with its frames holding up curtains. She crept to the bed, her pained leg dragging.

The bed lay neat and empty, not even a single ripple in the quilt. Her breath snagged on a sob. If Under was not here, she did not know if she could find the strength to leave with her injury. There must be something that could help her.

Turning to the bed stand, she pulled out a drawer. Her hand dove inside and felt around. She withdrew a packet as big as her thumb. Shakily opening the envelope, her fingers brushed on matches. Wander's eyes dashed to an unlit candle on the bed stand's surface. Picking out a match, she slashed the end against the envelope. She squinted in the moment the little stick burst into light. She spread the flame to the candle and blew the match out. She lifted the plate the candle sat upon and turned to the darkness of the room; it all dimly lit up.

Her heart jumped at the sight of a figure in an armchair on the opposite end of the room. "Under!" She recognized his raggedy coat and wilted appearance. His dark hair blocked her from seeing his eyes.

With the candle in hand, Wander slunk across the marble floor. Reaching Under's feet, she put the flame up to see his face. Every muscle in his body seemed loosened, his face slackened, his eyes closed, his arms heavily resting at his side—all completely relaxed as if he were enjoying the best sleep in the world like Aura described. Wander grabbed his knee. "Under!"

No reaction, not even the twitch of an eyelid. She set the candle on the floor. With the aid of the armchair, Wander managed to stand up. Her hands clutched at the collar of Under's coat and shook with all her might. "Please, please, please! You've got to wake up!"

His head fell back and forth with her shakes. When she let go his eyes cracked open. She adjusted her position so her head was in his view. "Aura's going to kill you if you don't get up! C'mon!"

His eyes drifted shut. "No!" She grabbed his arm and pulled. His body slumped forward like a limp doll's. She was half his weight. There was no possibility of dragging him out of the palace.

Pushing him back on the chair, she took a moment to think.

Using the wall to prop herself up, she limped out into the hallway. Bending by one of the guardswoman's bodies, she picked up the filled water skin. Slower, she made it back to Under.

Standing over him, she twisted off the cap of the water skin. She took a sip before pouring the entire thing over Under's head. The water sunk down through his hair. His body tensed. Seeing his eyelids lift was like the break of breath after nearly drowning.

"Under!" she got on her knees to look up at him.

He blinked at her.

"Can you hear me?"

He moaned and rubbed the side of his head.

"How do you feel?"

"Cold. Tired." He looked as though he'd fall back into a trance at any moment so Wander kept gently shaking him.

"Aura controlled your mind. We're in her palace."

Under squinted at her, his mind lost and confused. He opened his mouth to say something but hesitated. Memory and realization washed over him and his brown eyes went wide. "I . . . I attacked you."

"You didn't hurt me. This was from a guard outside. I killed them to get to you. Aura separated us and put me in a prison. Myth saved me. I have the key to get us out of here." Wander pulled the key out of her pocket and handed it to Under.

Getting out of the chair, Under sat on the floor with her. He had yet to speak without sleepiness in his voice. "The fox, where is it?"

"Myth told me that Aura is hunting it down. She wants me to save it."

Under seemed to wake more. "Was what Aura said true? The guardian has been controlling you?"

Wander nodded. "Masu, too, while he was in the forest."

Under sighed and shook his head.

"I don't know what to do," Wander said. "I'm having trouble believing what is real. My feelings may not be my own, or thoughts, or goals. Masu and I, we were just tools that the guardian played with."

"No," Under protested. "I'm sure that's not completely true."

Wander looked away to hide her crinkling face. Her throat tightened.

"Just the fact that you're confused and upset proves that's not true. Those feelings aren't the guardian, that's you."

He was right. She looked at his kind face and nodded. She fell forward and wrapped her arms around him in a tight hug. "I'm so glad you're okay." The smell of sewage still clung to his clothes. "We should escape this place and rest somewhere safe. Then we can plan what to do next." Wander stood up.

Suddenly her legs fell out from under her. Her hands catching her fall, she felt pain jolt through the tips of her fingers and up her arms. She let out a heavy breath.

Under's hands wavered around her, "Are you alright?"

Her entire body went cold, but every movement conjured a burning agony. Her skin felt like a leather cocoon to be torn off. What little contents her stomach contained swished around uncomfortably, making her insides ache for them to escape. She hugged herself and curled into a shivering ball.

"Wander, say something!"

She shook her head. One word and her itching throat would expand and jiggle like a tickling, fiery feather. She wanted to claw it out; even drowning in water would not satisfy the scorching in her gullet. Her fingers tore at her arms. Even to cry from the pain caused more pain. She did not remember agony like this since she woke in that forsaken bed after the fire had consumed her body.

Under crouched to her bent over body. "Are you. . . ?" He trailed off, realizing she was in no condition to speak. He put his hand to her forehead.

She blinked to let tears clear her vision. Under must have thought the weeping was from the pain. It was not that. She realized this was it: The fox had released her. All her fear of losing herself came to this one moment. She could still remember the smell of wildflowers, the sting of picking at her own scars, and the taste of fresh fruit served in a wood bowl.
There were no gaps. She still remembered Masu, the touch of his wings at night and his voice calling her

beyond the trees. She could still recall Roslyn's face peeking into her room, Ethan's bitter laugh, and Ms. Flinsler's unflinching face at the word *Mom* leaving Wander's lips.

This was the real her but weaker, much weaker.

"Hang on. I got you," Under shook his hesitation away. He scooped up her trembling body. She shut her eyes and pressed her head near his armpit. Her breath absorbed into his coat and warmed her nose.

Under carried her through the palace, sometimes stopping, other times turning around and standing still, Wander felt the guardian's release deepen. As she explored her own memories, everyone and everything suddenly became more precious. A sense of extreme loss hit her. In Under's coat, she let out a muffled sob. She had awoken from a trance. All this time she wandered with a sense of surrealism as though in some dream. Now she woke in a crisping, crumbled form with her living tragedy. She began to hyperventilate.

She wanted to start over with this warm heart. Instead of wandering away from Heathcliff, she'd save Roslyn and Ms. Flinsler. She would not kill, not Ethan, not anybody. But it was too late to change any of that.

Under gave Wander's body a reassuring squeeze. Wander shut her eyes, hoping to lose herself to a coma.

A voice hissed, "What are you doing?"

"She's not alright! She just collapsed shaking! Please, I don't know what to do."

"Come. Quick."

Soon the air of a new room sunk into Wander like bothersome sunlight on a hot day. She gasped and let out a cough that set her body aflame inside. Under set her down on what felt like a bed. Wander's fingers clutched at quilt-like texture beneath her. Opening her eyes, she saw a deep-green wall.

"Wander, can you say something?" Under asked. He stood at the bedside, Myth next to him. She wore a velvet robe and red eye patch with hair in a loose bun, her figure swaying as she leaned on a cane.

"Water," Wander managed to croak.

"Here," Myth hobbled away and returned with a silver kettle.

Under's fingers curled around the handle. Wander opened her mouth as he tilted the silver arm toward her mouth. The first drizzle of water missed, hitting the side of her lip and escaping down her cheek. Under adjusted and the water rushed from her tongue to her fire-pit throat.

"You're lucky you bumped into me," Myth said. "She appears to be in a lot of pain. I can sympathize." She searched about her room, opening cabinets and dressers. "I'll share some of my medicine with her."

With a brief moment of relief from her drink, Wander looked around the room from the bed. What the room lacked in size, it made up for in elegance. An entire concave wall of shelves was lined with books. Two dark green cushioned chairs sat with a tall round table between. The most one could fit on the table would be a kettle and two cups.

Myth's figure limped back to the bedside, her teeth grinding. She set a drawstring bag upon the mattress. She pulled the red string, the dark cloth opened, and she took out a syringe. Wander recognized the object from the Heathcliff doctor. In her other hand, Myth took out a vial of white liquid, like milk, except it swished around faster.

Under put his hand between Wander and the needle tip. "What's that?"

"Shy's Gold. My personal stash for when the pain is too much. I'm only giving her a little."

Under got out of Myth's way, and she reached for Wander's arm, her long velvet sleeve dangling down. The needle never came though, instead a shock of blue expanding into a branchlike shape snapped between them. Myth withdrew.

"What is this?" She hissed through her teeth. Her empty hand reached this time. The shock that occurred reminded Wander of little lightning bolts across a night sky. It did not hurt, but she flinched in surprise from the sudden light.

"What's going on?" Under asked. Myth massaged the second hand to get shocked. "I can't touch her. She can no longer touch spirits, as that ability was given to her by the guardian."

"Does that mean she is no longer under its control?"

"It appears so."

"I thought the fox would be controlling only Wander's mind. How is it affecting her body like this?"

"The only reason someone can feel their body is due to their mind," Myth said. "I imagine the guardian gave her body many benefits. The ability to touch spirits is only one of them. With burns like these from an elemental's fire, I would imagine an average human to always live in agony. I'm sure the guardian gave her mind the power to block out that pain. She likely had all the same benefits as Aura's Arms as well: nearly impossible to knock out, quick to heal, and immune to many substances such as poison and drugs. With all these benefits suddenly gone, I imagine her body is having a breakdown. She has been brutal to her body under the guardian's influence. Here," Myth passed the syringe to Under, "you are in a human form, so you can still touch her. Find a vein and stick it in."

Myth carried herself into one of her chairs, barring her teeth as she hit the cushion.

Kneeling at the bedside Under searched for a vein on Wander's arm. She looked away and Under's other hand held hers as he administered the shot. Myth rested her head in her hand while watching. "If you told me you were a shadow from the beginning, none of this would be happening. For my sister to find the truth about you before me, that is a great loss."

He ignored her, placing the medicine back in the drawstring bag.

Myth moved her gaze to the bed. "Tell me, Wander, I advised you to save yourself and you ran off to save this man. Are you happy? Now the guardian is probably dead, and soon you will follow."

Under stood up. "Leave her alone."

Wander attempted to speak only to erupt in coughs. Tears pooled into her ears. Under's hand came down and rested on her forehead.

"As she is now, she can't kill my sister. She won't be able to save Masu." Myth's single eye stared wide. "Without the guardian, I doubt she can even move on her own."

"Did you know this would happen all along?" Under raised his voice. "Did you know she was being controlled this whole time?"

"Unfortunately I learned the news from Aura. As Queen, she has more access to old texts and resources than I do. For me, Wander's abilities were merely serendipity. I did not know it came from a guardian. I did not even see the creature with you when we first met."

Wander's body began to feel heavy, warm, and sleepy. Despite that, her heart raced. She did not want to fall asleep for fear she would not wake up. Under's hand slipped away from her forehead. She wished she could grab him before he walked over to sit with Myth but her arms felt too heavy to lift.

"So the fox, it is dead? Does Wander's release mean it's dead?" Under asked.

"That is likely. Aura's Shadow probably succeeded in the hunt and is bringing the guardian's corpse back to bleed."

"And Wander, could she die?"

"At this point, that is probably a mercy."

Under rested his face in his hand, blocking his eyes and nose. A silence hung over the room. Wander wanted to lift herself up, anything to prove Myth wrong.

Instead she twitched, barely keeping her eyes open. Everything tingled, and she barely felt as though she were in her own body anymore.

"But there is another possibility," Myth said. "The creature could have let Wander go for a living reason. It may have realized their separation may be forever, so it took its lent power back. It may have lost interest in her."

With that, Myth clutched her cane and stood up. "I will seek my sister and see if the hunt was successful for myself. I will return with news. If anyone knocks, don't answer. If someone barges in, I suggest hiding yourselves or killing them as a last resort. I always keep my door locked when I'm not there so someone getting in is doubtful."

Myth locked the door on her way out. Her unsteady steps could be heard through beyond the walls with the tap of her cane against the tiles.

Wander looked over to Under. He rubbed his eyes on his sleeve. "Under . . ." she managed to get his name out. She swallowed saliva to wet her throat. "Don't worry."

He moved to sit on the bedside, the mattress sinking toward him. The whites of his eyes looked freckled with red. His throat bobbed as he swallowed and said, "Don't fight the medicine, okay? It's alright to rest."

"If Aura finds me," Wander whispered. Under bent down, his ear to her breathe. "If Aura finds me, kill me before she controls me."

"She won't find you."

Wander looked over to the silver kettle. Under read her mind, taking the pot and giving her a sip. With a hydrated throat, Wander said, "Now that I'm free, I feel like I've treated you wrong. My mind was in fog. I was always distracted while you suffered."

He shook his head. "That's not true. Now that you're free, you're just looking for something to be wrong that is not there."

She managed to smile. "You always know the right thing to say."

Wander shut her eyes.

Finally she let herself sleep. She spoke to Under as though she expected to not wake. This free Wander talked differently from the one he had traveled with. He felt as though he listened to a woman rather than a young girl. Maybe when death loomed, people became ageless.

If she died, what was next?

Since Alice's death, everything had barely kept together. Maybe humans all had that one thing that was their stable rock, and with it gone, their world couldn't be rebuilt. Wander however, he believed that if it was possible to start over with anyone, it would be her.

Under jumped at the click of the door. Myth slipped through, opening her door as little as she could. "The hunt is not over. My sister switched her strategies as well. The shadow is defending against another human attack. All her Arms are. The last place the fox was seen was the Sax Woodlands. Lucky for us, my sister does not yet know that Wander has escaped."

He lifted himself from the bed. "There is still time. We can save the guardian."

"Save it?"

Under looked back at Wander lying in the bed. "If I save the guardian, I can reunite it with Wander."

"You want her to live, even if it means she is no longer free?"

Under furrowed his eyebrows and frowned.

"I would like that, too." Myth gripped the knobs of her dresser. Pulling it, she gazed among folded clothes. Her hand searched under folds of red and extracted a sheathed dagger. She passed the case to Under. The burnt amber color of the sheath popped out with a fish and fern leaf design. A jade stone also popped out of the sheath like a strange button. The black handle had a white centered sphere with a faint drawing of a rhinoceros. Pulling the blade out, she revealed the steel had been decorated in dark swirling designs.

"That blade holds the ivory of a dead guardian. It passed through my family for many generations onto me. I used it in the Horizon War to kill Morning. I would like you and Wander to take it. It will make anyone bleed, human or spirit. It has even done more than that at times. It is a weapon of many talents. It is magic. When a guardian is killed, we leave nothing to waste. Their bones make horrifying weapons. We only bring those out when we feel we need the extra edge, which may come soon."

"You're giving it to us because you still want our help? To kill your sister?"

"Yes."

Under sighed as he sheathed the dagger. "Can you protect Wander while I get the guardian back?"

"Yes. Do you know where the Sax Woodlands are?"

"Yes, I've seen maps." Tucking the guardian-forged weapon into his pants pocket, Under approached the bedside. He gave Wander's hand a tight squeeze.

"Open your window, would you? I'm going to fly out of here."

As Myth unlocked her window and opened it to the cool night, he transformed. Every time he did, he felt his entire body go cold and fall into darkness. In the dark, he could feel himself swirling around his consciousness, like he became a pool of water. He built himself up. Veins, muscle, keratin, blood, light bones, eye coatings, skin—everything rose up with him inside.

He turned into a crow and landed on the windowsill. He saw the city of Dem blanketed in dark with spots of yellow glow where nightlife lived. Balloons hovered over buildings as commonly as chimneys. Every day the city must have seemed like a festival.

Letting go of the window frame, he took to the sky. He saw the outer walls of the palace painted with flowers. To think, someone who would kill entire populations of people took the throne of such a happy seeming place.

The world spun even under Wander's eyelids. The last she remembered, Under sat at her side, his weight shifting her own on a mattress. Opening her eyes, she saw a slumped woman as still as stone. Myth slouched in her chair with a book in hand. Her unpatched eye scanned the page.

Wander could not even hear her heart or flow of breath. No bird tweets, bug songs, rustling of leaves, creaks, water drops, whispers, not even the flip of a page lent her comfort. "Under?" she managed to mutter. Her own voice felt like a tickle.

Myth's eye darted up. "He is getting the fox back for you."

Her eyelids fluttered. The mattress felt as though it floated. Everything seemed off balance, like a river tide.

"Why?" Wander's voice came off strong for her dazed condition.

Turning her book over, Myth laid the pages open on her lap. "Is that not what you want? To live? To get off this bed? To protect your mind from my sister? To free Masu?"

Though Wander's face turned warm, she could not find any tears to release the agony when she said, "Masu was never free."

Myth folded her fingers over the book spine. "I think being free isn't about being yourself but being who you want to be. What people want and who they are are often different things. It brings up the question of what Masu would want. After learning his background, can you blame him if he wouldn't want to be himself?"

The concept splashed into Wander's mind, and her thoughts spun. Controlled by the guardian or not, Masu was happy. Maybe a part of him even knew about being controlled, and he accepted that fate.

Freedom for her could be the same. Even at the cost of her own will, she wanted to have power enough to save Masu. Between dying and saving him, even if he was a monster, she did not care. Whoever he was, she'd love him. Wander turned her head on the pillow, "There is a strange forest in the palace."

"The palace was built on what was once enchanted land. It was overseen by the stag guardian, Radinn. It was his blood that gave our first ruler, Rumor, her power. Back then, it wasn't a hunt. I think the guardian pitied her slavery and offered her a chance. Poor Radinn did not know he open the doors to his and other guardians' demise."

Myth leaned back, staring off into space. "Aura's path to being queen was different. She drank when she was ten back when our parents were still alive. I remember her coronation well. It was on a windy day and the cities' balloons all tugged at their homes. My sister stood on a stage in a gray gown with thousands of our people watching. I sat backstage, watching from behind a curtain.

"A wild horse was dragged out of the palace in chains. His hooves kicked, and his head thrashed like a sea monster's. I could tell the creature frightened my sister. Thousands of people watched as our father, pulled a sword from his sheath. With one mad thrust, he killed the horse. Our mother prepared a mug of the guardian's blood for my sister on stage. When my sister drank, she would not stop coughing. It was a bad sign too, for a ruler to choke on the guardian's blood."

Wander shut her eyes, feeling the heaviness of sleep beckoning her.

"We used to be so similar, my sister and I." Myth seemed to speak aloud to herself more than Wander. "When she became queen, I never felt more useless. That's why I talked her into letting me fight, despite the duty of the deviant ruler to be not allowing his or her own people to fight. I wanted to kill the ones who killed mother, father, and our baby brother. Then I did, and now I feel the cost in every pain my body conjures every moment of every day."

Wander tried to speak, only to let out a soft moan as she fell asleep.

"Forgive me," Myth turned the book so the pages faced up again. "I have spoken too much."

Chapter 15
Monksbreath Inn

"A sure way of making money is opening an inn. Awei is a world of travelers; however, some of those travelers could be slavers, spirits in disguise, or a wanted criminal. The innkeepers are either tough or don't care who walks in as long as they have coin." – Human Trade in a Spirit World

Wander woke facing the sky. Tree branches clouded strips of blue. Speckled orchids entrenched in the twisting wood. A bird's song brought warm memories of mornings when her greatest problem was trying to sleep under too much sunlight.

"I wish it could be this way." Whispers echoed through the wood. "Tracing our steps back, we could get there."

Her hands pressed down on dry soil. Something was wrong. She immediately knew when she saw her un-calloused and clear hands. Looking at her palms, she could make out every line like a map. She reached at her face to touch soft cheeks. She could even feel the peach-fuzz above her lips. For the first time in so long, she wanted to see her face, just one look to remember when she was not hideous.

But the moment she stood, the world shivered. Not only did the earth shake, but so did the sky. Even colors spattered. Wander hugged herself and shut her eyes.

"Mama!" said a voice.

Wander did not remember opening her eyes, but she saw a new place from so many angles. Trees twice as tall as the largest she knew with leaves shaped like hearts. The branches were so thick, entire gardens grew on them. On smaller branches hung lines of clothes billowing in the wind. At the top of the trunks, where branches exploded into veins, there were homes all painted white.

An entire valley had these trees. On the upper part of a mountainside though, the tallest tree with the widest branches stood out. The sun set exactly behind it, casting a monstrous silhouette. When darkness came, the entire valley did not light with torches, but crystals that reflected moonlight.

After those images, Wander found herself standing upon a branch as thick as a hallway. A child, even smaller than Roslyn, ran past her with downy wings, brownish, and soft.

The child rushed to meet a woman in white. Her black hair reached her ankles, and dark wings eclipsed the glowing crystals behind her. Getting on her knees, she greeted the boy at eye level. Her eyes glowed red, brighter than any gaze Masu had shown in the dark.

They embraced.

"Mama, what's that?"

"Just a little blood."

"Blood?" The boy pressed his hand to her breast. Looking up at the woman, Wander got a look at the young face of Masu. "Are you hurt?"

She shook her head, red lips curling into a smirk. "Mama never gets hurt."

Wander's ears rung as all the colors of the world shook, blurred, and froze for a moment. It all crashed down and up into a new memory.

The world had turned to daytime on a cliff side. Winds shook a green dress. A woman stood on the horizon. White feathers violently twisted off her and scattered into the air. Her blonde hair was still, braided intricately around her head like a crown. She hugged something tightly. Wander ran to the woman side to get a better look. Little Masu, eyes wide, clutched at her chest. Hiding tears, the woman's face buried into his black hair. She walked off the cliff and dropped.

Wander covered her ears and shut her eyes as crashing waves pummeled her hearing. Then everything was dark and quiet when she opened herself back up.

"This isn't a dream. My mind . . . it's not my own. Are you Aura? The guardian?"

The world shook and the colors blended, falling. The inside of Wander's head felt like something was scratching. She stumbled until she fell. Opening her eyes, as though it were all a dream, she found herself back where she started: a forest. Before peace could settle in, all the colors of life turned to flame. The brown bark of tree trunks brightened to blood red. Moss on the stones went orange, and the leaves blazed golden. Flowers became sunsets and ferns to fire. The soil became softer, like ash.

Whispers echoed with a chorus of different voices.
"Little lies for little people."
"He tumbled down and stopped moving."
"That's not me."
"I have to save him!"
Bushes shook and a figure stepped out, the dark silhouette of a man. As it neared, the shadow stretched up as tall as a dogwood tree, thin as a pole. Little arms bent at the elbows, and ended at dog-like paws. It wore the blackest cloak to cover its torso and legs, so dark that it seemed like the absence of existence, like a void.

The lanky creature's most striking feature was its head. It wore a long white mask with angled golden eyes outlined by red. The mask had red lips that opened in a snarl and pointed animal ears. Wander swore she saw very real similar ears flicking behind the mask. Its head was crowned with horns. Upon closer inspection, Wander noticed they weren't horns, but dead branches with bark peeling to show blood underneath.

The figure hunched down to look at Wander. Its human-sized neck angled forward like a horses. She expected noise from its size, but the entire world went quiet. She could not even hear her own breath. They stared into each other's eyes. Beyond the snarling mask, she saw only darkness.

"What are you?"

It did not answer.

She squinted at the animal mask, "Are you . . . the fox? The guardian?"

A vision played in her head. A familiar fox crossed the river to a tree, Wander recognized the tree from the Emerald Wilds. She called it the "bee tree" since she had once stepped on a hive near the roots. At the tree's base, the fox stuck its snout in a hole to meet another. A second fox, red, popped her head out. She sniffed him. Behind her, three bumbling kits whined as they came out of the hole. Young, their eyes were still closed. The red fox picked a mewling one up in her jaws and set it back in their underground home. The guardian helped, lifting the one kit similar to him, with a dark pelt, smaller than the rest.

Then the vision took a turn. Fire set to the tree. Wander saw the red fox inside, crouched, her body sheltering her babies. A burning branch fell upon the entrance. The force of the fall caused a crackling thunder of flame.

Wander snapped out of the vision to find the masked guardian near at her face. "I'm . . . sorry." The creature looked downward. She followed its gaze to the ash-covered soil. "So Aura was right?" Wander asked. "You are using me to kill her?"

It did not answer. Wander began to understand the creature could not speak, or simply would not. She had a feeling it understood her though.

"You made me kill Ethan. You made me a shield against the fire. You are the reason I almost burned to death."

The figure increased in size, like a bird ruffling its feathers.

"And you made Masu yours, too. Was Aura right about everything?"

Warmth spread around Wander's back. She turned around but nothing was there. Turning back to the guardian, she said, "You are also the reason I could fight, do magic, and live."

Wander stared upon the guardian's shadow paws. She wanted to back up, but the creature's form swirled around her like a snake upon prey. "If there was any chance to save Masu, I'd need your power . . . but then you'd have my mind.

"And you want Aura dead? As revenge for her killing the forest? What if I have to kill Masu to get to her and you make me do it?"

Wander went silent, staring into the void of the guardian's cloak. It was like the night sky, just needing a moon and stars. The being smelled like flames. She tried to make sense of where they were. A burning Emerald Wilds surrounded them, but it was impossible to be there. She saw the forest after the fire, and all had turned to ash. The last thing she recalled, she lay in a bed in Myth's tower room.

This world was the other one, the sleeping one. The one she always had difficulty remembering. Was any of this real? She had to treat it like it was, or the consequences could be foul.

She looked at Masu's feather on her right wrist. The guardian stretched taller, like he was prepared to pounce.

Wander's green eyes half opened to the sound of rainfall. Outside a window she saw a branch bob up and down from the storm. Her lips had stuck together, and she pulled them apart. She felt as though she could fall back asleep any second.

This was not Myth's room. Wander was boxed in by brown walls. She lay on a white bed with nothing else but wood furniture: a table, chair, bedside table, and a second bed at the opposite side of the room. The air smelled of mold.

Someone hunched over the table, head in hand, elbow on table surface. The figure blurred for a second. She recognized the thin body and dark coat. "Under?"

The head turned to show a single brown eye. Something in the look seemed feral, like a wolf in a cage. He rose from the desk and sat at the bedside, appearing more disheveled than ever. His hair looked to have endured rain and wind. It was not so much his body, though. His eyes did not shed that mad look on his face. His voice tried too hard to sound normal, rising higher than usual. "How are you feeling?"

"Better."

"We are back in human lands. I managed to get us a room in a small village. I got the guardian back. Is it controlling you?"

They looked at the foot of the bed. The fox curled and slept, still as a stone.

"Since I'm feeling better, I suppose so," Wander said. She tilted her head at Under. "Are you hurt? You don't look good."

"Just tired. We escaped one prison and ended up in another. This is the first moment of peace since before that crazy human battle. Feels like weeks rather than days."

Wander sat up, her body felt heavier than she remembered. Under offered a hand to lift her out of bed. She stood up, the tangle of sheets falling to the floor. For a moment she swayed, and Under tightened his grip on her. Recollecting herself, she managed to stand strong. After a couple confident steps Under let go of her.

"I never thought I'd say this, but I want a bath," Wander said

"I can get a bucket and cloth. The inn should have those."

While Under was away, Wander looked out the window at the storm. No people, just tapping raindrops. The branch of a tree in the window waved up and down at the mercy of wind and water. In the corner of the window, Wander noticed a tent of web on the outside. A black spider watched the storm pass as well.

She tapped the glass and the spider tensed. What did it know? Did it know of her finger tapping the glass, or did it stand, mindlessly scared of an unknowable threat?

She looked to the side; the fox sat up on the bed. "Are you alright?"

The animal stared in silence. It did not care about Under, she figured that out well enough. If Under was controlled by Aura to protect her, Wander might not be able to stop herself from attacking him. Under was already in a dark place. It's been that way since Alice died, but it was getting worse. Being with Wander could only make things worse. Her journey only brought more struggles. He should have stayed away, away from the war and her. He could be anything and can go anywhere.

"I'm back."

With a white cloth and towel lying over Under's shoulder, he shut the door behind with his foot. Water sloshed back and forth in the large bucket he carried with both hands. The handle of a second, smaller bucket was tucked through his fingers.

"Thank you." Wander helped Under ease the large container of water on the floor.

Once set up, Wander undressed. Her clothes stuck and peeled off her skin from the amount of blood and dirt accumulated. Most of the blood was from carrying Masu out of the human prison, darker and heavier than her own.

Under sat up in the chair, elbow on the table, his teeth gnawed on a toothpick. His gaze seemed withdrawn, angling toward the storm outside.

Wander held her blood soaked clothes to her face. She breathed in Masu's blood, allowing herself to dance on the edge of agony. Setting her clothes on the bed, she folded her legs as she sat naked in front of the bucket. Sinking the cloth in the water, she saw the rag come to life like a ghost underwater. She spun and pulled the towel around the space, pretending it were a white fish. She pressed the soaked cloth on her shoulder. She could not help but grunt, eyes shut, and shiver at the intensity of the chill the water gave her.

"You alright?" Under took a quick glance.

"Yeah. Just chilly."

"I can see if I can warm it up for you."

She resoaked the towel. "No. It's fine." She winced as she spread the cool rag across her outer thigh. "Masu used to force me to take baths. He tried to get me into the river, and I wouldn't go. He eventually tried to bring the water to me instead. I acted like he was trying to hurt me, running away at the mere sight of that wood bucket. He'd chase me, pouring water on me and then rub me with certain herbs to smell nice. Then of course he'd brush my hair. That was the worst. I almost fell out of our nest trying to run from him brushing my hair once."

"What was your hair like?"

"It was a little lighter than daffodil petals," said Wander. "And it was never straight." She put her hand on her bald and scarred scalp. "I miss it."

"Here." Under sat across from her. He scooped up water into the smaller bucket. "Put your head over the big bucket here. I'll pour this over your head for you."

Falling forward, Wander stared at her quivering reflection in the water. She preferred water to mirrors. Something about the rippling image had more beauty than a window or mirror could reflect. Water fell on her head. She remembered when Masu did it, her hair darkened, long and heavy, falling far past her face. Her reflection became a storm as the water returned to the bucket.

By the time her bath finished, the water had become dark brown.

She dried herself with the towel.

"We can get your clothes washed, too," Under said as he collected her cloak, socks, underwear, pants, and shirt.

"Under . . .I'm sorry I never told you about killing Ethan," she said. "It happened a couple days before I met you. Aura controlled him to take the fox, so the fox made me kill him. Back then, I did not know why I did it. I thought if you knew, you would hate me. Even now knowing I was mind-controlled, I still don't feel any better. It still feels like it was me."

Under's wilted look did not break. "I can't be mad at you. After all, I kept the secret about being a shadow for a while."

He left downstairs with her attire.

Setting the towel aside, Wander wrapped the bed's blanket around her. The fox jumped off the bed and sniffed around.

Wander remembered her enchanted sword. No, it was probably the guardian's. The sword was retrieved from the Emerald Wilds, so it must be the guardian's. That must have been why Wander took the sword from Heathcliff: the guardian wanted her to use it to fight. The magic from the sword must be what was left from the Emerald Wilds. If she were to fight Aura and her Arms, she was going to need the sword back. But Naktol had taken it.

The floor creaked as Under returned.

"Here, you should wear this gown while your clothes dry." Under pulled a white dress from beneath his armpit. Wander tugged the light dress over her head, her arms easily finding the short sleeves. Under helped, pulling the dress down her body.

The bed sank as they both sat down.

Closing her eyes, Wander took in the moment of peace. "I'm starving."

"I'll get you some food after I rest a little."

"Aura took the cloth I wrap around my face. Do you think we could get another?"

"I'm sure I can get something from a shop."

"Thank you."

She glanced out the window to see a two children running and jumping in the puddles. Their bare feet squished in the mud.

"Hey, Wander," Under's voice pulled her vision to their reflection in the glass. She could see him hovering behind her, staring at the reflection as well. "If the guardian is keeping you alive by controlling you, then what will happen after you kill Aura if that's the guardian's end goal?"

"What do you think will happen?"

He looked worse off from her question. "Whatever happens, I'll be there for you, okay? I'll try to keep you safe."

The storm subsided. The roof tapings stopped, and a peaceful silence was accompanied by sunlight in the window. Under left to shop for food and a cloth for Wander's face. Curling under the bed's quilt, Wander took a warm nap. She took in the moment of safety and comfort. If she ignored her hunger, she could almost feel as though nothing could be wrong. No Masu. No Aura. No other humans. Just she and Under. The curious and passionate girl in the Emerald Wilds felt like it was so long ago. The girl wanted to leave, meet new people, and see the world. Now she dreamed of that small world with just a couple people. Getting Masu back seemed unrealistic now. She could not even recall his voice or the expressions of his face. In the dream the guardian showed her, she saw his face and heard his voice only to lose them the moment she woke up.

"Can I really save Masu?" she asked, remembering she was not alone. The guardian jumped onto the bed with her. His snout nuzzled the frayed feather she wore on her wrist.

"That doesn't even matter anymore, does it?" Wander said. All that mattered was the guardian's goal.

Under returned with bags. Setting them on the table he pulled out an apple, a jar of nuts, and sandwich. He pulled a dark scarf from the bag and threw it to Wander with her now dry clothes.

She dressed herself. In the window, she watched her face disappear into darkness until there was nothing but her eyes left to see.

As she ate, she caught Under watching her. "What's next for us?" he asked.

Despite his casual tone, the question came at her like a knife. She knew what she had to tell him. There was no choice even, like trying to control a heartbeat. "You can't come," the words came out dead and toneless.

"What?"

If she did not wear the veil around her face, he'd see sorrow wrinkle on her face.

"I have to do the rest alone."

"Wander, that's—"

"Please."

His gaze wandered for a moment. With a conclusion, his eyes darted back to her. "It's the guardian, isn't it? It's making you say that."

"No." The guardian's will and her own were now completely blurred. There was no telling anymore. "I know I'm dangerous now."

He leaned forward, hand on the table. "All the more reason you'll need me. I need to stop you if you are forced to do something crazy."

"I won't act like a friend if you do that, so please, don't make this harder than it already is."

She did not realize how tense Under had become until he relaxed and shrank down, more wilted than ever. "I see."

"After I kill Aura, I'll be free and come find you," Wander put a little pep into her voice. "This isn't goodbye."

"Right." Under's sullen appearance did not dwindle.

"When Aura dies, we can stop worrying about everything."

"Is this because Aura controlled me?"

"No, but that's another good reason to go alone. She had you, and she was going to kill you."

With a scowl, Under shook his head but had nothing to say.

"I want to stay here for a while with you before I go," Wander told him. "I'd like a couple days of rest."

As the day passed, Under seemed to settle more into Wander's decision. He asked her what she would write if she learned how. "Memories," she answered. "So I can keep the good parts of my life."

Now even when Under smiled, he seemed sad.

That night when they went to bed, Wander could feel the guardian's slow breaths, his heartbeat against her legs. Across the room she watched Under's silhouette. He lay on his stomach, his hair covered his face, and one arm stretched out.

"Are you awake?" Under's voice startled her out of her thoughts. He shifted his head up from the pillow, half of his hair messy.

"Yes."

"I can't sleep," Under said.

As far as Wander knew, Under having issues sleeping was ordinary. She'd wake in the night to pee or jump up from a nightmare, and he would be awake to see. He never made a peep about his sleeplessness though, until now.

"Why not?"

"Just anxious I guess."

"Anxious?"

"Nervous," he said. "It's ridiculous though because I'm exhausted. I haven't slept since Aura's trance, and I don't think that even counts so maybe not since two days ago."

"You can talk to me until you feel better," Wander said.

Under laid back down to face the ceiling. "When Alice was a kid living with her father, I'd often sneak into their place at night. Alice would expect me. At night, I always got lonely, so I'd turn into some animal and tap on her bedroom window, usually as a chickadee.

"She'd get up in her nightgown and let me in. I never knew the warmth of a bed until I met her. She let me under the covers with her and her stuffed animals. She'd tell me about her day until she fell asleep. Sometimes she liked to read to me by candlelight when she got a new book. I'd sleep curled up in her arms as a dog or cat. Eventually I started to turn into her. Both of us, with the exact same face, voice, and features would talk until dawn about everything. We were so foreign to each other. Back then, you would not have believed it was me. I was inhuman with little concept of long-term emotions. I shape shifted all the time and gave scarce loyalty to a single form. Perspective was like running water, never the same. Because of that, there were endless things for a little girl to talk to me about. When Alice drew an original human body for me, I stayed in that form to be with her. All the other perspectives began to fade the longer I didn't change. My mind became more and more human every day. The world shrank, but it also deepened. I fell in love with Alice because of it. I think about her at night the most. We were always together then."

"I wish I could bring her back," Wander said. "I wish I could bring a lot of people back."

"People are meaningful," Under said. "But we're all stuck in a meaningless world. That's probably the most tragic part of living."

Wander sat up and the fox jumped off the bed. She looked at his silhouette across the room. "Can I sleep with you?"

Under scooted as far as he could in a bed meant for one person. Wander nestled close to him and nuzzled her face to his chest. One of his arms extended over her. She realized she was starved for this sort of intimacy. Feeling warmer than ever, she shut her eyes.

The rainy days passed Wander and Under like a dream because they slept through it all. On their last day, Under taught Wander how to follow a map, tell directions, and read some letters. That was the most fun she could remember having since their snowball fight.

"This is S and is looks like a snake. So remember the sssss sound." Under often compared letters to things in real life to match the sound. "M is for mountain, see the peaks? O is for orange. They're round. B. B is for . . ." He stared at the letter he drew.

Taking the page, Wander turned it down. "It looks like a butt."

Under sighed. "Sure. B is for butt."
The sun emerged the day Wander planned to leave. The muddy village of Monksbreath bathed in light, with puddles shrinking and people out in boots. Outside, Wander waited for Under. She would not leave him without a hug and a promise to see each other again. She leaned against the inn's wooden walls. The fox circled around her feet. The curious people who passed would look away the moment they met Wander's gaze.

Monksbreath was a quiet place. Even the children were rather silent. Maybe it was fear from bordering with the deviant lands. Or maybe the presence of rain had a way of making everyone sleepy.

Under finally came out of the inn. He stood straighter than usual. "I have something to give you," Under pulled out a sheathed dagger. "Myth gave this to me. It's made of guardian bone apparently. You'll need it more than me."

Wander unsheathed it to view the dark lines swirling in the steel. When she held the dagger, she could smell rot and flame. She decided to stick the sheathed blade into her boot. "Thank you."

The shadow dove both his hands into his pockets. His posture sagged. "I'm . . . not good with goodbyes."

Wander hugged him, her face against his lower chest. She did not realize how thin he was under the coat until her arms locked completely around his waist. Hugging her back, he curled downward.

"You take care of yourself, okay?" he said.

He could not see her cry. If he did, Wander was sure he would not let her go. With all her might, she held back her tears and sniffles. "What are you going to do?"

"I'll be in Willton, where you can find me."

"Okay." She did not know the right time to let go of the hug. When she pulled away, she turned her head to avoid eye contact. She became sure of her face getting red and her eyes watering. "Goodbye."

Chapter 16
Sollast

"Do you know why Sollast Castle is also known as the House of Wolves? Humans tamed the wolves. No spirit could, but we did. They saw something in us, and we in them." – Sollastian History

Wander kicked stones as she walked the road. Whenever a rock rolled off into the grass, she gave up time to find it and kick it back to the path. The fox led the way ahead. He always stopped to wait if Wander fell far behind.

The trail bordered farmlands of corn and wheat. Wander reached over the wood fence and pulled an ear of corn from a stalk. The stalk swayed forward and back with Wander's tug and release, its tassel bobbing in the sunlight. As she moved on, Wander peeled the corn of its dry husk to the gold inside. Her thumb ran across, admiring the smooth texture.

She stopped at the wheat fields. Wind sent blond waves through the meadow. A single oak tree had grown just right of the center. A land never looked more open and warm. The silence and isolation only brought out its welcoming.

As they neared Sollast, wagons, horse riders, and travelers passed. Parents moved their children to the other side of their bodies. Conversations fell silent as they saw Wander. The horses whinnied. Hooves tapped the earth. As more humans crowded the road, the fox got closer to Wander's feet.

Wild flowers bordered the trail. They left no scent, but the bees and butterflies did not seem to care. "You!"

The fox bolted into the flowers, but Wander froze.

A man in a belted blue tunic charged up. His left hand rested on the handle of a blade strapped to his side. His brown hair seemed soft and fuzzy like a squirrel's tail.

Wander clenched her fists. A power she did not understand buzzed in her palms. The world slowed, and her body felt lighter.

More men surrounded her, all armed with bows and blades. Four of them, two on each side, pointed arrows at her. The arrow tips directed to her legs.

"Are you Wander?" the man asked.

The path began to swell with humans. Whispers fogged Wander's ears.

"Yes!" Wander said loudly. She tried to raise her voice over the hums in her head.

"You are wanted for betrayal to the crown. Our Lord Naktol has ordered that upon sight, you are to be taken alive to her throne for judgment."

Wander's mind fuzzed. Her own thoughts and the guardian's power tried to imagine the best scenario for them both.

The human straightened his back. "You are unarmed. Come peacefully, and you will not be harmed."

"Alright."

"Then hands up."

Relaxing her hands, she raised them to the sky. Her cloak sank down and heavy onto her shoulders. The bowmen did not yet unwind until others bound her hands with rope.

"Nothing to see here!" One barked at the unwanted audience.

Despite Wander's tied hands, two men each clutched her upper arms as they walked into and through the city. Her eyes kept to the ground. The city street of cobblestone was not always even. Some stones were missing. Once in a while, she stepped over something forgotten, a feather, glass shards, and a torn leather bracelet.

This was for the best. She'll be escorted to her planned destination. The guardian's weapon was somewhere in Sollast's castle. She could try to make a deal with Naktol to return it to her. No, that likely would not go well. She had no friends here. Once inside, she might have to fight her way to the blade.

Wander did not know what a throne even was. She knew of the word *thrown*, but it was not a place. She expected something dark, another prison perhaps. But the throne room had no shadows. Rainbow windows brought in red, blue, green, and gold sunlight on the long sapphire rug and stone walls. The room was larger than any she had stood in before. Even with the extensive room, little furniture or art took space. As she slowed to admire the setting, a guard kneed her butt to move forward.

A silver and blue altar stood at the end of the long and high room. Three rounded steps came up the platform to a gray seat. The armrests were carved into wolves with azure jeweled eyes and black fangs. The seat's back extended three times taller than a regular dining chair. Its gray frame swirled like clouds. The chair had had a curtain on each side, like a window. The deep blue cloth had been pulled back with parts of a white design hidden in their folds.

Naktol sat in the altar's chair. She glowed in the gray seat, her silver hair and blue eyes contrasting with the dim shades. She adjusted her posture, unfolding her legs and lifting her chin. Two people, each in armor with a spear, stood like statues at her sides. An unarmed man stood behind, hands at his sides. "That's far enough," Naktol said.

Wander's captors stopped. "Take off the mask. I must know it's really her."

Hands grabbed at her veil and pulled. With her face free, she looked away.

"That's her, alright." The queen turned to her left. "Mard, see that these people are rewarded." The unarmed man bowed and strode down the altar. Naktol turned forward. "You may let go of her."

Mard motioned Wander's captors away. They let her go and exited behind her. With free arms, Wander picked her headscarf off the ground and rewrapped the darkness around her face.

Naktol sneered. "What do you have to say for yourself?"

Tightening the veil, Wander muffled her voice. "I have returned for my sword."

"What?"

She grew louder and her heated breath caught in the cloth. "I want my sword back."

The queen's face twisted as though she sniffed rotting milk. "What a laugh. You betray our trust, release Pitch, hand him back to Aura, and retreat to her palace in Dem. And you return and have the gall to look at me and ask for your sword?"

"No, you betrayed me. Masu was supposed to be unharmed if I distracted him. You captured him and nearly killed him."

"That beast killed Devon while you pretended to fight!" Naktol shouted. Her body lunged forward. "I heard from my scouts you did not kill a single deviant soul in Loreman. While you pretended to be one of us, the Wings killed my people! His hands have the blood of hundreds! Did you expect me to let him go? Are you so small minded and selfish to think that I would give into your whims at the cost of my people?

"Sara figured you out. You are no witch. You're a pawn of Aura. Just like her Arms, you are resistant to poisons. Her sedatives did not work on either of you. Perhaps your mind is not your own and you were innocent once. Maybe you're a victim, and Aura broke your mind. Of course she would use humans to get into my ranks and spy. I have a rule about prisoners who have escaped. If they cannot sit still, then they must be executed. But you're different. This time, I'll have you watched all the time. We will find what makes Aura's mind-control tick, even if it means drilling a hole in your head!" Naktol pointed forward. "Seize her." The guards at the sides stepped forward and marched down the altar.

Wander obeyed the humming in her head. She clapped her hands together. Between her palms she could feel buzzing. Her hands tensed, impossible to relax, her fingers trembled. She could hear hissing whispers layered with screaming and scratching like nails to wood in the back of her head. Forcing her hands apart, a dark ball of energy burst into being. It reminded her of a dark sun. The ball blasted forward between the guards. They stopped, holding their spears tight. The ball exploded into wisps that dove into the guard's bodies like flying locusts.

The guards simultaneously dropped their spears. One grabbed his head, fell to his knees, and curled into a shivering, crying ball. The other let out a scream, constantly rubbing his hands together and shaking his head.

Naktol shot up out of her seat. Her anger was briefly tamed by fear. "What is this?"

"Magic. And it's not Aura's." Wander opened her mouth to tell the truth, that the guardian controlled her but she could not. Saying it was as impossible as sneezing at will.

"Enough tricks then." Bravado returned to the queen's tone. Her arm reached behind her chair and pulled out a weapon. Wander had never seen such an object before. With both hands, the queen gripped long handle with a heavy steel ball of spikes. Wander imagined it was heavy by the way the queen held it, her hands far apart. She stepped down the stairs and passed her panicking guards. Her boots glittered in the rainbow light. "I'm not afraid of magic. You can surrender, or I'll break both of your legs if I have to."

She ran forward and swung down. The action seemed to happen in slow motion for Wander, and she managed to jump back out of the way in time. The rug sank into shattered marble under the weight of Naktol's weapon.

Wander threw her hand toward Naktol. A burst of air and sound came between them. The queen staggered backward. The blast hit Wander as well, her ears ringing and vision blurred as she saw two Naktols recover and make a second charge.

Her swing hit the wall this time, and Wander twisted out of the way. Before Naktol could pull the weapon from the stones, Wander clapped her hands together for a spell.

"MY LADY!" The double doors to the throne room were thrown open.

A woman stood at the threshold, legs shaking. "N-Naktol?" She looked to see the queen with her weapon launched in the castle wall, Wander standing at her side, and two guards crying and rocking on the floor.

"What?" Naktol shouted.

The woman braved the rage in the queen's tone. "We're under attack! Aura's Horns, Chant, and her Shadow are attacking the city!"

Naktol let go of her weapon, and it remained stuck in the wall. "Are you serious?"

"People are already pounding at the gates! It's a slaughter!"

"Dammit!" Naktol ripped her weapon from the wall. "Open the front gates but lock the castle. We need to keep people outside. Vernon, Edith, Miguel, and Juliet are in charge of leading people out of the city. We've planned for a situation like this. Find them. The army will distract the Arms and provide four paths to escape."

The woman nodded and took off running, leaving the doors wide open.

"I'll help," Wander said. "Let me fight them."

"Like you did in Loreman?"

"Where is my sword? I can save people."

"You came here to distract me from this! Aura sent you!" Naktol held her weapon high, prepared to strike.

Wander sprinted for the door. Her panic created a beat in her ears that drowned out whatever Naktol shouted. Stumbling out of the throne room, she took a right toward a crossroads of halls. Where is the sword? If the guardian can control her mind, then he must be able to read her thoughts. He was not here to lead though. Of course, he threw her into the fire while he hid away.

After running down a few corridors, Wander staggered to a stop. Doubling over, she covered her eyes. They stung as though she held a chopped onion close to her face. Rubbing them, she reopened to see blood on her hands. Were her eyes bleeding? Looking up she saw a white glow like fire beyond the walls. It's shape . . . a sword?

With eyes still pulsating with pain, her hands met the walls. The glow seemed far off in the distance. She followed the wall, keeping her gaze on the sword. Getting closer, Wander saw the glow intensified. Her hands trailed along until she touched a door. The strange vision dropped away, the glow gone. It had to be this door; the guardian had showed her the way.

Taking a breath, she smeared blood from her eyes to her sleeve. The door seemed ordinary, wooden with a gold knob. Wander tried to the knob. Locked. Of course. Gritting her teeth, both hands strangled the doorknob. "C'mon!"

A crash came from the other side. Wander yelped as a blade jammed itself through the top right hinge of the door. Pulling her hands back, she watched the steel emit a black fire as it struck down, breaking the hinge, the middle one, then the bottom. The door threw itself open, but opposite from where it was supposed to. It sloped back, only the lock still attached.

The guardian's blade lay on the ground where the last hinge broke. Before she could even bend to pick it up, the sword flew up, its grip landing between her thumb and index finger. Taking hold, she sprinted toward the exit.

Now that Wander knew her mind was not her own, the guardian appeared to use its power with more ease.

The training yard was chaotic with soldiers grabbing gear. Vincent roped a chain to his side. The best of the weapons were already taken for those leading safe parties out of the city. He pulled the bowstrings to test their feel. Selecting one, he emerged from the tent.

A group of soldiers loitered. "The rumors are true! Aura has a monster. It's now in the Trade District!"

Vincent's lips curled. "That's not a monster. That's Aura's Shadow. It changes form. It can be a bird one moment, a monster the next."

The warriors looked at Vincent's interjection like a couple of startled cats. "Does that mean it can be a human, too?"

"Yes. It can be anything."

"How are we supposed to beat something like that?"

"Get lucky and use your head." Vincent marched off.

He did not expect Aura to make such a bold move. All her pieces were here but two: herself and the Wings.

Naktol sought the protection of her daughters before anyone else. Vincent saw her before he sought a bow. For one moment, she was just a pleading mother. With wide blue eyes, she pulled Sara aside. "Take them with a small team. Take it slowly and safely. No one is to see them. No fire or blade is to touch them."

Vincent trooped to the gardens with the rest of the soldiers. Already the top heads of the army stood high and spoke loud. They stood on walls of one of the garden's many fountains. "Naktol is currently creating a defensive plan to evacuate civilians," said a scarred general. "If you are standing here, then your job is part of the offensive plan."

Something urgently tapped Vincent's right shoulder. Turning, he met the large brown eyes of a serving girl. Her hand waved for him to follow. They weaved through soldiers to the stairs of a castle entrance. Her chocolate hued dress twirled as she turned to him. "You are Vincent?"

He nodded.

"Naktol awaits you in the room ahead. She has instructions for you."

"Me? What kind of instructions?"

"She did not say."

With little to go on, Vincent wasted no time meeting the queen. Just up the stairs and through the door, Naktol stood with her back leaning to the wall. Her hand covered her lower face, her eyes in a trance of thought.

"Naktol." Vincent greeted her with a stiff bow.

"Thank goodness she found you." Naktol left the wall, standing taller than him. Sweat slipped down past her right eye.

"You have instructions for me?"

The queen seemed breathless. "It's Wander. She is part of all this."

The last he had heard of the "witch" was that she had been arrested by Sara for betrayal. After her escape, she became a wanted criminal with a reward great enough to buy property in the Gold District. He couldn't go by one day without seeing her wanted poster. They had two drawings side by side of her: one cloaked and other of her scorched face.

"Just before the attack," Naktol said, "my guards had caught her at the gates. She asked for her sword back. When my guards tried to take her away, she became hostile and attacked with magic. When I received news of the invasion, I got distracted and she ran off."

"The sword she wants is powerful," Vincent said. "I saw it cast magic when we first met."

"This is exactly why I wanted to see you. She is an unknown for the rest of the soldiers. I want you to find her, hunt her down, and kill her. Wander is under Aura's control and cannot be trusted. She is searching for her sword in this castle. I hid it in a room of other confiscated weapons on the left of the research tower door. Here is the key." Naktol opened her hand to reveal a silver key.

Vincent held out his hand and she dropped it into his palm.

"In the beginning, you did not trust her. I was a fool and ignored you," Naktol said.

His fingers closed around the key. "I will do my best."

Wander hid in the outskirts of the castle between a patch of raspberry bushes and a wall layered in red trumpet vines. Guards or masses of citizens clogged every gate. Wind carried smoke overhead. Distant screams broke the serenity of the flowers and castle.

Wander took hold to find a wooden grid beneath the vines, a way to support them to the wall. With luck, perhaps she could climb over. She tucked the sword into her pants belt. The blade was too large for such a holding, but it worked for the moment so she could climb. Clutching the wood frame, her feet found footing as she climbed up. The feat was far easier than tree climbing. Reaching the top of the wall, she got a full view of the horizon. Chant's fire had yet to reach the inner city. She seemed to work on the borders, aiming to close everyone in the confines of the labyrinth of buildings.

Rather than steady herself down, Wander decided to jump. She landed on her feet with no pain. Pulling the sword free, she ran toward the outer city. Chant would appear if she just followed the smoke.

People left their doors with sachets and backpacks filled. Even though the fire did not reach this far, they seemed prepared to abandoned their homes. Others ran with nothing on their backs. They ran faster than everyone else. A few were not as lucky, their bodies bloodied, shot, crushed, or burned. They limped and stumbled down the streets, some falling and failing to move anymore.

The further from the castle, the worse the conditions became. Bodies scattered the streets and arrows stood on their back like signs in the ground.

"HELP! MAMA!"

Wander spun around to see a child crying over a body. His little hands pushed at a fallen woman's shoulder. He began to cough in his cries. A yellow mist had swamped them, like a fog of pollen. Wander's sense of smell went numb. Her nose felt swollen and tingly. Her free hand tensed up with magic. She waved through the air and the mist cleared. Bending down to the child and body, she touched the woman. "She's dead," Wander said. "Run that way and don't breathe that mist." She pointed in the direction of the castle.

"No! No, no, no!" The child shook and remained locked in position. When Wander's hand reached for him, he screamed.

With no warning, Wander suddenly could not feel her own body. No weight, no sense of the ground, and no pain. Her hearing and sight blanked out for just a moment where she saw only white and heard dead silence. When her vision and hearing returned, the boy seemed even more frightened. His sobbing and shaking had grown more intense. Following his gaze, she saw an arrowhead stick out of her stomach. Turning around, she saw Aura's Horns holding her thick bow. The spirit reached over her shoulder at the many white feathered arrows, her long white hair held up in a bun. The roots to the sharp tips of her horns painted black. She wore gray and white armor, fitted like a corset with tiny vine-like patterns inscribed in the steel. Her hips held a belt of blue bottles and a couple of gray pouches. With a second arrow in hand, she took a blue bottle from her belt. She pressed the arrowhead into the bottle and held it upside down.

Wander put her hand at her back to feel the shaft of the arrow that had just hit her. Her fingers curled around the wood and pulled. Tearing the arrow out of her flesh, she threw the bloody thing to the ground. She felt nothing: no pain, no dizziness.

A second arrow came in the few seconds Wander looked away. Her hand shot up and locked around the arrow shaft before the tip could impale her neck. Throwing it down, she swung her blade to chop the third arrow shot.

Placing both hands on her sword's handle, Wander rushed forward. Aura's Horns pulled three arrows against her bowstring. She turned the bow horizontal and shot the three arrows. Taking a hand off her sword, Wander blasted the air between her and the Arm, sending the arrows flying off. More of the yellow mist dissipated, showing a browner world of road and dust.

The Horn seemed unfazed, standing her ground. Her white hair loosened in its bun. Wander did not stop charging. Swinging down her sword, the steel met with the bow. Whatever it was made of, Wander's sword seemed to bounce off the material. The Horn's free hand dove to her hip. Wander leapt backward to dodge the uppercut of a knife.

Backing up more for distance, Wander pointed her sword and stabbed into the dirt road. Looking up, she saw the similar spell she once used on humans. Vines burst from the soil around the Horn's feet. In bloodlust, Wander wanted to see the vines break the woman's neck. She wanted them to enter her nostrils, ears, and mouth, to destroy the puppet to the point of uselessness for its master. Make it beyond healing, without any escape.

Aura's Horns pulled a blue bottle from her belt. Pulling the cork out, she dumped a black liquid on the ground. The vines sizzled and withered. Stepping out unharmed, the spirit continued to sprinkle the dark liquid on the ground around where she stood. She encircled herself in the stuff.

Drawing in a frustrated breath, Wander ran straight for her. She let out a roar of anger as she thrust the blade forward. The Horn's gloved hand curled into a fist and aimed to punch the sword aside on its flat end. Wander saw the action and with delight she turned the blade. The Arm's fist hit the sharp end of Wander's sword, sending the blade back but at a cost. The skin along her knuckles opened to bone. Black blood drooled and curled along her fingers.

Unperturbed, the Arm drew an arrow and set it against her bow. She took more time in the shot than the others, the arrowhead pointing at Wander's shoulder. When she shot, Wander easily dodged but heard a scream.

Looking to where the arrows struck, she saw a human had been watching their fight from a second floor window. His head fell on the windowsill, the shaft through his eye. More screams came from behind him. Not all humans were running. They were also hiding.

Turning back to the Arm, Wander's heart dropped at the sight of an empty street. The woman had escaped. Wander looked back to where the child cried over his dead mother. Gone. At least he got away.

Moving through the city, Wander found alleyways of poison gas like before. When she came to those spots, she threw her hand up. Air burst from her palm. Her headscarf and cloak billowed, and the mist scattered. With the air clear, Wander moved on past the bodies of those who breathed the poison.

She had nothing to use against the fires she passed. The burned corpses looked like her, with patches of red and black skin. Some bodies still glowed with flame like a dying fire. Coughing rose from one of the burned corpses. Wander would not know if they were a man or woman if it weren't for the breasts. Every other definitive aspect of the body had sizzled until it withered. Stopping at the body, Wander sat on her knees. The woman's blackened lips spread to show white teeth chattering. Slamming her eyelids tight, she reopened them and let loose tears as she looked at Wander. "Help," she whimpered with a raspy voice.

Wander took her hand. "Can you get up?"

She cried in agony and her bleeding hand violently shook. No use, the woman could not even budge. Wander's mind drew a blank at any thought of a magical way to save her. Someone like Aura could heal her. Even with her skin and mind sacrificed to the guardian, Wander had no power like that. Did the guardian lack the power to save people, or was it that he didn't want to?

The quivering hand turned still and Wander dropped the arm to the cobblestone. Standing up, she turned her head to see a familiar face.

Vincent stood with a sword in one hand, a chain swinging in the other. Unlike everyone else Wander had seen outside the castle walls, he stood alive without a scratch. She could almost shiver with adrenaline by just looking at him.

A blood curdling scream roared from behind Vincent. Both he and Wander looked to see a man race out of an alley, his right arm holding his mangled left. A creature leapt out of the passage after him. Paws hit his back. He fell face first on the stone paved street. Dark lips curled in a snarl of sharp fangs and teeth. Its maw opened to crunch the flailing man. Blood and drool came down from its mouth biting down on the now silent and limp body. With the man still in its jaws, the animal looked up at Wander and Vincent with wide brown eyes. Wander recognized the creature. It was an enchanted wolf, just like in the Emerald Wilds. Some of them grew as large as the trees. Their howls always woke her when the moon was at its highest. But how was one here?

The wolf dropped its kill down and crouched. It growled, narrowing its focus on Vincent.

"RUN!" Wander shouted.

Vincent ran toward the beast. The wolf jumped forward, its shadow eclipsing Vincent. Wander almost looked away, prepared to see him get chewed and spat out. The wolf pounded onto him with its jaws wide and ready to chomp down on Vincent's head. Vincent launched his sword up through the creature's lower jaw. Pulling out, he stabbed up through the jaw again, again, and again. As the wolf moved off him, he managed to slice its chest as well.

Vincent rolled away. The wolf breathed heavy with blood pouring from its torn up jaw.

The warrior stood up, readying his sword for the next attack. The wolf's entire form was enveloped in darkness. The darkness fell to the ground in a shadow. Rising, the darkness spread to a creature of similar size. The shadow turned into a boar the size of a bear. Four tusks stuck out of its blood-soaked mouth. Dust flew up from the earth as the creature breathed. The wounds Vincent gave still bled from its jaw.

Maybe Vincent was in shock, or the boar was too quick. Wander could not tell as she watched the charge and maul Vincent. It pushed him to the ground, its tusks goring and beating at him.

Wander shot forward and sank her sword as far as its hilt into the boar's back leg. Clutching the handle, she endured the struggles of the boar as she pulled the blade further through its flesh. She tried to cause as much damage as she could, twisting, pulling, and pushing. She sent magic through the blade, and she squeezed plants through the boar's veins and flesh. The roots pushed through the wound for room.

Screaming, the boar backed away from Vincent. Dust rose from the streets as it struggled away. Wander pulled the sword out of the beast's leg. Roots dangled out of its gored wound, their magical growth ending with the separation from Wander.

The boar ran off. Vincent lay motionless. His head was turned away. Under his armor, she couldn't tell if he was breathing. She placed her hand on his bloody chest. "Don't touch me," he hissed weakly.

"You're alright?"

Vincent's hands blindly searched and reached around him. Wander looked over to where his weapons fell. Luckily, they were not near.

"I'm not your enemy," she said.

Vincent attempted to get up only to hiss in agony and lie back down. His body shivered. "You're one of Aura's puppets. It's obvious."

"Then why would I attack her other Arms?"

"To gain our trust."

"You can say that about anyone!"

"You're inhuman. You have powers similar to the others."

Wander opened her mouth but then shut up. Proving her innocence was impossible. Even if she could tell them that a guardian controlled her, they'd just be suspicious for different reasons. "You'll know the truth once I kill Aura myself. Maybe if I kill one of her Arms."

"Like your feathered friend? What makes him so different from them?"

"Let's get you out of the street. I'll help you get up."

Vincent groaned as she tucked her arm under his torso and pulled him up. He left a smear of blood on the road. She guided his arm over her shoulder. Vincent put weight on both his legs only to hiss in agony. "One's broken," he breathed, picking up his left leg.

"Okay, just lean on me. We won't move far."

She led him to the nearest building. The first room had a hall and stairs. Wander stared at the stairs then back outside. Vincent spoke through clenched teeth, "What's wrong?"

"We have to get you up those stairs. Aura's Horns brought poison that is like a heavy fog. I don't think it reaches high, though. You'll be safest there."

Wander set her sword against the wall. She and Vincent gripped both sides of the stair's railings and took one step at a time. The higher they got, the heavier Vincent felt. His movements slowed.

Reaching the top, Wander set Vincent down in a plush chair. His dark skin had paled, and his eyes closed as he took labored breaths. Wander moved to the nearest room and tore the white curtains from the windows. She returned to Vincent and pulled his shirt up. "Stop," he murmured, barely conscious.

"Let me help you while I can." For all she knew, the guardian's will could just pull her away from him, leaving him to die.

His tense body sank limp. Looking back at his face, she saw that he had fainted. Biting her lower lip, she bandaged his back wound with the curtain. She found another on his shoulder and wrapped around it quickly.

Rushing down the stairs, she grabbed her sword and left the building. In a run, she searched the streets. She could no longer chase the sight of smoke; it was everywhere. She moved back north. The victims moved toward the castle—and so did the killers. The destruction had moved inward while she attended to Vincent. Homes that were once just abandoned had now become hills of rubble. Glowing ashes moved slowly through the air like fireflies. Corpses lay in pieces, cooked, crushed, or arrow pinned.

Shadows danced in an alleyway and Wander lingered. As she neared, she could feel heat against her cheeks. A blast of fire roared from the passage. Glow and heat blinded Wander's vision, like planting her face into a pyre. Her knees locked and her fingers clutched at her sword handle. With all her might, she slashed the flames. An explosion of air staggered her back. The blast dispersed like splashed water. Despite not touching her, Wander could feel the heat crackle and singe her already deformed skin.

Chant stood in the passageway, glowing brighter than ever. Her usually orange hair had become gold and moved wild like grass under a water's current. A gold chest plate glittered with the reflection of flames. Her bare feet jingled with anklets. Looking ahead at Wander, a smile broke across her face. She walked through the now scorched alleyway, wood blacked and sizzling. "If it isn't our escape artist! I didn't expect someone like you to be here, at the heart of humanity."

Wander hesitated before asking, "Where's Masu? Is he alright?"

"You're not going to see him again," Chant said as her hand raised and a fire ball formed.

Wander charged.

Chant evaporated into a dark cloud. She flew past and behind Wander before reforming into her humanoid body. "Killing me is impossible you know. Even with a guardian's power, a human can't kill an elemental." She threw both hands forward and an explosion of fire blinded Wander.

This time Chant stood too close for Wander to prepare in time. She fell to her knees and slammed her eyes tight shut. Everything eclipsed in white. Her ears rang. Her head down to her toes went cold and numb. Whispers and tapping rattled in her head. She lost sense of direction and the feeling of the ground under her feet.

She felt like she fell back into her body as she flinched and opened her eyes. Heat and dark smears had scarred the alley. The walls Wander stood between were near completely eaten by the flames, showing the insides of abandoned shops. Her sword lay stabbed into the ground, though Wander did not remember placing it there. Her bleeding fingers uncurled from its handle as she looked at her hands and arms. The fire had hit her, though she felt nothing. Her entire body was like a rotten flesh cocoon, bleeding, peeling, and sizzling. Chant stood at the entrance of the passageway. The elemental's eyes stared wide, taking in that Wander somehow still stood alive.

Both of Wander's hands grasped the blade and pulled it from the street. Looking down, she saw her legs quivering, her pants in tatters from the fire blast. She couldn't feel pain, but her body could barely comprehend its own condition.

Chant's hand fell to her hip as she drew out a golden dagger and flew forward.

Wander turned to the building on her right and stabbed her blade through the weak wood. Her palms slipped around from weakness as she cast magic through the blade. She did not even know what for; she just did it in desperation. The entire structure collapsed into itself, starting with the roof. The walls broke apart and the debris of brick, wood, and furniture all poured into the alleyway, engulfing Chant.

Wander faced the other building. The sword glowed in darkness as she stabbed into the stone foundation. The chimney crumbled down into an avalanche of wreckage, piling on top of where the other building had collapsed. Staggering back, Wander took a few gasps of breath. She rubbed her finger under her nose and looked to see blood.

It was unlikely that the elemental just perished, but she was at least incapacitated for a while under all that weight. Straightening up, Wander walked out of the passage. As she moved through the streets, she felt fast pulsations in her heart. The screams and the crackling of wood sounded like dim echoes. Her vision fuzzed. Sinking the sword into the dirt, Wander leaned forward and coughed.

"Wander!" A voice cut away from the dim echoes. A tall figure rushed toward her. As he came closer, she recognized Under's dark coat and feminine face.

"My God, you're in tatters and bleeding everywhere." He took off his coat and placed it around her quaking shoulders.

Still crouched forward, Wander blinked up at the shadow. "What are you doing here?"

"I got worried. Then I saw this entire town was under attack, and I had to find you."

Wander let out a shaking breath. Warmth ran down her cheek as she leaned into his chest. Under's arms carefully wrapped around her, and he leaned his head down on her hers. She felt her warm breath against his shirt reflect back to her face. Shutting her eyes, she melted into weak relief.

"I'm so glad I found you."

She nodded against him.

He stepped back with hands holding her shoulders. "We have to get you somewhere safe."

Wander put her arms through the sleeves of Under's jacket, her fingers just peeking out at the ends. "I tried talking to Naktol. She thinks Aura's controlling my mind and wants me captured."

"After this attack, the humans will be more scared than ever. You should avoid them." He took her hand in his, "Come. Let's leave."

She nodded, fingers curled against his smooth palm. As they moved toward the city borders, Wander stared at the sky. When did it become night?

"What happened to the guardian?"

"He's outside the city, I think."

She looked at the back of Under's head. Warmth kept leaking from of her eyes. She wanted to say something, but no words came. His presence felt as comforting as food when starved or light when scared. He cared about her enough to come to this burning city.

A hawk flew over them. The bird dove to the street they faced and fell into a dark shadow.

Under stopped and pushed Wander behind him.

The shadow rose into the form of a large golden cat, brown fur hung around its neck. The beast let out a roar, showing white fangs. The colossal paws were large enough to cover Wander's entire face.

Under's body turned to darkness and fell to the ground. The shadow rose to a bear that towered over Wander and the cat. Landing on all fours, the bear let out a growl.

The cat's body went dark and fell to the cobblestone. It rose to the giant boar that had gored Vincent. Under changed again, this time into a creature Wander had never seen before. Like the boar, it had tusks. Its gray body rose to the size of some buildings. Its long nose was like a fifth leg, and its ears looked like blankets.

The giant boar sank into the earth as a shadow and the darkness rose and kept rising past the buildings. Wings cast out. A tail stretched out and whipped down on a building, crushing the roof. The black color faded to reveal another form unfamiliar to Wander. It was a scaled beast. Its bat-like wings spread darkness over roofs and chimneys. The limbs were cat-like, slim and calculated. Its neck was as long and thick as the trees in the Emerald Wilds, holding a head that seemed like a hybrid of wolf and snake. The reptilian face let out a howl that made Wander's ears ache.

Just when she thought the creature could not get more unbelievable, its maw opened to let out a scream of fire into the sky. Wander could feel the heat on her face from where she stood. The entire street glowed in dancing red. It looked down, its eyes dark gold with red pupils. The irises seemed like many arrows pointing at a single glowing red ball with dark shapes inside.

Under fell down and rose back up as his human self. Wasting no time, he grabbed Wander's hand, pulling her along an alley. As he led her, Wander looked up to see the beast stretch its neck. Its nostrils widened as it took a colossal breath inward. The monster opened its maw and blew out a lungful of fire. The entire alleyway glowed red.

Wander shut her eyes, preparing to lose all feeling in her body again. Instead, Under jerked her arm as they dived to the side. Opening her eyes, she saw they had retreated into a house. She could still feel the heat behind the wall. "What is that creature?" she asked.

"He turned into a dragon. . ."

"Dragon?"

The entire building shook. Wander and Under jumped back as dark claws stabbed through the wall and raked. "C'mon!" Under pulled Wander through the building and out another doorway before the entire building exploded in flame.

Under nearly tripped on a corpse, stumbling across the street to another home. The roof over her head did not stave off her nerves. They leaned against the wall by a window where Under glanced. Whatever he saw did not bode well for them as his head shot back as though to avoid something.

Between her heaving breaths, Wander said, "I think he can smell us."

"Maybe the smoke and fire will cover us."

"I can fight him."

"No, you can't."

"I fought him earlier. I wounded his leg."

"He's a dragon, Wander! He is the reason the deviants beat the winged beings. With Aura's healing, mind control, and his shape shifting, you don't stand a chance. No one does." He took her hand. "We shouldn't stand still."

Past a hallway and kitchen, they exited the back of the building to another street. Under tugged her arm more and more as she grew tired and slowed down.

They continued toward the city walls. Any sign of the dragon had disappeared. No roaring, fire blowing, shadows, rumbling, or flapping wings. Despite this, Wander could not be calm. Her entire body quaked. Under stopped. Wander followed his gaze to the right. A woman limped across a street. A mess of short blonde hair blocked her eyes. Her pants were stained with blood. She held a mangled left arm, looking frail enough for a breeze to knock over. The woman fell to her knees.

Under and Wander ran through an alleyway to get to her.

"Hey, are you alright?" Under asked.

She looked up with bright blue globes, blood spattered around her doll-like face. Darkness rose up and encased her body before falling into the ground. Before either Wander or Under could react, the shadow exploded into its dragon form. Until now, the shape shifting Wander had witnessed was graceful and labored like the slow pour of milk. This transformation was violent, like a wild animal tearing through a dark curtain.

The dragon's launched its maw at Wander. The teeth crunched her right arm before throwing her up in the air. Twisting in the sky, she saw the dragon's neck snap back to her like a snake as its jaws chomped on both her legs. Its head viciously shook back and forth. Her entire body went numb, but the sight of her legs between the monster's teeth was enough to thrust her heart and mind to utter terror.

The dragon let go of her. Hitting the ground knocked the sight out of her for a second. She heard the beast scream. When her vision returned, she saw an owl attacking its eyes. Diving down, the owl turned into Under. He scooped her up. She shut her eyes as she felt him run. Each moment lasted forever, every second with the possibility of death. She did not want to see it come for her.

She felt Under go up some steps. Cracking her eyes open, she saw a ceiling. Under hissed, falling to his knees and setting Wander on the floor. Looking up at him, she saw his right arm had been hit by something, the upper part red and swelling. His face eclipsed her vision. Brown eyes full of panic. "Wander! Are you alright?!"

"I'm alright." She tried to move, but her legs only twitched. Raising her head up, she easily saw where the dragon had chomped down.

"You can't walk?"

She kept trying to raise herself. She propped her torso up with her elbow, but the rest of her body had been too damaged. Under put his arms around Wander and tried to lift her up. One arm managed to lift her legs from under the knees, but the other only quivered under the weight of her back.

"His tail whipped me when he bit you. I think he did something to my arm." Under sat back, breath heaving. "I can't carry you."

"We can wait here. The battle will pass," Wander said.

"It's not safe. He's looking for you. He could crush this building like he did with my and Alice's home."

Wander's hand reached for his. "Let's chance it."

Under took her hand in his. Silence hung between them.

Wander wanted to shut her eyes and fall asleep. Even with Under's coat, her body felt cold. At this point, she did not mind dying. It felt like a lifetime since she lived in the Emerald Wilds with Masu. She could not remember what his voice sounded like. The things that she fought and sacrificed for had begun to disappear from her memory. It was like fighting for a vague dream now. With her mind no longer completely her own, she could imagine enduring things far worse than death, like fighting forever.

Her thoughts scattered when Under's hand squeezed hers. "I can kill him."

"How?"

Any fear, panic, or sadness had been replaced by stone cold seriousness. "This whole time, if I was brave enough, I could have just killed him. I could have killed him before all this, but I kept the idea out of my mind."

"What do you mean?"

"I'm a shadow just like him. Despite that, I stayed human while he killed Alice. I could have saved her. I could have stopped this all from happening."

"What can you turn into that would kill a dragon?"

"I can't make the same mistake with you. If you die here—"

"Under," her hand tightened its grip on his, "what would you turn into?"

"Even I'm not sure what would happen to me. If I'd be dead or—"

"Don't do it. If you're going to die, don't do it."

"No. I've got to do it. I'm the only one who can."

"Under—"

"I've been pretending I can't do anything."

Wander held his hand as tightly as she could. He had the expression of someone lost in a storm of thoughts. The sound of cracking fires outside surrounded the house. He shook his head and straightened his back. "I've got to do it."

"No!"

Under's eyes finally looked into hers. "It's going to be okay."

"Let's just wait for the battle to pass!"

Under bent his head down. His lips pressed against her forehead. Letting go of her hand, he stood up. Darkness rose up from his feet to his head. The shadow fell and rose back up into a clone of Wander.

Turning away, Under left the room.

Wander tried to move, only her arm reaching out. "No," she cried. "Please come back! UNDER!"

The only response was the crackling fires outside.

"Hey . . ."

Something nudged her side, awakening aches and pains along her hip and chest. Wander squinted open to brightness. Brown eyes framed in a helmet hovered over her.

"My God, are you alive?"

She turned her head to see the sight of floorboards and distant stairs. The air smelled of burning and sweat. Twisting her body, her legs peeled from the ground. Propping herself on her elbow, her head pounded. Once she saw the doorway, she remembered the sight of Under leaving. "What happened?"

"The battle is over. Aura's forces retreated."

Sunlight poured in from the windows and dust glowed.

Wander rubbed her head. "How long has it been?"

"It's been ten hours since the retreat. I'm with Naktol's military. We're searching for survivors."

"Where's Under? He's a man who is really tall with dark hair. He's pale."

"I'm sorry. I don't know who that is. If he was with you, he could be with the survivors' group back at the park. C'mon, I'll take you there. There's a doctor there who can help you."

The soldier lifted Wander in his arms. Outside, what was the scene of a nightmare had transformed into a sunny day. Men and women walked around in armor. Across the street, one kicked down the door of a house. Three talked on a porch. One held the hand of a hunched old woman, leading her northward. Next door to where Wander stayed, soldiers lifted rubble. One ducked under as they held a piece of roof. She backed out dragging a young man's corpse. She hauled him to the center of the street, where bodies lay in a perfect line.

Wander's heart quickened as she leaned forward in the soldier's arms. The bodies were many people of all sorts. A child even younger than Roslyn first caught her attention. He lay with a toy doll in his arm. Next to him, a woman lay with a bloodied chest. One soldier sat by a body, both her hands holding his hand, she cried silently.

No sign of Under among the bodies.

Turning her head, Wander's breath left her. A giant boulder silhouetted over the roofs of homes a couple streets down. "What's that?"

"I know it sounds crazy, but that's what saved us. A giant rock fell from the sky and crushed the dragon's head. With Aura's Shadow dead, the others retreated."

"How could that happen?"

"I'm not sure. Some of our people are looking into it."

Tears swelled in Wander's eyes. "Take me there, please."

"Why?"

"I might know what happened."

Her chest tightened as they neared the looming stone. The homes, people, and soldiers they passed all seemed in a separate world from her. A loud sobbing came from one window. Two soldiers helped a man with a mangled leg out of wreckage.

When they got to the boulder, she could see what became of Aura's Shadow.

The colossal body took up the entire street. Its wings shaded where they stood, like a massive tent. The tail landed on what used to be a shop. Seeing the scales up close reminded Wander of smooth jewels. They walked along its back to its neck. The neck bent backward, bleeding, and bone the size of tree trunks stuck out.

"Looks like the boulder crushed its neck and rolled up to its head," the man holding her said.

A group of twenty soldiers all stood at the boulder's bloody base, completely covering what was once the dragon's head. Wander shrunk when she saw Naktol standing among the soldiers. Naktol looked up and their eyes met. The queen ran to her and her helper. "Soldier! Where did you find her?"

"Um, just a couple streets west from here, my lord."

"Robert!" one of the soldiers shouted. "Do you not know who that is?"

"No!"

"Are you blind? She's unmistakable! It's Wander, you dimwit! Her wanted posters are all over the barracks walls!"

The soldier tensed up as the queen hovered over him.

"She was unconscious in a house! I just thought she was a severely burned and injured civilian. I swear!"

Naktol spoke. "Set her down and go back to work."

"Right away!" Despite his obvious panic, the soldier gently set Wander against the wall of a porch. He jogged off, glancing over his shoulder before he disappeared around a corner.

Naktol's shadow shaded over Wander. She seemed unarmed, but shined in silver armor. "What did you do?" the queen asked. She spoke plainly, not loudly or angrily.

Wander gazed away from Naktol to the gray boulder. The stone was flat enough to be a table on one side. The top pointed toward the sky like a mountain.

"I have a whole party of soldiers that say they witnessed you turn into a bird, fly over the dragon, and turn into this rock. Explain."

The vision of the rock blurred, and Wander slammed her eyes shut. She attempted to sit up, but her body wouldn't obey. She knew Naktol waited impatiently for an answer, but she could only shake her head. She opened her mouth and a wail emerged. She raised shaking hands to cover her face. The darkness of her palms could not erase the sight of the bloody stone. A hand touched her shoulder. She convulsed away and let out a scream. Despite her legs aching with resistance, she curled up into a ball.

She did not want to open her eyes ever again.

Even among rubble and bodies, Sollast regained its bird songs and blue sky. Volunteers came from various settlements with carts full of blankets, medicine, and food. Supplies for the burn victims were in the highest demand: ointment, disposable sheets, water, alcohol disinfectant, fish skin, and willow bark. Some people survived with burns as intense as Wander's, but the moment their tongues touched the relief of water their bodies died of shock.

Many were crushed by buildings rotted down by fire or by the dragon's rampage. Arms and legs dangled from rubble piles. The military's dogs would sniff the bodies out from the street. Barking, they'd climb the wreckage, and everyone would start digging.

There were a few miracles. Both citizens and the military worked together to dig through a mountain of debris with the dog barking and digging the hardest. With limited shovels, some people dug until their hands bled through their gloves. "They're alive!" someone shouted. A man and woman were pulled out of the wreckage, the two refusing to let go of each other, legs shaking, one crying. Their bodies finally in the light, they embraced.

While much of the military remained organized, the citizens became wanderers looking for those they had lost. When the military could not find a missing person's body, the citizens moved about the streets like ghosts. With the smell of smoke and rotting flesh still in the air, many people moved around holding scented cloth to their noses and mouths.

Despite his broken leg, Vincent limped through the streets to see for himself what was saved and lost. Within only a couple days, the name Wander murmured from everyone's lips.

"She turned into a bird, and that bird turned into the stone that killed the dragon. The little thing soared just above the dragon's head and then poof! She really was a witch."

"No, no, no. You got it all wrong. She's in the queen's custody right now, so how can she have turned into stone? I heard it was someone else's magic. Didn't the girl say that herself?"

"I heard the queen doesn't plan to kill her."

"My fiancé is in the military. She told me that Wander is in a cell, but she doesn't eat, speak, or do anything."

Vincent tried to view the stone for himself only to be stopped. The entire area had been fenced and guarded.

"It's really not worth seeing." The guard laughed. "Everyone's saying it's magical, but however you look at it, it's just a rock. Despite our orders, Stan touched it. Hell, he even punched it and bruised his knuckles. I swear it's just a rock."

The castle became a refuge for the most wounded. The best doctors traveled to the castle, each given a hall with an ever increasing line of patients. Vincent was one of those patients. He did not remember, but a military team found him stumbling out of a house during the battle. One recognized him from the barracks and carried him back to the castle for treatment.

What Vincent could remember was Wander carrying him upstairs, her grip awkward but strong. He could recall her standing in the middle of the street before noticing him, her dark cloak flowing with the ash carried in the breeze. She had that bastard sword in one hand and that dark feather dangling from her wrist.

Despite the doctor telling him to stay in bed, Vincent did not quit moving. No book, sickness, no man, or woman could keep him in bed during the day. He needed to see the destruction and repair of Sollast. Today though, he just wanted to move around. The gardens were the least crowded place he could find.

The battle never really made it to the castle. The dragon knocked down some walls but seemed to find more promise for victims in the city. In spite of not sustaining damage, the garden had still changed. With its lack of visitors, Vincent still could not escape what happened.

"Vincent." A man approached him out of the path to the hedges. "The queen wishes to speak with you."

Vincent stopped hobbling, his dark wooden crutches dug into the dirt. He nodded, knowing this would happen soon.

"She is in the southeast wing in the tearoom."

Vincent turned and made his way toward the castle doors. The queen seldom made appearances post-battle. If Vincent had any guess, it was that she was plotting. Aura had made her daring move. Now humanity had to answer. But how?

Fighting was impossible. Even without her shadow, Aura's Arms had an advantage. The deviant queen had no army, and for that, the humans thought they could easily win. They did not count on how magic could turn one spirit into an army. Through this massacre, they also learned of a new kind of deviant poison. Aura may not have an army, but she had her own people focusing on crafting weapons and contagions. With her Arms doing all the fighting, her people could put so much time and resources into science that tossed humanity into the dust.

While humanity's best bet for survival would be to scatter, that would mean they'd already lost. The winged beings also scattered in the end. Then they got picked off one by one for years and years. Vincent could take this meeting as a chance to warn Natal to not yet go on the defensive.

Sollast Castle's tearoom was a dimly lit place with a round white rug. Three screens boxed in the round table at the center.

For the first time, Vincent saw the queen without armor on. She looked frail, body draped in a silver dress. Her large feet were encased in sandals that looked like more of her daughters' taste.

Her hands cupped her steaming tea. "I was going to meet you in the tower, but then I remembered your injury."

With more effort than he was used to, he managed to sit across from her. He set his crutches against the table. "I would've been fine."

"Of course."

The queen's eyelids dropped to her tea. Her nails pinched the string of the teabag and pulled it to the side of her cup. "Would you like tea?"

"No, thank you."

"Straight to business then," she drank her tea quickly, like a painful shot of whiskey. "You cannot fight anymore."

"It'll take a while for me to fight again."

"Before I go into my plan for you, I'd like you to give me your honest opinion. Do you think humanity has hope of winning this war?"

Vincent could not find the guts to tell the queen there was no hope. No matter how hopeless something was, he could not bring himself to tell others. So instead of answering, he remained silent.

Naktol nodded, understanding the silence. However, instead of sorrow, her face brightened. "What if humanity wasn't alone?"

"What do you mean?"

"We can ally ourselves with other spirits. If we had even one of their kingdoms on our side, we could beat Aura. We'd no longer have to resort to just ranged combat. We would have people who could touch them!"

The rumors were true. The queen really was thinking of allying humans and spirits. Vincent never believed them because of the war. Why would the queen war with the deviants if she wanted spirits as friends?

"Don't tell me you're anti-spirit."

"Most humans are anti-spirit because spirits are anti-human. To most of them, we're animals."

"Well, we can change that. I've been writing to King Dim, Queen Whisper, and Queen Iris since I have been crowned. None answered my letters until now." The queen pulled a brown envelope from her side. She handed it to Vincent.

A rounded flap was folded down with a broken gold seal. Vincent opened the flap to see the actual envelope was the letter folded up. He spread the parchment to a cream colored inside with dark ink in elegant cursive.

Lord Naktol,

The Glowing Palace is holding the annual Moonflower Ball. The Moonflower Ball is an ancient tradition in lullaby society, and only for the upper class. The Ball is held for kings to choose a bride. Both my brother, Dim, and I extend a welcome to you and your kind.

However, there is a condition to be met for this welcome. Rumor has it that a human girl exists that can touch spirits. If she attends the party as a choice bride, only then are you welcome in our halls.

Sincerely,
King Fade

Vincent squinted at the words. The signature ended with a gray stamp of the lullaby's crest, a rabbit in a moon. He had never heard anything good about lullabies, nocturnal spirits who drank blood to survive, like bats. Their breath put anything but other lullabies to sleep. There were endless tales of lullabies having powers to put humans to sleep just by making eye contact. Keeping his mouth shut, he handed the paper back to Naktol.

Naktol tediously refolded the parchment. "Wander is a danger, but if we give her as a bride to these spirits, we could have an alliance."

"What happened to Wander?"

"She is my prisoner with eyes always on her. My original plan was to have her experimented with and executed, but this letter changed my plans."

"What makes you think Wander would go through with this plan?"

"That's where you'll help. Since we caught her after the battle, the girl is unresponsive. Something traumatic happened, or she's lost her mind. She doesn't speak, barely eats, and just lies in her cell. The guards have reported lots of crying to the point that they're feeling awful for her."

"What could I possibly do? Why me?"

"She knows you and—"

"That's not it," Vincent hissed. "You keep pushing me, and only me, to her. She knows other soldiers on much better terms. This is for a different reason. Both you and I know that. Why don't you just say it?"

The queen narrowed her eyes, "You are the only wind-born in my ranks. If you open that part of yourself to her, she will automatically feel closer to you."

Vincent did not know whether to feel relief or rage when the queen finally said it. This whole time, he'd been trying to be normal. The queen's fascination always sickened him. He knew it wasn't for talent or need; it was always for being wind-born.

Under the busy military barracks were the jail cells of Sollast Castle. Torches lit the short stone passageway to the guards. How strange it was to stay underground in the dark while all of Sollast attempted to recover from the destruction above.

One of Naktol's servicemen had aided Vincent down the stairs. The guards seemed to have expected Vincent. "It's the last cell on the left." One unlocked the barred gate behind them. The other guard handed Vincent a rusted key. They stepped aside as he entered another hallway. This one was bordered in prison cells with bars only wide enough for an arm to reach out.

To his right, Vincent made out a skeletal figure. A man, not Wander. The man lay on his bed with only underwear on. He paid Vincent no mind, their eyes barely meeting before the man turned his back to him.

Vincent had heard rumors that this place was meant for rogue spirits, serial killers, and criminals meant to remain secretly hidden.

Reaching the end of the hall, Vincent saw Wander. She sat on the edge of a bed completely sheltered in darkness. The silhouette turned to reveal a pair of green eyes stained and reddened. Her fingers pinched at the dark feather tied to her wrist. Her gaze held unpredictability.

Vincent took the rusted key and unlocked her cell while keeping his eyes on her. She faced away. Once inside, he locked the door behind him. Sure she could just kill him and take the key, but having to unlock the door might give the guards enough time to stop her.

Adjusting the crutches under each arm, Vincent hobbled in front of Wander. She did not look up or say a single word.

"Naktol has plans for you," Vincent said. "I've come to ask for your compliance."

To his surprise, she answered. It was only a mumble, muffled out by her veil.

He dared to step closer. "What did you say?"

"I don't know what that word means."

"What word?"

"Compliance."

Young wind-borns had trouble with words. Vincent tightened his hands on his crutches, not quite knowing how to feel about the familiar fumbling. "I am asking, will you obey Naktol's plan?"

"What is her plan?"

"It's to create an alliance with spirits. With their help, we can defeat Aura. The queen has written to the spirit kingdoms many times. Only now has one of them replied. The lullaby kings, Dim and Fade, are holding a special party. You have been invited."

"That's strange." No emotion in her voice. She spoke like someone barely conscious.

"I won't lie to you. The party is meant for possible brides. Both of the kings are choosing future wives. They want you to attend."

"I don't understand."

"They are interested in you because you can touch spirits. If one of the kings chooses you as a bride, the humans would automatically get an alliance."

"A bride . . ."

"A bride is a partner. In lullaby culture, though, you will be owned like property."

"Like a bed or basket?"

He nodded.

She took her time thinking, her gaze completely enamored with the floor. The other prisoner coughed from his cell. Vincent prepared for anything. She may have indeed lost her mind. She could laugh, cry, or just start screaming, and he would have been ready.

Her head tilted. "I'll do it."

"Really?"

"It's a good plan. Humans should ally with spirits."

"Why don't I believe you?"

She finally looked up at him. Her tortured eyes rimmed with redness, as though they had been trampled. "I have nothing left to lose."

More dangerous words were never spoken. Whatever happened to Wander, humanity would be lucky to get rid of her. She'd be the spirits' problem now.

Chapter 17
The Moonflower Palace

"If anywhere in Awei is like you are in a dream, it's the Moonflower Palace. It's not just because it's beautiful. It's a difficult place to remember after you leave if you're not a lullaby." – Travels of Manger

Wander lay motionless in bed for days. The guards brought her three meals, slipping the brick-like meat and carrots through the bars on a paper plate. She only ate a couple bites each meal just to calm her aching insides.

She could not end her sobs and shakes. Any self-reflection on her life felt like an endless darkness, a cave with the entrance blocked and with no light on the other end. Masu's feather withered like a flower on her wrist. She couldn't remember his voice, smile, or how he touched her. At this point, she could admit that she did not know why she still wanted to save him. She had sacrificed everything, and for what? If his mind wasn't controlled, he'd be a stranger. In the end the Masu that raised her was just a persona created by the guardian.

Wander tried to remember the joys of the Flinsler family. The way Roslyn held her hand and took her outside to play or Ms. Flinsler's care in making dresses. Ethan's judging glare from across the dining room table. Any recollection of them held no comfort. Chant burned Roslyn and Ms. Flinsler to death while

Wander ran away. Ethan died by her own hands. The family housed themselves in her nightmares, and now they stood in her waking mind around her like ghosts. Then there was Alice. Unlike with the Flinslers, Wander had witnessed her slow and sorrowful death. When she closed her eyes, she saw the image of Under bent over Alice's crushed form, trying his best to comfort her. The end of a life in its most raw and godless pose.

Under's vague death crumbled all foundation. To be a stone is no different from being dead. Rocks aren't conscious. They can't speak, breathe, feel, taste, or have thoughts. For Under, warm, talkative, and caring Under to change into something so cold, heavy, and silent . . .

Wander's fingers pulled Under's coat forward. She popped up the collar to brush against her cheeks and nose, taking in a smoky smell through her headscarf.

And what of herself? She was nothing. Just a weapon the guardian had to swing at Aura. Even now she could feel his will tugging at her to stay alive. She had nothing but that.

Three strangers and two guards gently approached Wander's cell.

"Wander?" A dark-skinned man stepped out of shadow. He dressed uncommonly, wearing a white robe with a gray undershirt and pants, his rope-like hair tied back into a thick ponytail with a white ribbon. "My name is James." His hand reached beyond the bars. Wander looked away, and James took his hand back. "I am from Illula, the lullaby capital. By King Fade's orders and Naktol's permission, I am here to help you through the Moonflower Ball."

"You don't look like a spirit," Wander said.

He laughed. "Far from a lullaby, I know. I'm human, born and raised in Sollast's borders. I moved to Illula later." He went silent, possibly expecting Wander say more. She had nothing. Raising herself up from the bed, she approached the door. James' smile faded when he saw her eyes.

"I'm ready to go."

"Not quite yet. It's a very fancy party. These two ladies here are going to fix you up. As a choice bride, you're going to have to present yourself well."

Wander looked at the two women. They did not look happy to be there. Neither of them made eye contact. Their lips compressed like they had eaten something sour.

After unlocking her prison, the two guards escorted Wander out. With a guard on each side, James, and the two women following, Wander treaded upstairs. The sunlight pierced her eyes when she emerged out to the military barracks. A hush passed through the busy soldiers. She felt eyes hit her at every direction. Mattresses lined the castle walls with injured. Some struggled to lift their heads to see her.

Few people treaded the castle halls. The guards led Wander to a room with painted screens blocking out all but the corner. Only a vanity and bench stood in the corner. The dark wood vanity had thin drawers, and the bench stood with curved legs. "Have a seat," one of the women said.

Wander sat on the bench. It took work for her gaze to avoid the mirror. She never wanted to look at herself again. Each day she only felt uglier, her skin like raisins, eyes tortured.

"I brought the dress," James said. "It should be behind the screens."

One of the women tapped Wander's shoulder. She immediately flinched. "Please undress."

Wander turned her back to the mirror as she unwrapped her veil. Her fingers caressed Under's coat. Before allowing sentiment to claim her heart, she shed it off and did not dare think of him more. She had to keep numb, to not reflect, and to just do what she was told.

The other woman pulled a white dress from behind the painted screen. "It looks rather plain for a bride. No jewels, corset, lace, or train," she said as she held it up to herself.

"If she were dressed in jewels with a corset, lace, and a train, the lullabies would think humanity was trying to show off," James explained. He went behind the screen. "No. If Naktol wants an alliance, Wander will need to dress modestly." He came back with gloves and white cloth. He and the women passed the garb to Wander. "I'm sorry," James folded his arms. "But unless Fade or Dim choose you as a bride, you are still a prisoner. We can't give you privacy."

Wander took a couple moments to understand what James meant. Sheepishly, she shed the last of her garments. Belt, pants, shirt, socks, and boots all came off. Once near nakedness, she made haste to pull the dress over her. She got lost, pulling her hands out where her head was supposed to be. The women helped guide her through the dress.

"Hm? What's this?" One of the women took Wander's hand and tugged at the leather bracelet, Masu's withered feather barely attached.

"Take that off."

Wander shut her eyes tightly when they took her bracelet. She did not dare look where they put it, probably in the trash.

They gloved her hands next, pulling little silk sashes to tighten them to her wrists before tying them into bows. James tediously wrapped the snowy hued cloth around Wander's head. His fingers kept pulling the cloth further down her forehead and the sides toward her cheeks. "We need to see the least amount of skin possible. We just want to see her eyes." They laid a second cloth over her nose, mouth, and chin and tucked away the sides into the headscarf. The women took silver jeweled pins and stuck the needles through the scarf and veil to keep them attached.

James stepped back, his fist covering his mouth as he examined Wander. "The skin between her eyes should be powdered. Also, lots of eye makeup will help and another cover up for her head."

James disappeared behind the screens again. The women soon blocked her vision holding dark pencils. "Look up for me," one said as her pen neared Wander's eyes. She obeyed and gazed up at the stone ceiling. Both women rubbed pencils around her eyes. The dry sensation made her want to shut her eyelids tightly, but she fought the urge.

She wanted her bracelet back. When she held that feather, she could remember burying her face in Masu's wings at night. She even remembered plucking them out before she understood him. When she did that, his wings would ruffle up, each feather rising like a ripple in water.

"Stop tearing. It'll ruin the makeup." Hands rubbed her tears away.

The women stepped back as James returned with a white cloth covered in flowery lace. "Perfect. And here's the finishing touch." He set the lace shawl on Wander's head. "Look in the mirror."

When Wander looked in the mirror, she did not even see herself in her eyes. Her eyes sprung out of the heavenly veil, dark makeup etched perfectly around them. She touched her covered cheek with her gloved hand.

"She's far better," one of the women said.

Outside the castle walls, Vincent waited in a black carriage with white vines painted all over the outside. He sat on a dark, cushioned bench seat. Dressed in a white robe, his head rested on a fisted hand as he looked out the carriage window toward outer Sollast.

Of course Naktol would send him to make sure Wander behaved herself. Her standards for him were becoming less thought out each day. He knew nothing of spirit customs. Few to no humans knew anything about spirit culture, especially for the lullabies. Lullaby breath put people to sleep, they lived by drinking blood, and like any other spirit they could not touch living humans without getting shocked.

Naktol gave Vincent a report on James. He was a prominent thief back when he lived in Sollast. He eventually became too well known. After everyone in the city and beyond knew his face, he escaped to the lullabies for refuge. Naktol believed for so long that they had killed him. It was only until the lullabies sent him to fetch Wander did the queen find out the lullabies had accepted him.

"I trust him less then than the spirits," Naktol said. "Treat him with as much caution as Wander."

"Why not send more soldiers?" Vincent had asked.

"James came with another letter from the kings. They said Wander could attend only with James and one diplomat."

He almost laughed. "I'm not a diplomat!"

"It is no great title. Outside our borders, all humans are diplomats, from the children in the streets to the farmers in the fields. You are going to this party as a representation of how humanity is. You are an injured soldier. The lullabies will notice."

"I'll show them we are weak."

"You say that like it's a bad thing. Do you think spirits think like us? They do not. We are at war with spirits. I once tried to show spirits we were strong, and because of one single misunderstanding, the deviants decided to kill us all. I've learned from that mistake. I will not show my sword to the lullabies. We will show them our weakness out of need for mercy."

Vincent pulled away from his thoughts. James crossed the bridge out of the castle gate with Wander holding his hand.

The Wander he saw was like an alter ego of the original. The original cloaked herself in darkness with wild eyes framed in cloth. She formerly walked like an untrained solider, her boots making too much noise and her body swaying. The original's back and neck leaned forward from the weight of her bastard sword. This Wander had turned the shadiness of her concealed face into something more beautiful and warm. She walked itty bitty steps with feet in hose and gold slippers, her gloved hand gently led by James. As she neared, he could tell she had cried. Even the makeup could not cover that her eyes looked like they had rashes.

"What are you doing here?" Wander spoke louder than usual. The white veil must be thinner than the black, making her voice less muffled.

Vincent straightened up and attempted to look less tired. "The queen ordered me to supervise."

"It's always you."

"I know."

Wander sat across from him. James came in after her and sat by Vincent's side. "It's a day's trip to Vivid Mountain. Dim and Fade's villa is at the top."

"I'd like to know what to expect at this party," Vincent said.

James leaned forward, elbows on his knees. "Well, have either of you had any contact with lullabies before?" The carriage began to move with the sound of donkey hooves clapping against cobblestone. Vincent hated to think their lullaby driver might listen in on their conversation. Carriage driving was an excellent placement for a spy.

Wander shook her head.

"Well, I should let you both know that it's taboo for lullabies to hunt humans and spirits for blood drinking. All the blood they drink to live comes from animals."

"I thought they thought of us as animals," Vincent said.

"Only the assholes think that."

"Am I going to have to drink blood?" Wander asked.

"No. Something else will be provided."

Vincent looked out the window. The carriage strolled through the queen's back road out of Sollast through the mountainside. This way, the carriage would not get attention from Sollast's citizens. If humanity had any strength left, Vincent could picture citizens throwing rocks at a spirit carriage. When trees cleared, the back road had a view of the golden and green patched valleys. The rolling southern mountains took over the horizon beyond the valleys.

"The lullaby kings are Dim and Fade. Dim is the older sibling by ten years. It's important for you to know that he has already been married once. His partner, Queen Floret, died of illness two winters ago. Because of this, he has to pick a new spouse while his younger brother picks his own for the first time."

Vincent could tell that Wander did not understand much, or even care to listen. She probably did not understand anything about human marriage, much less spirit marriage. How old even was she? Two years, maybe three would be Vincent's guess from her basic understandings but odd behavior. Like any wind-born, she was born in an older body, so guessing an age was difficult.

When he thought hard enough, this carriage ride was familiar. He could remember when one came for him. His mind trusting, hazy, and far too naïve to know what awaited him. Wander's eyes drew him out of thoughtfulness. She glanced at him as James talked. Vincent hardened his face so she'd look away.

"Dim also has a daughter, Bell. She's five years old. She's very shy, though, so she'll probably be hiding in her room through the whole event. Dim is very protective of her so if you see her, do not interact with her."

What James did not speak of was of a lullaby's abilities. Their breath knocked consciousness out of people. When a human slept, lullabies could touch them. They were known as the only spirits who could touch humans, but only when humans slept. Why would lullabies want to marry themselves to a human? Surely not out of goodness. They could not touch her unless she slept. While their breath could make her sleep, they could do anything they wanted with her.

"Also while humans and other spirits are awake in the day and sleep at night, it's the opposite for lullabies. So we are going to arrive at Vivid Mountain at night, but that's also right when the ball begins, because for the lullabies, their day is just beginning. I brought some strong beilit leaves." James pulled a dark blue silk cloth and unfolded it to reveal crushed leaves with a teal hue. "They keep you awake. You both should take some when we get to the mountain."

James crossed his arms and leaned back. "Now, tips for getting the kings to like you. I'd say ask them questions, but without sounding stupid or nosy. Don't take up a lot of space. Bow just your head whenever you meet someone. Act excited and grateful to be there."

"What's a bow?"

James smiled and shook his head until he realized she was serious. "Oh. Just dip your chin down until your eyes are at the floor. Don't take too much time to do it. It should only take a second.

"There will be possibly a hundred lullabies there hoping to be chosen as Fade or Dim's bride. Like you, they will also be trying to get the kings to like them. Do not make eye contact with these women. The brides of Moonflower Balls often challenge and fight each other throughout the evening. You do not want to get involved in that, as you are a strange guest that could easily be taken advantage of.

"By sunrise, Fade and Dim will announce their chosen brides. Hopefully one'll be you. The villa will be your new home and humanity will be saved."

Wander's eyes had cleared up, but they became puppy-like: pathetic, sad, and easily kicked down.

Could she really get one of the kings to pick her when her wretchedness overflowed through her covered body?

James spoke on and on throughout the entire day's journey. It was a wonder how his voice didn't tire. Did Wander really listen to everything the man was saying? "Now, Wander, whatever you do, don't show your face to anyone. If you do, your chances of being a chosen bride will be zero."

"Wait," Vincent perked up, "they don't know about her burns?"

James' eyes bulged. "No, and we best keep it that way."

"Are you serious? If they choose her, they'll uncover her and see that they've been tricked!"

"You do not know the social norms like I do. Once they choose a bride, they cannot change their minds. To change their statement would be the greatest taboo imaginable. It's the same with the alliance. They will not be able to break an alliance once it's made unless certain conditions are met. Wander will just have to stay covered long enough for both deals to be made." "Certainly more problems will come of this plan," Vincent said.

"The kings invited her themselves. If they had any issue, they could only blame themselves."

The sun ducked behind mountains. Smears of clouds glowed pink, like fluffy curtains backed by sunlight. Wander wondered where she'd stand when the sun rose back. Vincent gave her the comfort of distancing his eyes. He kept his gaze to the window at his side. It was obvious he did not choose to be here. James, however, watched her for the entire ride.

"You've been shaking for a while. If we can do anything to ease your anxiety, don't be afraid to ask."

"I am fine." Each word felt empty.

"Here, best chew these beilit leaves now. We're getting close." James passed on the crushed greenery. "Just chew and swallow. They're a little sour. If you still get tired throughout the party, I can give you more."

Wander took a pinch with her gloved hand. As James passed the leaves to Vincent, she unpinned the cloth that covered her mouth and nose. She revealed her mouth only for a second to take the leaves in before re-veiling herself. She sucked in her cheeks and pushed the leaves to the side of her mouth. By pronouncing them a "little" sour, James had prevaricated. The leaves reminded her of the time she bit into a lemon. Roslyn had laughed endlessly at the face Wander made. The rest of the day she tried to get Wander to try a lemon again just to see her funny face.

The carriage strolled through mountainsides, weaving side to side, descending and ascending. Cicadas joined the sound of donkey hooves against the dirt. Wander watched the passing of moss, ferns, and waterfalls until it was too dark to see much. When night fell, other carriages began to appear. Each emitted warm glows of silver and gold light. Round paper lanterns hung at each corner. The paint on the carriages' doors and bodies shone like moonlight. Tucked behind the curtains of the windows, Wander could just make out the silhouette of the riders. The donkeys that pulled these carriages had ears longer and fluffier than the ones Wander was used to.

"Ah, we are arriving during the rush," James said. "There is Vivid Mountain ahead and Moonflower Palace is near the top."

Ahead, two white spires stood at Vivid Mountain's base. They held up a canopy of iridescent lanterns, each color soft, as though diluted with water. When they entered through the spires, they witnessed a forest of lights. Lamps of rounded shapes seemed to float in the night. When they passed close by, Wander could see they dangled from something as thin as fishing line tied to the tree branches. Deeper in the woods, she saw a white doe leap over bushes. A squirrel of identical hue climbed on the treetops.

As the carriage moved up the mountain trail, Wander had to lock her legs and keep her back against the wall as to not fall forward on Vincent. He seemed aware, tensing up and making himself smaller against his space.

"The lullabies believe the top of Vivid Mountain is closest to the moon," James said. "Not by distance, but in spirit. You may notice that the animals and flowers glow pale as moonlight."

"The moon is everything to them. What sort of moon one is born under influences how others treat them. If one is born during a waning moon, they are known to be lesser. If another is born during a waxing moon, they are known to be better. As you can imagine, this has various levels. Someone born under a new moon will be treated like they are bad luck. New mooners are often loners and get trapped with the lower class jobs in the community. Full mooners are privileged and beautiful. Most of the brides you'll see here are probably full mooners. Rulers such as Dim and Fade are always born under a waxing moon. If a ruler has a new mooner or waning moon child, they are given to an orphanage. Most orphanages are filled with waning and new moon kids.

"You'll notice that the glowing marks on the lullabies all differ in some way. Each have different patterns, but all also have varying degrees of radiance. These markings are the physical brand of what kind of moon they were born under. Those that shine brightest are full mooners while the new mooners barely glow, if at all."

Wander gazed back out into the woods. James kept talking, but her mind drifted away. The lanterns reminded her of stars, and the stars reminded her of the nights in Masu's nest. She'd look up and out the window toward the spills of light in the darkness.

I want to die.

It was an exhausted thought like the desire to sleep, except Wander did not want to wake up. She wanted to be gone from everything except that one sliver of existence in the Emerald Wilds. A shorter but far better lived life. She could pretend she had died in the fire with kind memories and a heart still filled to the brim with love.

James straightened. "We're here."

Looking out, Wander saw a garden in front of a white five-floored manor. A path of stones twisted and turned around bushes dotted with little white flowers. White rabbits hopped about with no fear of the people mingling around.

The spirits seemed as delicate as spider webs. Every figure looked as though they had been bred out of snow and stars. Like James described, they had marks that glowed like visible veins on the body. Everyone had dressed to augment their natural beauty, their bodies veiled in fragile, translucent cloth to show off their marks. All possessed silken white hair. Some wore their hair wild with white roses, the curls flowing down to their sandaled feet. Most tightened their hair up in complex buns and braids with glittering pins and décor. Among the lullabies arriving and strolling about the gardens, some were cloaked in white and stood as still as statues. They held aspen carved staffs with lanterns hanging on the ends. Past the gardens, the manor's windows were larger than its doors. Each window blurred the other side like a river's surface. The doors to the inside hung open to show a deep purple rug.

James took Wander's hand and led her out of the carriage. Already others glanced and some stares stayed.

"Who is that?"

"Why is she all covered up?"

"A human."

The brides whispered in gentle voices.

One of the statue-like lantern carriers moved. His white cloak billowed as he walked, his face obscured by the shadows of his hood. He walked to Wander, Vincent, and James. "Is this Wander?"

James nodded. "Yes."

"Very good. The brides are gathering in the ballroom, waiting for Dim and Fade to make the starting toast. A human meal has been prepared. Follow me."

"Don't worry," James said to Wander, his hand still gripping hers. "Vincent and I will be right here with you."

Wander caught the gaze of one bride. The spirit's violet eyes were framed in swirls of the glowing light in her skin. Noticing Wander's gaze, a soft smile curled on the lullaby's pink lips.

James jerked Wander forward. "Don't make eye contact."

Up three steps, they came inside the manor. A dark dresser sat against the wall in front. Three pieces of wood smoked on an oil-spotted plate. The wisps smelled slightly different from the clouds that followed fire. A floral smell mixed into the smell of burned wood.

"Incense," Vincent said behind her. "Humans use it, too."

"I have never seen it before," Wander said. "Why would people want to smell smoke?"

"Most people think it smells nice."

Taking a right, they entered a chamber even larger and far taller than Naktol's throne room. The place lit faintly. Candles centered on scattered round tables of goblets. Cloaked figures stood at the walls with lantern staffs similar to those outside. The glass ceiling magnified the stars and complete moon. The greatest lighting in the ballroom were the lullabies. Their markings shined like white fireflies, and their snowy hair glowed in the dark. Wander never saw so many people in a room at once. Nearly all of them were women. The brides' were more elegant than Wander ever dreamed. On their heads some wore crowns made of dogwood flowers, white quartz, and crystals. Some had their hair woven with ceramic beads or swan feathers. Even their hands seemed dreamlike with bracelets that chained themselves up their hands to ring around their middle fingers.

Wander's legs froze. James tugged her hand to force her forward. Silence came over the lullabies like a breeze over tall grass to all those Wander moved past.

Peering over at the candlelit tables, she saw the goblets filled with a thick, dark red substance. Blood. A lullaby took a goblet into her flowered hand. Tilting the goblet to her lips, she took a sip. When the goblet lowered from her face, a red imprint brightened her upper lip before she pulled a cloth from her dress pocket and brushed it away.

"Here."

They stopped at a table distanced in the far corner of the room by a window to the outside garden. The window framed a view of rabbits with their noses twitching at the grass. At the table, the guard uncovered three silver platters. In the center lay round slices of meat with brown skin and pink innards. A glass bowl of blueberries sat on one side and on the other, a plate of dark mushrooms. Glasses crowded the side of a pitcher filled with water.

"I hope the food is good," James said. "As you can guess, the lullabies don't know how to cook or slaughter animals for meat. They probably got some books on cooking. Now I'll be gone for just a moment. I see a guard gesturing at me for a word." James slipped into the crowd of lullabies.

Wander took a handful of blueberries and slipped her hand under the cloth that covered her mouth. The berries tasted sour enough for her cheeks to pucker up. Vincent picked up a mushroom and brought it to his mouth.

"Hello."

Wander and Vincent turned in unison to see a bride. Her low ponytail of starlit hair extended down to her hips. Vines of little crystal flowers intertwined with her delicate curls. Her thin white gown of lace clutched to her curved body, revealing the markings that glowed on her cleavage, back, and arms. The marking reminded Wander of the shapes she'd draw on the sandy shores of the Emerald Wild's riverside, twisting, turning, with no sharp angles or straight lines.

Her blue eyes smiled while her lips remained still. "I couldn't help but notice that you both were forced to stand in a corner all by yourselves. Would you like to join me and my sisters?"

"No. We are fine," Vincent answered.

The bride scanned Wander, who gazed downward. The lullaby's toes intertwined with sandals of petite wildflowers. She must have expected Wander to say something, but only an awkward silence ensued.

Turning her back on the humans, the lullaby was about to return to the inner party when Wander's voice broke out. "Actually, I'd like that."

"Wonderful!" the bride waved her hand for Wander to follow.

Vincent's hand fell on Wander's shoulder, "What are you doing?"

"I'd like the company of spirits."

"But James said—"

That's when Wander blocked him out and followed the lullaby deeper into the dark ballroom.

"My name is Blur. What's yours?"

"Wander."

"My sisters are there," Blur pointed to two other brides standing by a table of goblets. One's hair was braided like a crown around her head with gold laced in. Her glowing marks drizzled down her skin like raindrops on glass. The snug dress she wore made a V down between her breasts to her stomach. The other sister fanned her face with a painted fan of cherry blossoms. Her pink lips shined and she possibly had the shortest hair among the brides, too short to decorate much. Her earrings dangled with white bird tail feathers.

Her markings twisted around her arms and legs like vines.

"Hello. Sheathe, Rein, this is Wander. Wander, these are my sisters."

Wander attempted the long nod that was called a bow. She guessed she did it wrong, as the brides giggled.

Sheathe continued to fan herself, her feather earrings dancing in the breeze. "Are you the human girl that can touch spirits?"

"Yes."

"I told you," Rein said.

"Yes, that explains it."

"But for star's sake, why is she wrapped up like a thief?"

"Yes, why are you hiding your face?"

Wander looked toward the goblets. A hooded white figure came with a massive jug of thick red fluid on her shoulder. It took some sort of talent to tip the jug and not spill as she refilled all the goblets with blood.

"I don't want too much attention," Wander said, "for being the only human bride."

"How strange. You still stand out," Rein giggled.

"So you really are here to marry Dim or Fade?" Blur asked as she playfully swirled the blood in her goblet.

Wander nodded

"Why?" Sheathe chimed in.

"Humanity needs an alliance."

"Right. The war," Blur said.

Sheathe snorted. "The humans got into that mess themselves. Everyone knows not to mess with the deviants."

Blur and Rein looked at Wander as though expecting a retort, but she said nothing.

"A marriage between humans and spirits would never work out anyway," Sheathe continued. "Even if you can touch us, you are still completely different. If we so much as breathe on you, you'd fall asleep. You couldn't even kiss Fade or Dim without holding your breath. And the blood! Human blood is red, the same kind of blood we drink. Humans are animals, and that's that. You both have the same blood. For Fade or Dim getting married to you, it would be the same as being bound to a dog! You eat like an animal, too, don't you? Meat, vegetables, and fruit. How would you even have meals with the kings?"

Hushed whispers took over the ballroom. Wander saw far in the back where the floor was raised higher, two men had come in. One revealed a buff body with only an opened up white robe and pants. His hair puffed around his head and thinned as it elongated down to his chest. He had brown eyes darker than the many blue eyes of other lullabies. The glowing marks on his chest and face were jagged like cliff sides.

A cloaked server passed a goblet to the man and a second to the other. The second seemed as scrawny as a dangling leaf. His hair reminded Wander of a horse's mane, long and windswept. He covered himself in a buttoned down jacket. His dark eyes matched the first. Wander could not see much of his markings due to his conservative attire. When his hand reached for a goblet, she could see glowing hills and swirls around his fingers.

The more muscular one held up his goblet. "Welcome," his deep voice spoke loudly so the entire ballroom could hear. "I am Dim, son of Fae and Sylph. My brother, Fade, and I are honored by the gift of so many visitors on this warm night. We are now opening the doors to the outer gardens and east halls so that the crowding may cease.

"While I wish everyone could have an equal opportunity to speak with my brother and me, I'm afraid the night will not last long enough. Due to that limitation, Fade and I will speak to only those who interest us. But do not worry, as tradition, those not chosen as a future queen will be compensated with royal gifts at dawn. When the first sliver of sun rises, my brother and I will announce our chosen queens."

Dim raised his goblet. "To rightly begin the evening, a toast to the moonlight that shines down on this mountain, to those who traveled far to get here, and to whomever is chosen to be our brides."

Fade's eyes looked directly at Wander. She looked behind her, then back at him to see a smirk lift one side of his face. He winked. Wander had no idea what that gesture meant or if it were even on purpose.

All the brides took a blood filled goblet. Rein smiled at Wander as she held her cup toward her lips. Everyone in the room raised their glasses.

Wander looked around until she found a goblet left on a table. She took the cup and raised it with the rest of the lullabies.

Then all the lullabies drank at once. What made them decide to drink all at once, Wander had no clue. All she knew was that the brides wanted her to lose. They were like everyone else in this world, curious, cruel, and together.

Wander unwrapped the veil that covered her mouth. She held it to block the view of the kings and brides as she chugged the entire goblet of blood. She had tasted blood before, but not this much all at once. Her entire body wanted to retch. What shocked her most were the gel-like clots mixed into the blood. The only thing Wander could compare the texture to would be a thick soup. Swallowing all the blood was the most difficult part. It felt and tasted as wrong as consuming her own dung. She shut her eyes and tilted her head back to quicken the process. She tried not to breathe through her nose. The steel stench only worsened the experience.

Emptying her goblet, Wander set it on the table. The taste still strong in her mouth, she recovered her veil to shield her face. The three brides stared at her in utter disbelief. The shocked face Wander took most joy in was Rein's mixed expression of disgust and bewilderment.

Doors opened all around the ballroom at once, and the brides began to disperse. Without a word, Blur, Sheathe, and Rein left.

"What do you think you are doing?" Vincent limped up from behind. "James said to stay away from other brides!"

"He also said we should trick the kings into an alliance without seeing my face. You didn't agree with that."

"You cannot trust him or the spirits."

Wander lightened her tone, "Whose side are you on?"

"What do you mean?"

"You're on Naktol's side, right? Do you think I should marry one of the kings for an alliance?"

"No one is on Naktol's side. There is no 'Naktol's side.' We are at a war where all of humanity could become extinct. There is only humanity's side. Naktol is just one human. So no, I'm not on her side. I'm just trying to help humanity survive."

"You didn't answer my other question. Do you think I should marry one of the kings for an alliance?"

"Maybe."

"Maybe?"

"After the attack on Sollast, Naktol is resorting to desperate measures. An alliance is definitely our best bet for surviving. Spirits see humans as animals. I wonder if they even would even shed a tear at our extinction. Humans haven't even been a part of this world for very long. All the spirits are familiar with each other. They probably think we deserve to die. They probably think we're idiots."

"Why would they think the deviants are right? Aura is so powerful. Don't they want to get rid of someone so threatening?"

"The war started over a land dispute. Humans were slaves to the winged beings until the winged beings lost the war to the deviants. The winged beings had the Setting Range, a long range of mountains filled with the largest trees in the world. It was all put to ruin by the war. It eventually was renamed the Winged Graves. The deviants herded us to ancient lands they were willing to give up. We eventually made our own city while the Winged Graves just sat there. That was hundreds of years ago though.

"Having the history books, Naktol thought we had all this land that we weren't using. She wanted to spread humanity back to its roots in the Winged Graves. Aura discovered us and said we weren't allowed in those lands. Taking Naktol's idea, she began to have deviants settle there instead. She had hundreds of years to claim that land. Naktol was furious and sent troops to attack. That's when the war began.

"I don't know much about spirits politics, but they probably think that humans started the mess. The deviants say that they won that land for their victory over the winged beings. But it, like most of their land, is unused and wild or enchanted. They just didn't want us to have it. We have struggled in this world, having been enslaved, eaten, and pushed around by spirits all through history. So Naktol snapped and wanted to get something for us. Everyone says deviants never start wars. But are the ones who start really so guilty? If a bully comes in and pushes you around, calls you names, are they suddenly a victim when you attack in fury?"

Vincent took a breath. "Sorry. Talking about this just ticks me off. I hate spirits."

"I'm sorry. I did not know or think of any of that before."

"I know. That's the worst of it. Despite having been enslaved, humans now enslave their own. Wind-borns like you and me are the first to be thrown under the wagon. It's so easy for someone like you to be taken advantage of, someone with the body of an adult but the mind of a child. All of Naktol's servants are wind-born. We are collected for our ignorance."

"Wait," Wander's gasped, "you're wind-born? Like me?"

"Not so loud!" Vincent hissed.

Wander smiled. "Thank you. Thank you so much for telling me."

"Don't get all giddy about it."

She lowered her voice. "I've never met another wind-born. You have to tell me about where you were born. Who raised you? What—"

"No. I'm not telling you any of that."

Wander frowned and gave a moment to think. "If you tell me your story, I'll tell you about how the boulder ended up killing Aura's Shadow." She mildly regretted the offer. Just saying the word *boulder* made her sink deeper into herself.

"Alright, that's a fair deal."

Wander had to think of where to begin. Would Vincent even believe her?

"Hey, is everything okay?" James walked up to them. "You both look a little shocked."

"It's fine," Vincent answered. "Some brides were just checking Wander out."

"Ignore them. This event is a breeding ground of gossip. Now's the time to wander around until Fade or Dim notice you. Don't look busy and definitely don't talk to anyone but the kings." He put his hand on Vincent's shoulder. Vincent immediately tensed. "Vincent and I will watch the competition."

"I thought we would stay with Wander."

"The party is more crowded than I anticipated. The kings will only approach a few brides. If we want Wander to be approachable, it's best not to stick with her like she needs to be protected."

Wander nodded. "I'm good at wandering." She turned and picked a door to walk through.

"Just don't do anything stupid," she could hear Vincent say from behind.

The opened doors that Wander chose had a cloaked guard holding a lantern at each side. Stepping through, she breathed in the scent of wisteria. Beneath moonlight, brides gathered in a courtyard bordered with open aired corridors. Sometimes when they moved, they blurred like a thrown torch.

At the center, a leafless tree grew taller than the corridors, its trunk and branches heavy with wisteria. At the courtyard's corner, a lone bride stared at something. When Wander moved in further, she saw the bride was looking at a barn owl. The bird's talons clutched at an iron perch that extended from the stone walls. One bride sat at a corridor window and watched the stars and planets. A moth flew near and landed on her dress skirt.

"Are you Wander?"

Shocked by an unfamiliar male voice, she turned expecting one of the kings. Instead a guard stood before her. He held a staff with a lantern of painted rabbits.

James said nothing of how to behave around the guards.

"Y-yes," she teetered out a response.

"Come with me. There is something of importance."

Wander looked around, wishing either Vincent or James were watching. Only the bride with the moth on her dress watched. When her eyes met Wander's, she quickly turned away.

The guard motioned to a closed door. Wander followed as he unlocked it with a key, and they both slipped inside. They ended up in a smaller courtyard possessing a dogwood tree, a table, two chairs, and a pond with lily pads. The guard moved under the dogwood, pulling down his hood. He revealed a face of angled glows, blue eyes, and fluffy white hair. He reached down into the side of his cloak and pulled out a letter.

"This is for you."

Wander walked up and took the sealed letter.

"I know what sort of person killed Aura's Shadow. The only thing that can kill a shadow is another shadow."

"Who are you?"

"My name is Many," he kept his voice in a whisper. "I am a part of a group of those who are supposed to be dead as far as deviants are concerned. This letter will lead you to us. We want to help you."

Wander looked back at the folded letter and back up at him. "I don't understand."

"I'm afraid that's the only information I can offer here. Everything will become clear once you read the letter. You mustn't show it to anyone else and once we leave this courtyard, you can no longer speak to me."

"I can't read."

"What?" The guard's stoic nature wavered.

She unfolded the letter and looked at the symbols. She could only recognize her own name at the top. Under at least had taught her to write her own name.

"I definitely can't read all this," she said as she looked upon the paragraphs and a map.

Many stood dumbstruck with a long silence. Finally having an idea, he folded his arms. "Then I'll allow just one close friend who can read to come with you. Someone you trust. Now I must go before we are noticed. Leave a while after me and do not associate with me for the rest of the ball."

"Associate?"

"Do not speak to me," he clarified as he left. His white cloak billowed behind.

Giving some time before she left, Wander folded the parchment and slipped it into her dress. When she left, she decided it could be best to go where there were no other brides. She wandered until she reached a vacant courtyard. Hopefully one of the two kings would notice her alone and they'd approach.

Finding a gray wood bench, she sat down. Laughter rose from behind her. Wander tensed up and realized she wasn't alone. Glancing sideways, she saw King Dim with a bride. She stood about half his height, her hands holding each other behind her back as they walked through a garden of white rose bushes.

"Is that so? Then what are your thoughts on having more children?" the bride asked. She brushed a lock of hair behind her ear to reveal crystal jewels.

"Sometimes I think that could be good. Other times I wonder if it would only make Bell feel forgotten." Dim pulled a white rose from one of the bushes and passed it to the bride. She dipped her ringed nose in the petals. Her eyes darted in Wander's direction.

Looking away, Wander got up and sought an exit. Witnessing the king and bride talk seemed inappropriate. The way the bride's eyes shot at her gave her a clue. Wander almost retreated to another courtyard when she caught something in the corner of her vision. A small figure stood at the end of a corridor. The child flinched when she realized she was noticed and disappeared behind the corner.

The little girl's withdrawal sealed the fate for Wander to follow. Wander tread through the corridor. Her shadow shrunk and rose with the passing of candlelight. Weaving around the corner, she saw the little girl had barely moved.

Her size haunted Wander with recollections of Roslyn. They had the same large brown eyes. This child however, was a lullaby. Like the others, her pale hair nearly glowed in the dark. Most of her body could not be seen under a blue quilt that she cloaked around herself. The little girl hid her face under the quilt.

"What's wrong?" Wander asked.

"You're not supposed to see me." Her voice was muffled against the blanket.

Wander wished to bend down to the same height, but her bridal dress constricted her. "Why?"

Her eyes peeped out. "I can't say." She scanned Wander from head to toe. "Why are you all covered up?"

"I think the kings will like me better if I'm covered up," Wander said. "If they see my skin, there is no way they would choose me."

The girl uncovered her face. "Does that mean we're the same?"

No burns covered her. Her cheeks looked as smooth as river stones. Wander shrugged, not knowing what her story could be.

"I . . . I want to talk to my dad," the child said. Her face reddened and her voice shook. "Juniper is acting strange, and it's starting to scare me."

"Where is your dad?"

"He said I can't talk to him until after sunrise. Today's really important, and he'll get mad at me. Can you help me?"

Wander nodded. The little girl led her further into the labyrinth of halls. The child moved like a ghost, her legs unseen under her quilt. As Wander looked around, she feared she had crossed a barrier to a more personal side of the mansion, no brides sat on the stones, and there were no guards with lantern staffs.

They entered an already open door. Certain aspects of the room were unlike anything Wander had seen. Mobiles of different lengths hung from the ceiling. Little stuffed animals with button eyes dangled down from some. Others were made of paper flowers. To examine all of them would take half the night.

Wander reached up and caressed a downy feather from one of the mobiles. At the end of the room a canopied bed sat under a window. A shelf of books took half of the adjacent wall. Dolls, glass animals, and teacups sat around the shelves with the books. A little round table held a mess of open books and colored pencils.

"She's here." The little lullaby squatted in a corner.

Over her shoulder, Wander saw a chubby white rabbit on a blue cushion. The animal lay on its side, its breath heaving.

"That's Juniper?"

The girl nodded and her voice clenched. "She's gotten worse! Is she dying?"

Wander stroked Juniper's thick white fur. "I don't know."

"Daddy would know."

"I can get your dad for you."

"He's going to be mad at me!"

"Would he want you this upset?"

The lullaby shook her head.

"Then let me get him. Who is he?"

"Dim."

"King Dim?" Wander realized she had little reason to be shocked. If the girl lived in this room, then her father being the king would only make sense.

"Yes."

"I'll tell him."

"Thank you."

"Just show me back to where I was."

With more haste than before, the girl led Wander back and sped back to her room even faster.

Dim still conversed with the same bride as before. They both held glasses of blood by the rose bushes. Their glowing skin shined out of the night.

Shaking off any care of what might ensue, Wander marched forward. It did not take long for the bride to stare her down. Seeing her eyes wander, Dim turned around. His stoic nature faded when Wander interrupted.

"King Dim?" Wander shakily bowed.

"Excuse me, we're having a conversation," the bride spoke from behind.

"Is something the matter?" Dim asked.

"Your daughter needs you. It's very important."

"What the matter?"

"Something is wrong with her rabbit."

With that said, Dim handed Wander his glass of blood. He left without a word toward the inner sanctum of the mansion.

The smell of blood made Wander want to vomit. She could reimagine its overwhelming taste and set the glass on a windowsill.

"I see what you did there."

Wander turned around to the abandoned bride. "You'll wish you didn't do that." She hissed as she charged past.

Curiosity getting the better of her, Wander managed to retrace her steps back to the lullaby girl's room. The door was left wide open. Peeking in, she saw Dim crouched down, his hand reaching something blocked off by his daughter's standing figure. She no longer covered herself in a quilt. Whatever she hid, Wander could not tell. She looked ordinary.

"Is Juniper okay?" Wander asked from the doorway.

The little girl moved aside to show Juniper with a litter of twitching babies. "She was pregnant!" the girl announced in a tone full of glee.

"Pregnant?"

Dim raised his cupped hands to his daughter, cradling a baby white rabbit.

The girl hugged herself. "They're so little!"

"Now, Bell, don't be too rough with them," Dim said as he gently passed the baby into her hands. "They are not toys. They're very fragile. Let their mother take care of them for the night." He stood up. "I have to get back to the ball. And you, who are you?"

"Wander. I'm—"

"Yes, my brother Fade wanted you meet you. Please, follow me outside."

Wander took one last look at Bell, who gently set the baby rabbit down to join the litter of five. She turned to Wander and smiled. "Thank you!"

Dim led Wander toward the outer courtyard until he took a sharp turn in the opposite direction. The mansion's halls got darker and darker until Dim's markings became Wander's beacon.

"Where are we—"

Before she could finish her question, Dim spun around and his hands clutched her shoulders. He threw Wander against the wall and closed in on her. His breath stank of blood. If not for the guardian controlling her, Wander would surely have fallen asleep to his breath. "Did you see?"

"The rabbits?"

"Don't play stupid. My daughter, why did you talk to her?"

His left hand left her shoulder and came toward her neck.

"Sorry, I wasn't thinking! I didn't know she was yours!"

"I don't care who you are, I'll kill you if you say a word about her to anyone."

"Why?"

Something in Wander's eyes or voice made Dim loosen his grip. "Bell's skin. You saw her new mooner skin."

Wander had to think back to what a new mooner meant. She realized the complication she had walked into. James had explained that new mooners were born without markings and were treated as the lowest of the low in lullaby society. Didn't he say that if a new mooner were born by a ruler, they'd get put in an orphanage? Someplace Wander didn't know of.

"I didn't notice," Wander told Dim.

Dim let go of her. "If this gets out, not only will you be in severe danger, but I will make sure Naktol loses her idiotic war as well!"

Wander raised her voice. "I'm not going to tell anyone!"

"You better not. Now I must attend to the brides. I'll be sure you're supervised."

On the walk back out of the dark corridor, Wander tried to breathe as softly as possible. A heavy silence fogged her and the king with only the tapping of their shoes on the floor making sounds. When they returned to the courtyard, Dim sped ahead and toward the ballroom.

I just ruined my chances, didn't I? Wander thought. She was not too surprised with herself. Taking her to a social event was not the best idea.

For the next hour, she strolled anywhere lit by lanterns. Moths bright as moonlight danced around the lit paper that shielded them from the flames. Brides all began to look at her strangely. Some whispered to those nearby while gesturing toward Wander.

Though her stomach growled, she didn't dare return to the ballroom. From what she could see in the windows, the whole place was crowded with whispering bodies. In the center of a courtyard, she sat on an iron bench under a tree of dangling lights. She shut her eyes and let herself believe the world had ended. If only she could block out the sounds of talk from the ballroom and the footsteps of passersby. She even wanted to return to the jail cell in Naktol's castle, a place to just wither away in private.

"I've been looking everywhere for you."

Wander's body tensed. King Fade walked up from behind and sat next to her. He smelled of the wisteria a couple courtyards down. He looked off to where Wander stared, in the ballroom windows.

"Sorry, I wander around a lot," Wander said.

Fade snorted. "'Wander,' I get it. How'd you get a spirit's name anyway?"

"A spirit named me."

"That's unusual. Spirits usually choose their own names."

Wander made eye contact with some brides through the window. They were watching them. When they caught Wander's gaze, they turned and shuffled away.

"Is it true that you're a human who can touch spirits?" Fade stared down at Wander's hands.

"Yes." Wander offered her gloved hand. He held up his own and shakily placed his thumb in her palm and cupped around her backhand. "I bleed red, too," Wander added, "if you want proof that I'm human."

"That's unnecessary, though I'm curious as to why you're all covered up."

"I don't want anyone else to know what I look like."

"I can understand that. Being able to touch both humans and spirits would make you a spectacle. Do you know how you're able to touch spirits?"

Wander tilted her head. The answer was the guardian possessing her, but she certainly would not share that even if she could. "I don't know."

"You know, if a spirit dies, a human still can't touch them. But if a human dies, spirits can touch them. Maybe there's something about you that's close to death that makes you able to touch spirits."

Wander shrugged and her dress tightened. "Maybe."

"Am I correct in that you're wind-born?"

"I am."

"So how old are you really? What has being wind-born been like?"

"I don't know how old I am. I was born in an enchanted forest where I was raised by a spirit. He took great care of me, and those were the happiest days of my life. The forest was burned down by Aura because she wanted the guardian in the forest to drink its blood for power."

"I'm so sorry. Did your spirit make it out—"

"I don't want to talk about that, please." The words she emitted were a soft, quick warning.

"My apologies. It's obvious you've been through a lot."

His tone was sincere. When Wander looked at him, she could sense anxiety similar to her own.

"No," Wander readjusted herself and took a deep breath, "you're just being nice. But could I ask you why you wanted me here? Why do you want me as a bride? I don't understand."

Fade let out a sigh. "Straight to the point then. It probably won't make much sense to a human, but none of the brides are here for me. They are all here hoping to be bound to my brother. No lullaby woman would be with me."

He pulled up his sleeve, revealing glowing waves. On his hands were hills, but as the markings reached up his arm, they made wide spirals. From his wrist, a full rotation went around until it touched his elbow.

"It's because of my markings. See the twists and turns? Did you see my brother's? His are sharp angles, the mark of being a man. All the brides here have markings similar to mine with soft curves. Basically put, they see me as a woman because we assign man and woman by our markings. I don't know if that's comparable to anything in human society."

Wander's unease diminished under curiosity. She tilt her head. "You seem to be a man though."

Fade laughed. "See? This is why I invited you. You see nothing wrong with me. Best of all, we can touch as though you are a spirit, too." Fade rose up and offered his hand. Wander stared at his hand for a moment before finally taking it in hers. He pulled her out of the seat, and they walked together. They followed the borders of each courtyard under the rooftops and wide stone halls.

Fade remained close enough to hold hands, but Wander's hand remained dangling at her side. The spirit's long starlight hair shined in the dark and softened by candlelight. She'd watch his markings brighten as they approached unlit corners and dim when they reached lantern light. While everyone was physically beautiful to Wander, she realized that spirits were particularly stunning. To see a spirit was like seeing a red flower in a white field. Around them, Wander's heart beat faster. They had something that contrasted against the world. Masu had such qualities, and she had taken them for granted. After enough time around humans, she could now recognize the strange beauty of spirits.

"So how are you enjoying Vivid Mountain?" Fade broke the silence.

"Without all the people, it would feel similar to my home. It feels enchanted."

"Dim and I were raised here, so I find the whole place sort of boring. I hope to go out and see the world sometime."

"I know what you mean," Wander said. "But there's no place like home."

They reached a courtyard where vines crawled up the stone walls. In the center, the ground sank down into a pond. Fireflies brightened the garden of water lilies. A willow tree's locks of green tipped into the water's edge.

Brides were scattered around. Three spoke in a corner while sipping blood. One watched the fireflies from the outer edges of the courtyard square. Two guards held lantern staffs, and one wandered with a tray of blood brimmed goblets.

Some comfort came to Wander at the sight of James and Vincent. The two guys mingled in the shadows. Seeing her, James gave a thumbs-up. Vincent looked utterly exhausted and bored. Whatever comfort got balanced out by Dim's fierce gaze. The king glanced at Wander as he spoke to a bride by the pond. She quickly looked back to Fade.

"So lullaby breath puts humans to sleep?"

"Are you worried about that? I'd never do that to you, and if anyone else did, they'd be punished."

"A lullaby once attacked a friend of mine. She wanted his blood."

"That's terrible. My father made hunting humans illegal."

"Illegal?"

"You don't know what that means?"

Wander shook her head.

"Wow. How young a wind-born are you?"

Wander shrugged. She swiftly turned the topic around. "But you can touch regular humans while they're sleeping? Why's that?"

"Can't say. I'm no scientist."

Scientist? Wander decided not to even bother anymore.

Fade stopped. A firefly blinked in front of his face. The insect landed on the index finger of his lifted hand. "Both humans and spirits can touch animals," he said. "Maybe there's just some spectrum we have yet to discover with spirits on one end, humans at the other, and animals in the center."

Wander looked for a firefly to catch. Finding one, she took both her hands and closed in on its fluttering wings. Her fingers made a cage around it until it landed on her palm.

Fade stepped up to her. "I answered your question as to why I want you as my bride. Now it's my turn. Why do you want to be my bride?"

The firefly crawled through the cracks of Wander's fingers and flew away. The question caught her off guard. She didn't want to be his bride. She didn't want to be anything right now. All she wanted was Aura to be dead. Fade was only a means to that end.

"I—"

A severe tug caught on Wander's veil. She felt a snap as what held her shroud to her face fell away. She attempted to catch the headscarf, but it swiftly pulled away, leaving her head bare. Every eye in the courtyard pierced her. One lullaby burst out into laughter, and the brides with her struggled to hush her up. Voices rose.

"Is that the human?"

"My stars, what is wrong with her face?"

"A monster."

Looking for her veil, Wander turned and saw the bride from earlier. It was the one who had been speaking to Dim before Wander made him leave. The bride's face was pale with horror. Somehow her bracelet had caught on Wander's headscarf. There was no doubt the bride plotted this to look like an accident in passing.

With tearing eyes and a tightening throat, Wander looked at Fade. His jaw had dropped, and he stepped back.

Wander bent down to the floor and curled her head down into her arms. She could not muster up a scream or sob, but she felt like rivers rolled down her cheeks. She felt as though all her insides had fallen away into a pit. She did not dare look at anyone's reaction anymore.

Feet shuffled toward her.

A strong grip took her wrist. "Get up," Dim said softly.

More feet moved along with the tap of Vincent's crutches.

"Don't touch her," Vincent said.

Wander looked up just in time to see a zap occur as Vincent tried to grab Dim.

A cloth suddenly fell on her head and blocked her vision. As she wrapped the cloth around her head, she realized it was a jacket with buttons. She covered all she could but her eyes. Fade stood topless over her, revealing all his swirling marks. "Let's take her inside."

Dim helped her up and led her toward the inner halls of the mansion. Vincent, Fade, and James followed. The corridors and candlelight blurred in Wander's silent crying. A door opened to reveal a living room with a couch covered in an iridescent sheet, walls covered in steel artwork, and a huge stump table.

Taking a sharp right, Dim opened another door to a moonlit bedroom. A table lay out for white star-shaped flowers to grow. Dim gently pushed Wander to sit on the bed by the door. "Stay here while we talk to your friends."

He turned and shut the door behind him, leaving Wander alone in the room.

Wander rubbed Fade's shirt to rid the wetness on her face. She clenched her teeth and let out a sob into the cloth. Pulling off her shoes, she curled up on the bed. She buried her face in the shirt while weeping. She did not care to listen to what everyone said in the next room.

"Hey."

Wander woke up in Fade's damp shirt. She rose up to see Fade's tall silhouette slink through the door. She scrambled to hide her face in the shirt. .

"No, no, it's okay. You're alright." He moved slowly to sit next to her. The bed sank with the additional body.

Wander looked away. "I'm sorry."

"Vincent and James explained everything. You have nothing to be sorry for. I'm the one who should be sorry. I'm sorry you've been put through so much."

"I did this because I want the humans to win."

"I understand. Your kind is losing and desperate."

Humankind was a complicated stranger for Wander, but Fade seemed sympathetic. Maybe it was okay to talk to him.

"I'm fighting for the spirit that named me. He is a winged being. His name is Masu, and Aura is controlling him."

Fade said nothing. When Wander looked at him, her eyes widened. The spirit rubbed the edges of his eyes.

"Are you crying?"

"I didn't realize how awful the war must be until now," his voice was strained. "You were listening to me complain about my markings while your entire body has been burned so awfully. I'm so ashamed. Vincent told me how young you are."

Wander shook her head. "No. You're nice. I'll be with you if you'll help the humans."

Three short knocks came from the door. "Come in," Fade said.

Dim, Vincent, and James came into the room. The spirit crossed his arms and leaned against the door once it shut. Vincent and James both stood in front of the bed.

"How are you doing?" James asked.

"I didn't like everyone seeing me," Wander said.

"There are few good-hearted brides at this ball," Dim said. "How they reacted to Wander's face proves that."

The humans and spirits went quiet. Conjuring enough courage to show her face, Wander looked up. Dim, James, and Fade looked at the floor.

"What's going to happen now?" Vincent asked.

"I can't marry Wander," Fade said.

Dim let out a sigh of relief.

Fade looked at Wander. "I know you won't believe me when I say it's not because of your burns. My reason is simply that you are far too young. You may look older, but your heart and mind are like little Bell's."

"But what about the war?" Wander asked. "Or finding a bride?"

"Could you be bound to a different human?" Vincent asked. "You wouldn't be able to touch her, but you'd get a bride, and we'd get an alliance."

A sudden idea, one that was not her own, ached and rolled in Wander's head. She knew it was not hers, but she had it bubbling in her mouth like the need to throw up. If she did not say the idea aloud, she knew she would be sick.

"Naktol's youngest daughter," she said.

Everyone looked at her with brows heightened.

"Aura will be after Naktol's youngest daughter to turn her into an Arm," Wander said. "That's what the Arms are. They used to be the children of the defeated rulers. I was told that the youngest is chosen. If

Naktol's youngest daughter is married to Fade, she'll be safer."

"You're right about the Arms," Dim said. "So there is a tactical level to that idea. That could sway Naktol a little."

"The queen could only agree to your terms if you play it tough," said Vincent. "Let her know that you're unhappy with her trick in sending Wander. Let her know her youngest daughter is the only way to gain your alliance."

Wander shivered and looked at the floor as the others spoke. She could not believe this idea was agreeable. Was this idea from the guardian smart? Or was it *vengeful*?

"What about Wander?" James asked. "She'll be in huge trouble."

"She'll have our protection and can stay in lullaby lands where Naktol and her guards have no rule."

Wander did not know what she did to deserve protection. It seemed too good to be true. Maybe the lullabies would use her in some way.

Dim opened the door. "I'll let you decide her fate, as risky as having her sounds. I have to see to the brides. We'll talk this over after sunrise." He left the room.

Fade looked at Wander. "Would that be acceptable? To stay here?"

"I may not stay," Wander said.

"Well, you can take refuge in our lands if need be." Fade walked to the door, "I should let you have time alone to figure everything out."

After Fade left, James broke the short silence, "Well, girl, you really changed the games."

Vincent rubbed the back of his head, "Naktol's going to kill me."

James put his hand on his shoulder. "I'm sure the good kings would let you stay if need be. Don't worry, the lullabies are going to change everything in this war."

Vincent cut in. "I wouldn't be too pleased yet. You're discounting that the deviants could also resort to alliance tactics. While the deviants have no military, the elementals do."

Wander remained in the guest bedroom for the rest of the party. Lying in the bed, she stared out the window with a view of an uninhabited courtyard. The outdoor square was larger than all the rest. Two sets of stairs came up and met on a balcony on the second floor. Violet flowers drooped like willow branches from their stone pots. Beneath the balcony on the wall, a creature's face carved from stone blew out water into a fountain. A statue of a woman looked up and reached toward the sky. The pale stone reminded Wander of this night's brides. The sun began to rise. Wander could tell from the blackbirds. The courtyard transformed in warm light.

Fade fetched her veil from the bride who had taken it and helped Wander put it back on her face. His markings glowed less in dawn's light, giving him a more human look.

"Who did Dim choose for his bride?" Wander asked as Fade secured the veil behind her ears.

"A cousin, Viola. It will be for convenience rather than love, I'm afraid. Dim was deeply in love with his wife and Bell's mother, Floret. Floret was a special woman who can't be replaced. I had a feeling none of the brides who came tonight would interest him."

"How are we going to get you married to Naktol's daughter?"

"We sent James and some guards to pass a message to Naktol for a meeting about an alliance. That will get her attention, and we'll meet."

"Can I be there?"

"Sure." He got up, and the mattress rose. "I know humans are used to sleeping at night, so you must be exhausted. My brother and I are going to sleep in a few hours and will be up at sunset. We still have guards making rounds around the mansion in the daytime if you need anything. They have been made aware that you and Vincent are staying."

"Where is Vincent?"

"Just a couple doors down. He expressed to me that it might be unwise for him to return to Sollast. His goal was to make sure Naktol's plan succeeded, and he obviously failed."

Fade bid Wander a good day before going off to bed. Emotionally drained, Wander hit the bed at daylight. She usually slept on her side or belly, but this time she stayed on her back. The songs of a mourning dove drove away any promise of sleep. She wondered where the fox guardian had run off to. The creature disappeared during her arrest in Sollast. Like Aura and her Arms, the fox could control Wander from a long distance. The guardian remained somewhere safe while everything else burned.

Rising from the bed, Wander strained to see the outside courtyard. Vincent sat by the fountain with a pencil and paper. In loose white garb, he almost seemed tranquil. He focused on the page. His crutches leaned by his side.

Wander left the bedroom and found her way to the courtyard. "You're not sleeping?" She sat on the fountain's edge with him. He covered his paper with a hand.

"You expect me to sleep in a mansion of spirits who drink blood? What about you?"

"The sunlight is bothering me, and I have a lot on my mind." She looked to his lap. "What are you writing?"

"None of your business."

"It's okay. I can't read."

Vincent sighed and uncovered the page. His pencil had shaded an artwork of the courtyard, detailed in the petals of the flowers and curled architecture around the windows. "I can't read, either."

Wander smiled under her veil. She couldn't believe they had that in common. Maybe most wind-borns never learned to read.

"My friend, Under, taught me how to spell my name. Do you remember him?"

"That tall guy. The one who disappeared before the battle at Loreman?"

"He didn't disappear. He turned into my horse for the battle."

"What?"

. "He wasn't human. He was a shadow. I know the deviants killed them a long time ago, but Under was definitely a shadow. He could change into anything he looked at for a while. He's what happened to Aura's Shadow. That giant boulder was him, and he can't change back. He was my best friend," Wander's voice tightened. "I didn't want him to get involved any more. A woman he loved died when Chant, Masu, and Aura's Shadow attacked Willton. I saw the whole thing. I wanted him to move on because everyone around me gets hurt."

"I'm sorry."

"He was too good to me. I wanted there to be someone who could always save me. I grew up with Masu always saving me, so I liked Under and let him get hurt."

She left a heavy silence. Vincent wouldn't look at her. She knew he might not believe her. She was not afraid of that. She was afraid of little any more.

"I . . ." Vincent looked at his drawing, "I was born in a sheep pasture. It was snowing. As you can imagine, I was bare and empty of any coherent thought. I would have frozen to death if the farmers didn't find me. They wrapped me in a blanket and brought me into their log cabin. Their little daughter, Lilah, named me Vincent. She let me sleep in her bed. I did nothing but sleep under a pile of blankets for the first week. I was spoon fed soup and water and slowly got stronger. I didn't understand language, walking, anything. They taught me. Like any wind-born, I imprinted. I got extraordinarily attached to the family. Like a duckling, I'd follow them wherever they went.

"I wore the farmer's clothes. I was much shorter than he, so I often tripped in his baggy pants. He taught me basic things that blood-born humans take for granted like talking and thinking rationally. Lilah was the one I liked the most because she treated me like a baby brother. She'd read to me, hold my hand, and teach me the fun things like what sounds certain animals made."

"That sounds wonderful."

Vincent puffed up and shook his head. "After a couple months, the family sold me to slave traders. I was sold for one thousand gold pieces, enough to buy a new house. They fed me and taught me only so I'd cost more. I'm sure there was little debate when they found me. They were a poor family."

"What are slave traders?"

"Sometimes people take other people and use them like you use a horse. You make them do all the work you don't want to do, and they don't get a say. When you become a slave, you stop being a person and start being a belonging to someone else. Slave traders look for wind-borns for obvious reasons. We make perfect slaves because we have no families and our undeveloped brains make us easy to mold into whatever they want. They hunt for wind-borns in the wilderness, but also buy them at a high price from anyone else who finds them.

"I was taken from what I thought was my home and my family and put in chains. We went to Windfalls, the center of the slave trade. It is where we are trained and sold. It is where wind-borns are conditioned to obey others. My life became early mornings, late nights, beatings, commands, and repetitive tasks. They even got me to break down when hearing a certain word.

They did everything in their power to control someone who had little will or resistance."

"What's the word?"

"That's something I'll take to my grave. It's a word people don't just say in common conversation. I haven't heard the word for six years, and don't plan to in the future. I'm sure you don't even know it. The word is meant to punish me if I don't follow orders. Every slave has a different one. We are taught to associate the word with pain and torture."

"That's horrible."

"What blood-borns don't understand is that wind-borns don't forget the people they imprint on. It's a bond that makes and breaks us. A day did not go by when I didn't think of those farmlands with Lilah and her parents. I missed their warm, decorated cabin, the sheep, the old dog that slept near the fireplace—every little thing. Eventually it hit me that they were the ones who sold me. To them, I was just money. After making me into an obedient solider, the slavers sold me as a bodyguard to a gang leader at Sollast's border. I was good at the job. It was not much better than Windfalls though, as the gang leader liked to show others how far he could push me. He'd give me seemingly impossible tasks, some of them nearly killing me.

"Then one day, a strange girl spotted me. I noticed she stalked the gang leader and me down the streets. Then she called out my name, and I realized it was Lilah. She was all grown up. She begged the leader to buy me. Of course he doubled the price of what he bought me for. It was something she could not afford."

Vincent let out a sigh. "Oddly enough, weeks later she returned with the money. The gang leader was surprised, but let me go. Lilah took me to the outer farmlands of Sollast. She explained she was betrothed to a rich man. She told me that her parents lied to her about what happened to me. They told her I was going to a place that could better take care of me. I think she expected me to be that same, fun, innocent boy she played with. I was far from it and not used to talking anymore. When she tried to make conversation, it was like she was talking to herself. She could not touch me without me flinching. She still tried to squeeze me into her life with her husband. The money that she bought me with came from him, and she convinced him that I could be a great worker for him.

"The husband caught on that Lilah might be attracted to me. Things got heated. Lilah would visit me at night crying when she and her husband got into an argument. It was a drama filled life, but it was the best part of my life. I managed to start talking again and stop flinching. I also began to love Lilah. When I was with her, I actually began to feel alive."

Vincent looked at Wander, devoid of any emotion. "Then she was killed by Aura's Wings. She rode to the nearest town and in that slot of time the Wings attacked. Just him. He killed as many as he could as they fled the marketplace. Her body had an arrow straight through her skull, so at least it was quick."

Wander felt as though she was going to be sick. Her heart raced, and she looked at her feet.

Vincent continued. "I got kicked out of the house by the husband, and I decided to become a soldier to kill what killed Lilah. Not long after that is when you and I met. When I learned you were windborn, I didn't want to treat you differently. When Naktol decided to marry you to spirits, though, it reminded me of when I was sold. That's why I didn't like it."

"Vincent . . ." Wander had no idea what to say. "Sorry" seemed pointless in the face of everything.

He shut his notebook. "Don't. The last thing I need is your pity."

She nodded. "Alright. Thank you for telling me everything."

"I'm sorry about Under. He seemed like a friendly guy."

"Thank you."

"I'm going to bed." Vincent got up with his crutches and hobbled back toward the guest rooms.

Wander stood up. "Wait." When he stopped, she said, "Do you still plan to kill Masu because he killed Lilah? You know that wasn't his choice."

Vincent faintly smiled and flailed his right crutch. "Do I look like I'm in a position to kill anyone?" He took a couple steps and then stopped again. "It's obvious you imprinted onto Masu like I did with the farming family. For that, I guess I am sorry."

Vincent disappeared into the mansion.

Wander bathed in the sunlight for hours with her own thoughts. Vincent's story took time to sink in. What makes a wind-born get born anyway? Why did he end up in farmlands while she woke in the Emerald Wilds? How easily could their fates have changed? No matter how hard she tried, she could not remember when she first woke up to the world. Her earliest memories were with Masu in the nest. Wander would give away part of her soul to remember every moment of the wilds.

"Is everything alright?" One of the white-cloaked guards walked out into the courtyard.

"It's okay. I'm just thinking," Wander told him.

Before he left, an idea flashed in her mind. "Wait!" She jumped up and ran to him. She pulled the piece of paper from her pocket given to her by Many. "I can't read. Could you tell me what it says?"

The hooded guard held the note close to his face. "It says: 'Lumin Village. Go to Tint's Hats. Find Tint, prove you are Wander. Bleed and shake her hand. Then you'll make new friends.' There's also a map of Lumin Village with a star on it. I imagine that's where Tint's Hats is."

"Thank you." Wander gestured for him to return the paper.

The guard held back. "What's this about? Who wrote this?"

With no plans to let him in on more information, Wander shrugged. "What's Lumin Village?"

"It's one of our hybrid villages. Spirits only. Probably not safe for a human. Who gave this to you?"

Wander opened her mouth, but no words came out. Her heart suddenly raced. She looked around but there was no danger. Unintelligible whispers crawled in her head. Numbness took over her left arm, and she raised it. Her fingers curled like talons before extending out to release a white flash like lightning.

The guard dropped the paper and covered his eyes.

Not knowing what she was just forced to do, Wander took three steps back. She grabbed her left hand with her right and held it down. Unlike lightning, the magic caused no sound; it may have even forced silence.

The guard uncovered his eyes. "What . . . what were we talking about?"

Wander still could not speak. She stood there trembling, trying to find words the guardian would allow. "N-nothing, sorry," she managed to say.

"Are you alright?"

"Yes," she tilted her head down. "I just need some sleep."

The guard left, his steps uneasy like he could faint at any moment.

Wander took Many's note from the ground and pressed it to her chest. *I made him forget. The guardian made me make him forget.*

At sunset, giggles came from the hall. Wander could not determine how much she had slept. Her time under the blanket felt like an infinity of waiting. The quilt was thin enough to let sunlight glow through. She stared at her bare hands. The skin around her wrists and fingers wrinkled with scars. When she got out of the bed, her body felt heavier than usual. Some clothes were left for her. She pulled up white pants to her hips and put on a white shirt. The long sleeves pleased her, and she adjusted her white wedding veil. No skin was to be visible.

After gloving her hands, she stepped out into the shadowy corridors. To the right, she wandered down the courtyards toward the ballroom. At night the whole mansion felt like a fallen sky of stars. At sunset, the place seemed ordinary, barren of the nocturnal animals and the flowers that blossomed only in moonlight.

"Did you get any sleep?"

Wander somehow missed Fade sitting beyond the brush. He sat on an iron chair with a garden table. A glass plate with edges rounded like petals sat empty on the table. As Wander gazed at the rich painted colors on glass, she thought the plate would be too pretty for food. Fade held a matching teacup; the blood could be seen through the glass.

The lullaby king smiled when he realized he had surprised her. "It's an early evening for me. Yesternight was stressful, so I had trouble sleeping."

Gathering herself to socialize, Wander held her hands together. "When do you think you'll meet with Naktol?"

"Well, we've been sleeping until just now. We are going to send the letter after some blood drinking. I imagine that as we are getting up, the humans are going to sleep. The human queen will probably read it at sunrise. Though she must be busy with the war, so it could take longer than that. I'm not sure what her highest priorities are."

Wander shifted her weight to her left leg and sighed, her breath warming the veil on her lips and nostrils.

"I'm sorry. We were too busy yesternight to send anything." He opened his mouth to sip more blood. As he did, Wander saw his crimson glazed tongue.

"I hope we can ally soon," she said. "I want this war to be over."

"I talked to Vincent earlier. He seems to think you're more personally invested."

"What do you mean?"

"Aura's Wings. You want him free, right?"

"Yes."

"You realize the humans will execute the Wings the moment he is free?"

"What about the lullabies?"

Fade chugged the last of his cup before standing taller than Wander. "If lullabies got to him first, we'd give him a chance to show that he's not dangerous, imprison him, and give him a proper trial. If the humans got to him first, I'm sure they'd kill him without even trying to talk."

Wander nodded and looked away toward the mansion walls. Night came fast. The sun had already ducked behind the mountain.

"I want to go to Lumin Village tonight. Do you know it?"

"It's a lullaby town on the edge of our territory. Spirits typically have hybrid villages on the edges of our lands. All sorts of spirits live there, not humans. Our hybrid areas are not exciting. Not many outsiders move there because they'd have to sleep in the day rather than night. Lumin in particular is very small. Why go there?"

"I'm meeting an old friend. I want to see him while I have the chance."

"Best get that done today then. I'll give you two escorts. You'll need them to travel there and possibly for protection. I'll also get you a more appropriate headscarf. You look a little silly with that fancy headpiece."

"Escorts?"

"Companions."

"Um?"

"People to go with you."

"I don't need—"

He held his hand up. "I want to trust you," he said. "But I am not a fool. You are important. I do not want you leaving until things are settled with Naktol."

Wander expected to lose control of herself at any moment. She could attack him, erase memories, or just start running. Her teeth chattered and gritted. Nothing happened. No whispers bubbling up in her head, numbness, or clenching fingers.

"Fine," Wander finally said. "That's fine, I guess."

A breakfast of fruit was set aside for Wander and Vincent in the ballroom. Vincent already finished half his plate. He seemed thoughtful, only greeting Wander with a grunt as she sat at the small table.

As she adjusted her new black and red veil to cover more of her neck, Wander noticed the lullabies removed all the tables from the ballroom except this one. With the room clear of bodies, the reflection of torches bounced off the shining marble floors. She spent less time eating than watching Vincent tediously peel his clementine. He tried to get every white sliver off the orange flesh.

"I should tell you," Wander said as she examined the apple slices; which the lullabies had cut into star shapes. "I'm leaving this place for tonight, but I'll be back. I'm going to Lumin Village. It is to get more help for the war, I think. Someone told me to go there for help."

"Can I come?"

Wander shook her head. "I think they only want me."

"Are you sure it's safe? Not a trap?"

She shrugged.

Vincent gave her an exhausted glare. "And the lullabies are alright with you just strolling out?"

"Fade is sending escorts with me."

Vincent finally took a clementine slice from the fruit's body. "Fine. Thanks for letting me know."

"I thought you would yell at me."

"I'm done trying to control you," Vincent said.

Wander's lips trembled. She just wanted to tell one person that she was already under someone's control. If she wasn't, maybe she could actually listen to others. Thinking of not going to Lumin Village felt the same as backing up into something sharp. The guardian wanted her to go. He wanted her to go enough to not allow her to even think otherwise.

Chapter 18
Lumin Village

"Despite their strange diet, lullabies are possibly the most open minded of spirits. After all, their hybrid villages invite all races. Even humans. It's rather experimental, but it gives me hope." – Naktol's Notes

In the middle of the night, a guard escorted Wander to a plain white carriage drawn by two white donkeys. Wander almost did not see the driver in the dark. He had no glowing marks and brown hair. She sat in the cramped space in the carriage. The guard came in after her, and the carriage began moving.

"I thought there would be two escorts."

"No, just me." The guard took down his hood to reveal a familiar face. The very same face that had given her the note about Lumin Village.

She recalled his name. "Many?"

"Yes. I was glad to hear you were going to Lumin. I volunteered to be your escort. Someone else was supposed to be here, but I told them that there was a change of plans and that Dim picked someone else."

"You lied?"

Many looked outside to the woods. "The place we are meeting is secret. I don't want other people to go."

"I want to know who you are and where I'm going."

"I'll show you."

Many faced his palms upward and took in a deep breath.

Darkness rose up from his feet, up his torso and through his arms until his entire body was encased in a shadow. His form shrank down to a pool on the carriage seat. A hand stretched out as a child-like form came out of the darkness. The black dissipated to reveal a dark-haired little girl in a blue dress.

Wander pushed her back against the wall of the carriage, and her heart skipped a beat. For a moment she thought this was Under. She did not let the thought live long, banishing it. If it were Under, he would be turning into himself.

"You are a shadow?"

The little girl nodded; she faced her palms upward and breathed. Shrinking back into a shadow and rising, Many transformed back into his lullaby form.

"Yes, and I am with a secret organization for those who are supposed to be dead. If people knew about us and the deviants learned about us, then we'd be in danger. That's why this is secret."

Wander knew what she wanted to talk about first. "The boulder that crushed the dragon in Sollast was a shadow like you. His name was Under, and he was my friend."

"We thought the boulder was a shadow's doing. That's part of why we decided to approach you."

Wander held her hands together, her thumb caressing the other. "Since you're a shadow, too, then you must know if it's possible for Under to change back. Maybe you could help him. He didn't know any other shadows, so maybe he was wrong about a lot of things."

"I'm sorry," Many sat back. "Shadows who turn into inanimate objects do not have the minds to change back. They only change back in songs and legends."

Wander's hands let go of each other, and she stared at her empty palms.

"I'm sorry, but I would not give you false hope." Many's hand touched her knee. "But it's okay, you've been doing good. One of Aura's most powerful Arms is dead. The lullabies and humans are going to ally. And with my people, you'll have a secret weapon Aura will never see coming."

"And what's that?"

"You'll see when you arrive. If you don't mind, I'd like to hear more about Under. We shadows rarely meet each other since we have no way to recognize one another. There are probably many of us scattered in the world of Awei, but only a few lucky ones are in my group."

Under's story was a good one, but as Wander spoke, she felt she gave him no justice. "Under doesn't remember having a family or being born. He just lived in a forest as different animals for a while before befriending a human named Alice. He wanted a body of his own, not something borrowed from someone else, so she drew a lot of pictures of an original body for him to examine until he transformed."

"You must have heard wrong," said Many. "If any shadow attempted that, they'd just turn into the parchment with the drawing on it."

"But all that is what he told me."

"Did Under think he had a family that he forgot?"

Wander shrugged again.

"We shadows don't have families. We are more like wind-borns. But it is a little more complicated. By example, let's say there is a little girl who loves her toy doll. She loves it so much that she keeps it for her whole life. The doll is passed down through generations of children that play with it and whisper secrets in its ear. The doll goes through nights, rain, and sunshine with emotions poured into it. So much occurs around it: celebrations, death, and life.

"Because of all these emotions poured into it, the doll gains a soul. The soul is trapped in a place with no way to think or live. It may exist that way forever. If it endures enough negativity, it becomes cursed, enough positivity, it becomes a blessed object. But there are some instances when it hatches into something else. That is a shadow.

"What little organization my people have left is access to old texts to know what we are. Most shadows today hatch into confused creatures. They stumble about through life, ever changing, but never reaching the point of personhood."

Wander played with the newfound knowledge. What counted as an object? Could a shadow be born from a house or a piece of clothing? A tree? Does what they hatched from form their personality? What did it mean to be a cursed or blessed object?

"How long would it take for an object to gain a soul?" Wander asked.

"Lifetimes seems like the right answer, but I'm not so sure. Some karma is born in seconds. Some people emit so much energy in their desires that it brings life to beings it was never meant to."

For the rest of the ride, Wander heard all about shadows from Many.

He told her of what he heard of shadows before their war with deviants, that they did not really have a king or queen ruling over them. "Anarchy" he called it. They lived in tents spread all around Awei. They did not see human land or deviant land, just land. The deviants did not like that, and that's what got the shadows all killed.

"You'd think shape shifters would be unstoppable," Many said. "But we had little to no organization. Even if we did, our powers would just have been turned against us. No power in the world can counter mind-control. Nothing. The shadow that could turn into a dragon, the one whose mind was controlled by Aura, he was the leader of our one attempt fight back against the deviants. When his mind broke, the rest of us either died or went into hiding."

Many talked through midnight. Wander hung on to his every word at the beginning. Within an hour, she completely spaced out. Sometimes she snapped back into the moment to realize the shadow was still speaking to her.

"Ah, we're here."

They exited the carriage. Wander had never seen such liveliness at night. The little town had round golden lanterns tied up to each other over the dirt roads. Spirits roamed around the market street. Wander could tell none were human just by looking at them. The lullaby's markings lit up their skin. Others wore masks, their bodies covered in tattoos. Some shopped in a tiny marketplace of open tents. Inside, Wander saw fire and welding, a faceless molded iron into a plate in front of a wide eyed child. In the child's arms was a lemur with orange eyes and a dark pelt. Outside of the tent was a rainbow street musician. She played some form of flute Wander had never seen before. It was a soft pink color bent into a sort of infinity sign. The sound the instrument made was joyous and high. For a moment, the world was beautiful and wondrous. When she remembered herself, the joyful sensation faded.

"This way." Many opened a curtained doorway to one of the smaller buildings. Wander stepped into a room bathed in candlelight. Stands and cabinets held hats of all kinds. She examined them one at a time. One was pink and felt like flattened straw, a velvet cloth tied between the crown and floppy brim. A smaller hat had dark feathers that Wander touched.

"Oh, Many! I'm glad to see you," a voice croaked from behind the back counter. A cane tapped against a wood floor as an old woman stepped out. A brown shawl was draped on her shoulders and messy silver hair hung down out of a gray knit cap. She seemed to be a deviant. Human-like characteristics but with the same odd tinge of surrealism that Wander sensed around spirits.

"Tint," Many gave the elderly spirit a gentle embrace. Tint's face barely reached the shadow's chest.

Her wrinkled cheeks lifted in a smile at Wander. "And who is your cloaked friend?"

"Wander."

"The human that Robin wanted to help?"

"In the flesh."

"Oh what a joy!" Tint came up to Wander and took her gloved hand in both of hers and made a vigorous handshake. "Welcome, Wander, welcome. Forgive me; we had no idea when to expect you. My place is such a dreary mess."

"Robin was right by the way," said Many. "The boulder that killed Arrow was a shadow, a friend of Wander's. His name was Under."

"Then he's a hero, your friend," said Tint to Wander. "Not just for saving people from one of Aura's Arms, but for saving the soul of that mind-controlled shadow. Arrow was like you, someone who came out of nowhere to fight the deviants and protect his people. They made him the thing he stood against. But now he can finally rest in peace knowing someone else is there to fight."

"I'm sorry," Wander said. "Did you know him?"

"No, but my grandparents knew him and told me his tragic story." Taking Wander's hand, the old spirit led her to a patchwork curtain between two hat stands. Unveiling the curtain, she revealed stone stairs that led to a source of light.

"Mist and Robin are downstairs. There are more of us, but they are not here today."

"That's fine," said Many. "This was Robin's idea anyway. Mist also has the access we need."

Wander stepped downstairs with Many behind her. The steps weren't even so she descended slowly.

The room below was lit with lanterns and smelled of dust. Boards were nailed to the walls and floor to cover up holes. Bookcases took a far corner. One shelf angled down from the weight of the thick texts. Some scrolls awkwardly stuck out from between the books. The floor was a mess of thin brown and red rugs, their patterns faded with age.

In a corner, a woman curled up in a rocking chair. She wore thick rimmed glasses and held a book over the arch of a bulbous stomach. Her brown hair was long enough to be mistaken for a blanket. Looking up at Wander, Wander saw that freckles took over her entire face from the chin up to her forehead.

"How are you feeling, Robin?" Many greeted from the stairs. "I brought a special guest for you."

The freckled girl's jaw dropped. She placed a sliver of cloth in her book before slamming the pages shut. As she rose from her seat, her brown skirt fell to her ankles. "Wander?"

Having reached the base of the stairs, Wander had a better view of the room. A woman got up from the couch to reveal her tall stature. Her brown eyes were framed by a dark face, her long hair sleek and dark. She wore an odd pink concave stone on her neck and dressed in pants and a black shawl. Her nose was pierced with a sapphire ring that linked to a silver chain that reached to her pierced ear. The chain was decorated in blue stones and beads.

"I'm so happy to meet you!" Robin took Wander's hand in both of hers. "I have heard rumors of your actions against Aura. You are connected to one of her Arms aren't you? The winged man."

Wander examined Robin. Were all these people shadows? Or were they deviants? The stormy woman by the couch did not seem like either.

"His name is Masu," Wander said.

"Wander, this is Robin and Mist," Many introduced them. "Mist is a shadow like me, but instead of living the life of a lullaby, she chose to live as water elemental."

Mist gave Wander a short nod.

"Robin," Many continued, "is a winged being but lives as a deviant."

Even with her face covered, Wander's shock showed. Her body froze up, and her eyes went wide. Robin's back was bare. How could it be?

"You're like Masu?"

"Of all the survivors of the deviants, our people are the fewest." Robin's fingers tucked into the bottom of her shirt. She pulled it up and turned around. Two parallel scars were torn down her back. Wander stepped closer. The scars replicated where Masu's wings started. Her hand hovered, reaching to touch. Robin pulled her shirt back down.

"Where did the wings go?" Wander asked.

"We have survived by hiding what we are. When I was born, my mother and father tore my wings off, like they did to themselves when we lost the war. A deviant doctor accepted high payment for getting rid of wings in secret during the genocide of our people."

"With Tint's age, she has trouble going downstairs," Many said. "But she is also a survivor. She is a horned being. She shaves her horns down to her skull, which is difficult, and wears hats to hide her identity. Horned beings have founded safe places like this."

"Wander, you can have my seat," Mist said. "I'll go and make everyone some tea."

Robin took Wander's hand and led her to the couch where they sat side by side. Many pulled the rocking chair across from them. His lullaby marks glimmered in the dim basement.

"Please, Wander, tell me all about yourself." Robin brushed her hair with her fingers. "I want to know about Masu, too."

Wander detailed her story to the spirit. When Masu was mentioned, Robin smiled and glanced at Many. When Wander got to the part of the fire and her body burning, Robin put her hand on hers. At the part where she killed Ethan, her voice choked. The guardian would not allow her to say anything about killing him.

"Are you alright?" Many asked.

Wander nodded. "Ethan was killed," she managed to say. "Aura killed him," she added in a lie. She kept hitting barriers where the guardian wanted silence. Nothing about him or Myth or various things Aura had said were allowed.

As Wander told the rest of her story, Robin's body seemed to press against her as if to protect her from the world she shared. When her story ended, Robin gave Wander's hand a squeeze. "Thank you."

Mist brought out four steaming cups of tea. Rather than joining Wander and Robin on the couch, the shadow sat cross-legged on the floor. Wander's ceramic cup was imprinted with little hummingbirds. The jet-black tea emitted steam hot enough to scald.

"I feel like a coward living among the deviants," said Robin. "Aura's people live naïve and happy. While Aura is evil to outsiders, she is a beloved leader to her people. Anyone who can make it to her palace with a terrible wound or illness gets healed by her magic. She has cured people's blindness and amnesia. She even helps those who are ill with sorrow or anger." Robin's hands tightened around her cup. "No one should have those powers. I think even she is under some sort of influence by drinking guardian blood. I mean, wouldn't that make sense? That could be why the deviant leaders are so merciless to people other than their own. At events, she keeps her Arms around her, and they remind me that I am not safe. Especially Masu, he terrified me the most because he is one of my people. He's Aura's favorite, too. She'd bring him everywhere to just stand behind her.

"Some damage she did without magic. Aura's kindness to her people made my parents confused and think it was our fault. That somehow we deserved what happened. I know our leader, Morning, killed Aura and Myth's parents and brother. That didn't warrant her killing everyone! I mean, what about Masu? He was just a baby, what did he do to deserve to be her slave? What did I do to deserve my wings being ripped out?"

"Calm down, Robin," Mist spoke. "You are getting fired up at someone who plans to kill Aura. The human has enough tragedies on her mind."

"Sorry." Robin took a deep breath. "Sorry. The point is that I don't want to hide anymore." She put her hand on her stomach. "Now more than ever. I want my baby to keep their wings. I want to raise my baby in a world where they don't have to hide."

Wander knew she was failing to understand something important when the spirit kept staring at her stomach. "Living without my wings is anguish because I still feel them," Robin said. "They are like ghosts at my back. I feel like I can fly but I can't. But then you came, someone whose mind cannot be taken by Aura. Not just that, but you want to free Masu, the prince of our lost kingdom. I want us to help you defeat Aura. I also want Masu to be free. I want to meet him." Her hand caressed her stomach. "I want him to teach my baby how to fly."

Wander looked back at her tea. "I don't know if I can free him. Aura told me he won't be the same person I lived with in the Emerald Wilds. His mind has always been controlled. She told me if I set him free, he'll be like his evil mother. If he's like that—" She sucked in her breath. What would she do?

"She's delusional!" Robin's voice rose. "Aura would probably say the same thing about me or any other winged being. That's how she thinks: that any outsider is like another outsider who wronged her."

Wander pulled her veil down and sipped the minty tea. She avoided the stares of the spirits, her eyes narrowing on the inside of the cup.

"We should tell Wander the plan about how we're going to help," Many said.

Wander placed her empty teacup on the floor. "If any of you are thinking of traveling with me, you shouldn't."

"Well, that wasn't our plan exactly," said Robin. "The reason we've survived so long is by hiding."

Mist straightened her back. "An Arm has been killed. That has never happened before. Also, if the alliance between humans and lullabies succeed, that will be new as well. It would be the first time the deviants fight two allied forces. I have little doubt that if the human-lullaby alliance succeeds, Aura will call upon the elementals. You've seen how much damage a single elemental can do. Imagine more of them. Not just fire, but forces of storms, quakes, and the sea. Humanity and the lullabies wouldn't stand a chance."

Many cut in. "That's why we're going to break the elemental-deviant alliance, so Aura can't do that. Without the elementals, she also will lose Chant. Chant is possibly the strongest Arm after Aura's Shadow."

"The plan is that I escort you to the elemental islands in the far west," said Mist. "Together, you and I will convince the royal elemental families to turn their backs on their alliance with the deviants. With that alliance broken, Aura would only have Masu and Red left to defend her in a battle."

"How would we do that?"

"Other shadows who live as elementals and I have been conducting investigations on the alliance. We've looked for anything we can say against the deviants and have found a couple things. It won't be easy though. The royal family makes decision through consensus, so we'd have to convince the four leaders: Caliber, Fury, Rush, and Ruin. We already have Rush on our side, and they will be your way in."

"Wander plans to be present at the meeting between Naktol and the lullaby kings for the alliance," Many said. "Once she does that, I can get her to you."

While Mist and Many continued to chat, Wander gazed back at Robin. The woman seemed kinder and more passionate than the average person. Robin noticed Wander's gaze and grinned. Wander spoke so only Robin could hear. "If Masu is free and I'm not around, would you take care of him?"

"He would be family here."

Wander let out a sigh, lifting a weight that she did not even know was upon her. "Thank you."

Chapter 19
Sollast

"The city didn't fall, but it was broken. Its people were broken. Rubble outnumbered buildings. Many had been burned and doctors were few. Scarred skin was going to be a common trait for the human race." – Records of the War of Arrows

Wander's return to Sollast felt unwelcomed before she even stepped out of her carriage. Most of the outer city had become ruins. Few buildings withstood the smack of a dragon's tail or the roar of Chant's fire. Nearly a week had passed, and the air still stank of smoke. Some of the humans stood or sat in a daze. Many wrapped themselves in blankets. The buildings that still stood were modestly guarded and faint whiffs of food came from the windows.

"The boulder is still there." Vincent pointed out of his window. The massive figure of Under's boulder could be seen behind the row of buildings they passed.

Wander only gave a quick glance before looking away. She could not stand the sight.

The inner city remained intact, but far more crowded, crowded enough that Wander no longer wished to look outside. She adjusted her veil, pressing the cloth further up the bridge of her nose. "I don't know if I should've come."

"Even if you changed your mind, one of Naktol's terms was for us to be present," Vincent said. "I have little doubt that she'll try to pull us into the issue rather than agree to the lullabies' terms for an alliance."

The carriage stopped only a few feet from open castle doors. Wander offered to help Vincent down from the carriage. The moment her hand touched his, he scowled and slapped her hand away. "I got it!" Since Wander had learned of Vincent's background, his personality made more sense. He tries to make himself the opposite of a needy wind-born.

Wander could not say for all wind-borns, but she knew she was just a little child in a larger body. Her struggling actions and mysterious appearance had made others mistaken her for someone who knew what they were doing. None of it was true, she was still Wander, that little girl who wandered constantly into the sharp jaws of danger who needed saving. She had the desire to be saved, to be dependent, and be taken care of.

The betrayal Vincent suffered as a wind-born had made him someone who never wanted to be taken care of. Depending on how her journey ended, Wander wondered if she'd end up like him. She was already close. Her desire to be saved and taken care of was what killed Under, the Flinsler family, and Alice.

Dim and Fade stood in the castle halls. The daylight from the windows made the usual glowing marks on their skin invisible. This time of the day was when lullabies would normally be sound asleep. They wore black cloaks not so different from Wander's, except the long hoods dangled down their backs. A wooden door decorated in vines of iron was at the wall behind them.

"Are you both ready?" Fade asked.

"Remember," Dim said, "it's we who are doing the talking. Don't speak unless spoken to."

"We're ready." Vincent spoke for them both.

Through the doors Naktol and four strangers sat at a round table in a round room. The human queen stood and the four others followed with a tilted bow to the lullaby kings. Naktol's fierce gray eyes met with Wander's and her upper lip twitched like a wolf about to snarl. The room was the base of one of the castle towers where walled off stairs rotated upward to another floor. Natural light glowed through stained arched glass windows. The stained glass had veins of bright blue that bordered designs of doves, howling dogs, and rolling hills. The arched windows were framed with thick black curtains.

Wander waited for everyone else to pick a seat. The kings sat themselves across from Naktol; Dim stood directly in her line of sight. Vincent placed himself by Fade's side. Wander wished to be by his side, but the space was taken by one of Naktol's people.

She sat by Dim and then realized everyone but her still stood.

Naktol planted her hands on the mahogany table. "Welcome, Dim, Fade. Despite the situation, I am pleased to finally meet with you face to face." One of the four humans on her table side began to take notes with a dark feather dipped in ink.

"This is the first time spirits have bothered to visit our land since our independence from the winged beings. I hope such an occasion would be celebrated, that humanity would finally be recognized as part of this world rather than ignored and pushed aside like in all other matters. I happily opened your letter with hope you accepted an alliance. Instead I had to read it over and over again, hardly believing what I was seeing. You want my youngest beloved daughter Sophia to marry you? I speak for all humanity when I say we are fed stories from birth, through childhood, and adulthood on the ways of spirits. And you probably already know that none of the stories are good. After our slavery with the winged beings, we saw spirits as people to be feared and hated. We told stories that rainbows would make us forget who we are, that elementals would destroy us, faceless would indoctrinate us, and that lullabies would lull us to sleep and drink our blood.

"But I was never afraid of spirits. This was because I saw the same patterns in my own diverse people. We misunderstand and fear each other for the smallest differences whether it is the color of our skin, our religion, or place of birth. I thought this was the same for our feelings about spirits. It was all just a misunderstanding. If we overcame ourselves, we could be strong with them. We could build a better and understanding world together. But here we are. It's just like in the stories. You want to take my child away. Why Sophia? My daughter is still so young. She's an idealist. She's been helping with the recovery efforts of this city. Humanity needs her now more than ever."

"You asked for Wander. I gave her to you. But it turns out you both are shallow. Once you saw the burns on her face, you lashed out at me with this ugly request. Humanity is in danger of annihilation by the deviants. I should be working to stop that. But here I am, protecting possibly one of the most precious of us from a whole different breed of spirits. So please, tell me some good reasons you kick us while we are down."

Dim pulled parchment out from under his cloak. Unrolling it, he squinted his blue eyes in the bright room as he spoke. "Thank you, Naktol. But I have to correct you in that humanity has done nothing but kick themselves since you've gained your independence. We spirits are old enough to remember details you have long forgotten. Let's discuss why you are in the position you are in. Humanity became independent by chance when the deviants extinguished the winged race. Queen Aura was much younger then, but she still had the courtesy to split the winged lands in half, half for the free humans and half for the victorious deviants.

"Hundreds of years later, you are queen. Maybe you forgot, maybe you didn't care, but you attacked the land Aura set for herself. Deviants never attack someone without being attacked first. Everyone knows that once someone starts a war with deviants, that the deviants are the ones that end it. Greed, stupidity, I don't know which, has gotten you into this war.

"My brother, Fade, invited Wander to the Moonflower Ball because she could touch spirits. Ignorance about our culture prevails even in other spirits, so I'll make this clear to you. My brother cannot find a lullaby bride because of his markings. You cannot see his markings now because it is daytime, but they are a woman's markings. However, my brother is a man in every respect. Our society is wrong in believing his markings make him a woman. But we are kings, and we know to tread carefully to make the changes we desire. The people have accepted him as a king, but not as someone worth marrying or even taking seriously at times. When it came for the traditional ball, I worried for him. A king requires a partner in our lands when he comes of age.

"Your need for an alliance and my brother's need for a bride seemed to match up. So we asked for Wander because she could touch him like another spirit could. But when we found out her true identity, I was disgusted. You think it's because of her skin? It's deeper than that. You sent us a child. Not eighteen, but possibly three or four years old. She's wind-born. She tried her best to blend in and managed to trick everyone for a short time. I'd like to add that she never betrayed you. Instead one of our jealous brides tore the mask from Wander's face to reveal her. I realized she was just a child the moment I saw her shut down and cower in the middle of the party.

"You did not just send us a child. You sent us a child prisoner. We learned it all from Vincent, who also told us about Wander's age. He would know. He's also wind-born. We learned about humanity's oppression of wind-borns. How does humanity expect to earn respect from spirits in light of that oppression? You were all once enslaved! Now you enslave each other?

"This girl is a child prisoner who has gone through psychological and physical torture. Burned by an elemental fire, chewed on by a dragon, shot by arrows, poisoned, gouged, and more. She has seen the ugliest side of reality: people burned alive, a friend tortured, friends killed, betrayal, and more. We listened to her story. She wanted to help you, Naktol, and you used her and betrayed her like the world already had. So, Wander is now under our protection."

"If not for Wander and Vincent's pleas," Dim continued, "we would not have even given you another option for an alliance. My brother asking for your daughter is a merciful opportunity. We chose your youngest daughter because she is the one in most danger. It is the youngest of the royal family that would become a new Arm for Aura. She would be captured and her mind broken. If her age is of concern more so than her safety, we can discuss your other daughters as well. So, what's your answer?"

Naktol's eyes never looked larger. "You're telling me that Fade can't marry a lullaby because of his skin?"

Her question was met with silence. One of the people sitting next to her stood up to whisper something in her ear. She pushed him away.

"That's asinine!" she yelled. "He could just marry a woman with male markings! He could just marry another man or no one at all!"

"In our culture—"

"It's all twisted!" Naktol shouted over Dim. "Your culture is wrong, just like the deviants'. Even if we did attack them first, that didn't warrant genocide!"

Dim kept himself calm in the face of Naktol's rage. "Spirits respect each other's traditions. Humanity has been ignored for the very thing you are doing right now."

Naktol shook her head, "Besides what makes us different, surely you would not put your people at risk just so one of you can be married? There is something you are not telling me."

Dim seemed actually happy from this question, "The deviants are a powerful bully of the world. Today they may kill humanity, but who is to say that they cannot decide to kill all lullabies tomorrow? Currently their genocidal culture is bound in traditional rules, and that's why their victims are so particular. But you surely must know as I do that traditions and rules change with time. It's only a matter of time before the deviants see something wrong with everyone and pick off the races one at a time."

"That is something we can agree on," Naktol seemed to calm a little. "Is that reason not enough on its own to ally with us? Why involve something as silly as marriage?"

"It's not silly to us. It is actually pretty customary in an alliance. After all, the fire elemental King Caliber gave his daughter to Aura as part of an alliance agreement."

Naktol crossed her arms and made cold eye contact with Wander, "And Wander, you don't know the full story about her. She is under Aura's mind-control. That is where her powers come from."

Dim put down his parchment. "What?"

"We conducted tests. She is immune to all the same things Aura's Arms are. It also explains why she can touch spirits. It explains how she can fight."

"No!" Fade spoke up. "Aura's Arms do not talk. She puts their consciousness in a comatose-like state. Wander is free thinking."

"That's what Aura wants us to think," Naktol said. "Wander is a spy. Even she may not be aware of it. And what of you, Vincent?" Naktol turned to him. "You fed me nothing but your suspicions. Why the sudden change?"

"I have not completely lost my suspicions," Vincent said. "To be honest, I have just lost faith in you. When Sollast was attacked, I saw that you sent your best soldiers to see your daughters to safety. Your daughters were already the safest of all your people. Even you! You did not fight. You panicked and remained in the castle. You even sent me to go after Wander instead of focusing on saving the city. I obeyed because I thought Wander could be attacking others. I was wrong. She saved me. She's probably the reason I'm alive. While I searched for Wander, I saw the devastation. Families were poisoned, chewed, burned, and broken all over the streets. I could have saved some, but I followed your orders instead. Now I'm ashamed of that."

"I am not perfect," Naktol clenched her hands. "I am not psychic or invincible!"

"I'm also wind-born," Vincent said. "You assigned me to Wander because of that. You have treated me differently when the last thing I wanted was to be treated different. Looking back on my life, I actually have a lot to be angry about with you. You are no revolutionary like you claimed when you took the throne. If you were, the slavery trade would no longer exist."

"Enough!" Naktol slammed her palms on the table. "I did not invite you all here to berate me."

"Agreed," Dim said. "Do you accept our terms for the alliance or not?"

"Not my daughter," Naktol's voice quieted down. "You will not have her or any of them. I'll give you land, money, labor, anything you want. Just not them."

Fade and Dim looked at each other.

"Please! She's only eighteen! She's my only blood child. She doesn't understand the world yet. My other children, they have dreams and have already chosen their futures."

"Mama!"

Everyone looked around for the source of the tearful voice.

A girl stepped out from behind one of the black curtains, her strawberry-blonde hair disheveled and her pale freckled face flushed. She wore a green and white gown of lace with pink flowers overlaying the white.

"I'll do it, Mama!" she cried.

The queen stood dumbfounded. "Sophia! You're not supposed to be here."

The princess shook her head. "No, Mama. I can speak for myself."

Naktol's eyes bulged, and she shook her head.

"I'll be fine," Sophia smiled through her tears. "We can't not do this. We need them."

"No. We can find another way. You can't trust them."

Sophia looked over at the kings. "Which of you is Fade?"

Fade timidly raised his hand.

"Sophia!" Naktol hissed. "Don't talk to them!"

"This isn't like you!" Sophia cried. "You are the one who told me you dreamed of peace with the spirits. I shared that dream with you. After the attack, I've never been more afraid. I've never felt more powerless. Then I noticed you've changed too. You don't eat or sleep. We are all worried. But now I can do something! I can help save us!"

"You can't live with them, Sophia. They are lullabies. Their breath puts people to sleep. They can take advantage of you."

"I brought this for Sophia," Fade held up a baby blue cloth with string on the four corners. "It's a breathing mask. As long as she wears it, our breath won't put her to sleep."

"No," Naktol said, "she is not wearing that thing."

Sophia embraced Naktol. The queen's armored body towered over her daughter's petite form. "Please, Mama. Let me be brave."

Naktol tensed up and looked at the kings. "Let me talk to her. Give us two hours."

Wander sat outside in the castle gardens. Bluebirds bathed themselves in a shallow fountain. Their feathers puffed and their heads shook as they ducked under the water and splashed it onto their backs. The grass looked soft enough that Wander wanted to pull her feet out of her boots and plant them bare on the earth.

It took a while to find a place with to one else around. The shouts of Dim and Naktol still echoed in Wander's head. Dim's defense of her made her tremble, and she did not know why.

"There you are." Vincent came around the castle corner.

"Have they come to a decision?" Wander asked.

Though there was room on the bench Wander sat on, Vincent remained standing. "They just called on Fade and Dim. We will know soon enough."

Wander looked back out to the birds.

"You've been here for the past two hours?" Vincent asked.

She nodded.

"I've got something for you. A servant passed it to me, saying it was yours."

He held up a bracelet. Wander recognized the brown leather. A dark withered feather dangled down. Vincent handed it to her.

She rolled the bracelet pass her left fist where the feather hung at her wrist. Her thumb slid down the quill. It looked like the feather had gone through a storm, pieces torn or frayed. Its spine could be so easily snapped between two fingers.

"I remember you wore that when I first saw you," Vincent said.

"The feather is Masu's. He made the bracelet for me." Wander caressed the feather. She wished she could feel more. The trinket used to feel like a sense of hope, a reminder of what she was doing. Now as she looked at the frail plume, she felt empty.

"You also had the fox pet. Did it die?"

"No. He's around somewhere. He left before Sollast was attacked."

"The creature has good senses."

"He's from the Emerald Wilds like me."

Vincent stepped away to go back inside.

"Wait!" Wander stood up.

She could not get a grip of her own free will, where it started or began. Now she tried harder than ever to express herself. She'd think of something only to have it erased from her mind completely and be left blank. Vincent looked at her while she struggled. For a moment, she forgot what they were doing.

Someone needed to know that the guardian controlled her. The guardian didn't want anyone to know. Why? Because they'd stop him? Wander's thoughts could not even enter the realm of possibility that the guardian could also be her enemy. Freedom was impossible, as she needed the guardian to survive her burns. So why tell someone? The guardian didn't understand some element of how people work. They needed to know. They just needed to.

"Well, spit it out."

Wander grabbed her head. "I can't."

Vincent looked around and spoke more softly, "Do we need to go somewhere more private?"

"That's not it. I actually *can't*!"

"You're not making sense."

"It's about what scares people about me."

"Your abilities?"

He was quick to catch on. She couldn't say it, but he did. If she could just lead him to the word she couldn't say and distance her thoughts from her words, she could get him to understand.

"They aren't mine."

"Are you saying what I think you're saying?" Vincent crossed his arms. "You're under Aura's control? It's actually true?"

"Not her."

His eyes widened. "Someone else has the ability to control people?"

Wander dizzied. The guardian wouldn't let her say yes. Vincent would have to figure out that her silence meant he was right.

"Well?" he still waited for an answer.

Without thinking, she turned away from him. She had to leave. Vincent grabbed her upper arm. He squeezed tight enough that she could feel his nails through the cloth of her shirt and cloak. He spoke in a harsh whisper. "Whoever is controlling you won't let you? Are they near?"

"I don't know."

Vincent looked around. "A deviant?"

"No."

"Give me a word. A single word as to who they are."

No word could come to mind. Everything in her suddenly locked up.

"What is the person's goal?"

"Mine."

"Are you sure?"

She turned around, hoping he could see her panic in her eyes.

Vincent's harsh gaze softened, and he let go of her arm.

"I need my powers to live. If I don't have them, my burns will kill me."

"If that's the case, why even tell me?"

"I'm feeling less like I am here. I don't know what *is* me anymore.

"For how long?"

"I don't know."

"Wander," Vincent got closer to her, "if what you're saying is true, then you are innocent. But the one controlling you can't be ignored. I have to know who it is."

Wander hugged herself. So many thoughts were blocked. She became stupid with no words to describe the fox. She could see him; she could remember what he looked like, his fur like a night sky splashed with dead leaves.

"He wears a coat as old as himself."

Vincent's soft face soured. "What the hell? Is that a riddle?"

Wander did not know what a riddle was. Any hope of Vincent getting through her tangle of words and meanings seemed unlikely. She knew if she were in his place, she would never understand.

Dim came around the corner. His pale body in daylight looked as delicate as a snowflake in the sun. He squinted, his pupils nearly gone in the light. "Good news," he said. "We have our alliance."

Wander found herself staring into space without thoughts for hours. Despite her open eyes, they saw nothing. She only came into attention when Vincent checked on her. His hand would take her shoulder or he'd call out. She no longer knew how many days had passed or what she needed to do next.

With the alliance came a lot of progress in Sollast. Spirit allies came from the east in carts pulled by pale donkeys. The lullaby forces wore dark hooded leather. For so long, the human army had only used range tactics. Now they had forces that could touch other spirits. The lullaby army was armed in swords, spears, and battleaxes.

Wander was attentive for various moments of the war meeting. Dim and Fade were very familiar with the deviants' tactics since they had lived long enough to see the war with the winged beings. "Aura is using the same plan on you as she did on the winged beings," said Dim. He pointed to the war map of Awei. Thick harsh lines divided the world by people. Wander wondered where the Emerald Wilds were. She looked toward the eastern seas where the paper was dyed a light green with few words or dots. The large ink spot tagged Sollast was tucked in drawn arches of mountains. Dim's pale finger connected the dots below. All were pinned down in needles with red flags. "All these have been destroyed?"

"Yes. Completely obliterated," Naktol leaned forward. She placed pins with blue flags around other dots. "These ones have been attacked as well, but there are still survivors and buildings left to recover. The white flags indicate what hasn't been touched by Aura yet. But it's all strange. She has not targeted my military. She has avoided them whenever she could. She has wiped many small villages off the map. None of our large settlements are unscathed."

"She's saving her greatest force for last," said Fade from the corner. "Aura knows her Arms won't survive your numbers. That's why she plans to keep your military alive to turn them against each other with her mind-control."

"That's what I feared," Naktol said. "I'm at a loss to counter that kind of magic."

"She's been whittling humanity down while playing it safe. Based on her attack on Sollast, I think she's close to targeting your army. She'll try to get all your strength in one place, and it'll be a bloodbath."

Dim's finger trailed west to wordless mountains. "These are the lands that started this whole war, correct? The Winged Graves. South of those lands are deviant farms. I say you take a piece of your army, and we will take a piece of ours. We should set up on the borders. It'll need to be strong enough to withstand her Arms, but weak enough that the loss won't make the rest of humanity fall should we lose.

"With that sort of force there, we could possibly lure Aura out to try to turn us against ourselves. That will be the chance to kill her and end the war. We can hide forces around to evade her attention. They can try to assassinate her."

Wander blanked out as the meeting pressed on. She heard Naktol's hopes that the lullabies' breath would put the Arms to sleep. They shot the hope down. "Aura's mind control will keep them awake just as it keeps them from feeling pain."

After the one meeting, Wander passed on attending others. She spent her time in the castle gardens in the day and a guest room at night. One night she heard voices outside. She looked out the window to see Fade and Sophia walking down one of the garden paths together.

The princess wore the mask he had for her at the alliance meeting. The cloth covered just her nose and mouth. Her strawberry-blonde hair rose up into a loose bun. She wore a nightdress. Maybe she rose from sleeping and met up with him?

Something that Wander caught at the alliance meeting was that Sophia asked Naktol to "let me be brave." But to be brave, doesn't one have to already be scared? Wander could not blame Sophia's fear. Even kind people can be frightening. People are complicated, like forests with some spaces in shadow with dead and mold, some spaces fresh and verdant.

Wander toyed with Masu's feather on her wrist.

A small band of spirits capable of magic came to Sollast. A rainbow was among them. Wander watched her enter the castle on foot. Castle servants and soldiers crowded around. The spirits were safely boxed in by four lullaby guards who cleared the way for the rainbow to walk.

"Give her space!" Naktol's voice boomed. Her tall form stepped down from the castle stairs. "She's here to heal soldiers!"

The crowd dissipated, and Wander got a better look as Naktol greeted the spirit. The women had smiling sky blue lips. Her teal and violet hair came down past her shoulders, the first layer coming together in a braid at the back. Black and gray spots speckled her hair like splashes of paint. One eye was gray and the other green.

She had on loose pants that billowed in the breeze like a skirt. Her feet nestled in dark sandals with anklets of blue and violet weaves. Her gray shirt was cut sort, revealing a stomach with no belly button, like Wander's. Maybe rainbows weren't born from blood, but from the wind like her.

"She looks ridiculous."

Wander looked to the side to see Vincent watched as well.

"The colors remind me of a bird or flower," Wander said. "Where did the spirit come from?"

"She's a citizen of the lullabies. She was apparently exiled from the desert where the rainbows live so she lives in one of the spirit hybrid towns the lullabies have."

"What do you know about rainbows?"

"That they don't let anyone come into their territory or let anyone go out unless they are criminals. I know many of them have magic powers. There's green magic, white magic, red magic, black magic—"

"Black magic?" Wander's fingers brushed harshly against her thighs.

"Do you know about black magic?"

"Not really. I just heard of it."

"It's pure destruction from what I've heard. I know this rainbow is a red mage. A healer."

"Why red? She looks more blue."

"It's not about how they look. It's about what they do. I don't know why the healers are red. Spirits are weird with their meanings."

"Maybe they can heal your leg?"

"That's the plan."

The rainbow followed Naktol toward the barracks. The spirit stopped and stared straight at

Vincent and Wander. Wander glanced at Vincent and back at the rainbow. The spirit's gaze could not be read. A simple stare, but a long inquisitive one.

The barracks had changed since Wander last came there with Under. Few soldiers were present. All of them had gone out of the castle to help restore the city. Those that were around did not stand on their feet. The silver and blue tents had rows of makeshift beds. Some were lucky enough to get a mattress; others lay on piles of rugs and clothes. The air smelled of pus and blood. There were no sounds of training. No release of bowstrings, hammering, or loud chatter. The drill dummies had some arrows left in their heads and shoulders. The winged dummy that they hung up in the sky to symbolize Masu looked like it would fall to the ground soon. A strong wind or other cause had messed up the mannequin's balance.

The thought of coming to the barracks did come to Wander. She was still fond of her memory with Under and a group of soldiers socializing and going out for drinks. But that was before the army turned on her.

Naktol, the rainbow, and the lullaby guards ducked into one of the small tents filled with crippled soldiers. Vincent sighed and sat in one of the outdoor wood chairs. "I might have to wait a while."

The sun had moved by the time the rainbow got to Vincent. She no longer had a queen or entourage of guards following her. "I'm told Aura's Shadow broke your legs," she said to Vincent. Leather gray gloves stuck out of her pants pocket, the fingers bunched together like rose petals.

"Just my left one."

The rainbow looked at Wander. She gave a little bow before sitting next to Vincent. "My apologies that I've taken so long. My magic is much faster when I can actually touch the wounded." She sat on her knees at Vincent's side. "Could you show me your leg?"

Vincent rolled up his pants leg to reveal swollen and bruised flesh. Her hands hovered near his leg and her once blue veins turned white.

"This will take a couple hours."

"You must be very patient," Vincent said.

He got the spirit to smile. "It's nothing compared to other magic. Some spells take generations for the green mages who practice in reincarnation."

Wander had no idea what reincarnation meant, but on the subject of magic, she had to ask questions. If Aura was right about Masu being a black mage, Wander had to know about the power. But at the same time, she did not want to give away that Masu could be a black mage.

"What other kinds of magic are there?"

"There are many more than most people know. Red are healers like me, green practice reincarnation, white creation, black destruction, blue movement, yellow time, purple hypnotism—"

"Hypnotism?" Vincent cut in. "Rainbows also know mind control?"

"Oh, not at all like deviants. We don't drink guardian blood. We're born with our abilities. Hypnotism only works with consent. We use that magic to help people be who they want to be."

Vincent glanced at Wander, and she nodded. He was still trying to solve the puzzle she gave him as to what was controlling her. Perhaps he thought it was a rainbow now.

"Black magic sounds dangerous," Wander said.

"Black mages are something that we struggle with. They are born innocent, but as their magic grows, they usually become evil forces with a love of killing and power. However, we've found varies ways to lessen that likelihood. Firstly, we raise our black mages with no other black mages near them. We try to teach them about love, kindness, and trust before their magic is awakened. We also give them a white mage partner to live their life with. The two opposite personalities usually find peace in being together. However, most young white mages do not like that life; so many black mages are denied that luxury. Many are doomed without help.

"I was exiled from the rainbow lands for healing rogue black mages. The rogues live in the wilderness as predators of anyone who pass by. They do terrible things like kidnap and eat children. They conjure storms at nearby villages. They lure people away from their loved ones and manipulate them."

"Then why did you heal them?" Vincent asked.

"Because I loved one."

A long silence fell over the group. Vincent eventually shut his eyes, though it was hard to tell if he slept or just relaxed. By the time the sun was setting, the rainbow drew her hands away. She pulled the gloves from her pockets and covered her hands. "All done. He should be able to walk without crutches now."

Wander stood up. Vincent didn't stir; he was sound asleep. Wander made a move to wake him.

"Let him rest. My magic has a side effect of making people sleepy. Now that his body is healed, he probably won't let himself rest again for a while."

Before the rainbow left, Wander's voice broke the silence of dusk. "Why did you bow at me?"

The rainbow looked over her shoulder at Wander. "I could sense your injuries and pain from outside the castle walls. It's something beyond any red mage's power. When someone's injury and pain is greater than our magic, they deserve worship and respect."

Wander wasn't sure what to say.

"My name is Love, by the way," she said. "It was a pleasure to meet you, Wander."

Many came to Wander the next day.

He approached her outside by the entrance where she spent most her time sitting on a bench. His gray eyes squinted so tightly, it was a wonder how well he could see. He put his hand over his eyes for a better look at Wander.

She had forgotten about him until now. She had forgotten what to do next.

"Finally found you." He released a sigh.

That was right. Wander recalled she and a shadow were to go to the elemental islands. To secure a victory against Aura, the queen had to lose the elemental alliance. With the human-lullaby alliance secured, Aura could call upon the elementals and be far stronger.

Wander stood up. "Let's go."

"You don't have any other business to take care of?" Many's face scrunched more as he lowered his hand from his face.

"I am not sure if Fade, Dim, and Naktol will like me leaving. They trust me little enough as it is. We should go fast."

Many nodded and covered his head in a dark hood as they turned to leave together.

Wears a coat as old as himself.

Wander's riddle danced in Vincent's mind.

Whoever is controlling her is a he and wears a coat. As old as himself? Is there some sort of spirit tradition that makes someone wear a coat their whole life? He had to keep an eye out for anyone wearing a coat.

When the rainbow visited and spoke of magic, Vincent thought he was onto something. If rainbows were so capable of magic, then maybe one was controlling Wander? Wander seemed to dig into black magic. Was that a hint? No, she's not smart enough to do that. Whoever was controlling Wander might be always one step ahead of Vincent, of everyone. If that's the case, could he even help Wander? Vincent stood up from his seat. The barracks bustled with newfound positivity after the alliance and the rainbow healer's appearance. Soldiers crowded around tables, no longer afraid to raise their voices and laugh. Craftsmen brought their weapons and armor for the healed men and women.

Wander would be in one of two places. She either remained in her guest room or sat on the garden bench by the castle's south entrance. The girl had no desire to speak, be entertained, or do anything but sleep and eat. Even her eyes rarely moved. In the passing days, her eyes would transfix on the grass or sky for hours. How long had it been true that someone was controlling her? If not just recently occurring, the puppet master must have changed his strategy. When Vincent first met her, Wander seemed more animated and prone to emotion. After the attack on Sollast, he noticed that she was different, quiet but still with stirrings of personality. Now she had become like a doll. Whoever was controlling her was extinguishing her spirit.

Then again, the girl had been through a lot. Her silence and inaction could be effects of depression. That could be true, but Vincent had to remain wary. Wander made an effort to tell him that his suspicions were not wrong. Someone out there was controlling her. Why?

She was not sitting on the outside bench.

Vincent entered the castle walls. He took comfort in the shade from the sun, which had been harsh for days. Wander was purposely assigned to a room near the barracks. The girl would sleep less in the coming days. With a battle planned and drawing near, the barracks would not be quiet.

He knocked on the door more for her sake than his. He knew Wander hated others to see her skin.

Vincent opened the door to an empty room.

He stepped out and began to search the castle. He looked out of each window, hoping to see her dark form wandering the gardens. His steps walked themselves faster and faster. Nothing. Nowhere.

If Wander was no longer here, he feared what that could mean.

Chapter 20
The Sharp Hills

"Either you're hiding something or you're nuts if you live near the Warding Sea. At least the Sharp Hills create natural barriers against the noise, wind, and salt." – Travels of Manger

No wagon or carriage awaited them when Many led Wander out of the castle. He traveled the roads least populated, the places marked with the most destruction; the humans' abandoned, ash covered rubble and fields that were once neighborhoods.

Following Many from behind felt like following a reflection. His cloak and hers looked to be of the same cloth. Seeing his hood up from behind, she wondered if she looked that mysterious to others. A kind and gentle thought came that the cloak was beautiful.

"Where are we going exactly?" Wander asked. The question came late, as did most of her thoughts lately.

"We are to meet Mist on the edge of the Sharp Hills. It's the edge of deviant territory. The land is rural and barely used as the deviants think the land is cursed."

"Why?"

"It's where they falsely believe the last horned beings died. The last ones were said to be a family of poor farmers. They think the land is cursed with angry ghosts. I suppose that's the closest they can get to guilt. It's a suitable place for us to set out to the Western Isles. Robin lives in the Sharp Hills, and she has been sheltering a way for us to take safe passage across the sea to the islands."

"I've never seen the sea," Wander said.

"Few survive even stepping near. We are going to travel like the deviants and elementals. We will take an airship and fly high where no monsters or waves can catch us. It's the only way to reach the islands unless you're a sea elemental. Mist and Robin know how to operate the balloon, but only Mist will go with you. We don't want to attract too much attention to our group."

Outside Sollast, Wander found calm in the trees and barren dirt paths. The sounds of crickets echoed from the woodlands. Many kept ahead of her. "So, Wander, what do you think you'll do once the war is over?"

"If I could do anything, Masu and I would be together in a different enchanted forest."

"You'd find another? Wouldn't that be dangerous?"

She shrugged. "We'd find ways to survive."

But maybe they wouldn't. The guardian finding them curious and useful might be the only reason they survived in the Emerald Wilds. The fox gave Masu the tools to survive.

"If the deviants lose the war, the next plan would be to dismantle their logic of genocide," Many said. "That would be the new goal." The shadow stopped. "We are far enough from the city. I'll transform, and you can ride on my back. We'll arrive much faster that way."

Many took a deep breath and raised his hands, his palms facing up. Darkness took his body from the feet up. He shrank away to a shadow on the earth. He took much longer than Under. The grounded shadow dallied, the edges quivering. The darkness rose back up into the form of a pale donkey. Many bowed his front legs so Wander could climb on. Her hands clung to the tuft of hair on the back of his neck as he took off running.

They did not cross paths with anyone. Not even a patch of farmland could be seen across the rolling hills. A rafter of wild turkeys wandered the landscape. Sometimes a cloud blocked the sunlight, and the land darkened. The sunset cast the sky to a pink and purple haze. Wander realized she couldn't remember the last time she had eaten, yet she felt no hunger.

They ducked through a forest path. The screams of crickets and frogs joined in with the sound of Many's hooves. Wander stooped down to avoid branches. Night had fallen by the time they left the forest. Wander knew just from the landscape that they had reached the Sharp Hills. She had never seen the land jagged before. Each hill seemed to be a serrated boulder with a mixture of grass and moss blanketing most of its surface.

Many kneeled as a sign for Wander to get off. He turned back to his lullaby form. His markings glowed completely in the night. The markings zigzagged like mountains across his arms. The edges of his face glowed with tiny stair-like markings as thin as veins. His white hair contrasted gently in the night like a dying fire. "We're very close."

They strayed from the path and weaved through the hills. The sky distracted Wander, as she could see the entire galaxy above them. The silhouettes of deer timidly stepped over the hills. Managing to stop, gazing at the sky, Wander realized she could hear a far off roaring. A breeze was constantly flowing. A shiver went up her spine. "What's that sound?"

"The sea. It's about five miles from here. A ways off, but you can still hear and feel it."

A lantern appeared on a hilltop. A woman's silhouette stood, her long hair flowing in the gusting wind. Her hand waved in front of the light. Many and Wander approached to see Robin. The woman carefully stepped down from the rough hill. She wore a simple brown dress and hefty dark boots. Many greeted her with a hug.

"I'm so happy the alliance worked," Robin said as she led them through the hills.

They came to a shack. Upright logs held up a porch with rickety stairs. The wood was old and warped from the elements. Mist stood on the porch waiting for them. Her breasts were covered a blue cloth that strapped both around the back of her neck and behind her back. One leg was bare up to the thigh from a thin clothed skirt. Anklets and toe rings decorated her feet in sapphire stones and silver. Her right ear looked like it wore armor, a chain of metal triangles imbedded with sapphires linked from her pierced ear to her pierced nose. Many gave Mist a hug.

A white bird with black accents flew by and squawked. Robin forced open a sliding door to the inside of the shack. The walls smelled like rain. The wood floor was covered in mats and rugs of different shapes, colors, and sizes. A low table centered the room. Pillows were strewn about.

They stepped inside. Some art hung from the ceiling, paper orbs and cubes on beaded strings. At the table's center, a bowl was filled with sand with various shells placed in a symmetrical pattern. Off to the side a curtain lead to what seemed to be a kitchen. Wander could sense a small flame beyond, probably cooking.

"I was thinking you guys could spend the night," Robin said. She adjusted the pillows so they sat around the table. "But Mist wants to leave tonight. I think that's dangerous."

"I don't sleep," said Mist. "And Wander can sleep on our way there."

"And what of the danger?"

"I'm a sea elemental and a shadow. We'll be fine. I have traveled over the sea night before."

Wander spoke up. "I'd rather not wait, either."

Robin's face softened and her eyes got large. She looked at Many and back at Wander. "Are you sure?"

Wander nodded. "The humans and lullabies are working hard toward a battle to end the war. I want to be there when it happens."

"See?" Mist said. "We can't afford to relax. Rush is also expecting us. Let's get to the balloon."

Across the shack was another door to the outside. Robin slid it open to reveal stone steps up a craggy hillside. The breeze grew to a gust as the group traveled up the hill. At the top was a flatland.

"Ah, you already pulled it out of the cave," Many said.

A colossal brown blanket of cloth took the hilltop and spilled over the side. Rope came down from its four corners to a wooden construction. The wood was like a stretched bowl with two small benches nestled in it. One bench was at the front, the other at the back, each just big enough for a single person to sit on it. Wooden handlebars extended up from the bowl on either side of the benches.

"I had us test it this morning. The patch we put over the hole seems sturdy." Robin bent down by the cloth and picked it up to gaze over. "A lot of snails got on it while it's been in the cave."

"How does it work?" Wander asked. "How can it fly?"

"Sit here and hang on tight while I fire up the balloon," Mist patted the bench in the stretched wood bowl.

Wander sat on the bench. She noticed handles on the sides and grabbed them. Mist raised her hands level to her chest. From the feet up, she disappeared into the dark. When she reformed, Wander felt a sudden heat emerge. Mist became shorter, blonde, her skin tan with patches of white, eyes orange, she wore something similar to before, but now the clothes were yellow. Fire burst from her palm.

"Are you sure you can turn into a powerful enough fire elemental to handle this balloon alone?" Many asked.

"Yes," Robin said. "Maybe Many should go as well."

"That's too many people for this small ship," Mist said. "Enough worrying already."

Robin and Many watched as Mist handled the ship. She spread the blanket out. Once done, she sat on the bench across from Wander. The heat her body emanated was far weaker than Chant. Chant's heat was like the same fire that consumed Wander's skin. Mist felt more like a campfire. The shadow's hands dipped into the blanket, and she cast heat under it. The hot air expanded slowly. Wander scooted as far as she could on the bench, away from Mist's hands. Wander nearly jumped out of her seat when fire suddenly surged out of the shadow's palms. The blanket expanded upward until it floated up toward the sky. Mist began to shoot fire up into the balloon.

Their seats began to leave the ground. Wander tensed up and clung to the handlebars. The ground fell further and further away until Robin and Many looked up and waved. "Don't look down," Mist told Wander. "Not here, and certainly not when we are above the sea."

The shadow's blonde hair billowed in the wind. Wander's vision was hindered by the quaking of her veil. Her cloak flowed and pulled at her back.

Mist still held both her hands upward, releasing flames into the balloon. "I'm going to make sure we're high enough so the sea waves don't get us."

Wander tried to keep her gaze anywhere but down. On the horizon where the sky met land, the land proved to be a darker shade. A mountain moved quickly across the horizon and Wander realized the sea might be closer than she thought. That was no mountain . . . that was a sea wave.

She looked up at the brown balloon. In the bursts of fire, she saw its patched brown color. Despite their ascension, the stars did not look any closer. The roar of the ocean became greater and greater. Insurmountable fear suddenly gripped Wander. On the horizon she kept seeing mountain after mountain of waves dash across the world. The higher the airship rose, the more waves she could see beyond land. The sea took over to the end of the world.

The air tasted like overcooked fish dipped in salt. Once they were higher than Wander believed possible, Mist said, "The sea wind will keep trying to force us out. But don't worry, I'll turn into a storm elemental and guide us. Just hang on."

Mist transformed again. This time she became a tall being with bright red eyes. Her long white hair was disheveled and nearly glowed in the dark. The disappearance of her fire elemental heat woke Wander to the cold air. Mist's body then got caught in the wind like a sheet of paper before disappearing. Wander's heart dropped as the ship began to fall. She looked down and could see where the land met the sea. Each mountain of water crashed upon cliffs in a firework of foam and salt.

A blast of air, stronger and warmer than the sea wind, hit the ship. The air blasts kept coming, hitting the side of the ship and pushing Wander out toward the sea. The ocean's roar got loud enough to remind her of thunder. She would cover her ears if she did not have to cling to the handlebars. The crashing of waves were intense enough that some droplets of foam rose all the way up to touch the airship.

Mist reappeared on the ship in her storm elemental form, her long white hair wildly flying. She breathed heavily from her efforts to push the ship past the sea wind barrier. Raising her palms, she turned back into a fire elemental. She drew a deep breath before punching fire up into the balloon.

The airship rose up and away from the sea.

After several long streams of flame, Mist transformed back into a storm elemental. She became wind again and steered the ship as it slowly dipped. Once close enough for a huge wave to hit, Mist returned as a fire elemental and helped the ship ascend. Wander grew less tense with each passing of the pattern of ascending and descending. Hours into the journey, few to no waves were in sight. The sun began to rise over the flat platform of a world of water. Sunrise reflected in the sea, like a sun rose in an underworld as well.

Mist turned back into her fire elemental form and collapsed on the bench across from Wander. Looking up at the balloon, she lazily pointed her hand up and puffed out flames. "We . . . should have the wind . . . on our side now," she spoke through exhausted breaths.

"I'm amazed you could keep that up for so long," Wander said.

She smiled and grunted. "Don't compliment me. Elementals are just overpowered. That's why I like them. That's why I decided to live as one."

"Why a sea elemental?"

"Because I can breathe under water. I can turn into water. I also like sea elemental culture. We build our villages in lakes, some deep, some only rising a couple feet into our homes. I know the lifestyle and people are mysterious to visitors and strangers, but after living as a water elemental for thirty-seven years . . . I wouldn't trade that life for anything."

"You go into the ocean? What's it like?"

"There are endless wonders. There are ruins and trinkets long forgotten. There are seashells larger than me and reefs as big as castles. You can find sunken homes and jewels. There is so much life, too. The fish do not fear sea elementals."

"It sounds like a dream."

"Yes, but it can also be anyone's nightmare. You can go deep down where the sun no longer reaches and the ground is unknown. I knew a sea elemental once lost for years in an abyss. She no longer knew which direction was up or down. She had not seen color for years. Outsiders talk about the beasts the most. They get as large of the sea's mountainous waves. I'm sure you've heard of the megalodons that eat whales and hydras whose entire bodies have never been seen at once. Even the monsters are a danger to sea elementals."

Mist looked down at the ocean. Her blonde hair blew wildly. "You may not believe me, but the sea sometimes lures people to die in it as well. The cases are rare and scattered, but I know of them. Only the water elementals have a word for it. We call it 'The Inducing.' For us, when we are lured there, we cannot die so we turn into water instead. We just become water and never turn back."

Natural wind guided their ship for hours. Mist shot fire upward into the balloon to keep them up high. She told Wander that some creatures were even known to jump out of the water and eat sky faring ships. The shadow seemed to enjoy such horrifying stories. "The fire and storm elementals honestly have the best tales," she said, "because they fly these ships. They see the monsters from a safe distance to tell the tale."

With time, Wander no longer feared staring down at ocean. But she once looked down to see the entire sea a darker shade than before. The sky was cloudless with no excuse for the sea shadow. As she looked out to the horizon, she saw the edge of darkness made the shape of a fin. Some creature as large as a body of land was moving under the sea.

Wander's heart raced, and she turned to see Mist already was pumping the balloon with fire. "Let's hope we see only the silhouettes," she said.

Farther into the journey, Mist began to ask Wander more questions about herself. They began with Masu, then the Emerald Wilds, and drifted to Under.

"So he didn't know there were other shadows?"

"No."

"Did he wonder?"

"Not out loud. He said he loved being human more than anything."

"I see. It makes sense. I mean, the reason shadows formed an anarchist society is because we all had such different paths we could take. We integrated ourselves in wolf packs, human villages, or just changed every day. Many is desperate to find more shadows. I think being a shadow makes him feel like he fits in nowhere. For me though, being a shadow means you can fit in anywhere. You just need to find the right place."

"I don't think Under liked being a shadow," said Wander. "He didn't like copying other bodies. He wanted his own. A human drew an original body for him out of her imagination. She drew it in many ways for him to study. That's how he got his original body that he always used.
At least, that's what he told me. When I told Many that story, he didn't believe it."

"That is a difficult story to believe," Mist said. "But Many and I have different theories about our abilities. Many thinks we are all equal, that we all work with the same rules. We all can examine something and turn into it and that is it. I think shadows work more like elementals. As you'll see in elemental society, some are more connected to their element than others. Some fire elementals shine brighter while others look more deviant or human-like. Some sea and storm elementals can barely keep a corporeal form while others can barely turn into a breeze or puddle.

"Shadows could be like that. Some may turn into something without so much as a thought while people like Many and I have to focus for a time. The world isn't fair. Some people are born with better abilities than others. So maybe Under was just a really powerful shadow?" She sighed. "I guess we'll never know now."

A snail fell from the hot balloon and down toward the sea. Wander was surprised the creature held on for so long in the wind.

"You can curl up in the middle space of the ship if you want to sleep," said Mist as the sun began to set. "You can probably fit your legs under your bench and your head under mine. I can stand on my seat. I don't need to sleep."

Wander agreed, though this ship would be on the upper part of her list of most uncomfortable places she'd slept. She managed to lay her body across the small ship. The ship's borders tightened at her head and feet with little room to stretch. She stared at the panels of wood with a crack of dusky light.

Wander dreamed, and she knew she stood in a dream. She stood in the ashes of what was once the Emerald Wilds. Everything smelled like rot and death. Shriveled husks that were once trees twisted in the gray ash. Animal corpses lay about, their bellies crackling with a fire's heartbeat.

She wandered but ended up nowhere. Everywhere looked the same. More dead animals, more dried and charred trees. Once in a while, a dark feather fell from the sky. She'd look up but there were only dark clouds.

Chapter 21
Lotus Lake

"Few are adventurous enough to visit the Western Isles. A pity though, as elemental culture is the most fascinating culture of Awei. They have also been part of the world for the longest too. They've seen many civilizations rise and collapse." – Fire, Sea, Storm, and Earth

"We're here."

Wander woke under a starry sky over the sea. She sat up, her side that lay against the wood aching. In awe of what she saw before them, she quickly stood up. A cluster of mountains stood over the sea, some tall enough to reach the clouds. Their peaks were white with snow and ice.

"Those are the Storm Peaks," Mist pointed to the tallest mountains. "As the name suggests, the peaks are always enduring blizzards. It's always raining on the mountains' seaside. It's also where many hurricanes hit. The storms live there. So you can see why we don't land there."

Turning into a storm elemental, Mist shifted their course around the Storm Peaks. Wander sat down and held the handlebars. As they flew to a different angle, Wander saw an underwater crater, just close enough to the surface to be seen in the moonlight. Beyond the underwater crater were cliffs that matched the might of the sea waves. The cliffs bordered land with no plants. It was just a landscape of dirt and village clusters, dry, crusted, and sometimes hilly.

"What's that?" Wander called to Mist.

Mist reformed on the ship to answer. "The Ruins. That's where the quake elementals live. They shake the land, which traumatizes any life but their own. They turned their mountains into landslides long ago." She pointed farther. "See beyond the Ruins?"

Wander raised her gaze to a dark horizon of mountains. She would not see them from this distance at night if not for the fire. The entire mountain range was on fire. Rivers of glowing red and gold poured down the sides. Dark jagged mountains glistened with red veins.

"That's the Range of Light. It goes without saying what elementals live there."

"What about your home?"

"Sea elementals don't have established borders. You can just find us wherever water is. My home is Lotus Lake, which is between the Range of Light and Ruins."

The ship eased downward toward the sea.

"Where are we landing?" Wander asked.

Mist craned her neck over the ship, her ghost-like storm elemental hair whipping and swirling. "We can't be on the ship when it lands."

Adrenaline claimed Wander's heart. "What?"

"I should've told you earlier," Mist's crimson eyes looked at Wander. Wander hoped for a joking smile on her lips, but she looked absolutely serious. "How did you think someone like Robin got this ship? It crashed, and we salvaged it. That's why we need to jump."

Wander looked down at the torturous sea. As the ship eased down, the violence of the wind thrashed in her ears. "In the sea?"

"It's okay. I know the water here. I'll protect you."

Wander hugged herself and shook her head.

"I am a shadow who can turn into all four types of elementals. With me, you'll be fine. It'll be a rocky ride, but we'll be okay." Mist transformed back into a sea elemental and offered her pale hand. Wander only hugged herself tighter.

"If we don't jump, we'll be arrested, and the elements will keep their alliance with Aura. I assure you, they already see this ship that they don't recognize. They will send people to investigate."

Wander tried to make the choice quick and painless. She shut her eyes and grabbed Mist's smooth and cold hand. The hand curled into a fist around her hand. She kept her eyes shut, only to feel Mist jerk her forward and off the ship into the open sky.

Mist hugged Wander's body into hers as they fell. Wander clenched her mouth shut to not scream. The air sliced at them. Wander's cloak battered against her legs. She knew any moment they'd impact with the sea. They fell so fast, she knew she'd feel the debilitating force at any second. The only warning Wander received was Mist's hug tightening.

The moment they hit the sea, Mist's body disappeared.

Wander opened her eyes to bubbles through the sea's surface. She sank down headfirst into the dark abyss. The water suddenly gained a current that struck her back, forcing her upright. Seeing the moon beyond the sea's surface, Wander reached up and kicked. The water pushed her upward until her head burst out from the ocean. Her soaked headscarf clung against her skin. The water pushed her toward the cliffs where the waves slammed and exploded. If Wander hit the cliffs with that amount of force . . .

Mist's head broke the surface.

"Where were you?" Wander shouted over the waves.

"I guided you up! Now stay close!" Mist's body filled with darkness and sank into the sea. The shadow reformed into a bearded man. His long dark locks and beard floated on the water's surface. She grabbed Wander's hand. "Hold onto my back. We're going to ride a wave. Hold your breath and don't look behind you." Mist spoke in a man's voice.

She helped Wander crawl onto her wide and muscular back. Wander gave away her extreme fear in her desperate grip and trembling body. She closed her eyes and pressed her face against Mist's shoulder. Though Mist told Wander to hold her breath, the force of the wave knocked the wind out of her. Water rose up her nose. She peered over Mist's shoulder to see the impending cliff side. The moment they hit the land, a bizarre phenomenon occurred.

Mist exploded through the land. Her entire body vibrated as the rocks before them burst into sand to sink into the sea. They fell through a waterfall of dust, mud, and sand, hit the earth and tumbled. Wander let go of Mist and erupted in a coughing fit; her nose felt swollen with water.

"Not yet," Mist grabbed Wander and pulled her up. They stood in a dark cave. She spoke quickly in her man voice. "The sea will fill this place if we don't tunnel up quick. Follow me."

Mist stomped and clenched her fingers as she motioned her hands downward. Earth fell into dust and sand, forming a slope upward. She ran up, and Wander followed while coughing and snorting.

When seawater rushed into their cave, Mist turned around and threw down her hands. The ceiling fell in a muddy form and swirled into stone, blocking the sea from coming in. Cutting away the sea, she also cut away any light.

Wander fell on her knees, coughing in the darkness.

Mist spoke, "I'm sorry. I suppose this is a bit much for you."

"No," Wander managed to say. "It's fine."

"Come, I'll tunnel us upward. Hold onto my back."

The dark was like none Wander stood in before. She could not see her own hands even as she held them in front of her face. Her hand reached and her palm rested on Mist's tunic. Her fingers clenched on the cloth and followed as the shadow strode forward. The ground at times felt soft and sinking, other times like flattened stone. The air smelled like rainfall. Mist carved a tunnel that sloped upward. Her breath heavily drew in and out.

"If the earth feels like it is shaking, do not worry. We are under quake lands. We are probably not the only ones changing the land."

Mist had proven tremendously strong. Throughout their journey she had kept the balloon up and going with fire and wind, transforming back and forth without sleep. Now she had pushed Wander through the sea and land. "You're very powerful," Wander said. "You've trained yourself to be any kind of elemental. So why haven't you tried to fight Aura yourself?"

"It doesn't matter how powerful I am," Mist answered. "Mind-control trumps anything. Aura would just make me kill myself or my friends. You are the only one I know who can face her without that fate."

"I don't know if I'm strong enough."

"Aura may be asking herself the same question."

Mist and Wander emerged from the earth not too far from Lotus Lake. The sun began to rise over the mountain ranges surrounding the island. The smell of rainfall stuck on white-barked willow trees. A yellow frog hopped into a stream that glittered like crystal from the stones underneath.

The shadow changed herself from her muscular old male body back into her sleek and graceful sea elemental form. "Come," she said, "this stream runs into my lake." She nearly skipped in her steps by the stream, a gentle smile on her face. She was excited to be home.

Each step in the grass sank from the soft mud. At times the stream sloped down and rushed through slippery stones. Some silver minnows jumped the stones, fighting against the current. The willow forest opened up to Lotus Lake. The body of still water was large enough that Wander could not see the other side. Violet lotus flowers and lily pads spread across the lake's surface. At the center of the lake was a village a quarter submerged in water. The walls of the homes resembled the white willow bark. They had no chimneys and glassless diamond shaped windows.

Mist stepped into the lake and the lily pads caressed her knees. "Isn't it beautiful?"

Wander nodded in awe.

"Take off your shoes. Roll up your pants, and shorten your cloak."

Wander hid her shoes in a patch of cattail grass. She rolled up her pants to reveal her scarred legs. They were not so bad compared to the bottoms of her feet that had been nearly deformed in Chant's fire.

The lake's water gave Wander a chill. Her hands darted around as she tried to balance on the muddy moor. Mist giggled and took Wander's hand to help her walk. Tiny bites nibbled around Wander's legs and feet, but she did not mind. They got to the village's edge. On the side of a home, a log had been nailed to the wall on the water's surface. The turtles that rested on the log slipped down into the water. Many of the elementals stopped and stared. A couple rose out of the water.

Everyone's hair was sleek and smooth like Mist's. The sea elemental's skin was either pale as clouds or black as night. They covered their breasts and hips in light, colorful cloth. No one seemed old, and there were no children. One dark-skinned man with a blue headband held a struggling duckling in his hands with a group of friends. A woman's white hair was pinned up in a bun with a red lotus flower; she held another woman's hand when she saw Wander.

"Mist." An elemental with fogged up eyes stepped out of her home. She wore a necklace of mollusk shells. "Someone very important is here waiting in your home."

Horsetail reeds grew around the walls of Mist's home. A shroud of pink and violet seashells tied up in an elaborate web by a doorway. Instead of a door, a fishnet hung where the water entered, probably to keep out unwanted creatures like snapping turtles or large carp. Gigantic smooth stones were placed about the house for seating and arranging. Light poured in from a hole in the ceiling. Strings of turquoise and green sea glass dangled down from around the borders of the hole. Ceramic pots hung down from hooks on the walls and ceiling, many holding flowers and ferns. Light emitted from a doorway.

"Hello?" Mist called as they stepped through the fishnet.

The water rippled as a figure walked out of the side room. A plate with a blue paper lantern, painted with a delicate depiction of a koi, floated by their side. The figure had the longest hair Wander had ever seen. Their dark mane floated on the water's surface like a shadow. Their flowing white dress moved in the water like a ghost. A necklace of thin red coral spread out on her pale skin.

"Your honor!" Mist bowed low enough that her face almost hit the lake. She jerked Wander, and Wander copied the bow. "I am so sorry! My place is awful. I did not ever expect you to come here!"

Wander glanced and Mist's grip clenched for her to stay down.

"The family has received word from the deviant queen," said what Wander assumed to be a sea elemental. Their voice was calm and feminine. "She wants us to lend her a small army. I came here because of the abrupt urgency. I suppose this is Wander?"

"Yes," Mist remained bowed. "She has just arrived."

"You both may stand."

"Wander," Mist said, "this is Rush, the ruler of the sea elementals."

Wander looked into a pair of dark green eyes. Rush stood around the same height as her and Mist. The ruler had a far different bearing than Naktol, Aura, or the lullaby kings. They seemed serious, cold, and more otherworldly than an ordinary spirit.

Rush's pale hand pressed against Wander's cheek. "Do most humans cover themselves so?"

"She covers herself to hide what Caliber's daughter, Chant, did to her," Mist explained.

Rush's fingers pinched at the edge of Wander's veil and began to lift. Wander shook her head and stepped back.

"You survived Chant's flames? A human cannot do that."

Mist sat on a stone and folded up her wet legs. "That is why she is here, your honor. She has survived much and can touch spirits."

"Caliber will sense Chant's mark on her."

"Is that good or bad?"

"I am not sure. The fire king is hungry to burn the mainland with Aura. He will be the most difficult to sway. Seeing that Wander has encountered, been consumed, and survived his favorite daughter will just complicate matters."

"What of the others?"

Rush stuck their fingers in the lake surface and played with the water. "Ruin and Fury are leaning toward supporting Aura as well, much because of Caliber."

"Why are you different?" Wander asked.

"Perhaps it is in the seas' nature to doubt the fires. They look to the horizon while we look down and deep. While risk and change excite us, I feel like we should not ally with anyone. The elementals should remain untamed and alone, that is what makes us who we are. The family called a Conflux today, a gathering where all the leaders meet to make a decision to lend Aura an army or not. They are waiting for me. Once I enter, I cannot leave until we come to a consensus. That is why I came here. Mist has been a lead organizer against the alliance with the deviants since it has begun. She told me you were coming. You may be the voice we need to change minds."

"What's a consensus?" Wander asked.

"They all need to agree," Mist explained.

Wander pieced everything together. "Wait. Rush, does that mean you agreed to the deviant alliance in the beginning?"

"If reason does not sway us, brutality does," said Rush. "We can physically fight and kill each other until everyone agrees. We can also starve. It took weeks for us to come to a consensus. I will admit I could have put up more of a fight. I did not see much harm in the alliance at first. Now I fear Caliber would be prepared to kill to get his way."

"Where is the Conflux this time?" Mist asked.

"Fusillade Manor, in the Storm Peaks."

"That's no place for a human."

"This island is not a place for anyone but the elements," said Rush. "Dress warmly, Wander. The cold at that manor could be enough to kill you."

Chapter 22
Fusillade Manor

"The storm elementals' Fusillade Manor is an agonizing journey and even worse destination. The snowstorms sting and blind you. Whatever the manor looks like on the outside, we can only imagine." – Fire, Sea, Storm and Earth

Mist bid her neighbors goodbye at the center of Lotus Village. A dark skinned sea elemental with the fluffiest dark hair approached. Even coming from water, her hair managed to come to life and bounce under the sun. She was taller than all others, her cheeks full of freckles, her bosom layered in shells. Her arms hid in blue roomy dress sleeves. She gave Wander a kind smile.

"Abalone." Mist bowed her head. "I know you were excited to meet Wander, but I'm afraid we already have to go. The sudden Conflux was unexpected."

Mist turned to Wander, the lotus flowers drifting at the lake water swished. "This is the leader of Lotus Village."

Wander copied Mist's bow.

"Do not worry. Rush explained when they came. And I understand the Conflux is at Fusillade Manor, a place too cold for a human."

"I'm sure I'll be alright," Wander said. "I can survive things other humans can't."

"I still collected these." Abalone stepped aside to reveal a little canoe. The boat was layered in furs, black, white, and brown. "The bears that roam the peaks have fur that can keep you comfortable. The boat is for your journey upriver. A tiring journey for a splasher, but Mist is strong, and Rush is legendary. You will be there in no time."

Wander tried to enter the boat on her own, only for the construct to nearly flip over. Some sea elementals giggled, shaking their heads. They came over and held the boat and one helped Wander get in.

"She's worse than a splasher!" one laughed.

"What's a splasher?" Wander asked.

"We do not have families," Mist muttered. "We are like wind-borns. We call recently born sea elementals splashers because they are clumsy and playful and make the water splash."

Abalone aided Wander in covering her in furs. She draped the black fur, then draped some white, some more white, brown, then four more furs. Wander never felt thicker.

"It's hot," she said.

Abalone laughed, "You won't be hot when you get there."

When Rush emerged from Mist's house, everyone but Mist bowed before turning into water. The boat Wander sat in rose a little.

Rush's green eyes nearly glowed in the sunlight. Their pupils shrunk far more than a human's. "Mist, ride my current," they said. "Wander, stay in the boat."

Mist put her lips to Wander's ears. "Do not be alarmed. Rush is powerful. Their body can turn into a greater amount of water than any other sea elemental. They bring the might of the sea, so hang on tightly."

Her heart already raced. If Mist had enough caution to warn Wander of power, then it must be an understatement.

Mist dove under the lake and her body's silhouette disappeared. Rush followed, their white ghostly dress faded under the water. For a moment, it looked as though Wander were alone in the village. There were only fish and minnows under the water. The water then rose. Then it rose even more. The boat rocked. Wander's gloved hands clawed at the boat sides as the water spun the boat in circles. The lake bubbled and swished as though possessed by a river's rush.

Wander looked out at the lake's horizon. The entire body of water had been taken over, the once still waters now violent and shaking. Geese and ducks took to the sky, honking with panic. The logs that were once full of turtles sunning themselves were now empty. The lily pads and lotus flowers moved like trees in a harsh storm.

The boat rocketed forward, jolting Wander to clutch the boat sides harder. The lake gained a current with a mind of its own, guiding Wander as fast as if she were falling. Past the homes to the lake clearing, the boat dashed toward the east river. The river's mouth rushed over smoothed stone. Wander braced herself for the impact of two forces of water hitting each other. She prepared to feel the grating of stone under the boat. But the boat rose as the water that took the lake surface gathered around the boat like a hoard of insects. A wave of water hit the river, paving a deeper and wider path for the boat to flow.

The river water moved with no resistance. Wander looked out at the thick swamplands passing her faster than on horseback or carriage. The trees passed so quickly, her furs and cloak tussled in the wind. For a moment, she felt sick to her stomach. She stared at the bottom of the boat for a time. Rush's water covered anything that could harm them. Rocks, logs, even animals. The water just engulfed the creatures, no longer to be seen as they swiftly passed.

Even waterfalls did not stop them. No matter the size, enough water collected to jump the boat over the stones and earth in a violent wave. During those waves,

Wander pressed her body down into the boat and clung as hard she could.

As they approached the Storm Peaks, Wander covered the sides of her head with her hands. The wind howled and grazed against her ears. The sound and sensation felt like ice water and nails. Swamps turned to cloud cloaked mountains. As the land around became whiter, the air began to sting. Even the soft wind seemed sharp. Wander shut her eyes to protect them from the wind's bite.

By the time they reached the mountain base, the entire landscape had paled, and the sky cried drops of ice. The waterfalls came more often. Sometimes the river branched off like a crossroad. Mist and Rush must have known the right way, as they selected where to go without the slightest hesitation. As they climbed the mountains, the trees became bare boned and trembling. Any life probably lived in a white body that blended into the snow. Farther on there were no trees to be seen. They had reached the fog of clouds so thick that Wander could not see beyond the boat.

Then Wander heard a crunching ahead. She leaned forward to see the river had iced over. Mist and Rush's waves broke the frost into slush, carving the trail. They had to do this for the rest of the journey.

As they went higher, the most violent and cutting wind came. Even shutting her eyes, Wander felt like her eyelids were being lashed. She covered her whole face with her gloved hands. Her thumbs tried to reach for her ears that rung with the gust's howl.

When the boat stopped, Wander cracked her fingers to see. In the second she saw just the blizzard. Her eye dried up in the iced air. She re-covered her face.

"C'mon!" Mist shouted over the howling. "We're here!"

"I can't see!" Wander shouted back.

Someone grabbed her upper arm and pulled. She stood up only for someone to hit the back of her knees and make her fall. She fell into someone's arms. All she could see was a blizzard. She shielded her face from the cold.

"If she touches the water here, she'll freeze," Rush shouted. Wander realized Rush was the one who held her. "I'll carry her in."

Wander felt Rush run. They ran until the howling and blizzard stopped. Rush set her down and Wander opened to eyes to a high arched ceiling. They stood in a long and epic arched hall. The inside seemed to be completely made of stone. The walls had prominent cracks. Every couple meters a torch was lit in yellow fire.

Outside the door was the blizzard, a rain of blurry snowflakes.

"Welcome, Rush." Two elementals guarded the door. They both bowed. They wore white dresses. Their gray hair was wild like weather beaten tall grass.

"You are the last one to arrive. The doors will now close," one guard said. Their hands clenched into fists and swung in the air. A howl screeched through the hall as the wind claimed the stone doors, slamming them shut.

Mist put her hand on Wander's shoulder. "Let's go."

As they followed Rush down the hall, Wander asked, "What were those elementals?"

"Storms. Red eyes, gray, dark, and white skinned," Mist turned and said with a smile. "You'll notice that all elementals wear dresses. We don't like pants."

Wander couldn't help but laugh. "I prefer pants to dresses. They cover me up better."

"Some elementals like to just be nude. We don't have much of a sense of shame."

"Shame?"

"Embarrassment?"

"Ah. That must be nice."

Mist's smile quickly faded, and Wander wondered if she had reacted wrongly.

Rush's ghostly dress dragged on the stone floor with their sea of dark hair. "The first part of the Conflux will just be the family talking," she said. "I imagine Caliber is going to be as hostile as ever. Ruin and Fury are probably siding with him. You both will sit with the rest of the witnesses. Once the first part is over, the family will separate into their rooms to think and talk to the people. That's when both of you do what you've come to do. The key is to talk to each family member separately."

They passed two crossroads and went straight. They headed for a colossal stone door. The door was bordered in letters Wander couldn't recognize. At the door, Rush stopped. They squinted as their fingertips gently caressed the stone handle.

"What's wrong?" Mist asked.

They pointed to the wall. "Stand there."

Mist led Wander to the wall, their split shadows dancing in the torchlight.

Rush pulled the door open. A burst of fire as large as the 15-foot-high door pulled out of the opening. It overtook Rush like a wave, their dress and hair flailing until it couldn't be seen in the heat and crackling flame. A monster of gold and red took the hall.

Mist pushed Wander back. Wander blacked out for a second. In the eruption of light and heat, she nearly fainted. Her entire body trembled. She could remember the feeling of fire at her running feet, the moment when she was completely engulfed in bubbling skin, bloody, cooking, screaming but unable to move as she held the guardian under her. Sensing her fear, Mist held Wander tighter.

The fire dissipated with Rush still standing. Steam hissed and emanated from their body in a fog. They looked unfazed, emotionless, their gaze forward did not falter.

"Took your damn time!" a voice boomed from beyond the door. "What kind of tricks are you trying to play?"

"Peace, Caliber," Rush said. "You nearly killed some witnesses."

"That would be on your head, not mine. Let them in."

Rush gestured for Mist and Wander to come. Trembling, Wander only backed into the wall and shut her eyes.

"It's okay. He's not going to hurt you," Mist gently said as she guided Wander forward.

Wander shook her head but walked with Mist. They entered a dome large enough for a group of winged beings to fly around. The stone coliseum was completely bare. No seats, not tables or even a rug, just an empty vast room of echoes. Three prominent people stood at the center. How they stood and dressed immediately gave away that they were Caliber, Fury, and Ruin.

Caliber was the most obvious of them. His red curly beard ended mid-chest. His flaming head of hair took up one side of his head, covering one eye. The other side of his scalp was shaved short to reveal swirling dark tattoos. His orange eye was framed with a menacing low brow on tan skin. The fire elemental wore a crimson dress with golden letters weaved around the border. The dress ended at his bare feet, making Wander realize no elemental seemed to wear shoes. Golden armor covered his torso and shoulders. He seemed muscular beneath the dress and armor, his structure large and pulsating.

Wander guessed Fury to be the thin, nearly skeletal woman with bright red eyes and an angular face. Her black body was draped in a thin dark dress. Her cheeks and shoulders were blanketed in freckles. Her white hair looked unnatural as its messy contortions defied gravity.

Ruin looked younger and more human than the others. Mud colored eyes looked out through shaggy brown hair. His skin was dark like clay with dark swirling tattoos around his arms and face. Under dark armor, he wore a brown dress. Upon a closer look, Wander saw Ruin was hurt. A chunk of his neck was gone as though a bite had been taken out. He did not bleed, his insides had only darkness.

"What is that flesh being under those pelts doing here?" Caliber asked. His bright eye stared at Wander. "They are not welcome at a Conflux, Rush, and you know it."

"You are making up rules," Rush said. "Why not have her here? What can a lowly human do to our pride?"

"Who is she?" Fury asked. Her voice was beautiful and songlike.

"Wander. You may know her as the human who can touch spirits."

Whispers erupted in the outer boarders of the dome. In the shadows, elementals sat on the floor. They stared. Mist took Wander's hand and led her to the dark border with the crowd. She sat on her legs, and Wander sat cross-legged.

"Why are there no chairs?" Wander whispered.

"The family has to stand," Mist explained. "Sitting shows weakness. We have to sit on the floor and stay low because we have to be humble to our leaders."

"What happened to Ruin's neck?"

"Looks like a physical fight already occurred. It's probably Caliber's doing."

Wander turned her attention to the torch lit center.

"Is that why you were late?" Caliber said. "You think bringing a human will change anything?" He laughed. "Humans are weak. They are not only trapped in flesh, but have no power over this world. They don't deserve respect, much less my attention."

"Are you unaware that Wander survived your daughter Chant's fire?" Rush asked. "That demands your respect."

Whispers from the witnesses filled the dome. Wander scooted closer to Mist as Caliber stared into her eyes. Even meeting his gaze made her eyes sting and tear up.

"How could she survive?" Ruin asked. "Do humans have a way to endure the elements?"

"If so, she has not told me or anyone else," Rush explained.

Caliber grinned. "Then you finally did something right." He walked toward Wander with his two hands curled into fists. "We can get that information out of her right here. That'll help us decide."

Mist hugged Wander to her. Rush sped in between Caliber and the two of them. "The human is not here to suffer harm," Rush's voice echoed through the dome. "She is here to share knowledge. None of us but Chant have seen the war, and where is she? Wander came of her own free will. She will speak to each of us when we separate."

Fury crossed her arms. "That sounds fair to me. Besides, we're losing focus."

"That's right," Caliber said. The room cooled down. "While you were late, we decided to provide Queen Aura with a band of forty elementals, ten from each of us. That should be enough to wipe out the humans and then some."

"And what do we get in return?" Rush asked.

Caliber looked at the audience. Someone stood up and walked out from behind Wander and Mist. A fire elemental woman who was far dimmer than the rest of her peers, she looked like a human with a mysterious warmth and glow. She walked toward Rush. She bowed and handed them a scroll. Rush unrolled the parchment and scanned what appeared to be a map with notes.

"Land," Caliber said. "Queen Aura offered to give land from the Winged Graves for the elementals."

"The same land that began this war." Rush spoke to them as they stared at the map. Rush shook their head and handed the map back to the fire elemental. The fire elemental turned and disappeared back to the audience.

"I don't approve," Rush said.

Caliber's lips curled. "Of course you don't."

"We'd be breaking our oldest oath, we are not to settle there. We'd wreck the land and the people there."

"We discussed that," Ruin cut in. "The oath we gave was so long ago, either those today do not care or do not remember. The winged beings, horned beings, and shadows are gone. The humans are ignorant about us. The faceless don't care. The rainbows have cut themselves off from the world, and with the lullaby's human-like lifespan, they have likely forgotten."

"Queen Aura remembers," Fury said. "She mentioned she'd let go of the oath in her letter asking for aid."

Mist breathed. She took Wander's gloved hand and held it tightly.

"Queen Aura is an ignoramus then," Rush said. "That land is right next to deviant territory. We would undoubtedly hurt our neighbors by just being there in a rain of fire, ice, sea, and earthquakes. They'd get plagued by us."

Caliber shrugged. "The deviant queen has offered the land nonetheless. The pain to her people would be her own doing."

"Would it be? The deviants are loyal to their creeds. If we kill just one of her people without allowing her proper retribution, the queen would wage war with us like she did with the winged ones, horned ones, shadows, and humans. We would be the next race to be eliminated."

Ruin and Fury gave each other looks of uncertainty.

A laugh boomed through the dome. All eyes turned to Caliber, who roared with laughter. His visible eye was wide. "You really think low of your people, Rush, to think the deviants are something to fear. The reason the oath occurred so many years ago was because they feared us. They feared what we could do if we shared the same land. We only agreed to it to give them a chance to live and perhaps grow to be a challenge to us. It's been long enough. The mainlanders have wasted their lives doing the work for us by eliminating each other. We can easily kill them all. A mere rogue hurricane, tidal wave, fire, or earthquake kills them. Imagine when we put strategy and power behind the natural world, what damage—"

Rush interrupted. "Your dreams of war and ruling the world have clouded your judgment. You say the mainlanders have eliminated each other. You're right, but you're ignoring the fact that they were all eliminated by the same beings, the deviants.

"You forget that our people feared the shadows, people who could turn into anything, including any elemental. Despite their disorganization, such a power seemed unstoppable. The deviants killed them. They killed the people who we believed more powerful than us! Power doesn't matter against the deviants. Their leader takes the minds of others. Their enemy's powers become theirs. How could we ignore this?"

"Rush is right," Fury said. "Perhaps we still give Aura the army and ask for something that wouldn't be as risky?"

"No," Ruin said, "our alliance with her has already given us the other resources we wanted."

Rush got closer to Ruin. "The point of the original alliance let our elementals into Dem and its seashores. I'll admit that I am pleased with those conditions. I am also biased because only my people can use the sea. I think we should end our alliance with the deviants altogether. Our people should retreat back home. We should not have gotten involved in this war to begin with. Queen Aura can control minds, and we have opened ourselves to her."

"Are you kidding me?" Caliber shouted. "Not only do you want to deny us the opportunity to spread to the mainland, but you want us to withdraw what we already have?"

"We are powerful beings, Caliber. Powerful beings should be responsible and wise, not throwing our weight around and flaunting it. Why kill others when we can use our power to better ourselves? I know Ruin's people have been suffering from illness. We could focus on helping them. And Fury, you've expressed desire for adopting forms of study from the mainland like astrology and mathematics. We could work together on putting those into our educational systems. And Caliber, your daughter Chant can come home. Surely you miss her?"

"We can do all that," Caliber said. "And take the land."

"We haven't done any of it because of our focus across the sea!" Rush said. "You had your chance to prove we could, but instead you dug deeper into claims for the mainland. It's bordering on obsession."

"The mainland has resources the Western Isles do not," Caliber continued. "How do you suppose we will adopt anything or grow when our people aren't even allowed across the sea and no one, save Wander, can survive the trip here? We are stuck. Our people are meant to move. We are meant to take over."

He turned to speak to the audience and the room got warmer. "Rush weaves a story out of specific paths she has chosen for us. So many circumstances: First we kill deviants, then Aura finds out, then we don't allow her a kind of vengeance, then we get our minds taken, then we lose to her. These things are not going to happen."

Rush looked to Fury and Ruin. Ruin looked away, making the dark hole in his neck more visible.

"He's right," Fury said.

Ruin nodded.

With no warning, no expression, Rush exploded into a wave of water. The entire room cooled and darkened like the feeling of a cloud blocking the sun. Half the torches went out. The air tasted of salt. Mist hugged Wander to her, and they scooted further back into the shadows together. The seawater rose and charged into Caliber. When the water hit him, it twisted up like a geyser. His bare feet left the floor as he was thrown into a pillar. Before his body hit the stone, it burst into smoke.

The smoke soared through the column. Rush's water refigured itself into his person-like shape. Caliber's smoke dove down and formed into his flaming figure while still in the air. Holding his hands together, a surge of flame formed, and he sliced it through Rush. Wander covered her eyes, the sight nearly blinding her.

When she uncovered her eyes, she saw Rush's body fall in sizzling halves. They formed into water again, and the sea wave shot at Caliber. He blasted white fire into the wave, and the whole thing nearly evaporated into mist, searing and sweltering.

The mist fell down like rain and pooled into Rush. Their right arm turned into a tentacle of water and shot at Caliber.

"ENOUGH!"

Caliber's voice roared like thunder. His left arm melted into what seemed like liquid fire, something Wander had never seen before. He lashed it like a whip and collided with Rush's water. Their arm immediately became steam. Caliber's liquid fire fell on the stone, dark and bubbling.

"You cannot kill me like you did the past quake king! I am stronger than he ever was. We are matched."

Rush straightened their stance. Their voice hinted at no emotion, as though the brutal fight did not just happen. "This will be an awfully long Conflux then."

Fury and Ruin, who watched the whole thing happen, also seemed unimpressed.

Ruin raised his arm. "I vote for a break."

"Seconded," Fury said.

"Fine," Caliber and Rush spoke simultaneously.

Everyone spread out throughout the ruins beyond the dome. Rush remained in the dome center. Mist quickly walked to their side, and they spoke. Wander stood up and approached where Caliber's liquid fire mixed with Rush's water. Bending down, she examined the dark muck that was born from the fight. Heat rose from the hardened bubbles. The stone floor underneath had dipped.

"Are you alright?" Mist asked Rush.

"Splendid," Rush spoke in a short, aggressive tone. "I need some time alone."

Mist bowed. "Of course. My apologies."

The shadow motioned for Wander to follow. The two walked out a far right corridor to a hall filled with chatting elementals.

"I thought Caliber was done for."

Voices bounced around the arched walls.

"The quakes really need a better leader. Ruin is a pebble runt."

"Shh! Don't say that so loudly."

"Civil war? Not possible."

Wander looked at Mist as they walked. "I'm hungry." If not for the guardian's magic, she'd probably feel as though she were starving.

"There's no food allowed here, I'm afraid," Mist said. "I'll make you a fish feast when this is over."

"Is Rush okay?"

"Yes. They just need to cool down."

"Did they really kill the last quake king?"

"I wasn't there at the time, but yes. I heard he wouldn't agree to a certain distribution of land so Rush killed him in order to enforce a consensus."

Wander looked out at the elemental crowd. Many seemed to stick to their categories, storm, quake, fire, and sea.

"I know it looks bad to humans when a ruler tries to kill another," said Mist. "But this is normal in our system. It's what we believe is right. Without the killing, we would be stuck with no progress. It takes years for mainlanders to create change. They kill many and nothing changes. For us, it's just one Conflux and one life."

"How often do Confluxes happen?"

"Whenever at least two from the family believe it's necessary."

A fire elemental suddenly joined them, a large orange and hairy man who felt like a bonfire when near. "King Caliber demands Wander see him."

"I'll come along," Mist said.

"He will kill you. Wander only."

Wander trembled, but no one could notice under all her layers unless they hugged her.

"If he kills her—"

"You're the one that brought her here."

Wander gave Mist a terrified look. The shadow looked lost. Her expression showed that her mind darted around for ideas.

"Walk or I'll have to burn you," the fire elemental grunted.

Wander drew in her breath. "Okay."

She followed him through the maze of corridors. The crowds of elementals never thinned. Perhaps many waited out in the corridors instead of watching in the dome. Wander would have preferred that. Of course, like all places, there were the stares. Their eyes were colors of ice, fire, and mud.

The guard led Wander up some stairs that ended with an empty doorway. She counted twenty-one steps to try to calm herself. The fire king had to be beyond the threshold. She could feel him. Her eyes teared up and stung. Her body felt faint. If she got near enough, would she catch fire? Not again. Never again.

The guard stopped. "In!" he ordered.

Wander stepped inside. Behind her, the guard remained to safeguard the only exit. Caliber stood in an unfurnished room. Unlike the manor dome and corridors, the ceiling was like a normal house. The fire king looked out a rectangular window at the blizzard outside. Wander could see nothing beyond swirling flakes of snow. The wind howled endlessly. Without looking away from the window, Caliber spoke calm and soft, "Unclothe yourself."

"What?"

"If you really survived the flames of my daughter, my beacon of light, then you need to prove it. You will not freeze, not while I stand in this room with you."

Wander feared any protest would be met with Caliber's roaring fire. She took the cloth that shielded her nose and mouth and pulled down. With the other hand, she unwrapped her neck. She pulled down her hood.

"All the way," Caliber said. "Just your face won't do."

She unbuckled her cloak, pulled off her shirt, and nearly tripped over to pull off her shoes. She did not wish to untie their laces because she did not remember how to retie them. She pulled off her pants quickly, just wanting the whole examination over with. The king circled her, his one golden eye wide.

She shut her eyes, trying not to lose consciousness when he neared for a better look at her back. She could not control her body as it trembled. She could remember the feeling of being so hot, that it was as though she were freezing. The first time she felt her cocoon cage skin was when she woke from Chant's fire. The desire to just tear it all off to a bloody core ravaged her when she wasn't covered up.

"Are you scared?" Caliber asked. Wander could sense a smile made through those words. "You should be. I can turn into smoke and dive my way down your throat into your lungs. I could melt your eyes out of your sockets. How about my daughter, did she terrify you?"

Wander shut her eyes. She could not tell if she cried from the stinging or out of the memory of burning. She nodded.

"To survive and to live are two different things for us elementals. Rush may be right in your survival, but your life is extinguished. You're just walking burned meat. In that sense, you are probably my daughter's greatest work. She has marked you, and you are a sign for everyone else to fear her, to fear all elementals. "

Wander gulped and spoke. "Do you know how this happened?"

The fire king stopped circling her. He stood in front of her gaze, "Tell me."

"I lived in an enchanted forest, the Emerald Wilds. Chant burned the whole thing down. She burned my home, my body, all the animals, the trees, even the river had dried. I just . . ." Wander hesitated before saying, "How is that destruction something to be proud of?"

She half expected the king to explode in laughter or shout, but he remained calm.

"What is destruction?"

"When something is destroyed, it's broken, gone."

"Things are never gone. Something had to replace it."

"The Emerald Wilds became a wasteland. My body turned into this. Everything changed."

"*Became* and *turned* are the key. We elementals don't know of destruction. We don't know that mainlander word. There is only creation, never destruction. Destruction is a word made by those immature and selfish enough to think their opinions matter in this world.

"My daughter created what you are. She created what the Emerald Wilds is. Your word, *destroy*, is simply just a form of creation you don't approve of. But change and creation is nature, and the elementals are its heralds."

Wander looked down, unable to meet his gaze any longer.

"Dress up and leave," Caliber said. "Your journey here is a waste. You do not know us, our history, and our ways. I'd kill you now if my daughter hadn't already marked you."

Wander just wanted to get out of the room. She got dressed, and the fire guard stepped aside for her to leave. Mist had waited nearby for her, the shadow's figure leaning against the corridor wall. Noticing Wander's return, she immediately straightened, approached, and gently set her pale hand on the side of Wander's covered cheek. "Are you alright?"

"He was too smart for me," Wander said. "He's too powerful and smart."

"What do you mean by smart? What happened?"

"He also told me destruction doesn't exist, that it's just things changing. He said everything in a way I never thought of before."

"That's just a culture difference. It has nothing to do with intelligence."

Wander wasn't so sure what a culture was. So much now seemed above her reach.

"What now?" Mist asked.

"You're asking me?"

"This is our chance to change minds."

"Caliber won't change."

"He has to. One way or another." Mist walked back toward the inner halls. Wander followed, the air cooling the more distance they put between themselves and Caliber's room.

"We should talk to Ruin," Mist said. "His neck was injured, likely due to a disagreement. If that's the case, maybe we can get him on our side."

They passed through the halls most crowded with elementals. Bodies crowded together. Wander felt chills and heat waves with each being she passed. As the crowds thickened, Mist took Wander's hand so they didn't separate. They came to a hall parallel to the empty one that led to Caliber's room.

"Fusillade Manor has four corner towers," explained Mist. "Typically that's where the leaders go. The whole property, however, is cared for by Fury and the storms."

They went up a couple sets of stairs to the tower entrance. "Lord Ruin?" Mist knocked on the brown door inlaid with iron.

A young girl opened the door. Her large brown eyes looked up at the human and shadow through messy brown hair. Black tattoos marked her brown skinned cheekbones, dainty and curving like branches.

"Ruin doesn't want to talk to any sea elementals," she said. "He wants time to rest."

Before she could shut the door, Wander's gloved hand grabbed the knob. "I'm not a sea elemental. I'm human."

The girl glowered.

"Let them in," Ruin's voice came from within the chambers.

Her face still in a frown, the girl let them inside. Like Caliber's, the room was dull and empty like most of the manor. The back wall even had the same rectangular window with a view of the vicious snowstorm. Ruin leaned against the right-most wall with his arms crossed. His veins showed in his hands and arms. A taller quake stood with him dressed in a white robe. She examined the hole in his neck.

"This will take a visit to the Mud Cracks," she told him. "For now, you should wear something like a scarf. Don't let anything inside you. If you do, you could get very ill."

"Fetch me a scarf then," Ruin covered the wound with his hand. "I'll deal with these visitors."

Wander pulled one of the smaller black pelts that Abalone had pinned around her neck. Holding the fur herself, it seemed to once been on a weasel, the short legs still attached. She held out the fur. "You can use this to cover your neck."

Ruin tilted his head. "You're Wander?" He took the fur and wrapped it around his neck. "If you think kindness will get me to change my mind on the alliance between the deviants, you're wrong."

The woman who examined him gave a short bow and left the room. She passed Wander and smelled like rain puddles.

"Was Caliber the one who put a hole in your neck?" Mist asked. "It looks like he melted that piece of you right off."

Ruin let out a soft chortle. "Would it surprise you that I started the fight?"

"Yes actually," said Mist. "That's not like you."

"I'm a king," he hissed. "Very few really know me. I attacked because, like Rush, I disagreed with Caliber. I think the deviants are dangerous, too dangerous to tag along with."

"Then why did you vote for the alliance to begin with? You seemed very willing back then."

"I changed my mind because I know more now."

Mist seemed skeptical, even disturbed. Ruin's reason seemed sound to Wander. Knowing things as they were now, she'd do many things differently.

Ruin sighed and stopped leaning against the wall. He walked past them and to a quake that came to the door. The elemental bowed and handed Ruin a piece of paper. Ruin unfolded the parchment and read. In only five seconds of reading what appeared to be a long letter, he crumpled it up in his hands. He turned back to Wander and Mist. "Everyone wants something, but I'm sure you both know that the strongest always wins. Why come to me? The power is all with Rush and Caliber. Either of them could kill me if they wanted."

"Rush will protect you if you side with them," said Mist. "They—"

Ruin interrupted. "I don't trust them or any of you sea elementals. I was there when they killed King Sudden over a dispute of land. I could do nothing as your people flooded the Dust Flats." He dropped the crumpled paper to the floor. "No. I'm sticking with Caliber. He will protect me from Rush. He's the only one who can."

Mist glanced at Wander. She looked a little embarrassed. She was hoping Wander would say something. Wander wanted to leave. Talking, fighting—it was all the same struggle here. She could not leave though, not until this was over. Aura had to die, and the only way she could do it is to break this alliance. Wander's head ached. Her tongue felt fuzzy, and her heart throbbed. For a moment, she feared she was about to do something beyond her control.

As Wander fought the odd sensations, Ruin's face noticeably softened when he looked at her. Though he said nothing, his warm browns eyes seemed welcoming. Did he pity her? It did not matter. If Wander was about to lose control, she did not want Mist involved.

The two spirits still bickered as Wander emerged from her own thoughts. "Mist, I can speak alone with him."

Both fell silent. Mist looked notably upset. "Alright, but keep it civil," and quickly walked out. She actually seemed to desire to leave.

Once she left, Ruin nodded at Wander. "Thank you." He started a slow pace around the room, waiting for Wander's argument. Wander had an odd feeling in her gut. She remained silent, trying to determine what was going on. It was like her body was trying to tell her something. Her body was controlled by the guardian, so maybe he was trying to tell her something. He was exerting a feeling, not an action.

The feeling expanded when she looked at Ruin. When her gaze reached his eyes, she realized the feeling. It was a kind of pity. There was something they had in common, but what?

"You seem sad," Wander said.

"It's hard to be happy at a divided Conflux."

That wasn't the right answer, or maybe Wander was lost. She stepped over to the crumpled paper on the floor. She picked it up. Her fingers began to smooth the page. Ruin's slow pace snapped into a run as he snatched the parchment from her hands. "This is none of your business!" Some spit hit her face.

"You acted like it was trash."

"It is trash."

"Then why can't I see it?"

"It's private trash."

Words bubbled from her mouth that didn't feel like her own. "Who wrote it?"

Ruin stuffed the letter between his dress and armor. "If you want to know my business so badly, then what about you? To have survived Chant's fire, you must be full of secrets."

"See this?" Wander put out her left hand. Masu's dark feather dangled. "It belonged to a spirit that raised me. He raised me until our home burned down. He was taken and enslaved by Aura. You might know him as Aura's Wings. At the beginning he was the reason for many things." Her voice softened. "Now, I don't even remember his voice. I don't remember his face when he was angry, happy, or sad. Now I don't even know if he was free when he was with me. I don't know if he can be saved. I don't even know if I can be saved."

"Then why did you come all the way here?" Ruin asked.

"I suppose in a strange way, Aura has enslaved me, too. When she dies, I can be free."

Ruin's shoulders relaxed. Wander's tragic tale may have won her some level of trust. Since leaving the Emerald Wilds, Wander discovered that people like vulnerability. It was not so different from the animals.

"Have you met Chant?" Ruin asked. "I know she burned you, but have you met her?"

"A couple times, yes."

Ruin touched the armor plate where he tucked the crumpled parchment in. "The letter is from her. She has been writing to me every week."

"What does she say?"

"Every letter is the same. She's homesick and lonely. She wishes to come home. That's why I was against it. Then, as usual, I'm the one who gets beaten at a Conflux."

"Why would Caliber not care about what she wants?"

"He doesn't know what she wants. Chant has only told me."

"Why?"

Ruin stared at the ground. His brown hair blocked his eyes. "She and I came into this world around the same time. You're wind-born right? Elementals are similar, but we all call the ruler of our kind our parent. We are raised by the community and see everyone as a sibling. But some of us are stronger and get noticed by the parent of the community, like my father or Caliber. Caliber took Chant under his care as my father did with me. Because of that, she and I met at every Conflux." A small smile began to stretch Ruin's face. "We hated politics, and we would be bored. We had each other though, so we'd play. We'd fight. We'd do all the things best friends did. Chant wanted to go the mainland in the beginning, so I supported the alliance with the deviants. But now she's paranoid. She constantly wonders if Aura is controlling her mind without her knowing. She wants to come home where her friends are and where she knows she is free."

"But why didn't she tell any of this to Caliber?"

"She wants him to be proud of her. She is one out of thousands of fire elementals. The reason Caliber has asserted her as a front-line daughter, someone who can even replace him, is because of her strength and pride. She loves that and doesn't want others to know she is weak."

"Does Caliber know you love her?"

"Now wait a moment," his voice picked up. "I said nothing about love. Caliber doesn't know anything about us, and it has to stay that way."

"He should know. Then he'll be against the alliance."

"No. That would go terribly for me and Chant. There's no way I'm doing that."

"I can."

"No." His voice hardened. The warmth he had before when talking about Chant dissipated, leaving him menacing. "You will not tell a soul."

Wander's eyes widened as a clever idea came to her. "Then vote against the alliance," she said. "Do that and I won't tell Caliber about the letter."

Ruin's jaw dropped. His entire body suddenly looked as though it got larger. "Are you blackmailing me?"

Wander shrugged, having no idea what that word meant.

"Well, you are in no position to do that! Caliber won't believe you."

"But does he believe you?" Wander asked.

Ruin squinted and got close up to Wander, his tall form looming over her. "I can kill you right here. I can kill you the moment you say my name or Chant's to him."

All Wander could do to match his intimidating loom was to widen her eyes. "You can't kill me," Wander said. "Just like Chant couldn't."

Either he was going to start a fight or he was going to vote against the alliance. Whichever he chose, Wander succeeded at what she needed to do. She could never win against Caliber, but Ruin seemed delicate enough to break. Bracing herself, she took a chance and turned her back to him. When she did not receive any sort of physical harm, she walked out and did not look back.

The corridors were empty. Wander expected that Mist would have waited right outside. Only the sounds of the howling wind outside made it to the halls. Adjusting the pelts around her body, Wander backtracked to where all the elementals bantered and waited. Far enough, she began to pass groups of elementals. Waves of heat and cool traveled across her body with each cluster she passed. She made sure not to make any eye contact.

"Wander! I've been looking all over for you!"

Mist popped out of the crowd, her silken hair dancing with her slightest movement. "Good news," she said with a smile. "Rush has convinced Fury to vote against the alliance. You won't have to talk to her. How did it go with Ruin?"

"I'm not sure."

Mist's smile quickly faded.

Wander continued, "Either he will vote against the alliance . . . or I'll have to fight him."

Mist looked around. Wander guessed she disliked the idea of anyone overhearing their conversation. A couple elementals may have heard. "That's not good," she said. "Maybe we can get Rush to visit him. Or maybe we can try—"

Wander flinched at the sound of a deep bell ring that echoed throughout the building. Everyone else quieted and began to move back toward the center dome.

"Dammit!" Mist hissed. "The Conflux is returning. If this doesn't work, we'll have to try again tomorrow if we can."

"Sorry," Wander said.

The tone of Mist's once frustrated voice completely changed. "No, no, no, Wander! It's not your fault. I know it's scary and difficult for a human here. You did your best." All elementals that stood in the hall began to move in the same direction like a stream. "C'mon," Mist took Wander's gloved hand. Even through the furs, Wander could sense her chilled skin. They followed the crowd back to the dome.

The crowds that sat at the edge of the dome had become more divided. The fires collected together, making the walls and pillars around them dance in shivering light. Quakes sat near them, their numbers far smaller with more space between them. The storms sat at the quakes' other side, whispering and being the chattiest. Sea elementals were like the quakes in number, maybe even smaller. Mist and Wander sat in the front.

Caliber, Rush, Ruin, and Fury were already waiting at the center. Fury and Rush seemed to casually speak with smiles on their faces while Ruin and Caliber stood still and silent as stone.

A hush took all the elemental as Fury spoke aloud, "Rush and I struck a deal, Caliber. I'm backing out of the alliance."

The torchlight in the room wavered. Everyone began to chatter. The sea elementals around Wander softly cheered with soft laughter and sighs of relief. Ruin and Caliber's surprise matched each other, their jaws dropped. However, Caliber's expression quickly changed to ferocity. "What, dare I ask, did they offer?"

"I offered her land and knowledge, Caliber," Rush said. "I offered to not flood the Storm Peak's base as well as access to the undersea library."

Before Wander even asked, Mist explained in a whisper, "Every family member has a library no one else can access, not even their own people. The oldest books in the world are there."

"You will find more land and knowledge on the mainland," Caliber said. "Do not listen to their threats or gifts. You know in your heart that my way is right for the people."

"Maybe for yours and Ruin's, but not mine," Fury spoke with eloquence. "If the mountains get crowded, the storms have the sky. We do not need to colonize, because we are far from miserable. A risk for anything more would only be a product of greed, not charity."

Rush had that tranquil stare in which it was impossible to discern what they could be thinking.

"A tie then," Caliber crossed his arms. "You're only making this harder on yourselves. We'll have a longer Conflux, or we're going to have to fight two on two."

Wander prepared herself to stand and speak up. If Ruin would not say anything, she'd have to cause chaos. Maybe Caliber would attack her and think she was lying like Ruin predicted. She had to try. Rush and Mist might try to protect her. She stared at Ruin, who was already staring at her. She sat up, about to rise to her feet.

"Actually," Ruin spoke. His eyes darted to Caliber. "I have to deny the alliance as well."

The room got hotter, and the torch fires wiggled. Ruin shut his eyes. Caliber burst into flames that shot at Ruin. He reformed inches from Ruin, and his flaming hand shot through the quake king's chest. The fingers and entire hand broke through like a finger to mud.

Rush and Fury acted immediately. The sea ruler ruptured into a wave of water, and the storm queen blasted into a blur of wind. They intertwined as they turned into ice around all of Caliber's body. The room got freezing.

Ruin pulled away from Caliber's impaling hand. Black blood splattered on the dusty dome floor. His breath came out in white puff clouds from the sudden freeze. His shaking hand covered his wounded chest. Some quakes in the audience stood up, conflicted about whether to get involved.

Caliber broke free of the already melting ice. He charged at Ruin. Wander stood up and darted between

Ruin and Caliber. Mist shouted after her, but Wander could barely hear her over the ringing that took over in her head.

Caliber stopped his fist mid-swing from punching Wander. "What are you doing!?" Caliber shouted. His close breath scorched like hot steam.

The melting ice broke into Rush and Fury's forms. Rush hurried to Wander's side, prepared to stop Caliber if he tried anything.

"I made Ruin change his mind because he listened to me," Wander said. "You didn't, so I couldn't tell you that your daughter wants the alliance to end as well."

"Don't you dare speak of her!" Caliber hissed. Fury squeezed herself between Wander and Caliber. He shouted, "My beacon is no coward!"

"Wander—" Ruin started.

"She thinks Aura could be mind-controlling her," Wander said.

"And how would you know what my daughter thinks?" Caliber asked.

"Aura captured me and took me to her palace," Wander explained. "I escaped her prison and tried to find a friend she imprisoned somewhere else in the palace. In my search, I broke into Chant's room. She has many un-sent letters of concern and homesickness."

She saw Mist mouth "What?" in the background over Caliber's shoulder.

"Why would the letters never get to me?"

"It could be because Aura won't allow it."

"I need evidence."

"Your daughter is the evidence," Wander said. "She should be here. She of all people should have a say in this."

The room temperature evened out and Caliber lowered his fist.

"I have a compromise," Rush stepped between Wander and Caliber. "Let's investigate Aura's influence over Chant. Then we will have another Conflux to decide about the alliance."

"Aura wants the alliance as soon as possible, or else she could lose the war."

"That's her problem," Fury said. "We need to take care of ourselves before anyone else."

Wander turned to Ruin. He stared at her in disbelief.

"You got me," Caliber said from behind. "I'll agree to an investigation."

"As do I," Fury said.

"Ruin?" Rush called.

His eyes peeled away from Wander. "As do I."

The rest of the Conflux and the journey back to Mist's home was all a blur for Wander. She was glad none of the family attempted to ask questions or promote discussion at the Conflux's conclusion. She was starving and needed to rest.

She could not determine what time of day it was until they were far from the Storm Peaks, away from the blizzards and clouds. Once they reached the flatlands, it was sunrise. Wander wished she could sleep on the boat, but the ride was not calm enough. Like they did on the way up, Mist and Rush's water forms guided her down the rivers and streams. The waterfalls were more frightening on the way down than up. Her heart would escape from her chest every time as she clung to the boat sides.

When they reached Lotus Lake, the boat parked in front of Mist's house. Rush and Mist emerged from the lake water. They helped Wander out of the boat and into the lake. As they spoke, Wander looked around. No one else seemed to be in the village. They could all be underwater or traveling.

"I knew you could help us, Wander," Rush's voice interrupted her thoughts. "Thank you."

"We didn't break the alliance, though," Wander said. She felt fish or some sort of creature nip at her pants under the water.

"An investigation could take a very long time," Rush said. "You just need to end the war in the time we gave you."

"Wander," Mist cut in, "what you said about Chant . . . was it true?"

"Do you doubt her after how far she's come to help?" Rush asked.

"Oh no. I beg your pardon," Mist said. "Of course not."

Rush smiled gave Wander a subtle wink. "Perhaps we will meet again, Wander. I must return to the sea now."

"Goodbye," Mist bowed, and Wander copied her. Rush sank into the water, their dark hair spread and sank deeper until their form disappeared.

Mist lead Wander into her home. Wander sat on one of the smooth stones under the opened ceiling bordered with strings of turquoise and green sea glass. She folded her arms on another stone that she guessed was like a table and planted her face down.

"You seemed exhausted," Mist said. "Are you hungry?"

Without picking up her head, Wander nodded.

"Like I promised, I'm making you a feast," she said. The sounds of splashing made Wander peek out of her arms. Mist dipped her hands in a section of the lake house fenced off with nets. She pulled out a live catfish from the lake.

Turning her face back down into darkness, Wander listened to the sounds of chopping, cutting, and the clanging sounds of pots. She remembered Ms. Flinsler's cooking. It sounded like this in the mornings, afternoons, and evenings. Three times a day. Roslyn was sometimes asked to help. She was so small that she had to stand on a stool to reach the countertops.

Whenever they worked with something sweet, the child hid bites of raw food for herself and Wander.

Shutting her eyes, Wander tried to think farther back. In Masu's nest, the sounds must have been different. He only had what the Emerald Wilds provided. He had a garden, she remembered that. He also used the garden as bait for animals and laid traps.

Wander wondered if she had memories or if she was making up a story. None of it felt clear. Perhaps eventually all memories turn into stories and no one knows what really happened.

True or not, she let her mind frolic in those stories until she fell asleep.

Chapter 23
The Winged Graves

"You get a sense for when a land is about to become enchanted. I've felt it at the Winged Graves. It's spooky, like ghosts are watching you. And I know many ghosts would live in that place." – Ivy's Compendium of Enchanted Lands

Mist and Wander were guided back to the mainland by an air balloon driven by two storm elementals. The ride felt far smoother with fewer drops and shakes. The boat attached to the balloon was more spacious as well.

Wander sat on the floor and stared at her knees where her pants were thinning. Mist stood up with one hand holding the rope to the balloon. She looked to the sea, dark locks flying wild in the wind. Sometimes her hair whipped against Wander's face.

"Do you think Ruin will be okay?" Wander asked.

"He comes off as weaker than the others, but he's still an elemental," said Mist. "He's one of the more human of the elementals, but he still endures like the rest."

Wander leaned her head back and looked at the sky. She realized that once you reached high enough, there were no birds.

They landed in an unfamiliar place. A mountain's cliff side littered with stones in dry grass where the colossal sea waves could not reach. Wander no longer wore the pelts given to her for the Conflux. As she stepped out of the boat, the mountain breeze made her shiver.

"Hello!"

The ghostly lullaby form of Many waited for them. He ran over to hug Mist. He wore a dark cloak, likely to block out the sun. As the two shadows spoke, Wander looked out toward the land. Huge trees, the biggest she had ever seen, were beyond the mountain. Their branches were warped and twisted by the constant sea wind. Their roots must have been deep to stay upright for so long.

"Wander," Mist dragged her attention back. "I'm going back home. Many is taking you back to Sollast. The humans and lullabies are preparing for the battle at the Winged Graves. You should join them and make sure they win. The elemental investigation will only give them so much time to stop Aura."

"Thank you."

"I know we'll see each other again," Mist said. The shadow waved before she ran off the mountain's cliff. In midair, her body turned into water and fell into the sea. The two quiet storm elementals took a balloon back into the sky with them. It was now just Wander and Many.

"So," Many started as they walked toward the twisted woods. "How were the Western Isles?"

"Different."

Many gave a short laugh. "Mist tried to convince me to live there a long time ago. The culture was too brutal for me."

They walked toward the forest.

"Where are we?" Wander asked.

"The edge of the Winged Graves, north of deviant territory, west of human lands. This is what the humans and deviants started their war over. I'll admit, it's not so lovely by the sea, but the land gets far more lush and green farther in. Don't worry though. It's safe. The humans have already secured a space that is safe for us to cross. I'm going to take us to Sollast. Rush sent a letter to Naktol to explain your absence and victory at the Conflux, so you should be greeted warmly."

Many turned into a pale donkey and sat on his front knees for Wander to get on. Once on, she clutched his short and stubby mane as he took off to the forest. Wander made sure to look around at the land that belonged to the winged beings. If the war between deviants and winged beings never happened, this land could have belonged to Masu. It would have been a strange reality. The trees were thick enough to build rooms in. Some of their roots had surfaced and softened with moss, ferns, and little wildflowers. Their bark was dark and smooth, as though they had been skinned in rainfall. Leaves and flowers grew in the branches above. Orchids nestled and leaves had the shape of teardrops.

Wander spent most of the trip looking up. The branches were wide enough to be like twisted sky-paths. At times, she even saw nests. Not birds' nests, but winged beings' nests, tree houses reclaimed by nature in waves of green and speckled in flowers. Some were half destroyed, the guts of the home visible to show furnishings. Animals thrived in the treetops. Huge snakes, large enough to eat Wander, curled up and watched her pass by. She feared they'd act like the ones in the Emerald Wilds and drop on top of her. Perhaps they decided she was moving too fast. She saw monkeys with bright butts and others with tails longer than their bodies. Parrots as iridescent as flowers flew away or remained and watched from the tree sides. Some of them had feathers lengthier than Wander's arm and others let out bizarre screams.

Eventually they left the forests into the familiar sight of human farmlands. Not all was familiar. Fences remained intact, but the farmhouses and barns had crumbled. If Wander had to guess, these places were the first to be attacked by Aura since they were so close to the Winged Graves. They passed soldiers. The men and women broke their strict concentration to stare at the cloaked girl riding a white donkey. They must be heading for battle toward the Winged Graves. They wore armor and quivers full of arrows with long bows.

After a long stretch of seeing no one, they passed one group Wander had to stare at twice. It was a wagon full of people in rags . . . in a cage. They curled up and some cuddled one another. The man who drove the wagon horses had a collection of whips by his seat. Wander wanted to look at the situation further. The desire nearly made her fall off Many's back. She wished he would've stopped. But he kept moving forward, Wander looking behind her at the caged people who gazed back.

When they neared Sollast and no one was around, Many hinted for Wander to get off by bending to the ground. She hopped off, and he turned back into his lullaby body.

"We're close. Let's go."

They walked a couple miles to the outer walls of Sollast. The farmlands had crowded with both human and lullaby soldiers. The humans rode their horses, and the lullabies rode their donkeys. The humans wore a mix of brown leathers and silver armor. The lullabies wore dark cloaks and hoods like Many to shield their eyes from the sun. As they neared the city gates, they reached the familiar face of Naktol. The queen stood out not only in height but in a mighty elegance. She wore a white dress combined and woven in with silver chainmail and armor. The silver armor brought out her gray eyes.

Naktol approached, casting a shadow to Wander. Many backed away into the crowd.

"I thought you had turned on us again," Naktol said. "But I received a letter yesterday of where you were. The ruler of the sea elementals, Rush, wrote to me. They had never done that before. To my surprise, they thanked you, saying that you had put the alliance between the deviants and elementals at pause. Is that true?"

Wander nodded.

"Why did you not tell us where you were going?" Naktol asked.

"I was short on time. If I told you, I don't think you would have trusted me. Or you'd send others with me, and that would not have helped."

The queen sighed. "We have not trusted each other. That is true. So why are you here now?"

"I want to fight. I was hoping to get my sword back."

Naktol took a long, cold stare at Wander. "You will have it."

Wander followed Naktol into a tent full of quivers and arrows stacked on boxes. The queen stepped aside so Wander could see her sword at the far end. The two-handed blade lay in its sheath and harness on a table.

"I brought it to see if anyone else could hold it," Naktol said. "But I suppose it chose you."

Wander took the sword and belted it to her back.

"It's your last chance, Wander," Naktol said. "Before the battle, it's your last chance to tell me your real story."

Wander took a long look at her. "If we win, I'll tell you my story."

When she emerged from the tent, she could not find a single friend in the crowd. Many had gone. She was to travel with the main army back to the Winged Graves. There was nothing more to do but wait for the end. She sat where the dirt paths dipped into farmland. She tangled her fingers in the grass and listened to the wind. The army scared off the company of any wildlife. The air smelled of sweat and flame. A deer could likely hear the clanging of feet in armor from across the fields and hills at the edge of the woods.

"Hey." Vincent's voice came from behind. He stood in leathers and armor. A roped-up ball and chain was equipped at his hip. Wander could remember how he could use the ball and chain to pull Masu out of the sky. Dark stubble covered Vincent's chin, cheeks, and upper neck. His dark figure cast a shadow over where Wander sat. Giving up on Wander's response, Vincent sat on his knees. "How are you?"

"I don't know."

"You made everyone think you were going to betray us again."

"Did you think so?"

"Of course."

She smiled under her veil.

"You got your sword back," Vincent said. "I imagine Naktol will talk to you about this, but you're probably the only one who has a chance of killing Aura. She can't take your mind, so we want to put faith in you."

"It's always been my plan to kill her."

Eventually the last of the army moved. Horses and donkeys traveled together. When called upon, Vincent separated himself from Wander. With no animal allowing her to get close, Wander walked. Her dark cloak stood out in the sea of armor and hooves.

The whole time she felt herself being watched, even when she took a break to pee in the woods. The dark spaces between trees did not reveal any people. No branches snapped and no bushes shivered. Returning to the army, she joined the lullabies. The humans and spirits travelled together but separately, with the lullabies in the back. The spirits stared less. They also spoke among themselves less. The humans joked, whispered, and shouted over the sound of horse hooves on the road. Among the lullabies, there was only the sound of their travel and the woodland birds.

Wander walked slower at the road's edge, letting the lullabies pass. Unlike the humans, the spirits were equipped with both melee and ranged weapons. Wander figured humans would fight ranged since they could not touch spirits while the spirits fought melee. However, the spirits had both while the humans only had bows and crossbows. With Aura's power, the coming battle will to fold the army against itself. Wander realized the lullabies probably had the ranged weapons to kill humans.

"Wander," a gentle voice came from the army. Fade strode up on a white donkey. He stood out a little from everyone else; his animal's back was draped in a white blanket with golden flower designs. His hands clutched white reigns etched with complex markings. The donkey struggled as he tried to get close to Wander, shaking its head. "Good job with the elementals. That probably took a lot of courage."

She thanked him, and they walked side by side for a while.

"You know, Aura has a shield made of guardian bones," Fade mentioned. "If you swing that sword with too much force, it'll shatter on that shield. Enchanted, blessed, cursed—none of those can beat guardian bone. I just hope you know how to fight. You may be a magical human, but you can't out-magic a spirit. She has probably drunk a lot of guardian blood before this battle. My people have seen sightings Aura's Arms around our enchanted forests. She has been hunting. She may even be hoping to drink enough to control you."

Could that be possible? Could Aura out-maneuver the guardian and take Wander's mind?

Wander wanted to change the subject. "Where is your wife?"

"Sophia is not here. She is back in Sollast. She got to visit her mother there and now she is governing it with her sisters while we are gone.

"To be honest, I feel bad about what I've done to her. She speaks little and has issues staying up in the night and sleeping in the day. She and little Bell are inseparable, but I wonder if I should let her go."

The army entered the Winged Graves. As they did, Fade bowed his head down. All the spirits fell into a even quieter, haunting silence.

The back of the army came to a huge encampment under the trees. It was like a city poured into a forest. Tents, clanging, laughter, moss, birds, bark—the two worlds were together. Everyone had something to do. Before Wander realized it, Fade had left. Everyone went in a direction with a purpose, maybe to grab food, talk to a friend, or sharpen an arrow. Horses and donkeys were tied to any low hanging branches or stuck out root. Torches were speared into the earth to prepare for sunset.

Wander followed the borders of the camp. She watched the roots as she treaded along. She was not the only one who sought privacy. She listened in on a couple who hid behind one of the thicker trees.

"No matter what, I'm not letting them kill you."

"Lisa, you shouldn't have come if you're not prepared. Everyone here knows we may need to kill each other."

"This battle is a suicide then! We and Shiya should just go. We can find another way."

Wander made sure to walk around the couple without them noticing. She found others alone. They sat scattered, silent or crying with heads between their knees. Fear was beating in them. Wander found her own space on an unburied root. She sat down and set her elbows on her knees. She blanked out for a while until the Winged Graves darkened. The silhouette of a bat darted clumsily in the air for bugs. Lightning bugs shined blue light every so often in the dark.

She began to hear whispers, as though the forest were enchanted. The trees began to feel larger than they were before, or maybe she just felt smaller.

A black fox walked out of the darkness. He approached Wander. There was no mistake, the guardian of the Emerald Wilds had returned. He had thinned since she last saw him. Now he looked the size of a street cat. Wander had so many questions that she knew would not get answered. Why did he leave? Where had he been? Why come back now?

Perhaps he brought her to this very place to wait for him. Maybe this whole time he got what he wanted. He pushed her through her journey, taking her will and mind even when she did not know. He could be here to watch Aura die. After all, that was his goal all along.

Wander was called to a large tent with many others. Naktol, Fade, Dim, a gang of lullabies, and a gang of humans stood shoulder to shoulder around a huge stump. The guardian stayed near Wander's feet. Everyone was so focused, they did not notice him. Parchment had been spread across the stump with details Wander could not read that pointed at various circles. She could recognize various images like trees, stones, and a river.

She recognized one of the humans. His red hair had shortened to his scalp, but she still recognized Felix. He had dark circles under his eyes, or maybe it was a trick of the torchlight. His eyes darted away from Wander's the moment they met. After the Harlequin Wilds, Felix was one of the only people who made Wander feel like a hero. He was someone she did not hurt, someone who she actually saved without any strings attached. He even treated her well. Now Felix would not even look at her. She figured he and the whole army abandoned any like of her after her arrest at Loreman, maybe more so after she played a part in trading Naktol's daughter for a spirit alliance.

"My friends," Naktol began. "You are here because you are instrumental for the hope and finality of the coming battle. Each of you will be briefed for your task. I ask all to listen, because working together and knowing what everyone is doing is crucial. Then we will get to questions."

She turned to Wander first. "Wander, your job is simple," Naktol said. "I gave you your sword so you won't hold anything back. You must find Aura and do your best to kill her and kill anyone in your way, even if it is my people or the lullabies. I'm sure Aura will control minds to try to stop you.

"We have no idea where the deviant queen will be. We don't know if she'll hide or trick us by even tucking herself in our ranks. Whatever happens, it's your job to find her."

Naktol turned to the human gang. They did not wear armor, only dark cloth with many pockets. Three, including Felix, held crossbows and two were equipped with longbows.

"Felix, Delora, Shanise, Meg, and Ralph, you are my scout team," said Naktol. "You not only have the skills necessary, but you volunteered to take down Aura. For that, you will be known as heroes no matter what happens. Your instructions are to follow Wander from the treetops. Her activity and abilities will distract Aura from any chance of noticing what's above in the trees. Once Wander reaches Aura, you must back her up and shoot arrows at the queen. Make sure the first arrows hit, because the first shot will make Aura know your presence."

This time Dim spoke.

"Drift, Suffix, Ladder, Pour, and Negate, your jobs are exactly the same, but you're the back-up's back-up. If the arrows do not hit or the plan somehow fails, you must step in. That means either killing

Naktol's mind-taken scouts, killing Aura yourselves, or both."

The humans and lullabies took long stares at each other.

"My brother and I are remaining in the camp to order people around," Dim said.
Naktol scowled. "As will I."

"I have a question."

"Yes, Meg?"

"If Aura can't sense people who are hiding, then how did she control the minds of entire towns? People had to be hidden indoors. Her Arms are often distant from her. This doesn't make sense."

Fade answered. "Aura can sense other people through the senses of people she already controls. That's why no one outside this tent will know where you are. Few to none even know there will be a scout team hidden. The Arms are a whole different story. They have been around Aura so long that they are extensions of her. She knows their minds well enough to control them from across the world. Now that doesn't mean anyone the Arms see can be mind-controlled. Based on her actions, I think there is a limit to the second-hand mind-control. She likely needs to be somewhat near the premises."

Naktol quit looming over the map. She straightened up and made sure to make eye contact with every human as she spoke. "I wish I could fight with you. I know we are going to have half our number when this ends, if we're lucky. Also I know I have not been grateful enough." She turned to the lullabies and bowed her head, "Thank you for all you are doing."

Wander half expected Naktol to turn to her and do the same. After all, she had not treated Wander well. She had made her a prisoner when she truly did wish to help. But Naktol did not turn to her. Despite having her sword and a role to play, Wander was not trusted. Were the scouts also there to watch her to make sure she does not betray humankind?

"Good luck," Naktol said. "And if there is a God, I hope it watches over us all."

The army set out. From the sky, Wander imagined they looked like a mass of ants that gathered around a fallen fruit. She did not know what was customary in a battle, but a lot of people moved in the same direction. They had no form and spread out a little. Perhaps they knew too much strategy was pointless.

"If they don't know the real plan...they must feel hopeless," said one lullaby. Wander believed he was Ladder because he was super tall.

"They do have hope," another lullaby answered. "They know about Wander."

Wander and the scouts stayed behind in the shadow of a tree. As the scouts spoke among themselves, Wander watched a horned beetle make its way from a root to the base of the tree. The guardian remained at her side. The fox sat, waiting. Wander was concerned about his safety. Without him, her mind could be controlled. He couldn't fight and if he died it was all over.

A lantern was lit from Naktol's tent. The small flame looked like a star that had fallen into the forest.

"That's the signal," Felix said.

The scouts ran up one of the low, twisted branches. Wander waited until the lullabies and humans were high enough. They spooked an owl that flew away with ruffled feathers. Once she could no longer see their arms, she gave the fox a look. Was he really going to follow her into battle? With a deep breath, she began in a walk that slowly turned into a run, the trees passing faster and faster. The guardian leapt over the roots. The night was so dark but Wander knew the direction of the battle. She decided to begin there, but to try and not get caught inside the chaos.

She began to hear shouts, cries, and screaming. The main battle was near. In the distance she began to see silhouettes fighting one another. The sight nearly looked supernatural, like the silhouettes could belong to ghosts. The forest could be presenting an ancient memory with shadow puppets.

People out there were killing each other.

Wander's adrenaline mirrored the situation she was in. She began to shake. She did not know if it was her own fear or the guardian's control, but her gut told her to avoid the battle. She turned left and ran. The cool night air began to ache in her chest as she breathed. Her teeth clenched and her feet felt heavy when they hit the ground. Something caught her leg and she fell, hitting her face into the rough soil. Looking behind, a root stuck out and caught her ankle. The scouts above must doubt her. She certainly would, especially after this clumsy mistake.

A shade of something darker than the night air stood out on the ground by Wander's face. Grabbing whatever it was, she stood up and held it to filtered moonlight. It was a big black feather, too big for a crow or raven. Her breath began to shake and she looked around. Dropping the feather, she sprinted in the opposite direction from the battle.

Wander's heart jumped when she saw two silhouettes. One was unmistakable. They stood under a colossal tree that looked like a gate. A giant hole somehow formed at its base and the earth filled in. Or maybe two huge trees had leaned toward each other and became one.

Aura and Masu stood in the center. Wander had to stop and take in the image of the two standing together. Aura wore a gray dress covered in armor. Her shoulders, chest, and down her arms were all plated in steel. Her thick dark hair was wrapped up in a braided crown. She held a round white shield with a buck inscribed on its surface. The deviant queen's purple eyes gazed coldly back at Wander. Moonlight showed deep red lips.

Masu's hair had lengthened to the point where Wander could barely see his eyes. At the back of his head, his fluffy hair was nearly shoulder length. He stood expressionless with a two-handed sword. Aura had managed to dress him in full bodied armor.

Without a word, Wander drew out her enchanted blade. Her breath settled a little as she charged forward. Aura turned her back to Wander and walked toward the deeper darkness, the back of her gray dress billowing in the breeze.

Masu charged forward and his sword met with Wander's. His strength pushed her feet back. The blades let out a sound far louder than Wander expected. It did not sound like steel-on-steel, but more like an odd bell. For the moment they were locked, Wander got to see his red eyes. She did not remember how bright and bloody they looked. No other spirit had the same gaze. Masu's eyes nearly glowed in the night, like a monster's.

Wander maneuvered her blade up and knocked Masu's back. She quickly looked behind her. The guardian sat there, waiting. Why wasn't he afraid like the many times before?

Looking back at Masu, she saw he just stood there with the sword held up. Aura was not going to make him kill her. Aura simply has him here as a guard. If Wander tried to go any farther, he'd attack. If she did not, he'd leave her alone. But she no longer had a choice. Wander's head ached as she pointed her sword to the earth and stabbed.

Vines had barely emerged from the ground around Masu before he flapped his wings and flew just enough to dodge the plants. Pulling out her sword, Wander tried to run past while he dodged. Masu slashed the air, and Wander fell to the ground. She smelled her own blood before sensing anything else. She brushed her hand on her upper arm and looked to see blood. Her side had somehow been slashed. Masu slashed the air again.

Wander picked up her sword and blocked an invisible force.

His sword was enchanted.

Wander stood up and charged at him. She jumped and swung her blade down. Masu easily blocked the hit. With magic surging through her body, Wander managed to twist in the air, rapidly hitting a second time on his right arm. The armor cracked and black blood oozed out.

Neither took a single breath before they hit again. Masu moved for a stab, and Wander side-stepped. She threw her arm out and sent out an explosion of air. Masu did not even waver from the force. He cut through it, and Wander had to block his sword's magic. Masu kept cutting. He slashed and slashed. Wander could not keep track of every angle he slashed. She could not block every single one, so she just focused on her head and chest. Her legs got clobbered in cuts until they were trembling. The lower half of her cloak had torn up. Despite the loss of blood, she remained standing. The guardian was not going to let her go lose consciousness.

Masu had become no different than that boulder Under turned into. Masu, Under, and herself, they all had little to nothing of themselves left inside them.

Wander let out a scream and stabbed her sword downward. As vines rose out of the ground, Masu flew up to dodge. She blasted an explosion of air from her palm. The blast caught Masu's wings and sent him falling back. He fell on the ground, his sword still in hand.

Her heart racing, Wander pulled her sword out and sprinted to Masu. Reaching him, she stabbed down on his stomach. The sword punctured through the armor and into flesh. He let out a gasp of agony. She nearly heard his voice as he trembled under her violence.

Wander froze up and just stared down at Masu with tears in her eyes. His gasp brought up the most faded of feelings in her. She wanted to stop, to comfort him, to save him. She wanted to stop even if it meant him killing her.

He swung his sword up and slashed from her hip up to her shoulder. She pulled her sword out of his stomach and limped a couple steps back. Her right arm hugged her bloody left side. Masu used his sword to help himself up.

A chain flew out from the darkness, wrapping itself around Masu's sword and pulling it away.

The chain led to Vincent who emerged from the dark. With another chain, Vincent lassoed Masu's left arm. "GO!" he shouted. "FIND AURA!"

"His sword is enchanted!" Wander shouted back. "You can't beat him!"

Vincent pulled with all his might on the chain connected to Masu as Masu began to flap his wings.

"Who said I'm here to beat him?" Vincent said. "GO!"

Sheathing her sword, Wander limped through the gate-shaped tree as quick as she could. The fox followed behind.

Wander had distanced herself so much from Masu and the battle, she wondered if she got lost. The scouts above her were silent. She could not even hear their footsteps in the silence of the woods.

How large were the Winged Graves? How far in its depths could Aura have hid? If Dim was right, she could not have gone too far or else she could not mind-control any of the army.

The guardian sniffed the earth as he followed Wander. Her gut had brought her to Aura and Masu before, so she trusted her gut now. She kept moving further south. When she found Aura, would she even stand a chance? She still bled. If Masu killed Vincent, he could likely just follow her blood trail straight to her.

She no longer felt any pain though. She felt little to nothing overall.

They came to a beautiful open space under moonlight. Little white wildflowers grew among matted down grass. Deer must sleep here in the day. Wander looked up at the night sky at the nearly full moon. Then she looked around. The fox had disappeared.

A force hit her knees so hard that Wander felt her bones break. Even the guardian could not numb the pain and shock as she fell, chest down on the matted grass. Her broken body trembled as she lifted her head to see Aura emerge from the forest. She picked up the shield she threw at Wander's knees.

"You had no chance," she said from above. "I'm surprised you somehow got past my Wings, but you have still lost."

Picking up her head more, Wander scanned the area for the fox.

"Are you looking for your scouts?"

Wander looked up at Aura, who remained serious and cold.

"They have all killed each other by now."

Aura waited for the words to sink in. Even in this wretched moment, Wander caught a whiff of a sweet smell from a flower.

"Did you really think you had the upper hand on me with your alliance making and breaking?" Aura asked. "Deviants are most dangerous on their own. For the past couple of days, I have hunted and drank the blood of many guardians. My powers have evolved. I had spies in your ranks and knew about the scouts the moment that plan hatched."

Wander tried to flip her body around so she faced the sky. As her arms pushed her chest off the ground, she began to shake. Blood dripped from her body to the grass.

"You are alone," Aura said softly. "Just like you always were."

Wander's arms could not hold her weight, and she fell to the ground.

"I never mind-controlled Chant," Aura said. "I respect rules, just like I respect the rule that I cannot kill anyone with my own hands. That is why you're going to wait here until my Wings catch up to you. You aren't going anywhere."

Wander began to feel heavy.

"Your master, the fox, where is he?"

"I don't know."

Aura focused on the glen's edge, looking for any sign of movement. She looked back at Wander. "He left you."

Wander shut her eyes and focused on steadying her breath. If she curled a little, maybe she could slow the bleeding.

Without another word, Aura turned and strode back into the woods. Her footsteps sounded light against the knotty grass.

Wander let herself drift away into unconsciousness.

The candle in Naktol's tent blew out. "Damn," the queen turned to the stump. "You'd think trees would block out most of the wind."

"This place is haunted," Fade said. "That is without a doubt." The darkness made his markings glow. The sight was like if stars were lines

"Shouldn't the ghosts be biased and haunt Aura instead?" Naktol smiled when she got the lullaby king to laugh. He laughed like a kid.

"You have a point," he said.

The lullaby king drank blood from a one of Naktol's wine glasses. She tried to pretend he was just sipping on red wine. Naktol got up and her long fingers searched for matches on one of the tables. She felt a quill, extra candles, and finally the box of matches.

Fade's tone softened. "My brother has been gone too long."

Dim had left a while ago to answer an emergency. One of his people came running in, calling for assistance, too panicked to explain. Naktol and Fade offered to go as well, but Dim said he'd be fine alone.

Naktol swept a match against the box's rough side. She set the newborn flame on the candlewick. Fade's markings disappeared in the light.

"Fade!" Dim called from outside. Naktol thought it could be someone else because Dim had always sounded calm since they first met. This voice was panicked. But when they ran out of the tent, it was definitely Dim. He used a tree to help him stand. His right hand covered a bloody wound on his left shoulder. Fade ran to his brother's side, catching Dim as he tried to walk further.

Naktol went back in her tent and grabbed her weapons belt. She emerged, buckling the front of the strap. "What happened?"

Fade looked down at his brother. "He fell unconscious."

"A wound like that? It doesn't look like he lost a lot of blood," Naktol said.

Fade explored Dim for any more wounds. Nothing.

"I need you to take your brother and clear the encampment of anyone who stayed behind," Naktol ordered. She unstrapped a mask from her belt. One of her scientists had created it after getting his hands on one of Aura's poisonous gases. She strapped the black leather mask over her nose and mouth. Her breathing was a little more labored.

Fade carried Dim away and past Naktol's tent. Naktol strapped on an extra layer of armor on each of her forearms before she walked in the direction Dim came from. As she suspected, the forest terrain had become misty. She recognized the mist from her people's descriptions of the attack on Sollast. She pulled out a bow and held it out in front of her eyes. Standing her ground, she was ready to aim and fire.

A dagger shot out from the darkness. Naktol threw her forearm in front of her face as the sharp weapon hit her armor. It was thrown with enough force to stick into the metal. Lucky enough, it did not reach her skin. It was likely poisoned. She pulled the blade out by the handle and threw it to the ground. Aiming where the weapon came from, she shot an arrow. She did not get the satisfying sound of an impact.

Aura's Horns emerged from the darkness. Her white hair was the first thing to see, as it nearly glowed in the dark. Her gloved hand held Naktol's arrow. A small ivory shield was strapped to her left forearm. She dressed in a white dress, armored around the chest, hips, and shoulders. Her horns were painted jet black.

Naktol shot again three times. Aura's Horns caught all three in her shield. Naktol had trained her entire life for close combat. If she knew she would be a leader in the War of Arrows, she would have chosen her expertise differently. No. There was no way she was going to fight this from a distance, like children throwing snowballs. She could not stand it and could not win.

Dropping her crossbow and drawing a sword, the queen charged forward. She took the blessed blade in both hands, preparing to push the sword through the Horn's heart.

The Horn responded with a charge of her own.

The spirit and human impacted each other in a storm of electrical shocks. The Horns punched Naktol's sword back with her shield. That was the one sensation before Naktol's and the Horn's bodies flew back from the invisible force that kept humans and spirits apart. It was the first time Naktol felt that force. It made her heart race and her teeth chatter. Gripping her sword correctly became difficult after the sudden shocks.

The Horns threw five darts that Naktol caught on her forearms. Naktol threw her sword. It spun and the tip struck a couple inches just below the horn's neck and above her armor. Of course it hit, it was a blessed sword after all.

The queen rushed toward the spirit. Trying to ignore the shocks, her trembling hand managed to grip her sword's handle. She ripped it out of the Horn's body. She made sure to gore the wound as much as possible, hoping shocks could even go inside the spirit's body.

It felt so good to fight, so good to see an enemy and just fight back. No mind control, no tricks, no arrows.

A stinging sensation shot through Naktol's neck.

Letting go of her blade and reeling back, she grabbed a dart that landed by her throat.

Wounded, the Horn shakily walked forward.

Naktol's vision blurred. She lost feeling in her arms and legs as she fell to the forest floor.

The Horn walked past her and toward the encampment.

The fox emerged from the bushes and approached Wander. She stank of blood. Little life was left in her abused body and soul, just like that time he used her to shield his body from Chant's storm of fire.

Unlike that time, now the guardian also had little life in him. Without his forest, he was destined to wither away eventually. No magic could stop that. But he hoarded and stored enough power to see the end of this. He had to be selfish in times of pain and struggle to keep it. No matter what, Aura was going to die, even if it meant giving his soul to another.

The guardian tucked his snout under Wander's shoulder and dug his way beneath her body. Her blood smeared on his fur coat. Under the safety of her body, he laid down.

Wander felt a lump under her body sink away into nothing as her chest and stomach eased slowly back down into the grass. She let out a cry of pain as something crawled inside her legs and clenched at her bones. She found enough strength to turn to the sky. Her legs tore away from a network of roots that burrowed into her flesh. She managed to stand, her broken legs somehow healed. No, the roots had repaired her bones. Her enchanted body rose from the ground. Peering into the woods, she saw it no longer looked so dark. She could see beyond into the dark columns of trees to the light of green and life.

She walked in the direction Aura would be. She thought she would be shaking, but she wasn't. Her body never moved with more calm.

This was the longest night Aura could remember. The deviant queen climbed to the top of a colossal log and sat down.

No matter how she controlled him, her Wings took a long time to return. He was not dead or free. What was stopping him?

While her body sat in the desolate dark, her mind fought a war. They were all so afraid until she took control. She eased their fears and the moment they reached toward the feeling of hope she offered, they were hers. No one was killing themselves quite yet. Every single one had to fight. With the lullaby alliance, the army was larger than she imagined. She even figured she controlled less than half of the army, maybe a large third. With their minds taken though, they could fight better than the others. They would not faint or hesitate.

Aura picked up her head as a figure walked out of the darkness. Rather, a piece of the darkness came out as a figure. It was Wander, walking on somehow healed legs. Her green eyes were glowing. The human

514

approached so silently, Aura wondered if this were some pretender.

She stood up on the log, prepared for anything. Wander jumped supernaturally high, her sword raised above her head. Aura nearly tripped as she dodged. The human cut down and through the entire log. As she slashed through the wood, a hoard of termites poured out into the open air. Aura jumped down from the log onto the earth. Wander remained on the log, staring down at Aura with wide glowing eyes.

Aura's mind darted around as to how any of this was possible. The guardian. It had to be the guardian. He was going to use all his power on this one pawn. She might be no different from Aura's Arms now.

Aura's heart raced. She had to lose her fear. Something or someone was stalling her Wings and she sent her Horns too far to get back anytime soon. She could bring the army here to Wander. She just had to give them time to get here. She had to protect herself without killing Wander.

Wander took another leap and swung her two-handed sword down at Aura. The deviant queen put her shield between them. For fear of the impact, she held the shield with both her hands. She felt Wander's blade shatter above her. The shards splashed over her shield and around the twisted roots.

Wander and Aura both jumped away from each other. Wander looked at the empty handle that she held. The sword had completely shattered with not a bit of steel left to stand. Aura took a breath of satisfaction. Guardian bones, the most powerful material in Awei. Blessed, cursed, and enchanted items did not compare. This shield had been passed on through generations of the royal family. It had never failed them.

Wander's left arm held out the handle and branches poured out from where the blade used to be. Aura backed up and watched the magical branches meet with the shattered blade shards. The shard themselves grew branches that intertwined as they met with the others.

Aura aimed at Wander's knees and threw her shield with a spin.

Wander dodged enough to get one leg out of the way. The shield hit her right leg and it buckled. The sword had collected all its pieces and the branches shrunk as the blade pulled together. Aura put up her right hand. The thrown shield flew back to her, spinning, it managed to hit Wander's upper left arm. Now a leg and an arm were broken.

The impact made Wander drop her sword. With her unbroken arm, she lifted the healed sword.

"What are you going to do?" Aura shouted. "It'll just shatter again, just like your bones! I'll just keep breaking them!"

Wander stabbed her sword into the forest floor. Hissing in agony, she managed to stand by leaning against the log.

The earth shook. Something curled on Aura's foot. She looked down and saw the tree roots that covered the forest floor had sprung to life. They grabbed at her ankles, curling upward like snakes. She managed to escape the roots only to get entangled in taller ones. The entire forest had turned against her. The thick roots tried to pull her down. She turned the bladed sides of her shield to the roots, trying to cut as many as she could.

There were too many.

She screamed as one impaled her leg, the wood sharpening and harpooning her right thigh to the log. The roots had overwhelmed her until she could no longer move. One leg was pinned, the other tangled. Roots even curled around the log from above and pinned her arms along with the shield. Lastly was her neck.

The deviant queen managed to turn her head enough to see Wander limp toward her. One of the roots crawled up Wander's pants and to her knee. A loud crack came from Wander's body, and she yelped, but then her once broken leg straightened and walked. Branches and roots not only pull her sword together when it broke, it did the same for her body. She could definitely not be called human anymore.

Wander's silence sent chills went down Aura's spine. She struggled but the roots only tightened. Feeling less space for her neck, she kept still. Wander walked in front of her.

"You got me," Aura said. "But please don't kill me. I can give you what you want."

Wander tilted her head a little to the left.

"I'll free my Wings. I promise. I don't break promises. I'll free him. That's what you wanted all along, right?"

Tears swelled in the wind-borns eyes and she shook her head. "You have no idea how much this thing wants you dead." She began to reach downward.

Aura knew she could not appeal to the guardian. The creature was corrupted with a bloodlust for her. Her only chance to survive was for Wander to break free of the creature.

"Wander," she began, "if you kill me, Masu's mind will break! He has never been free before. I've been supporting him since he was a child. When I wasn't there, your guardian took my place. Without either of us, the Masu you know will be broken. His dark magic will fester. If you love him, set me free. I'll give him back to you, just as he was."

Wander shut her eyes and shook her head. "I can't." She pulled out a sheathed dagger from the inside of her boot.

"Please! Fight it!" Aura begged. "My people, they will suffer without me! If I die, my magic will all go away! That means those I've healed will be undone, and that includes Masu! I've healed hundreds, Wander, some of them children. I've healed ailments both physical and mental. My death will plague hundreds. My people will not be able to recover. Please!"

Wander pulled out the dagger and stabbed Aura's heart. It impaled through the steel like butter. Only one weapon could ignore armor so easily. It had to be guardian bone. Managing to look down, Aura saw the familiar handle of Myth's dagger, etched with the image of a rhino.

"That's my sister's," Aura whispered. She looked back at Wander.

"Your sister wanted you dead all along," Wander said. "She gave me this dagger."

Feeling death's breath near, Aura's eyes reddened with tears. "My sister would never kill me." Aura began to hear whispers and her body got heavier. The air became cold. She shut her eyes. The roots tightened more until she could no longer breathe.

Wander fell to her knees. Pain and awareness poured back into her as the fox's magic weakened inside her. She burst into tears and buried her face in her hands. Everything crashed down. Part of her expected everything to become okay when Aura's heart stopped beating. She was wrong, so many were still dead and she was still charred beyond recognition. She still felt scared, sad, and angry all at once.

"M-Masu."

He was free, whatever that meant. She was not sure she wanted to find out. She hugged herself and stood up. She wandered back from where she came from. After backtracking to the glen where Aura broke her legs, she moved back to the gate-like tree. The woods had become dead silent. Wander's heart pounded in her ears. Vincent and Masu were no longer there. A splatter of blood darkened the grass. Vincent's chains lay limp on the earth. The splatter became a trail into the woods. Taking a shaky breath, Wander followed. The trail changed from droplets to smears. She realized she had little to no magic and no weapons. Maybe that was for the best. She did not want to fight anymore. The sword of the Emerald Wilds could stay in this forest.

"Wander!" a hoarse voice called. Vincent noticed her before she saw him curled at the base of a tree. Getting to his side, she saw wounds scattered all over his body, scratches, stabs, cuts, burns—so many different kinds. One of his eyes had swollen and purpled.

Wander immediately held his hand. She knew he probably would not like it, but she needed to hold someone's hand. "Are you alright?" she asked.

"Does it look bad?"

She nodded.

"Did you kill Aura?"

She nodded again.

Vincent turned to spit some blood on the ferns.

"Where is Masu?" Wander asked.

"He changed."

Wander squeezed his hand.

"And it wasn't good," he said. "Wounds just magically burst all over his body. His face . . . he screamed. He looked at me with this furious glare. Then his hand summoned some dark . . . it was dark magic. Everything blackened. There was so much pain that I could not fight. When I came too, I saw he transferred his wounds to me. He completely healed himself. Then he flew off."

Wander ducked to get Vincent's arm over her shoulder.

"You're not going after him?" Vincent asked.

"Let's get you to safety first."

She tried to lead Vincent back to camp as fast as she could. It was not fast. His legs trembled as he tried to find footing along the complicated web of unearthed roots.

"How'd you kill her?" Vincent asked.

"Stabbed her."

"You look better than how I last saw you."

"I healed, but it wasn't my choice."

"It was the thing controlling you?"

"He's not controlling me anymore."

"What?"

"It was my fox, Vincent. He was the guardian of the forest that Aura burned down. He wanted revenge and used me to get it. Now that Aura's dead I'm free . . . sort of. I think he left part of him for me so I could live. Or maybe so he could. I guess that's my reward."

Vincent sighed, "Your riddle sucked."

"I don't even know what a riddle is!"

Vincent weakly laughed. "Wind-borns. We aren't good with words, that's for sure."

They began to pass bodies. Arrows stuck out of everything: trees, bodies, and earth.

"Look," Vincent pointed.

A perfect circle of blackened terrain was ahead. Within the circle, plants drooped and withered. Instead of bodies, there were only skeletons. The grass and soil had turned black.

"Black magic," Vincent whispered.

Wander maneuvered them around the circle and kept moving.

"WANDER!"

She stopped. A figure ran in the woods, leaping over roots. His arms were up. He stopped in front of her, a human. He breathed heavily and pointed to the right.

"The battle has ended! Is Aura dead?"

"Yes."

"We have a new problem. Her Wings is out of control." The man wiped sweat off his forehead. "He has entered the battlefield and is decimating people with black magic! We are retreating. Naktol and Dim have fallen. Both have been poisoned by Aura's Horn in an ambush."

Wander passed Vincent to the human. "Take him. I'm going to stop the Wings."

The human shook his head. "I don't think anyone can. We'll need powerful magic users, rainbows."

"I'm going to try."

"King Fade said he doesn't want to retreat without you. What do I tell him?"

"Tell him he can do whatever he wants, but I'm not leaving without trying to stop the Wings first. If I don't return soon, just go."

"Wander," Vincent said, "don't die for him."

Wander turned and ran in the direction the human pointed. She occasionally leaped over a root or body. She began to run past living people. The living searched the dead for survivors. Others urged the retreat and ran for the camp.

One noticed Wander. She pointed. "He's that way!"

Wander nodded and followed the directions.

Others began to join in. "He's over there!"

Wander got to a point where people did not help. They merely ran. She was close. She came to a still silhouette of someone with a cane who stood among corpses. Wander slowed down. It was Myth. The deviant blended to the darkness with cloak and hood over her head.

"What are you doing here?" Wander asked.

"To make sure you succeed," Myth said.

"I did. Aura is dead."

Myth nodded. "And yet your people are now getting slaughtered."

"Masu."

"Yes." Myth tucked her hand into her cloak. She drew out a sheathed dagger and held it out. "Take this."

Wander took the weapon. The handle was inscribed with an animal just like the other. The animal had large ears and a nose that reached to its feet.

"Another dagger?"

"The same as mine, but this was my sister's. It's also made of guardian bone. You're going to need it to kill Masu."

"Kill him?"

"Yes. You will have to, or else we will perish."

Wander shook her head. "No, I can't."

"It's not the man you knew," Myth leaned forward on her cane. "The tame man you knew was created by a guardian. This monster is what is real. But you know what else is real? Everyone else. Surely there are people worth saving? Think of your journey since the wilds burned. Think of the people you've met. They will be in danger. They are afraid, and have every right to be. I know you don't think you can do it. Everyone who knows you probably thinks you cannot, either. That's why they are retreating. But I know better. I know, despite everything, you can do it. Because the Emerald Wilds is not the only life you know now."

Her hands shook, but she placed the dagger in her boot.

"Good luck," Myth said. She turned and disappeared beyond the columns of darkness

When Wander found Masu, she had to stop and keep her distance. His profile stood between the dark columns of trees. All around him, the bark of trees began to peel, leaves deadened and fell, ferns shriveled, and grass blackened. The feathers on his wings puffed up, making him look larger than Wander knew he could be.

Raising hands full of tense fingers, Masu aggressively pulled off the armor that weighed him down. He stared down at the steel breastplate. His eyes were the most frightening thing about him in the dark. Their bloody color glowed dimly through shaggy locks of dark hair. He stood over bodies. Like the trees, their skin was flaking away.

Wander saw moonlight bounce from an arrowhead that struck down from the trees. Some hooded figure with white hair, a lullaby, prepared to fire at Masu. The spirit sat on a branch.

Trying to shake off her fear, Wander raised her hand to get the lullaby's attention. If the lullaby noticed, Wander's warning was ignored or misinterpreted. The bowstring snapped as the arrow was released. It was shot with such force that the arrow impaled all the way through the center of Masu's left wing.

Masu's eyes amplified in size and fury. As he turned to find the source, the lullaby threw a knife into his left shoulder.

Wander's feet could not move as she watched. Masu hands rose up toward the sky, grabbed and clenched. His fists glowed violet as he swung violently down. His magic forced the lullaby to crash down to the forest floor. The lullaby was momentarily stunned. Masu looked down at him, wide and unblinking. His left hand began to tremble, and he raised clamped up fingers. As he did so, the lullaby's body exploded.

His death happened so fast, there wasn't even a scream. Everything had burst. His eyes became black blood spatters. A mixture of red and black mucus now oozed from his filled mouth. His legs and arms twisted from the impact of whatever happened inside them. Bones had to be broken to get in the position they ended up.

Wander could no longer control her breathing. Her breaths came out loud and fast. She could taste her heartbeat in her throat. She had to do something. No force pushed her to fight anymore. She had to be brave by herself. Still drowning in fear and not wanting to be seen, Wander slowly bent down and pulled out Myth's dagger. She charged.

He heard her steps and turned around. With his turn, he sent a dark force at her from his left hand. It appeared too fast and close to dodge. The force sent her flying until her back hit a tree. Blood gushed from biting her own tongue, and her senses fuzzed from the impact. Opening her eyes, she saw Masu walking toward her. His sinister eyes look directly in hers. There was no recognition. He looked at her just as he did that lullaby. His fists began to clench, preparing some kind of horrid spell. She tried to get up only to fall back. Masu's single spell that pushed her back had also damaged her. Pools of blood began to darken and expand all over her clothes. Something had to be broken; breathing began to hurt.

The guardian was no longer here to fix her body. He was no longer here to force her to get up and succeed. He was not here to numb her mind. The image of Masu blurred as tears began to rise. With an outcry of agony, she managed to bend herself. She picked up Myth's dagger from the ground. She could barely muster to energy to squeeze the handle. She pointed the tip at Masu. When he got to her, he just stood over her and stared down. Wander began to wheeze. With a whimper, she slashed the dagger at Masu's legs. He stepped back so she could not reach far enough.

Masu sat down so the two of them were eye level with each other. Her skin felt like it was on fire. Though Masu did not seem to be doing anything, he must have been the cause. Just being near him caused people pain. Knowing this was the end of her life, Wander let out a sob. She thrust the dagger weakly at him. Masu's hand grabbed the sharp blade. He squeezed it as she kept trying to move the dagger. Black blood dripped down from his palm and dripped onto Wander's knees.

Wander did not want to look at him. She gazed away from him and toward the earth. Her shoulders trembled as she cried. She did not let go of the dagger, and neither did he. She wondered about letting go. If the world was this meaningless a place, then just let it do its worst. Let him kill her.

"Wander?"

She stopped breathing.

"Is that you, Wander?"

Wander looked back at him with tear stained eyes. Masu's feathers had flattened. His red eyes looked through his dark shaggy hair, no longer glowing. He no longer looked mad or even emotionless. He looked . . . scared.

For some reason, the situation became more frightening. Any hope at this point felt like insanity. Her entire body began to tremble like a leaf in the wind. She would not dare hope. She had seen the world and what it offered her. He was gone; he had to be.

"Wander," Masu said softly. His bloody hand let go of her dagger to reveal an impressive slash wound on his palm. "It's me."

Wander held the dagger with both of her shaking hands. Sniffling, she shook her head. He leaned closer, and she pointed the dagger at his face, shaking her head faster. His eyes began to glisten and water up. His voice had tightened, "What happened?"

Wander could not begin to believe what was happening, let alone explain what had happened before.

Some tears rolled down his cheeks, "You're so hurt."

Her trembling hands dropped her dagger. She opened her mouth but no words came out. Her arms reached out to him and he took her in an embrace that she dreamed of for so long. What happened next felt like melting. The two of them cried into each other. Masu's hug rekindled the needy child in Wander. She buried her head into his chest and his head rested on her shoulder.

"I'm here now," Masu whispered as he rubbed her back. "It's alright."

By the time they calmed, dawn had come. Light began to shine on treetops and sink into the ground. Memories, regrets, and so much more had to happen later. Wander's weak body shivered even when the sunlight began to touch her. Masu lifted her hurting body into his arms.

"Let's get you some help," Masu said. "You've bled too much."

He carried her through the Winged Graves. What were once dark columns now were colors of chestnut and chocolate. Delicate green stems glowed in daylight. All would seem peaceful and well if not for the many bodies they treaded over.

Wander could feel Masu's heartbeat. He was calmer than before, but he was not calm. His heart felt like it was about to explode. It beat faster when they walked over corpses. She was afraid to tell Masu about anything just as much as she feared to ask him what he remembered. Maybe it would be best for him to not remember anything, and they needed to start over. But how did he remember her? The guardian controlled him when they lived together.

A gentle smile came over Wander as she found her simple answer. She had been controlled by the guardian since the fire, but she still remembered everything. She would have done some, maybe a lot of things different, but she still felt connected to those she met.

But at the same time, were they really free? How were they, a spirit and human, still able to touch?

"How do you feel?" Wander asked.

"My head hurts, but I'll be okay," he said.

"It's going to take a long time to explain to you everything that has happened. A lot has happened."

"I think I'll be able to remember some things with time."

Masu did not seem to know where he was going. Wander did not want to give him directions to Naktol's camp. She did not trust the humans or spirits with Masu. They'd want to kill him.

"Why are you covering everything but your eyes?" Masu asked.

"I don't look the same anymore," Wander said. "I was burned in a fire."

"I think I remember a fire. Flying over it."

"That's when we lost each other."

Masu's grip on her tightened.

She began feeling lighter and lighter. "At some point, I gave up," Wander whispered. "I gave up on you. I don't know when, but I did. Our lives together began to feel like a dream and it just began to fade more and more until it felt like a lie." Her head turned to look up at him. "Do you promise that this is real?"

"It is real."

She felt like sleeping but she did not want to go to sleep. Breathing still hurt. She wanted anything to keep her awake, anything to lessen the pain in her chest. "Can we play the word game? I learned a lot since the wilds."

In his shock, Masu agreed.

"Stars."

"Stairs."

"Stole."

"Sister."

"Silly."

"Symbol."

"Sat."

She shut her eyes, "S . . . Stairs."

He gently shook her, "You already said that."

Wander opened her eyes but Masu had become a blur.

"Sister, huh? That's a new word."

She shut her eyes again, she let go and floated away.

Chapter 24
The Crescent Rest

"Maybe the lullabies have the right idea about the moon, the dark, and soft glows. On the final battle, I looked at the stars and felt God, a feeling of being small but brave." – A Soldiers Journal

"Where is Wander?" King Fade entered the medical tent.

The doctor was in the midst of stitching Vincent's cuts as he sat on a wood box. She just started with one on his back. The sting of the disinfectant was still fresh on his wounds.

Wincing from the pain, Vincent said, "She's gone to the Wings."

"That's suicide. We're getting reports that the death of Aura awoke dark magic in him. He's killing everyone thoughtlessly." Fade looked at the ground. "I'm going after her."

"You'd only make it worse." Vincent said. "Leave her."

"He's here!" A human nearly tripped over himself as he tumbled inside the medical tent. His voice picked up once inside. "WE'VE GOT TO RUN! HE'S HERE!"

Adrenaline claimed Vincent's body, and he began to shake.

Fade tried to grab the human and got shocked. "Who?"

"The Wings! He killed Wander!"

Vincent stood up. His doctor gasped and he felt the twine in his skin jerk.

Shock had taken Fade. The spirit's jaw dropped a little, his body frozen.

Despite the doctor's panicked gestures for Vincent to sit back down, he grabbed his shirt and pulled it cover his head. He grabbed his chains from the ground and took a crossbow. Barely any thoughts passed through his head other than killing the Wings. At some point, he actually began to believe Wander. He believed in that fairy tale story of hers of a spirit and human living together. Her eyes shined when she spoke of him. She believed he was real.

She was just like so many wind-borns: naïve. She was like all that are used and thrown away. That creature . . . the guardian threw her away. She believed its lies. Of course she did, she was only a child.

Vincent walked outside into dawn. The air had warmed, and the forest began to look a brighter shade of green. When he entered the medical tent a while ago, the encampment was teaming with people with reports and need of medical care. Now all were scrambling. The panic had not yet become violent. Already some soldiers rushed out with weapons from other tents. Vincent joined them as they ran through the forest. All held bows and crossbows. All were human.

"HALT!" someone in the front shouted.

They reached a part of the forest covered in shade. Branches thick with leaves above quivered in the breeze. Beyond the front, Vincent saw the top of dark wings. A hand rose above everyone's heads and motioned them to circle around. The humans encircled around an intimidating scene.

Vincent's crossbow aimed between red eyes that glowed in the dark shade. The Wings stood straight-backed. His hair looked wilted, covering his eyes as he looked down at the figure he held. Wander was in his arms. Her cloak had been torn into shreds. Blood stains gored her clothes.

"DROP HER!" a soldier shouted.

The Wings looked around him. As outmatched as he seemed, Vincent had heard tales of dark magic that could kill armies. Maybe they were just tales, but he could not be sure. The Wings looked back at Wander. His grip on her tightened, his fingers digging into her upper arm and thigh. As he bent down, everyone prepared to fire.

He set her body on the earth.

"BACK UP!" the same soldier shouted.

The Wings obeyed. He took four steps back and dots of sunlight through the leaves danced on his dark hair. The humans behind him backed up as well, never ceasing to aim for his back and neck.

A soldier set his crossbow down and walked in a crouch toward Wander's body. His hand was shaking as he checked her pulse. As he calmed a little, he put his ear on her chest.

Vincent felt his heart in his throat. He did not take his eyes off the Wings. The spirit was visibly upset. Tears rolled down from the Wings' eyes. Dark mages were known for emotional imbalances. He may not be crying for her. Or maybe he was . . . despite being the one who killed her.

The soldier picked up his head. "She's alive!"

A visible relief came over the team of humans, their shoulders less tense. Even the Wings did the same.

"Take her to camp!" another soldier shouted.

Derrick tucked his arms under Wander and lifted her. The circle let him through. Vincent's body had calmed immensely, like a giants hands that gripped him tight had let go.

"HANDS UP, SPIRIT!" a soldier shouted.

The Wings looked forward. "What are you going to do?" He spoke. His voice sounded sincere.

Hearing a voice come out of him put everyone in momentary shock.

Shaking off the shock, the same soldier shouted, "You are to be executed here and now for your crimes against humanity."

The spirit shut his eyes. "And what about Wander?"

"If she survives, she'll be the hero who brought you and Aura down."

A mix between a sigh and gentle sob came out of the spirit. With shaking hands, he put his arms up.

"ON YOUR KNEES!" the soldier commanded.

He dropped to his knees in the soft forest grass. He looked at the earth. Vincent heard the sound of bowstrings tightening.

"What's your name?"

All the soldiers looked at Vincent. He was surprised to hear his own voice too.

The wings looked at him. "What?"

"Your name," Vincent said.

"M...Masu. It's Masu."

Vincent's brows furrowed. "Do you know who I am?"

"What?" Masu's face began to match the confusion of the fellow soldiers.

"Not my name," Vincent said. "My face. Do you know my face?"

They had only just beaten the life out of each other hours ago.

Masu looked wide-eyed and frightened by the question. "No."

"What's the meaning of this?" a higher ranked soldier barked.

Vincent ignored her. "Masu! Do you remember killing people? Do you remember killing anyone?"

Masu did not answer and only looked more scared.

"ENOUGH!"

King Fade had snuck up behind the soldiers. Two moved for him to enter the circle. His pupils looked nearly gone in the morning light. His white robe flowed with the wind. "Important voices are not here to make a choice. A group of soldiers should not decide this man's punishment."

"Naktol's plans were to kill all of Aura's Arms," a soldier said.

"That does not seem fair does it? He was mind-controlled."

"He wasn't when he used dark magic!"

Fade turned to the other soldier that shouted, "Let the spirits worry about the magic. The bird spirit appears to be surrendering."

All the soldiers exchanged glances.

Fade walked up to Masu. "If you promise not to hurt anyone, we will take you into custody. You will be given a trial to decide what happens to you."

Masu nodded and softly said, "Okay."

"If you'll make that promise, stand up and listen very closely to what I say next while taking in a deep breath."

Masu stood up. Fade approached close and leaned toward Masu's face. He whispered something, a few words. Vincent could not lip read. As the King whispered, Masu took a deep breath and something came over him. His eyelids dropped and his entire body went limp and fell into Fade's arms.

Everyone lowered their weapons.

"What did you do?" a soldier asked.

"I'm a lullaby," Fade said. "Our breath puts people to sleep. Did you forget? It works for about an hour. I'll have a soldier keep him asleep until he's somewhere where he can't hurt anyone."

The soldiers, still a little shaken, began to move back to the camp. Their fingers were red from tightening their bowstrings. Fade ducked himself under Masu's arm and carried him. The king was scrawny and thin, but he seemed to handle the weight of a winged being well.

Vincent approached Fade. "How are Naktol and Dim?"

"My brother is hanging on," he said. His voice softened, "But your Queen, she is dead."

Wander stood in the ruins of the Emerald Wilds, unable to breath and freezing cold. The husks of dead trees began to fade away like melting snow. Whispers began to hush. The guardian appeared in the distance. He was in his dream form, a shadow, tall, a dark tail sticking out, dead crackling branches on his head like horns, and masked with the face of a pale smiling fox with red lips.

He moved closer and closer.

When the whispers silenced, so did everything else.

Dead silence.

The fire that crackled in the guardian's branches died. He began to crumble into ash, starting with the dead branches.

He got closer and closer as he began to crumble away.

Wander could not move.

He got close enough to touch her.

Two shadowy paws rose out of his dark form. They reached up and took the fox mask off. The entire time, the mask still blocked out the guardian's face from Wander's view. He moved the mask over her face, turned it around, and placed it on her face. Once on, her body warmed up, she could breathe again.

Once her eyes could see through the eyeholes, his head was gone, and the last standing piece of his form crumbled away.

The humans and lullabies parted at a crossroads between Sollast and the northeastern mountains. Post-battle felt surreal. The balance of death and victory had the humans and spirits quiet.

Bodies of those that perished in the final battle had been piled into wagons. The piles were blanketed in tent covers to shield them from the sun. When Vincent saw a bare hand stick out of one, he discretely tucked it back under the cover. The hand felt cold and had drops of morning dew.

Queen Naktol had her own covered wagon. Her body was wrapped carefully in a white sheet and placed between two crates of arrows. She perished of hydra's tears, the same poison that had killed many of her people. The poison caused some of her veins to purple. Vincent watched as she was wrapped up by soldiers. Fade said it was a quick death. Hydra's tears were meant to kill sea monsters. Nobody smaller than a whale could possibly survive or even struggle. Queen Aura probably got a shipment of the poison from the elementals. Only sea elementals could possibly get their hands on hydra tears.

The spirits put Masu in handcuffs. They kept him sleeping for the entire trip in a heavily guarded covered wagon. Wander was in a medical tent with the red mage rainbow, Love. If anyone could save Wander, it was probably someone with magic.

When the humans and the lullabies parted, the wagons with Wander and Masu went with the spirits. Though Wander was now a human hero, there was little humanity could do for her condition. Vincent put himself in charge of guarding Wander, so he went with the spirits.

By night they arrived at The Crescent Rest, a known paradise for old and injured lullabies. The Crescent Rest was like a castle without towers with stone walls five stories high. Ivy clutched to the edge of windows covered with violet curtains. The building stood in the middle of land surrounded by a blue lake shaped like a crescent moon, Lake Crescent.

The wagons filled with injured stopped at the garden's edge. Aloe plants, lavender, and white lilies grew inside the fence while grapevines lay across the weathered wood.

Vincent's eyes darted to Masu's wagon. He urged his horse forward to trot by Fade's donkey. "You're bringing him here as well?" Vincent gestured to Masu's wagon.

"The only reason your soldiers did not die when you surrounded Masu was because of Wander," Fade said. "He knew you all could help her, even if it meant his death. What I meant to say is if Wander and Masu are near each other, we can easily control them both."

"And if Wander dies?"

"Then killing him would probably be best."

Two nights passed. Vincent tried to sleep in the day and wake at dusk as the lullabies did. The place had filled with no bed to spare so he slept in a chair in Wander's room. Human medical rooms were white and bright, but the lullabies kept it dark with a deep purple rug and curtains. Instead of white sheets, Wander laid under a quilt made of hexagonal designs of purple, blue, and black. Her body was bare for a time so the doctor could treat her. The girl's skin was a collage of scars and burns.

"Her skin is all layers of screwed up," was what the crude doctor said. "Scars upon scars upon scars. The girl cannot even sweat. It's hard to imagine how she lived the way she did."

Vincent found no reason to keep what he knew a secret anymore.

"She was mind controlled," he said from the wooden chair at the bedside. "Not by Aura but by a guardian, a fox."

"Really? A guardian?"

Vincent shrugged. "That's what she told me when I last saw her awake. I think it doesn't control her anymore. That's why she could tell me."

"I've never heard of a guardian doing that to someone. It would explain how she lived." The doctor sighed. "But her freedom may be what kills her." After he did what he could, the doctor gently slipped a white nightdress onto Wander.

At midnight a young lullaby in a white spring dress, possibly seven years old, came by to Wander's room and set a vase of lavender at her bedside table. The lavender was tied in a bouquet with a red bow and little bell. Her large brown eyes looked at Vincent. She had no markings, but her white hair gave her away.

"Who are you?" Vincent asked.

"Bell," she said.

"Are you a patient?"

She shook her head. "I'm waiting for my daddy to wake up."

Dim woke up later the next night. Bell and Dim's new wife held his hand and walked around the halls. Dim and the woman's markings had them glowing like fireflies in the halls. The king's bare feet sank into the plush hall carpet. His eyes had dark circles under them and he needed a shoulder to lean on once in a while.

He noticed Vincent outside Wander's room. Vincent fought the urge to run back instead out of habit of avoiding small talk. Bell noticed Vincent first and waved, alerting Dim to the human's presence.

"How's Wander?" Dim called out.

With no escape, Vincent approached the spirit king. "Hasn't woken up, but she's alive."

"That girl has been through enough," Dim said. The grip he had on Bell's hand tightened. "Whatever happens, she deserves some peace. As for the winged being? Meet me later to talk about him."

They met later, away from Dim's family. The lullaby looked out the back windows at Lake Crescent.

Herons stood on legs taller than the deep water, their long beaks pointing down at the reflection of the sky. A lullaby doctor helped a patient walk out to one of the small docks.

"No one has told you about the Wings have they?" asked Dim.

"No."

"He is awake but not well in the head. He is being kept in a secure room for patients whose minds break. It's in the basement, a place with a lot of security."

"What do you mean by 'not well in the head'?"

"He is getting more and more chained up each day," Dim said. "Not for our safety, but for his own. The man is hurting himself in any way he can. He's biting his own arms and hitting his head against the wall. I'd hate to think what he'd do with dark magic. We've kept a dragon's eye amulet around his neck to lock his dark magic."

Vincent had heard of dragon's eye amulets. The stones were known for the vibrant outer colors, dark centers, and being found in the ocean. Since the ocean was the most dangerous place in Awei, the amulets were rare, hoarded by the sea elementals to sell to rainbows for insane sums of gold.

"Has he spoken at all?" Vincent asked. "Have you tried talking to him?"

"Yes. Sometimes he's incoherent, other times he's responsive. He usually hurts himself when others aren't looking."

"What are you going to do?"

"My brother thinks he should be given a chance if Wander lives," Dim said. "Fade is sensitive to others' feelings, often at the cost of being a good leader."

"So you think differently?"

"There is no question in my mind that the Wings should be executed," Dim said. "I visited him. The Wings may not know it yet, but living could be worse than death. Even if Wander lives, he should die.

The reports of his dark magic I read from the battle are horrifying. Rainbows have published endless books on dark magic, and from them I know that the Wings should not live. He will get worse. Aura's mind-control surely has given him psychological damage and trauma. Trauma, mistrust, and anger feed dark magic. And I'm sure the Wings are full of all of that right now."

Vincent kept quiet. He had no rebuttal or support to offer.

Wander heard the song of a whippoorwill and could smell lavender. Her entire body felt weighed down, dry, and hot. She opened her eyes up to a dark ceiling. The back of her head lay deep in a pillow. Her heart began to pound fast as she remembered Masu had been holding her. She turned to a curtained window and empty wood chair. On her other side was a bed stand with a vase of lavender that was close to sighing away into a wilt. Placing her hand down on the mattress, she tried to raise her body. She fell into the bed and let out a yelp, pain had made individual heartbeats around her arms, stomach, and chest. Her mouth bit into the pillow to muffle her scream.

This time expecting the pain, she rose up and hissed, bandages around her body crinkled and stitches under them pulled. Stumbling out of the bed, she caught herself on the wall. With no idea of where she was, she decided to follow the wall. Remaining hunched, she followed the wall out of the room into a corridor. The windows outside showed a night full of stars.

Wander's body became light as she saw spots blot out her sight. Arms caught her as she was about to fall over. She looked up at Vincent to meet a face that looked like it saw a ghost. Before she could talk, Vincent wordlessly pulled her back inside the bedroom. She could do little to push against his efforts as he put her back in the bed.

"Where's Masu?" she asked as he laid the sheet and quilt back over her hurting body.

"He's in the same building," Vincent said. "He's safe."

Wander let out a long sigh and her body relaxed. Shutting her eyes, she let some tears flow out.

"How are you feeling?" Vincent asked. "You've been out for six days."

"It hurts, but I've hurt worse."

Vincent left her to tell the others, whoever they were. Wander still did not know where she was. Past the pain and heat, her muscles felt like they had been stretched and worn. She pulled out her left arm out from under the blankets to see Masu's feather still dangled from her wrist.

Lullabies followed by Fade and Dim came back with Vincent. Fade gently touched Wander's shoulder as he explained what happened. Everyone wore a gentle smile. But Wander only half-listened to everyone who spoke.

"Is it true that you were mind controlled by a guardian?" one of the lullabies asked. Wander assumed he was a doctor.

She nodded. "A fox. He was from the Emerald Wilds. He's the reason I burned, but also the reason I lived."

"What else was the creature responsible for?" Dim asked.

For once, Wander could say it all. "He's responsible for killing Aura," she told them. "He gave me the ability to touch spirits and hold the enchanted sword. He gave me my magic. Sometimes he pushed me to do things, feel things, think, and say things that I would not have otherwise."

"But we are spirits, and we have been treating you. We could touch you. What does that mean? Are you still under the guardian's control?"

Wander shrugged.

Some of the smiles dissipated. For a moment, Wander wondered if she had just made herself turn from a patient to a prisoner. The doctor scribbled notes. Vincent's eyes looked to the floor. The lullaby kings glanced at each other.

"We will find out," Fade spoke up. "While guardian magic is not common knowledge, I'm sure there are experts out there. I'll dig through our resources. Surely there is someone who can clear up this unknown. For now, you should rest."

"I'm not staying here unless I can see Masu."

If there was any hint of joy left in the room, Wander had just kicked it away. "I don't think that's a good idea," Dim said. "We did not know that Aura's mind control was also neutralizing his black magic. Black mages are dangerous."

Wander spoke thickly, "I don't care."

Dim raised his voice. "Excuse me?"

Fade cut in. "We can talk about it."

"If I don't see him tonight, I'm leaving."

"You are in no condition to leave," the doctor spoke.

"I'll manage."

The meeting parted with an air of unease. Vincent straggled behind, seeming split as to if he should stay behind or not. Wander ignored him and looked out toward the purple curtains. She heard his footsteps leave.

After a nap, Wander awoke to a lullaby bringing her some food. The woman helped Wander sit up. Her entire back, butt, and legs all pulsated in pain as Wander rubbed against the sheets.

"Here you are," the lullaby set a pink plate on Wander's lap.

Nuts rolled on the surface. It was just a plate of uncooked nuts. Some weren't even edible nuts. Horse chestnut, buckeye, and black locust were mixed with pine, walnut, pistachio, and acorns.

The lullaby picked up a buckeye and gestured an offer to feed it to Wander. Wander pressed her head back into the pillow. "No, I can do it myself."

She expected the lullaby to act insulted, but she nodded with a smile and left. Wander ate what she could and snuck the horse chestnuts, buckeye, and black locust under the pillow and mattress. She tried to eat an acorn but immediately regretted the decision when her teeth felt like they were about to break.

Someone knocked on the wall as he came in. Wander spat out the acorn tossed it behind the bedframe. She took the whole plate and tipped it so the rest of the inedible nuts went behind the bedframe as well. With the nuts off, she saw the pink plate had a delicate painting of flowers at its center.

Vincent came in with slow steps. He sat in the wood chair at her bedside. Before he could open is mouth, Wander had to ask. "What have you been eating?"

It took a moment for the confusion on his face to evolve to understanding and then laughter.

"I've been making my own meals with what I can find. It's not much though. Raw vegetables and fruits here and there."

"Can you get me some?"

"Yes, but I imagine this other information I have is more important to you," Vincent said. "You can see Masu. The kings decided to entertain into the possibly that seeing you could make Masu calm down."

Wander nodded.

"I'd thought you'd be happy."

"I'm worried about us."

"It's alright. You both are getting taken care of. You both are free and safe."

Wander winced as she scooted up on the bed to sit straight. "I'd like my cloak and headscarf. I don't want Masu to see my burns." Masu was the only person in the world who knew what she looked like before the fire. He could look at her all covered up and still see a beautiful girl with golden hair underneath.

Since her old garments were tattered from the battle at the Winged Graves, Vincent scrounged for other clothes. He managed to find a brown hooded cloak and black scarf to wrap around her face. After applying ointments on her burns, a doctor helped her dress. Every little space the fabric moved across her skin felt like fire. She cried but found little shame in it anymore. For the rest of her life, this pain was going to be a part of her. She no longer had the guardian to numb it away.

"Are you ready?" Vincent asked.

She nodded.

Her heart raced in the small amount of time that she lay alone. She straightened when she heard chain links rattling outside the room.

When Masu came in, two guards helped him walk. His massive wings were wrapped in chains. His wrists were locked together in handcuffs. The clothes from the battle were gone, replaced by pants and no shirt. A bright amulet hung down from his neck. It looked like a blue cat's eye. As Masu got closer, the color began to show different shades. The various shades looked like thin blades of grass in a pool of water.

The guards gently sat Masu in the wooden chair. One seemed to hesitate letting go, for fear he'd fall over. "You have an hour," the other said. They left Masu and Wander alone.

When they left, Masu's cuffed hands grabbed Wander's. She forgot how much darker his brown skin was against hers. He put his elbows on the bedside and held her hand to his forehead. For a moment all was quiet. For the moment, she just enjoyed looking at him as dawn began to rise in the window.

"I'm sorry," he said softly.

Wander's other hand joined his to feel them quivering. When he raised his head she saw tears stain his eyes. Sucking in the pain, she sat up and scooted to the edge of the bed to be near him. She put her arms out for a hug.

The impact of Masu's body was enough to make her scream. She clenched her teeth and only made it worse as she hugged him tighter. He sniffled and rested his face in her right shoulder. He smelled like blood and sweat. She had dreamed of being in his arms again. Now that she was, despite the physical agony, she was also in a state of euphoria. She remembered him feeling stronger, warmer. Now she could barely feel him beyond the hot cocoon of charred and scarred skin. Even his breath against her ears would sting if it was not blocked by her hood.

"I remember now. I almost killed you. I don't know what happened to me."

"It's alright," Wander tried to summon calm over emotion. "You were confused. It's okay."

"I remember some more things too," Masu said as their hug broke. "I remember flying over the wilds while it was on fire. I remember choking on the smoke and waking up with a woman. I explained who you were to her, and she told me you were dead. She made me rest for a while . . . and then things started to get odd. I got really tired. I slept, but I wasn't really sleeping. It was like . . . I was curled up in a warm shell. If I ever had a passing thought of doing something, I'd only get more and more tired. But then I woke up and I did not want to fall asleep again. I did everything I could so I would not fall asleep again." Masu paused and shook his head. "I don't make any sense do I? Nothing is making sense to me."

"No. I understand," Wander said. "I know what you mean. I can explain what happened."

Masu squinted at her. His hands reached toward her scarf. She gently took his hands before they could reach her. She teared up and her voice tightened. "A lot happened. I promise though, I am Wander. You can't see that in my face anymore, but it's me. So please, just remember what I used to look like."

Something in her words hurt him. She could tell from his expression. Taking his hands in hers, she sniffled, "Can I tell you about what happened to me?"

He nodded.

"After I burned in the fire, I was found by a human village outside of the wilds," Wander explained. "A very kind family took care of me. But it didn't last long. A fire happened there too and only . . . my brother Ethan survived," Wander said. "We traveled to find other humans, but then I killed him."

"What?"

"I did not know why at the time. But far later I found out it was because I was under mind-control by the guardian of the wilds we lived in, a black fox. He stuck with me after the fire. I thought he was just an animal until I met the deviant, Queen Aura. She wanted him and I didn't understand why. Aura mind-controlled Ethan to grab the guardian so the guardian made me kill him. Then I found out Aura was mind controlling you. Then . . ." Wander choked. She shook her head as she spoke through tears.

"I made a friend, Under, and I loved him and he's gone. I saw his partner die. The family that adopted me, Under, Alice, and so many others died because of me. Wherever I went, the fire followed. Everyone with me suffered. And through it all, I was looking for you. I thought I was, but at the same time, the guardian wanted me to kill Aura. At some point, I started to just think of killing Aura. At another point, I just wanted to die. I thought you were gone for good because the guardian controlled your mind in the wilds while you raised me. I thought that maybe when you were free, you wouldn't even be you."

"Wander, there are still many things I don't remember," Masu said. "But you are not one of them. I remember you the most." He smiled and squeezed her hands. "How could I forget you? You're the only person in the world I know. Even if I knew other people, none of them would be you. You are like a piece of me."

Wander sniffed. Her scarf had dampened from her crying.

"But mind-control," Masu said. "That's . . . is that really what happened to me?"

Wander nodded. "You were mind-controlled all your life. Before the wilds, Aura controlled you. The guardian then controlled you. Then you were brought back to her after the fire and got controlled by her. That's why you didn't remember anything before the wilds. It's why you never wanted to leave. It's why you could touch me, a human. The guardian made it that way."

Did he know he was a prince to a now almost extinct people? Wander decided to leave all that for later. Perhaps it was also better to explain black magic later. A lot of things will be cleared with him over time. Already they had a lot of progress. He just received a lot of information to settle on.

"What happened to the guardian? Why can I still touch you?"

"The guardian controlled me while Aura controlled you. He isn't controlling me anymore I think. But I don't know why I can still touch spirits. I mean, I'm definitely me. His one goal was to kill Aura and I did that. Now I think he's gone. Maybe he just left a piece for me to keep."

Wander lay back down in the bed. This time she could not hide her whimpers. Masu struggled to stand up under the weight of his chains as he helped her ease down back onto the mattress. Masu's handcuffed hands held hers as the room brightened with morning sunlight. The steel chains of Masu's wings began to reflect little lights on the ceiling.

"What happened to your forehead?" Wander noticed a purple bruise beyond his dark shaggy hair. "Are the people here hurting you?"

"No, no, they aren't. Don't worry about it."

Upon closer inspection, Masu did not seem well. Darkness claimed the skin around his eyes like a raccoon. His lips were cracked and dry. His arms were marked in scratches, bites, and bruises. Was he lying? Why would he do that?

She remembered the looks of Dim, Fade, Vincent, and the other lullabies when she mentioned Masu. Then she came to a decision.

"Let's go."

"Hm?"

She squeezed his hand. "Let's leave this place."

"Why?"

"So we can both be free."

Masu licked his lips and his eyebrows furrowed. He let go of her hand and pinched the bedsheet.

"What's wrong?" she asked.

"I . . ." he attempted to find what he wanted to say. "I don't know if I should be free."

She reclaimed one of his hands in hers. "I'm not leaving without you. I have to leave, and I will not leave without you." As he still looked unsure, she added, "You should be free. I know you should. Neither of us will be free if we stay here."

"How?" he whispered. "How would we get out of here? You're hurt, and I'm a mess. Where would we even go?"

Wander winced as she sat up and rolled her legs off the bed. Taking a deep breath, she stood up. Masu flinched, prepared to catch her if she fell. She grabbed the chains around Masu's wings and unwrapped them.

"Can you fly?" she asked.

"I don't think so. I feel weak."

"That's fine. We'll walk. Maybe find someone who can give us a ride. Find a way to hide your wings. Maybe a really big backbag."

"Backpack?"

"Yes." She set the chains on the bed and took Masu's hands in hers. "We'll also hide the wrist chain until we can find help."

"Who will help us?"

"You'll see."

Pain was not going to lock her here. After all she had been through, she could handle this. She limped over to the window and felt around for a way to it to open. Masu got up and unlatched two knobs clearly visible in the center. Together they pulled up the window. A welcoming breeze caressed them. They had the luck of being on the first floor.

"Well," Masu turned to her, "let's go."

He tucked in his wings and stepped up on the windowsill before jumping.

Beaming, Wander tried to do the same only to stumble and nearly fall out. Masu offered his hands. She took them and held her breath as she jumped.

Epilogue

A week had passed since Naktol's funeral. The silver-haired queen's ashes joined many human heroes at the edge of an enchanted forest. It was known as Highhaven and sat at the top of the mountain that towered over Sollast's Castle. Her three daughters, Gwen, Mae, and Sophia came out of carriages in heavy coats.

In the snow, each of them spread their mother's ashes. Though the guards warned them not to go beyond to edge of the forest, Mae swore she saw human footprints and followed them. The guards chased her screams to find her alone. The princess swore she heard whispers and saw a giant white bear.

Queen Gwen was crowned the next day. Her blood was not royal, but Naktol adopted her for the task of ruling humanity in a future that came too soon.

Fade released Sophia to join her sisters and told her she did not have to come back. But two weeks later she did.

The reconstruction of Sollast was going to last for many years. The outer city was filled with encampments of those with no homes. But joy was still found among the tents and campfires. Humanity never felt so united.

Queen Gwen had decided to keep the boulder that killed Aura's Shadow as a reminder of the Battle of

Sollast in the War of Arrows. A fence was built around the colossal stone and a memorial was placed on the ground for the lives lost when Aura attacked Sollast.

According to some Sollastians, the stone sometimes felt strangely warm to the touch. It became a site of paranormal rumors, as some children claimed they heard whispers around the memorial stone and some dogs would bark at the boulder for no reason.

News of Wander and Masu's disappearance spread fast all across Awei.

Ivy, a lullaby scientist who studied guardians, was brought to a meeting between Dim, Fade, and Gwen.

"I can tell you a couple things," Ivy said. "Firstly, that the Emerald Wilds was a very, very powerful enchanted forest. The power comes from age, and few people have settled that far east to disturb the lands there. But the fire from an elemental is also incredibly powerful. When that much destruction comes to a land under a guardian's control, that guardian can snap. Guardians are highly intelligent and know the concept of revenge. Wander's guardian must have used her to get back to Aura. It was even smart enough to know that Chant wasn't the one who decided for the forest to be destroyed. A young guardian would have targeted Chant instead. If Wander is still alive and able to touch spirits, I'd hypothesize that that's because the guardian warmed up to her during their time together. Or maybe since she was born in its forest, it saw her as its final descendant and gave her life and power as its last will.

"That poor creature probably strained itself in trying to stay alive. Guardians need their land to live. Its magic was probably the only thing keeping it alive, but it also knew its magic was the only way it could control Wander and kill Aura. Though it did not look it, it must have been suffering until the end."

Vincent worked on rebuilding homes and schools in the outer edges of Sollast. Despite how much the world changed, he remained antisocial. Moments of joy and reward for him came from progress like when a family could move back into a home and no longer live in a tent.

A strange occurrence happened, however, when he helped a mother and child. They were two of many burn victims from the war. Vincent had become used to the sight of bodies scarred or charred in some way. The woman had somehow lost a hand, her sight, and had burns up her legs and arms. Her daughter was always at her mother's skirt. The girl's entire body was draped in blue except for her brown eyes.

"You're a soldier aren't you?" the woman said as she tapped her stick around her new home. Her daughter already made herself at home, coloring figures in chalk on their doorstep.

"Was," Vincent said. "I don't think I'm up for it anymore."

"Did you by chance meet a man named Ethan?" she asked. "I haven't seen my son since my village burned down. He'd be the type to join the army."

"I'm afraid not," Vincent said.

"What about Wander?" the little girl asked.

"Shush!" her mother hissed. "We do not speak of her. She's the one who brought the fire and left us. Her and her . . . creature." As she walked away, the woman mumbled, "I should've listened to dear Ethan. I wish I never took her in."

Teary eyed, the little girl returned to her drawings. Vincent moved on, but could not sleep that night.

Tint's hat shop's basement in Lumin Village was Wander and Masu's home for a long time.

The old woman quickly grew fond of Masu's excessive politeness and Wander's gratefulness. She sent letters to Many, Robin, and all others she knew she could trust about Masu's arrival. She fed them and let them sleep anywhere they wanted on her two extra beds and couches. Over the course of travelling there and staying, Wander explained what had happened to Masu in more detail.

He constantly seemed to be in a state of shock. Often times he just stared into space. Some would guess that he was sleeping but his eyes were wide open. He also began to act strangely. Masu began to cover his ears, shake, or bite himself if someone touched him too gently or whispered. Wander learned to hold him tightly, which always seemed to calm him down.

Once over dinner, Masu could barely stay awake. His head kept dipping and rising like sea waves. Seeing him sleep had become rare. At night, Wander would wake up alone and find him sitting up in a chair across the room. He did not seem to do anything but think deeply. He also barely ate. With each meal, he only took a couple bites and would scoot the plate toward Wander to finish.

"Masu?" Tint noticed as well. "You don't have to eat if you're sleepy. Why don't you go lay down?"

Masu left toward the bedroom without a word.

"That poor man," Tint said after a sip of her favorite red wine. "I suppose it's a battle to live normally after all he's been through. But Robin and Many are visiting tomorrow. Others are going to visit next week. Maybe making some new friends will cheer him up."

After Wander ate and helped Tint with the dishes, she peeked into the bedroom she and Masu shared. He sat on the bed's edge with his back hunched. His right hand clutched his lower left arm.

"Are you alright?" Wander came in and got a closer look to see blood oozing out from under his hand. Without a word, she ran back to the kitchen for alcohol and took a pillowcase off of one of the couch pillows in the living room.

She came back and took Masu's hand off the wound. He revealed a slice, like a long and deep scratch. He tensed and groaned as she poured alcohol on the wound. Tearing the pillowcase up with her hands, she bandaged the cut. "What happened?" She followed Masu's eyes to the bloody knife on the floor.

"I did it to myself," he admitted.

Eyes wide, she turned back to him. "Why?"

He teared up as he said, "I don't want to sleep."

She shook her head. "I don't understand."

"I'm scared that I might not wake up."

"Masu, you will wake up. You always have."

"You don't understand. I've been remembering more. When I feel tired, comfy, or even safe . . . it's like when she controlled me. Those are the things that she used to keep me under control. But when I feel pain . . . I know I'm free."

She squeezed his hand. "You are free. Aura is dead."

"I once thought you were dead, too."

"Did you see me die? I saw Aura die."

"But I didn't."

"Masu, do you trust me?"

He let out a sigh and shut his eyes. "Yes."

"Then you can trust that she is dead. I am going to protect you. Not just me, but Tint and the people you're going to meet tomorrow. You never have to be afraid of sleeping."

"Alright, just two hours. Then can you wake me up?"

Wander nodded.

Masu lay on the bed. "Could you also stay here while I sleep? Don't touch me . . . just . . . to watch over me?"

"Of course."

Masu laid on his stomach and shut his eyes. The dragon's eye amulet given to him by Fade and Dim remained around his neck. Masu said he felt like it was important to keep on. Tint recognized the trinket as something to negate magic. As long as he wore that amulet, his magic hopefully won't work or influence him. However, it was best to keep secret since it was like wearing royal jewels.

Wander sat on her knees by Masu's bedside. He had already fallen asleep. She folded her arms and set them on the bed's edge and laid her head down.

Finally, she was home again.

The deviants' nation became a dark and frightened land. Queen Aura's death fueled anger and panic in the deviants who had known peace for hundreds of years. The rebirth of illness and injury among those that Aura healed had shaken every community.

Parents awoke with children dead in their beds. Legs broke under people who stood for years. Some remembered they once wanted to die. Others forgot their precious memories. It was quickly called The Lost Night.

Thousands of deviants crowded outside the palace in Dem, but none were allowed inside. Myth ordered that all doors and windows be sealed and the outer walls to be surrounded by guards.

Myth, the crooked and ever hurting deviant, limped through the palace halls. Her orders were stern, a powerful voice booming out of her frail cursed body. There was only one deviant she allowed from outside. Myth strolled through her sister's favorite garden with the willow tree. Aura often hid behind the branches to read, write, chat, or play with a guest. It was a good place for her ashes to rest.

"Long time no see."

A man stepped out into the garden. He held his hands behind his back and wore his finest robe. His dark hair was combed back into a ponytail and tied up with beaded lace. A lock was left on the side of his cheek.

"Pitch!" Myth said.

"Should I be more formal?"

"I am not queen yet," Myth said. "I want to give the people time to mourn for a little before we heal."

He slowly approached. "I came bearing you the gift you asked for."

"So soon?"

"Didn't you know? I had it all this time."

He revealed his hands. His palms held a glass bottle the size of a finger filled with a red liquid. He passed it to Myth. "And there is more where that came from."

Myth shut her hand with the bottle. "I knew I could count on you."

He gave her a showy bow. "I will see you . . . tonight."

Myth waited too long for this moment. She entered the shelter of the willow tree where no one could see her. She uncorked the bottle and chugged the blood.

Right as the blood eased down her throat, Myth felt pains she had had for so long begin to numb. Her mind felt as though a fog cleared in her head and chest. Weight lifted off her shoulders. She let go of her walking stick and straightened her back. Her fingers dug into the back of her head and tore the ties that bound her hair up in a bun. The dark waves fell to the middle of her back.

She was finally free.

Allison Stalberg grew up in North Carolina but dreamed of other worlds since she was a little girl.

She studied English and sociology at Guilford College and currently works as a freelance writer and journalist. *Wander* is her first book.

She still lives in North Carolina happily with her family.

To learn more about Awei, visit her website at theaweiseries.com